I0831830

A NICK FISCHER NOVEL

THE GIRL FROM CALI

G.D. OBERMILLER

Published by Frio Press LLC

2025

This is a work of fiction. Names, characters, places, and incidents either are the product of the author's imagination or are used fictitiously. Any resemblance to actual persons, living or dead, events, or locales is entirely coincidental.

Cover design by Christian Storm
Interior layout by Lisa Gilliam, lisagilliam.com

ISBN: 978-1-7376459-8-6 (paperback)
ISBN: 978-1-7376459-7-9 (ebook)

For Kyle, Ruby, Jiaen.
God Bless the Child That's Got His Own

PROLOGUE

Maya Chavez and Lori Kostoch held hands to keep from falling as they raced down the narrow dirt path leading to the secluded beach on the Pedernales River outside Fredericksburg, Texas. The girls wore cutoff jeans, flip-flops, and T-shirts over new micro bikinis they'd purchased at the mall seventy miles away in San Antonio. They knew the tiny swimwear would drive every boy at the annual end-of-summer kegger crazy and make every girl jealous.

Lori was short, blond, and head cheerleader for the Battlin' Billies. She was born and raised in Fredericksburg and had been planning for her senior year since kindergarten. Maya was also born in Fredericksburg but had spent the last eight years in Southern California, a part of the world that was a foreign country to rural Texas teens. She was tall and willowy with startling green eyes and long raven hair that flowed loosely below her shoulders. Her exotic beauty was a mixture of Spanish heritage from her SoCal father and German from her Central Texas mother. Unlike Lori, she wasn't looking forward to her senior year as a Battlin' Billy. She'd never planned on returning to live with her rancher grandparents. And any hope of blending in was quickly dashed when she discovered that it didn't matter where she was born. Since she'd lived in SoCal, everyone considered her an outsider. They called her *the girl from Cali.* The nickname stuck.

The designation came with its own set of expectations. When

Fredericksburg teens heard *SoCal*, they thought of popular gangster rappers on social media who romanticized drugs and gang life. Maya knew the images distorted reality. The SoCal she'd lived in did have drugs and gangs, but it also had malls, parks, movie theaters, and places for teens to hang out besides remote beaches on rivers in the middle of nowhere. But in the complicated hierarchy of high school social status, the outsider mystique put her on equal footing with Lori and the popular crowd, so she let them think what they wanted. After graduation, she would be on her own, and as far from Central Texas as she could get.

It was August, the sun was down, and the summer heat lingered in the night air like an unwanted houseguest. Cooler temperatures were still a couple of months away, and this year's *Farmer's Almanac* called for shorts and T-shirts through Halloween. The sky was clear and far enough from any big city lights to expose the hazy tail of the Milky Way.

The girls followed a well-worn caliche trail curling through prickly pear cactus, live oak motts, and spindly mesquite trees. They wound their way over a limestone hill toward the echo of a thumping bass rhythm blasting from portable speakers. The kegger was in full swing. The glow of the bonfire on the horizon drew them like moths to a porch light.

Maya carried a red-and-white canvas tote bag she'd been given at registration. It was stenciled with the stylized head of the billy goat school mascot and held a bottle of cheap vodka, two plastic quarts of lemonade, and two beach towels. She'd stolen the vodka from her mother, knowing that by this time of night, her mother'd be too drunk to remember whether she'd lost it or polished it off by herself.

Maya's foot slipped on a loose rock, and Lori caught her before she could fall.

"Don't break the bottle," Lori squealed, holding Maya upright.

"No worries. It's plastic." She reached into the bag and brought out the vodka.

Lori noticed the seal was cracked and an inch of clear liquid was missing. "You started without me."

"It was like that. My mom never brings home a full bottle," Maya said, handing it to her.

Lori twisted the cap off, took a drink, and gagged. "Gross."

"You gotta mix it with lemonade. Otherwise it tastes like cleaning fluid." She poured equal parts vodka and lemonade into a plastic cup, a recipe she'd learned by observing her mother, and handed it to Lori. "Now try it."

Lori drank the mixture. "Yeah, better. You can't taste the booze." Both girls giggled.

They paused to catch their breath on the last rocky bluff overlooking a U-shaped bend in the river. White limestone rocks covered the sandy beach below and glowed yellow in the firelight. The stagnant air was thick with pungent cedar smoke that hung in the shallow river gorge like evening mist. In the late summer, the water level was low, but the bend formed a pool nearly always over four feet deep and perfect for swimming.

Fredericksburg high school students had been partying at the river bend for as long as anybody could remember. It was isolated, and trails on both sides led through dense brush, making escape easy in case local cops, the landowner, or an overprotective parent tried to raid the gathering.

"I thought this was a school party," Maya said, studying the older men around the bonfire. She didn't recognize them from senior registration.

"It is," Lori said. "Don't worry, the guys we want to impress will be here."

"You mean Owen?" Maya teased as she followed Lori down the bluff.

"What?" Lori pretended innocence.

"Don't *what* me. I saw you drooling over him at registration. You wanna cuff him."

Lori laughed. "Okay, it's time, right? We're seniors. You can't graduate without a steady boyfriend."

"Who made up that rule?"

Lori rolled her eyes. "Hello, everybody knows that. Come on." She took Maya's arm. "Owen made me promise to bring you. He said he had someone for you to meet."

Maya let Lori drag her a few steps closer to the fire. Then she realized she'd been set up and pulled Lori to a stop. "Wait, who is it?"

"I don't know. Don't worry. I'm sure he's fine. He's a friend of Owen's," she said as if that was all the explanation Maya should need.

Maya took a drink of the vodka-lemonade mix, hoping it would give her courage. She knew she needed to show off a little skin to keep up the bad girl image. "Hold on a sec," she said, dropping the bag and pulling off her T-shirt. Her bikini was bright red, with spaghetti straps and triangles of thin cloth that barely contained her small breasts. Lori covered her mouth in surprise.

Maya raised her arms and shimmied like a belly dancer. "You wanted to impress 'em? This is how you do it, girl. Take it off," Maya insisted. She felt a little lightheaded from the booze and the sudden shaking.

"No way."

"Chicken," Maya chided. "Let's blow their minds."

Lori chewed her bottom lip. "Give me some of that," she said, reaching for the vodka mix. She took a drink, then pulled off her T-shirt, revealing a strapless kelly-green version of Maya's bikini.

It worked. The young men around the fire noticed them. One broke away from the group and ambled in their direction. He was six feet tall with an angular body, muscular arms, and a cocky grin. His shock of disheveled blond hair covered his ears, and around his neck he wore a braided shell necklace. Maya recognized him and relaxed a little.

"Hey, Lori," the boy shouted over the music. "Didn't think y'all'd show."

"Told ya we'd be here," Lori shouted back. "I brought Maya." She gestured with both hands and bowed as if introducing a celebrity.

Maya arched her back, posing to give the boy a good look at her figure.

His eyes settled on her exposed skin and his grin got wider.

Lori slapped him on the shoulder. "Hey," she shouted. "What about me?"

He put his arms around Lori and kissed her. "Just teasing ya. Did you bring booze?"

Maya held up the vodka. "Of course."

He put an arm around each girl's waist and led them toward the bonfire. "Come on. I want ya to meet someone."

The music was deafening, and the throbbing bass vibrated deep in Maya's bones. She searched closely for other familiar faces. There were a few, but the group by the fire were mostly older, in their twenties or thirties she guessed. They wore long shorts that sagged below their waists. A few wore wife-beater T-shirts, but most were bare-chested, showing off a collection of tattoos. As she got closer, she noticed the men formed a circle around two older-looking women in sequined bikinis who gyrated their hips to the music as if they were on a strip-club stage.

One of the men stepped forward. His blond hair was long and tied in a thick ponytail. He was bigger than the others, with tatts covering his steroid-enhanced muscles. The most dominant artwork was a red-and-green oriental-style dragon that wrapped around his chest. The head of the beast covered his right breast, and red tongues of fire shot down his chiseled abs.

"Meet Dragon." Owen gestured toward the man with the tattoo. Owen pointed at Maya. "This is the girl I told ya about."

"You're the girl from Cali?" Dragon said in a raspy baritone.

"Yeah," she said, becoming uneasy. This wasn't what she expected. She knew she could pull off the Cali girl image if it meant intimidating a few high school girls and flashing skin at some of the local boys; they were all rednecks. But this guy was older, and she had to admit, handsome. He had prominent cheekbones and a square chin. A chill ran down her spine as his eyes seemed to bore into her. She glanced from his face to the dragon tattoo. She was attracted and repulsed at the same time.

Dragon grinned and focused on Maya's skimpy bikini top. "You ready to party?"

Maya felt her cheeks flush and hoped the man didn't notice in the dark. "Always down to party," she said, waving her arms in the air and nodding her head to the beat of the music. If she stopped the act now, she'd be humiliated.

"You're looking fine, girl," Dragon said. He took Maya by the wrists and twirled her with his powerful arms like a marionette on a string. His alpha-male cockiness and brute strength gave him total control over her and everyone there.

"Take off your shorts," he said. "Let's see the rest of it." It wasn't a request.

Maya looked around for Lori and found her hiding behind Owen.

"Don't be shy. Show us what you got," Dragon demanded.

There was no turning back now. If she hesitated, word would spread quickly that she was a fake, and she would lose her special status. Senior year would be a bust.

She smiled, hiding her nervousness, and unbuttoned the top button of her jean shorts. As she pulled the material loose, the other men pressed in around her. She let the shorts drop to the sand. Two guys tilted their heads back and howled like wolves.

Dragon shoved Owen aside, grabbed Lori, and tossed her beside Maya. "You too, girl."

Lori looked to Owen for support, but he wouldn't make eye contact. The other faces in the crowd stared like shelter dogs waiting for supper. Lori undid the top button of her shorts. Her face flushed.

Suddenly, all the men howled, then closed in around them. A hand grabbed the string that secured the tiny red top to Maya's neck. She crossed her arms as the flimsy material slipped down. The men laughed. Cedar smoke, body sweat, and cheap cologne overwhelmed her. She swooned and fought back tears. A hand grabbed her butt. Another tugged the string holding her bikini bottom. Her throat was tight. What had she gotten herself into? Maya clung to the bikini bottom with one hand and held her other arm across her breasts. She tried to scream, but the sound caught in her throat.

A rough hand grabbed her hair and forced her head down.

Then, as quickly as it began, it was over. Dragon was beside her. The man who'd grabbed her hair was on the ground, bleeding from his nose.

Dragon put his hands on her shoulders. "Sorry. These dudes're animals." He picked up her shorts and handed them to her.

"Thank you," Maya whispered. She retied her string top and pulled her shorts back on.

Dragon lit a joint and inhaled a lungful of smoke. He held his breath for what seemed like a full minute. Then he smiled and exhaled, holding the joint out to Maya.

She hesitated. She'd tried marijuana in California under similar circumstances. Someone had a joint and passed it around at a party. Dragon insisted with an expression that implied she didn't really have a choice.

"You sure you're from Cali?"

Maya nodded, put the joint to her lips, and inhaled. She tried to hold it, but immediately coughed violently. It was stronger than the stuff she'd tried before.

Dragon laughed. "Relax your throat, girl." He brushed her long dark hair over her shoulders. His smile was suddenly warm and friendly. His eyes engaging. All his focus was on her. Time stood still.

Her eyes flicked to the figures by the fire and the empty sand around her. Lori had disappeared with Owen somewhere in the dark. She was alone with a strange older man. Panic started at her stomach and rose into her throat. She knew she should run, but even if she got away from the river, she had no idea where she was.

The man saw her fear, put his warm hand on her bare shoulder, and smiled. Maya tried the joint again. This time she followed Dragon's advice and felt herself relax. A warm sensation slowly crept over her fingers and toes.

PART ONE

Missing Person

"Der Geist der Vorfahren lebt in uns."
The spirit of our ancestors lives within us.

German Proverb

CHAPTER ONE

Dozens of Fischer ancestors scowled down at me from framed photographs lining the ancient limestone walls of my small childhood bedroom. Some were tintypes, some sepia tone, some black and white, and others were color prints yellowed with age. Five generations encased in dusty glass, and all except the ones in color were stern and unsmiling. I'd read someplace that the cold expressions in old photographs were the result of the extended period of time it took to expose the film. The subjects had to pick a pose they could hold, or risk blurring the image. This may be true, but as a kid, I thought the old folks could read my mind from beyond the grave and disapproved of my plan to escape chores and play hooky. For the longest time, I was certain Grandpa'd hung the pictures to make me feel guilty and keep me in line. It wasn't until I realized that he'd slept in this same room as a boy that I made peace with their ghosts. There'd been fewer photos seventy years ago, but I wondered if they'd made Grandpa feel guilty. It was one of the many questions I never got a chance to ask him before he was murdered.

Dawn had come and gone hours ago, but I was still in bed. The recent stint in the hospital with the hourly bed checks had ruined my circadian rhythm. A steady bar of morning sunlight reminded me of the lateness of the hour, cutting through the small window and casting shadows on the photos. The limestone block house was built by the first Fischer to immigrate from Germany over 160 years ago. With my dad and now my grandpa gone, I was the last of the family line, and the photos once again made me feel guilty. This time for not providing an heir and not protecting Grandpa. So far, I hadn't been able to hold on to a girlfriend long enough to add any more branches to the family tree. It wasn't as if I wasn't trying. My latest prospect seemed promising. Her name was Kelly Hoffman, and she was a former Marine lieutenant working for the Texas Tech police department in Lubbock. She'd helped me out on my last investigation and stood her ground with a tactical shotgun when things turned western. Had she left me alone for the final showdown, like I'd asked her to do, I'd be pushing up bluebonnets beside Grandpa instead of rehabbing on the family ranch. She'd stuck with me in the gunfight and stood by me in the hospital while they dug a .38 bullet out of my chest and refilled my blood supply. Those were qualities Grandpa would have appreciated.

I cleared my throat and spoke. "She's coming back today for Oktoberfest. So, cut me a little slack. She may be the one." I waited, but the old-timers didn't respond. They were a hard bunch to please. No matter, I had a good feeling about Kelly, but time would tell. I'd said the same thing about my last girlfriend until she double-crossed me and almost got me killed.

I took morning inventory of my battered body. Everything hurt. I crossed the morning five-mile run off my to-do list. Experience taught me that recovering from a gunshot wound was a long and arduous process. It wasn't just physical. My head was holding back my recovery. Continuing the bloodline was only one of my worries. Now that Grandpa was gone, I had to figure out whether to keep the ranch or let it go. After two months of lying on my back and deliberating, I still hadn't made up my mind. On the one hand, there was livestock to feed and daily ranch maintenance that couldn't be neglected. On the other hand, staying at the ranch meant an hour-and-a-half drive to San Antonio where my fledgling private investigation and security business was, I hoped, still waiting. I couldn't be a Gillespie County rancher and a successful San Antonio private eye at the same time. Something had to give.

The tinkling of silverware downstairs reminded me there was another problem to deal with besides the family property and my romantic relationships. The problem of an uninvited guest with her own agenda that threatened to upend any of my plans for the future.

"Breakfast!" Helen yelled from the downstairs kitchen in a shrill singsong voice. She'd shown up for Grandpa's funeral and never left. Now, every conversation included a hint at staying longer. Not just till after the Oktoberfest weekend but indefinitely. Last night, I'd found her empty suitcase on a shelf in the barn. When I confronted her about it, she said it took up too much space in her room.

The smell of pancakes and sausage mixed with coffee told me she was working overtime to worm her way into my good graces after that incident. I had to admit that I was less than a gracious host and threatened to pull the welcome rug out from under her feet. I blamed it on my weakened physical condition. But who was I kidding? For me, "gracious host" was an oxymoron. I didn't want or need a roommate.

She said she wanted to take care of me, at least until I got on my feet. The wounds were sore as hell, but I could take care of myself. I didn't want to be nursed by a woman who hadn't been around to take care of me since the seventh grade. That was the year my father was elected sheriff of Gillespie County and the year Mother Helen walked out.

"Nicky, are you gonna sleep all day?" she yelled again. Her voice sounded exactly like when I was in elementary school, same singsong intonation, and the same veiled threat that there would be consequences for remaining in bed.

What irritated me the most was that she called me *Nicky*, like I was still in the third grade. It added to the odd feeling of seeing my ancestors staring down at me from the limestone walls. They all seemed to want the answer to one burning question: *What's next?* Would I keep the family ranch and stay in my old hometown of Fredericksburg, or would I sell out and return to San Antonio where I had a fixer-upper in the King William district near the Alamo and a private eye business? Maybe I would return to law enforcement like my father, or maybe finish my last year of law school, take the bar exam, and pursue a more lucrative and less dangerous profession. I was at a crossroads and having my estranged mother around didn't help.

I stared at the old photos. "Okay, I'll figure it out. You're lucky I don't put y'all in a box and store you on a shelf in the barn." They stared back. Unsmiling. I could tell they didn't like that idea.

"Nicky?" Helen called again, using the same singsong veiled threat.

Even recovering from a bullet wound, I couldn't sleep late in my own house. I stood on the worn wooden floor and stretched my arms toward the high ceiling. Each day, I tested my range of motion, anxious to get back to one hundred percent, but knew that achieving that may take six months or longer. The thought of another week with Nurse Helen made my skin crawl.

Her sudden interest in me and the ranch was motivated by money. She couldn't fool me, and she didn't have to spell it out. The Fischer family ranch sprawled over four hundred acres along Grape Creek, less than fifteen miles from Fredericksburg, Texas, a town that had evolved from a small agricultural community into a popular German-themed tourist attraction. The transformation started in the seventies following LBJ's tenure as president. The nearby Johnson ranch was known at the time as the Texas White House and had attracted national attention. A town that otherwise would have died out like so many other small rural Texas communities now boasted more than sixty wineries, dozens of retail shops, and a handful of German-themed restaurants. It also supported a world class World War II museum named for Admiral Nimitz, another one of Gillespie County's famous sons. There was money here, and Helen could smell it. The annual Oktoberfest weekend celebration alone attracted twenty-six thousand visitors last year and the festival committee expected thirty thousand this year. Before he was murdered, Grandpa'd turned down several very generous offers to buy the ranch. The investors wanted to turn the old homestead into a bed-and-breakfast.

"Do you need some help?" Helen called. Her designer boots clacked up the ancient stone steps, and I quickly slipped on a pair of jeans and hustled into the bathroom. She was my mother, but I'd stopped thinking of her in that capacity twenty years ago, and I wasn't about to let her walk in on me in my underwear.

"I'm coming," I said, closing the door before she could reach the upstairs landing.

"Let me help you change your bandages." She let herself in the bedroom and called through the bathroom door.

"I can manage," I yelled. I stripped the bandage off my chest and winced in pain when it caught the chest hair that had started to grow back. The edges of the wound were still red and raw, remnants of an infection that only recently had begun to recede. The .38 slug was going to leave a nice scar about three inches above my left nipple. I checked the other wound on my upper arm where a .308 rifle bullet had taken out a chunk of my triceps. It was clean and healing, but still sore. The wounds were courtesy of a corrupt state politician. He'd covered up the murder of a young woman found floating in the San Antonio River because the perpetrator was the grandson of his benefactor, a wealthy businessman. I'd been hired by the girl's mother to find her killer. In the final showdown, I put a .45 round through his brain, but not before he got off one lucky shot.

I held my arm up so that the wound was visible in the mirror over the sink. The new scars added to the constellation of marks across my forehead that I'd picked up on my final overseas deployment. Being a Marine and now a private detective took its toll. If I kept this up, I'd look like Deadpool before I turned forty. "Maybe you should start wearing red tights and a mask," I said to the scarred image in the mirror. The image smiled. "At least you still got a sense of humor."

Helen knocked on the bathroom door. "You all right in there? Who're you talking to?"

"Give me some peace. I'm talkin' to Deadpool." I definitely couldn't take six more weeks of her nursing.

"Who?"

"Never mind. I'm fine. Go back downstairs. I'll be down in a minute."

"I'm just trying to help."

She sounded hurt. I didn't care. I'd been asked how I was doing more times in the weeks following Grandpa's funeral than I'd ever been asked in my entire life. I was going stir-crazy from too little activity. The ranch house didn't have a television or internet, and I'd already read the collection of history books I'd brought from San Antonio. The daily ranch work was great for increasing stamina, but it was no match for hitting the bags and taking sparring time in the ring. It'd been months since I'd stepped foot inside Lucky's boxing gym and strapped on the gloves. I missed it. The workouts always took the edge off my frustrations.

I finished applying fresh bandages, then waited till Helen's bootsteps retreated downstairs before I emerged and finished getting dressed.

When I walked into the kitchen, Helen served me a plate of sourdough pancakes topped with three sunny-side-up eggs, fresh hash browns, and a side of venison pan sausage I'd made from last year's deer meat. It was my favorite breakfast as a kid, and other than migas, it had always been my go-to morning meal.

"Thank you for breakfast," I said formally. It was easily a two-thousand-calorie meal that needed to be followed by a day of manual labor. My plan was to saddle my horse and ride the property boundary, fixing fences, then spend a few hours on my makeshift outdoor pistol range. I hated losing my edge.

Helen watched me use my fork and knife to reposition the eggs on top of the pancakes. I reached for the ketchup, not looking up, bracing for her usual litany of morning suggestions for my future.

"Would you like some juice?" She held up an orange juice bottle.

"No, thanks. I'm watchin' my weight." I said it with a straight face.

She nodded gravely. One of the many things that annoyed me about her—she didn't get my jokes. She poured herself a glass of juice and sat down to watch me eat, as if I were a toddler in a highchair. At fifty-five, she wore her hair dyed blond and pulled into a girlish ponytail. She wore jeans tucked into stylishly sequined cowboy boots and a white, long-sleeved western shirt. The silver bracelet on her wrist was embedded with turquoise and a matching pendant hung from her tanned neck. The only weight she'd added in twenty years came from silicone gel breast implants. I'd heard rumors of other boyfriends over the years, rich rancher and real estate types, but she claimed to be single now. I hated to admit that she was a good-looking woman who didn't seem old enough to be my mother.

"I thought I'd go to town this morning and pick up something for dinner before the Oktoberfest crowd gets too bad. What would you like?" She sat in Grandma's place at the end of the long wooden ranch table nearest to the gas stove. She had served me in Grandpa's place on the opposite end, but I'd moved my plate to a side chair. I wasn't ready to take over his position at the table and definitely didn't want Helen taking over for Grandma.

"I'm goin' to the festival tonight. I won't be here for dinner," I said. She was filling in dates on the calendar as far ahead as she could, another one of her calculated moves to ensure she could remain on the ranch.

"Oh, that's right. Your girlfriend is coming."

"She's not my girlfriend, but yes. Kelly is coming for the weekend."

She picked up Grandpa's stovetop percolator and poured us both fresh coffee. It was weak and undercooked because she wasn't used to boiling coffee on a burner. "I don't know why Granddad never used a coffee maker. This kitchen hasn't changed in fifty years." She topped off her cup with French vanilla creamer. "Will you two be staying at the ranch? I could cook for you tomorrow."

A family meal with Kelly and Helen wasn't on the top of my to-do list. "I found us a motel room in town. But thanks for the offer."

"I'm looking forward to getting to know her. She seemed like such a nice person when she was here for the funeral. And she stayed with you in the hospital. I think she smitten." She said the last part as if teasing me about my date to the junior prom.

I bit into the deer sausage. The flavor brought back fond memories. The recipe was as old as the homestead, and I focused on those pleasant thoughts to keep my temper from flaring.

"When are you going back to Colorado?" I decided to plunge into the deep end and sink or swim. I was raised by a no-nonsense Texas lawman and a taciturn rancher grandpa who were both blunt and to the point. What few social graces grandma tried to bestow on me went out the window when I joined the Marine Corps.

Helen stirred the creamer into her coffee. "Don't you want me to stay?"

I took another mouthful of egg and pancake, trying to decide how best to put into words what I wanted to tell her.

I swallowed the food. "No," I said, as tactfully as I could.

Helen went to the sink. Grandpa didn't have a dishwasher. There wasn't room to install one, and he scoffed at the idea of wasting money or water on modern conveniences.

"You need someone here. You're not fully recovered, Nicky." She began scrubbing the mixing bowls vigorously.

"I've been taking care of myself for a long time."

"That's not fair. You know your father had a lot to do with me leaving." Her voice took on a familiar whiny edge.

I took a bite of sausage, thinking. I didn't know that, but I didn't want to get into another argument about why she left, or why she didn't make any effort to contact me until after high school. I told myself I was over it.

"I'm sorry," she said. "I just thought..." She stopped working and leaned against the sink. "With Grandpa gone, can't things be different? We're the only two left."

I looked up from my last bite of pancake and egg. Tears were forming in her hazel eyes. She was going to pull out all the stops. I took the bite and handed her my empty plate.

"Why don't you cook that deer roast that's in the fridge? If we have time, I'll bring Kelly by for lunch tomorrow." I knew I was only putting off the inevitable. There was no "we" when it came to the last of the Fischer clan. The sooner she realized that, the better. But I didn't want to start my day bathed in alligator tears.

Before she could reply, Sam, my chocolate Lab, exploded off the porch in a rage and stationed himself in the ranch yard between us and an as yet unseen morning intruder. Sam's sunny Labrador disposition toward strangers had soured on my last case after a man broke into my house in San Antonio, offered him a tainted hamburger, then shot him in the head. He'd fully recovered, but the stranger, who turned out to be an SAPD detective, had taken his innocence. Tires crunched on the gravel and an ancient Dodge Ram slowly appeared, winding its way up the driveway from the front gate.

Helen looked over my shoulder and recognized the vehicle. "I forgot to mention, Helmut Geisler called the landline this morning before you got up."

"Why didn't you tell me?" I found my boots in the mudroom and slipped them on.

"It was so early, I wanted to let you sleep."

I waved to Helmut through the window, then called to Sam. "Calm down, boy." He ignored me and kept barking. He recognized Helmut but had an ongoing rivalry with the blue heeler perched on the toolbox in the bed of his pickup.

Helmut nodded. His expression was hard to read. He could win the lotto, witness the birth of his grandchild, or lose a family member and he'd still wear the same weathered look. Like my grandpa, he was from pioneer stock who were so accustomed to hardship that showing emotion wasn't an option.

"Did he say what he wanted?" I asked Helen.

"He wants to hire you. I told him you weren't ready to go back to work."

More of her suggestions for my future. I didn't bother to reply. The woman was exasperating. I opened the screen door and stepped outside.

CHAPTER TWO

Helmut Geisler carefully unfolded himself from the cab of his dusty Ram pickup. He reminded me of a strip of latigo wrapped in Wranglers and a faded blue work shirt. Neither he nor his sweat-stained Stetson Rancher hat had changed since I was in grade school. And no matter the circumstances, I still felt like I was eight years old when he came to visit.

His blue heeler stayed on the toolbox, matching Sam bark for bark. Helmut raised his hand. "*Platz!*" he commanded in German. Both dogs obeyed. Sam glanced at me quizzically. He didn't speak German but knew better than to cross the old man. I nodded, and Sam took off toward the stock pond. The heeler jumped down and ran after him, temporarily pausing their rivalry for a dip in the cool pond water.

"*Guten Morgen. Wie geht's?*" Helmut said, delivering his German with a nasal Texas twang. He extended a callused palm. Despite his eighty-plus years, his grip was still strong and firm.

"*Morgen*, Helmut." I knew a little more German than Sam from listening to Grandpa growing up. But if things got more complicated than "good morning," I usually smiled and nodded my head. I regretted not learning more, but by the time I went to high school, the language was long out of fashion.

He surveyed me and then the ranch yard, lingering on the patches of weeds along the corral fence, the loose tin flapping on the barn roof, and other signs of neglect that were never visible while Grandpa was alive. "Still recovering from your wounds, I see." He chastised me like a schoolboy.

What he meant was, had I been physically able, I wouldn't have neglected the ranch upkeep. It was one more thing to feel guilty about. The Geisler family'd been in the area as long as the Fischer family. He was one of the few left, now that Grandpa was gone, who still spoke Texas German, kept their ranch precise and orderly, and remembered the stories about life on the Texas frontier.

"Good that Otto got his hay in the barn," he said, chinning toward the hay loft. Otto was my grandpa. He was going to add, *before he died*, but he stopped himself. Instead, he said, "Almanac says it will be a mild winter, but we won't get much rain. Might need to buy feed before spring."

Helen'd said he wanted to hire me, but I was starting to wonder if he'd come over to make sure I wasn't running Grandpa's ranch into the ground. "Coffee's on. Come in and have a cup," I offered. Maybe he would cut me some slack and get to the point if he had a cup of coffee in his hand.

He looked past me to the front window, where Helen stood staring at us.

"Is it safe then, to go inside?" he asked with a twinkle in his eye. He knew my family history as well as I did. There weren't many secrets around the old-timer network, of which, until recently, my grandpa'd been an intricate part.

"She was just goin' to town for groceries."

"So, she's staying then?"

"For now."

He waited for me to say more. When I didn't, he let it go and nodded. "I could use a cup."

We walked inside, and he hung his crusty Stetson on the peg in the mudroom.

"Good morning, Helmut," Helen said.

"*Morgen*, Helen."

"How's your wife?" she asked.

"She's up and around. Busy with the fall garden. Says death will come when it comes." Helmut's wife'd recently survived her fourth heart attack.

"Let us know what we can do to help," she said, then put a hand on my arm. "I'm going to town. If you think of anything you need, you have my cell phone number."

Helmut and I watched her jump into her white Chevy Tahoe with green Colorado plates and kick up a cloud of caliche dust on her way to the front gate.

"You two gettin' along?" he said, pulling out a chair and sitting at the kitchen table.

"We have our differences. But you know where that comes from."

Helmut nodded but didn't say anything, his curiosity satisfied. I tested the coffeepot to see if it was still hot, then poured us both a cup. "It's weak. Helen hasn't figured out how long to let it boil."

Helmut sipped his coffee. Said, "Ya." Referring to the coffee. We sat in silence for a long minute. Helmut would get to his business in his own good time. We listened to the dogs return from the pond and shake themselves dry. Sam gave a low growl to assert his dominance on the home turf before both flopped together on the front porch. A mockingbird in the live oak tree behind the house sang his repertoire of melodies accompanied by the flap, flap, flap of the loose tin on the barn roof.

Finally, Helmut cleared his throat and said, "My granddaughter's missing." He took another sip of weak coffee. True to form, his customary stern expression didn't change.

I waited for him to fill in the details. Men like Helmut and my grandfather chose their words carefully and used them sparingly, mindful of not wasting more than necessary. I inherited the taciturn trait, which drove my last two girlfriends crazy and probably cost me a few clients, but as much as I tried, I'd never acquired the knack for idle chitchat.

"Her name's Maya Chavez," he said. "I think something's happened to her."

He plucked a picture from the wad of receipts and scraps of paper in his breast pocket that, like most old-time ranchers, he used as a filing cabinet. I took it from him and studied the young girl's green eyes and olive complexion. The picture looked clipped from a school yearbook. Her dark hair was long and flipped over her right shoulder. The smile on her face showed intelligence and a touch of youthful defiance.

"You might remember my daughter, Anna. She ran off to California when Maya was in grade school. Last spring, the knot head she married left her high and dry. She started tendin' bar and drinkin' most of her paycheck. Left Maya on her own most of the time. One thing led to another, and they ended up coming home during the summer."

I topped off our coffee cups and waited for Helmut to fill in more details. When he didn't offer any, I pressed him. "What makes you think something's happened to her?"

"She didn't take anything with her. Not even her toothbrush. All her clothes are still in her room. What girl would up and leave like that?"

"Was she angry enough to run away?"

He sipped his coffee. "Well, Maya wasn't happy to be here. I know that much." He stared out the kitchen window in a rare moment of self-reflection. Helmut and my grandfather were products of their environment, unforgiving semi-arid hill country, and descendants of pioneers who'd delt with Comanche raids, drought, disease, and bandits. They passed down a pioneer spirit that didn't include asking for help or sharing feelings. Confiding in me and asking for my help was like pulling cactus tines from his bare feet.

"What makes you say that?"

"I don't think that youngin wanted to leave California for her high school senior year," he went on. "She'd spent eight years in that cesspool of Southern California. It warped her thinking. And her mother... Well, her mother never used any discipline on her. Then she came back to Fredericksburg. Hell, you know what it's like. You grew up here. Our biggest event of the year is Oktoberfest."

I did know. Until I left to join the Marine Corps, my idea of a traffic jam was following a flatbed trailer full of hay down a one-lane road. "Did you talk to the sheriff?"

"I filed a missing person report with Detective Zeller at the city station back in August. He didn't do a damn thing. Since Maya just turned eighteen, the meathead said there was nothing else he could do. She was free to take off if she wanted."

"That part's true. Maybe she caught a bus back to California."

"That's what Zeller said, but I think that's horse shit. I told you all her stuff's still in her room. Even if she was mad enough to take off, she's a smart girl. She would've said something and packed a bag."

"Did Zeller check her cell phone records?" I asked.

He looked puzzled for a moment. Like my grandpa, Helmut had a landline in his kitchen and still wrote the occasional letter to his cousin in New Mexico.

"Ah," he said, remembering. "I gave him the number I had. He said it wouldn't help. Something about the kind of phone it was."

"A prepaid phone?" I asked.

"Ya, that's it." He dug into his shirt pocket filing cabinet. "I have the number here." He sorted through the scraps at arm's length, not bothering with reading glasses, then handed me a number written on the back of a gas receipt.

"She hasn't tried to contact you?"

"Haven't heard a whisper since she snuck out the window to go to a party on the river."

"She snuck out?"

"I told her she couldn't go. I know what goes on down there. So, naturally, she went anyway." He stroked his gray whiskers. Another moment of self-reflection. "Her mother used to pull the same stunt, and when I put my foot down, she did it anyway. She'd leave when she thought I was asleep and wouldn't come back till the next day. Crazier than a March hare."

"Did she walk to the river? That's fifteen miles from your place."

"No, the Kostoch girl picked her up outside the gate. I recognized her vehicle."

"Lori Kostoch?"

"Ya. She's a senior this year too."

"And you think Maya's in trouble?"

"I'd bet my prize goat on it. I feel it in my bones." He fixed his rheumy eyes on me. "I've tried to find her myself, but I've gotten nowhere. Hell, ten years ago, I would have turned the town inside out. But now..." His voice trailed off, displaying emotion that he wasn't accustomed to using. "It's hell gettin' old. I know you're recovering from that business with your grandpa, but if you could look around, I'd be much obliged."

I rinsed my coffee cup in the sink to give him a moment to compose himself. "I'll look into it," I said.

He stood and produced a small wad of bills from his wallet. "I can pay. I know you do this for a living."

I waved off the money. "I don't know if there's anything I can do. Let me ask around first. Fredericksburg's still a small town. You said she went to a party on the river. Somebody's bound to have seen something. If I get a lead or think I can help, we'll sign the paperwork and make it official. We can negotiate payment then.

"It's your call," he said. The brief emotional self-reflection was safely tucked back inside his rawhide exterior.

I walked him out to his pickup and waited while he folded himself back behind the wheel. "*Hier!*" he yelled to the blue heeler. The dog obediently jumped into the back of his pickup and settled down on the toolbox. Sam barked a warning, reasserting himself as master of the ranch yard.

Helmut started the engine and put the vehicle in gear. "*Danke. Halt dich munter*," he said out the window. It was a salutation I'd heard all my life. According to Grandpa, it meant something like *keep your chin up*.

"*Halt dich munter*," I said. Helmut drifted down the hill toward the front gate.

I scratched Sam behind the ears, careful to avoid the fresh scar from the bullet wound. "Rehab's over, ol' buddy. Time to get back to work."

CHAPTER THREE

It was Oktoberfest weekend, Fredericksburg's biggest event of the year. Every weekend brought tourists from around the state to browse the boutique shops on Main Street, taste local wine, and sample German cuisine, but on the first weekend in October, the population tripled. The Fredericksburg Chamber of Commerce advertised the town as *the polka capital of Texas*, which would seem to have a limited appeal, but Main Street was bumper to bumper, and parking was scarce, so the slogan seemed to be working.

Kelly was driving down from Lubbock, a five-hour drive that would put her here in late afternoon. My plan was to nose around and ask a few questions about Helmut's granddaughter while I waited. If I was lucky, I would find her and take her home or at least get a lead on where she went and set Helmut's mind at ease, leaving me to focus my attention on Kelly. The relationship showed promise, but it was still too early to tell. If finding Maya proved more difficult, I would have to call my partner in San Antonio and launch a full-scale investigation, and the chance of a hot and heavy romance would evaporate like valley fog in the afternoon sun.

As I dodged road construction crews and weekend tourists on Highway 290, the main road from Fredericksburg to Austin and the large population centers in Texas, I wondered why any teenager ran away from home. A parent conflict seemed the most likely. In Maya's case, according to Helmut, she preferred life in Southern California to rural Central Texas.

He also said her father had left and her mother was stuck in the bottle. I could relate. I'd lost my dad at fourteen. He was murdered serving a warrant on a meth crew cooking drugs in a trailer outside of town. By that time Helen had already moved out. She wasn't on the bottle like Maya's mother, but the effect was the same. I went to live with my grandparents to finish high school. I know they had their hands full with me. I was angry at the world, and even though I loved to hunt and ride horses, I had a chip on my shoulder and something to prove. I waited until after graduation and did the most radical thing I could think of—I joined the Marine Corps. At the time it seemed like the fastest way for a broke teenager to see the world. My exploration started in Southern California with bootcamp in San Diego, then moved up the coast to Camp Pendleton. From there, I went to Camp Lejeune in North Carolina, then Iraq and Afghanistan. My journey ended four years later in the Landstuhl Regional Medical Center in Germany. Not exactly a whirlwind vacation, but the effect was the same. When the hospital discharged me, I couldn't wait to get home.

It could be that Maya needed a similar escape and her grandpa's wish to get her back would have to wait until her adventure had run its course. If that was the case, there was nothing I could do. Like me, she might have a chip on her shoulder and something to prove to the world. I wouldn't recommend the Marines to her, but maybe she'd found a substitute.

Maya's mother, Anna, worked at a local motel. Helmut wasn't sure what her schedule was and didn't have her cell phone number, because both changed every few months. She lived in town while Maya lived at the ranch. According to Helmut, that's the way she wanted it.

It was midmorning by the time I pulled into the Super 8 motel. The parking lot was already full. Every room for rent in town and the outlying bed-and-breakfast houses sold out months in advance. I parked in the fire lane, got out, and leaned against the battered grill of my ten-year-old F-150. The local cops were lenient on parking violations during the festival weekend. A bead of sweat formed under my black Resistol cowboy hat and trickled down my forehead. A lot of guys in Central Texas still wore straw hats till after the first of October because of the heat, but mine was new and had a great George Strait crease that I hoped would impress Kelly.

My pearl snap shirt was already damp. The sun was out, and the sky was clear. By noon the temperature would be in the eighties.

I recognized Anna Geisler-Chavez when she emerged from a ground floor room pushing a service cart. I hadn't seen her in ten years, but behind her pinched mouth and spiderweb of wrinkles, I saw a clear resemblance to her father. She stopped to light a cigarette and stare at a family of four piling out of a minivan as if she resented the extra work they represented. She wore a frayed Metallica T-shirt over worn jean shorts and looked like she could use a beer.

"Hey, Anna," I said, taking a few steps toward her. I didn't want to come on too aggressively for fear she'd bolt into one of the rooms. She had a reputation for being flighty and probably owed money to half the people in town.

It took her a few moments to recognize me. "Hey yourself, Nick Fischer."

"Busy weekend, huh?" I was working on my meaningless friendly chitchat.

"You come by to tell me that?" So much for idle prattle.

"Actually, I came by to ask you about your daughter, Maya. Your dad said she was missing. He hasn't seen her since the middle of August. The tenth, to be exact. He's worried something might have happened. Have you heard from her?"

"Guess that kinda proves the old man couldn't handle her either. She's at that age, you know? She's a wild thing. My ol' man thought he could break her like one of his quarter horse fillies. Ha. He's livin' in the nineteenth century. Always has been." She blew smoke through her nose and cocked her left eyebrow. The menthol smoke smelled like it was laced with cheap vodka. If she was fishing for sympathy, she wouldn't catch any from me.

"So, you haven't seen her?"

"Zeller already asked me that. I told him what I knew. What's it to you?"

"I'm a private investigator. Helmut thought I might be able to help. He's worried about her. I told him I'd look around. He said y'all weren't speakin' to each other."

"You got that right. The old bastard took my daughter away from me. I got nothin' to say to him."

"You're not concerned that Maya's been gone for six weeks?"

"Maya's not my responsibility no more. Helmut took me to court."

"I didn't know that." Helmut had left that part out. "Do you think Maya ran away?"

"I did when I was her age. I know what that old fossil's like. He never leaves that patch of rock he calls a ranch except to go to church, the feed-store, or the auction barn. He never took a day off, even for his daughter." She was bitter at the world for not treating her right.

"Did you ever think he was working all those long hours to support you? He gave you a home and a place to live."

Anna looked at me like I'd just slapped her in the face, not expecting to be called on her bullshit. "You call that a home? He worked me like a hired hand. I slaved for that old man. And for what? He didn't pay me nothin'. He won't give me no money now."

"Why'd you move back here if you didn't get along with him?"

"He owes me. I'm his only daughter. The old bastard won't be around forever."

"He doesn't owe you a damn thing." I let my anger get the best of me. I couldn't help thinking of Helen's return looking for a handout after Grandpa died.

Her bottom lip trembled. She covered her face to hide her tears. She didn't want to listen to what I had to say. There was obviously more to their story than Helmut had told me. Somewhere along the way, father and daughter had gotten crossways with each other. I didn't want to dig too deep unless it would help me find Maya.

I tried to soften my approach and redirect the conversation before she completely shut down. "Do you have any idea where she might have gone? Was she close to anybody back in California? Maybe your husband's family?"

Tears streamed from her bloodshot eyes. "Ex-husband," she corrected. "I don't know. Maybe. I don't know."

"Helmut seemed to think she wanted to go back."

"She didn't talk to me." She dried her eyes with one of the clean white bath towels she was carrying on her cart. After a deep breath she said, "Can you find her?" Somewhere beneath her bitterness, she was concerned. Once she understood she wasn't going to get any sympathy from me, the reality of Maya's absence hit her for the first time. "I miss her. I really do." She'd been so focused on her resentment for her dad and her own problems that she'd forgotten how to be a mother.

"I'll do what I can. If she does contact you, give me a call." I handed her my business card and got back into my pickup. Before I started the engine, I saw her sneak a sip from a pint bottle of vodka hidden under the clean towels.

CHAPTER FOUR

I took the side streets to avoid the downtown festival traffic. Fredericksburg only had one main street, appropriately named "Main Street," that ran east and west and bisected town. There was an empty parking space behind the Catholic church, and I pulled in to jot down a few notes and call my partner, Skeeter. Full-scale investigation or not, I had a feeling I would need his help. He was house-sitting for me in San Antonio and recovering from a gunshot wound of his own. The last case had almost laid waste to the entire Fischer Private Investigations firm—all two of us.

Skeeter had been a four-year starting defensive tackle for the University of Texas and was drafted by the Washington Redskins before their name change. But on draft night, a car accident took his best friend's life and left him with a metal prosthetic hand. Instead of an NFL career, the six-foot-seven three-hundred-pound gentle giant turned his attention to computer science. He'd always been a techie and he had a knack for online research and, my worst nightmare, social media, which he engaged in like an overgrown teenager. I was the last generation to be born without a cell phone in my hand. I didn't get one until after I mustered out of the Marine Corps and wasn't interested in all the ways the younger generation kept in touch. Every teenager on the planet had a digital trail. I needed my partner to track Maya's.

He answered on the third ring. "Davis and Fischer Detective Agency," he said, imitating a cheery answering service voice with his deep baritone Texas accent.

"You're feelin' your oats today."

He chuckled. "I's well rested." He exaggerated a black southern accent to amuse himself.

"When did you change the business name?"

"I deserve a promotion, boss man."

"Remind me why I need your assistance."

He shifted smoothly into a pedantic professor voice. "Because, my friend, you are a cowboy detective stuck in the nineteenth century, and you would rather ride a horse or operate your ancient pickup in pursuit of a quarry than join the modern age and access the internet superhighway."

"Good point. How's Rose?"

"Never lets me forget trash day."

"She does like a tidy neighborhood."

Rose Gustafson was my next-door neighbor in the old King William area of San Antonio just south of downtown. It was named for Kaiser Wilhelm I of Prussia and built by prosperous German businessmen in the nineteenth century on the banks of the San Antonio River. The houses were the ornate Victorian style and those that were maintained or renovated gave the area an old-school charm. Like many vintage neighborhoods, it had experienced periods of neglect, but was currently undergoing a renovation and a surge in home prices. I'd purchased a Victorian fixer-upper on the fringe of the district with the idea of doing the renovation myself and making a profit on the resale. That was four years ago. I hadn't had time to devote to the project. Rose's house was in pristine condition. She was a retired university biology professor who was born in the neighborhood and liked to keep track of everything going on around her, including the lack of progress on my home repairs.

"She's keeping me supplied with homemade chicken soup."

"Ah, that's why you're so perky this morning. You must be ready to get back to work."

"I like the sound of that. Please, tell me this is a paying job."

Skeeter was wary of my habit of taking on work for clients who couldn't afford the full service. I had to remind him frequently that when he was in jail for capital murder, I took on his case pro bono. At the time, I hoped that my success would jumpstart my fledgling business. His mother was at her wits end and desperate to free her son, but she couldn't afford to hire a lawyer or one of the big agencies. When I found the killer who'd set him up and gotten Skeeter off the hook, I became royalty in the Davis household. The success solidified my reputation as a private detective and Mrs. Davis's word of mouth jump-started my business. Skeeter was so grateful that he volunteered to help with my burgeoning client list. It didn't take long for me to realize that I couldn't get along without him, so I hired him full-time. I'd gotten into the business because I didn't want to sit behind a desk or take orders from law enforcement bureaucrats. I'd read the fictional exploits of Marlowe, Spade, and Spenser during rack time on deployment, but the modern-day detective couldn't pound the pavement like Marlowe unless he had a computer sleuth partner.

"No payment yet," I said and heard him sigh in disappointment. "Need I remind you how my business model works?"

"No, I'm clear. But a paycheck once in a while would be nice."

"Fair enough. We're checking out a missing person for an old family friend. He's willing to pay, but first I wanted to be sure there was something we could do."

"That high-minded moral integrity is gonna drive the firm into bankruptcy."

"If it does, we're in the wrong business."

He chuckled again. "All right cowboy, I trust your instinct. Who's the missing person?"

"Her name's Maya Chavez. She's eighteen and a senior at Fredericksburg high school or would be if she'd showed up for class. Her grandpa is Helmut Geisler, Grandpa's rancher buddy. You met him at the funeral."

"I remember he looked like he'd just stepped off the set of Lonesome Dove."

"That's him. Maya disappeared in August after a high school kegger on the Pedernales River. It was supposed to be a back-to-school party and a celebration of Maya's first year at Fredericksburg high school."

"Where'd she go before that?"

"She and her mom lived in San Bernardino."

"The Inland Empire. Why'd Helmut wait so long if she's been gone since August?"

"He tried the local cops first. It sounds like they asked around town, but since she just turned eighteen, they didn't investigate any further. They told Helmut she probably went back to California."

"She got relatives there?"

"Yeah, her father's side of the family. But Helmut says she didn't take anything with her. No suitcase. Not even her toothbrush. He thinks something happened."

"Hmmm," Skeeter said. I could hear his finger tapping on a keyboard while we spoke. He could type faster with five fingers and a metal hook than I could with ten. I gave him Maya's burner phone number and all the details I'd gotten from Helmut and Maya's mother, which weren't many.

"Let me know what you come up with?" I said and disconnected. There was no point in talking to him any further. The tapping sound and his "hmmm" meant he'd already jumped down the internet rabbit hole.

I broke out a blank spiral notebook from the pickup console where I kept a stash ready for new cases. Always the optimist. I wrote *Maya Chavez* on the top line, thought for a minute, then wrote: *Missing*. I was really making headway. *She'd left without telling her family or packing a suitcase.* I wrote, *Last seen at a kegger on the Pedernales. Ties to Southern California.* Next, I wrote *Helmut Geisler, Grandpa.* Helmut hadn't told me about Maya's legal status or that he'd taken his daughter to court. I made a note to follow up with Helmut. I wrote down Maya's mother's name. She didn't seem to be close to her daughter and had complained more about Helmut than the fact that her daughter was missing. I was starting to get the picture that Maya's home life was less than ideal and could provide a motive for running away.

I tapped my pen on the notebook while gazing at the arched windows and stone buttresses of the old Gothic building that had housed the original Catholic church. Gazing was a tried-and-true detective technique. When I didn't have a lead or didn't know which steps to take next, I gazed blankly at buildings, or preferably, Hill Country landscapes, and waited for my subconscious to piece together a clue or someone to hit me over the head and tell me to go home.

A steady stream of festival attendees flowed toward the Marktplatz, the park in the center of town that was fenced off for Oktoberfest. They wore more lederhosen and Tyrolean hats than I'd seen on my tour of Germany. Some of the costumes were authentic felt and leather, worn by the hardcore fans with German roots or too much money to spend. The thrifty, casual weekender sported graphic T-shirts stenciled with lederhosen or dirndls and plastic hats. After my discharge from the Landstuhl medical center, I had a couple of days to kill before my flight stateside. I spent it in a rented Volkswagen cruising the backroads of southern Germany searching for traces of Fischer ancestors. I tasted plenty of quality beer and learned that modern German folks dress pretty much like people in Texas, minus the cowboy hats and boots. I even met a man named Fischer from a town that figured prominently in my family lore, but he didn't seem interested in our possible shared ancestry. His loss.

After ten or fifteen minutes, a Toyota Landcruiser parked next to me, and a group of college-age students got out to admire the building. They took selfies and probably posted them on Instagram. The group crowded in the vehicle reminded me of what Helmut said about Maya's last day. She'd snuck out of the house to go to the party, and Lori Kostoch picked her up. Bingo. Gazing had done the trick. I knew the Kostoch family. They were farmers who ran a produce stand south of town and sold hay. Grandpa had purchased a truckload from them last winter. Lori's mother had been at Grandpa's funeral. Lori's father had been a Marine and was killed in action in Iraq before I was on my first tour. I wrote her name down under Anna's. Even though Fredericksburg was overflowing with newcomers, retirees, and entrepreneurs trying to cash in on the tourist boom, all the older families that had been around for a few generations knew each other and kept in touch through the old-timer network.

I found a number for Kostoch Farms and called. Lori's mother answered, and after catching up and accepting her condolences once again for Grandpa's death, she told me that Lori had a job at the German Café on Main Street and was there now working the busy festival weekend. The café was a landmark for tourists and a regular meeting place for locals. Since it was almost lunchtime, I figured it was a good time to have a chat with Lori and see if the *jaeger schnitzel* was as good as I remembered.

Despite overindulging at breakfast and getting no physical exercise, I was hungry.

I glanced at my reflection in the rearview. Damn, that was a fine-looking hat. I got out and decided to walk the two blocks to the German Café. I had the last parking place in town, and I needed to work up an appetite.

While I waited for a table, I searched the staff for Lori. Her mother said she was short, athletic, and blond. That narrowed the list to half the teen girls in town. Three of the workers matched that description, so I asked the hostess if Lori was working. She pointed out a teenager hustling out of the kitchen, carrying two plates of German sausage with generous sides of potato salad, sauerkraut, and red cabbage.

When I was finally seated, Lori stopped at my table a little out of breath and flashed a cheerleader smile. She was appropriately dressed in a blue cotton dirndl and could have easily made the cast of *The Sound of Music*. I slipped off my sunglasses so she could swoon over my big hazel eyes. I'd been told they were engaging and hard to resist.

"Hi, I'm Lori. What can I get you to drink?" she asked.

"Hey, Lori," I said, flashing what I hoped was a friendly smile. "I'm Nick Fischer. I was a Battlin' Billy back in the day."

"Oh, yeah..." She didn't recognize the name. "In town for the festival?" She was distracted and in a hurry to move to the next customer. I could understand, but I needed her attention. So far, my dashing good looks and new cowboy hat weren't working, so I decided to try my sense of humor.

"Actually, I'm a professional polka dancer. You can catch my demo at seven in the American Legion tent."

Her face lit up. I had her attention.

"Really?" she asked sincerely.

"Do you like polka?" I asked.

"Of course." She was a true daughter of Fredericksburg.

"I'm just kidding. Actually, I'm looking for Maya Chavez. Her grandpa, Helmut Geisler, asked me to help him find her. She hasn't been around since August. I'm a private investigator." I dug out my license and held it up. The corner of her mouth twitched. The cheerleader smile faded. "Sorry, I didn't recognize you. We're so busy. I'm sorry about your grandfather."

I nodded. "Thank you. Did you and Maya go to the kegger on the river together?"

She looked nervous.

"Hey, I'm an alum. I partied at the river too."

"Okay, yeah. I saw her there." She glanced around the jam-packed café again, this time checking to see if anyone was listening to our exchange. "No, I haven't seen her."

"When did you see her last?"

"That night, I guess."

"Did you talk to the police?"

"No," she said quickly. "Why would I?"

"Because she's missing, and her grandpa's concerned."

The color drained from Lori's cheeks. "Okay, yeah. I did talk to a policeman. But I don't know anything. I—I wish I could help," she stammered.

She seemed not to know what to do or say next and had changed her story twice in less than a minute. I handed her one of my business cards embossed with two crossed swords above the words *Semper Fi*. She studied it.

"My dad was a Marine," she said.

"I knew your dad. I'm just here to help Helmut find Maya."

She chewed her bottom lip, still not sure whether to trust me.

"If you think of anything that might help me find her, give me a call." She had more information but for some reason was too scared to share it with me.

"Sure thing, Mr. Fischer," she said.

I had to stop myself from looking around the room to see if she was talking to me. Nothing brings home the inevitability of aging more than returning to your hometown after fifteen years and being called "mister" by a local teen.

"How's the *jaeger schnitzel*?" I switched topics to the menu and Lori relaxed.

"Still the best in town," she said, regaining her confidence.

"Sold. And bring me a Spaten Doppelbock." There weren't many places that had dark German beer on draft. More calories. I heard a faint ding from the bell at the cash register and was reminded that Lucky's boxing gym was calling my name. I needed to get back to my regular workouts or start buying bigger Wranglers.

"Anything else?"

"*Nein danke*," I said.

She rolled her eyes and gave me a teenage chuckle. Every tourist she waited on tried to speak German on Oktoberfest weekend. It was like going to a Mexican restaurant on Cinco de Mayo and ordering with a Spanish accent.

When she brought the food, I thought she might add more details about Maya. Instead, she pasted on the cheerleader smile and made a point of not making eye contact.

I drank the beer and polished off the schnitzel. It was as good as I remembered. Then I waited for Lori to reappear with my bill so I could ask a few more questions. She never came back. Another waitress brought my check. The café was too busy to look for her, so I took the check and walked to the register. Lori had written her name on the bottom in girlish script with a heart in place of a dot above the *i* in her name. Below that, she'd written, *Ask Owen Bauer*.

CHAPTER FIVE

I was at a crossroads, literally and figuratively. Literally, my pickup sat at the intersection of Main Street and Highway 16. A thirty-foot travel trailer and a dozen vehicles parked in front of me waiting for the light to turn green. I could stay on Main and continue east out of town and back to the ranch or I could turn south on Highway 16 toward the high school. Figuratively, the choice was between chasing a runaway or impressing a new lady friend. If I went back to the ranch, I could shower, shave, and pack an overnight bag in time to meet Kelly at the motel for our weekend rendezvous. If I turned south to the high school, I could catch Owen Bauer when he finished football practice and question him about Maya's whereabouts.

Since Helen'd extended her stay, I had to scramble to find a room at the Best Western to accommodate my out-of-town guest. It wasn't exactly a love nest, but Kelly was a Marine and a down-to-earth country girl raised on a farm in rural Lubbock County. She didn't seem to be impressed by excessive money or a flashy lifestyle—a welcome change from my last girlfriend.

Would she also understand my need to turn up a trace of Maya before any hope of finding her evaporated like the Spaten Doppelbock at the German bakery? No one I'd talked to, so far, had told me everything they knew. Helmut and his daughter Anna gave conflicting stories. Lori seemed to skip over key information. Like any other case, I proceeded with the idea that the more people I talked to, the closer I'd get to the truth. I didn't believe in Santa Claus, ghosts, or that people could disappear without a trace. If you looked long and hard enough, there was always a trail to follow. When the light turned green and the traffic dispersed, I glanced at my reflection in the rearview mirror. If given a choice between work and romance, Grandpa would advise work. Besides, how could Kelly reject such a handsome cowboy? I grinned and turned south toward the high school.

Something about Maya's disappearance was beginning to worry me. She was eighteen and had every right to live life on her own terms. But there was something brewing below the surface. Call it a hunch. I knew I wouldn't be able to rest until I found her and made damn sure she'd made the decision to leave of her own free will.

It had been over ten years since I'd pulled into the Battlin' Billies stadium parking lot. I saw the team on the gridiron and fought the sudden urge to sprint to the locker room as if I was late for practice and facing thirty minutes of extra wind sprints. The pickups in the lot were newer, and the gunracks were empty, no doubt a new rule designed to keep students safe. My generation brought our shotguns and rifles to school so that we could be in the field hunting as soon as the bell rang or practice was over. Times had changed.

It was early afternoon in October and still hot outside. Not the sticky, humid-hot of San Antonio because the town was sixty miles further away from the Gulf of Mexico and a thousand feet higher in elevation, but hot enough that watching the football team do bear crawls made me break out in a sweat.

Head coach Rocky Velosic was on the field wearing one of those straw field-hand hats with the extra-wide brim, torturing the team with end-of-practice conditioning. It was the same drill we both hated when we were on the team together. It was a cakewalk compared to Marine boot camp, but at the time, all my teammates thought we would die. I waited in the parking lot until the drill was finished and the coaches and players ran into the locker room. I'd see Rocky later, at the festival. He was the talkative type. If I said hello now, I'd have to spend the next hour catching up on the local gossip, so I stayed in my pickup and waited for Owen Bauer.

His family was a fixture in Gillespie County. Like the Geislers and the Fischers, the Bauers traced their family roots to the original settlers. They farmed, raised cattle, and at one time owned a dry goods store on Main Street that was now an upscale restaurant. I'd heard Owen's dad, Mike, invested in a winery and opened a tasting room. Owen Bauer made headlines in the local sports section last week. As an ex-player, I made a point of keeping track of the team and the ups and downs of the current head coach who'd been my teammate. Owen was the senior quarterback and, according to the paper, having an outstanding year.

Twenty minutes later, Owen walked out of the double doors under the stadium. I recognized him from his picture in the paper. He had thick blond hair that was damp and disheveled from a shower and tucked under a red team cap. The brim was flat, like he'd just picked it off the shelf, and he wore it covering the tops of his ears as if he needed the extra skin protection.

"Hey, Bauer," I called through my open window before he could reach a brand-new Ford F-250 4x4 pickup. His family had money and Owen was flaunting it. I wondered how his teammates felt about the new wheels. He turned toward me as if he expected the paparazzi and dropped his team duffel bag to the parking lot.

"Do I know you?" he asked. The kid had a cocky chip on his shoulder that could have held up the north end of the stadium.

I got out and walked over to him. "Nick Fischer. I used to play ball here back in the day." I held out my hand and he shook it. He hadn't completely forgotten his manners. "I was on Coach V's team." That got his attention. "How're y'all doin' this year?" I wanted to make him comfortable before I got to the serious questions.

"I think we're goin' all the way," he said, putting on a goofy grin and launching into what sounded like a rehearsed speech. "If our frontline gives me the protection I need, I'm gonna beat Coach V's passing record." Rocky was a local legend. It wasn't enough to win our team the state championship, but it did launch his college career at North Texas, and it eventually landed him his dream job of head coach at his alma mater.

"Enjoy it while you can," I said. It wasn't what he expected to hear. His goofy grin faded, and I caught him focusing on the forehead scars visible under my hat brim. It was time to switch gears.

"Who are you again?" he asked.

"Nick Fischer. I did play ball with your coach, but I'm a private investigator now." I showed him my creds and let him look them over for a moment. He seemed confused. "I'm lookin' for Maya Chavez. She went missing from the end-of-summer kegger on the river. I understand you where there that night."

His eyes flashed recognition, and his tan face turned crimson. Lori had been right. He knew something. A little switch went off in his brain. He blinked a few times in rapid succession before the goofy grin returned.

"Maya who?" he lied. The kid needed to work on his delivery if he was gonna play college ball.

"Chavez. New student. Her grandfather's Helmut Geisler. You know him?"

"Sure. Everybody knows Mr. Geisler. He's her grandpa?" I guessed Maya hadn't shared her family history. He picked up his bag and tossed it in the back of his shiny new pickup. "I'm drawing a blank on the girl."

"You're gonna have to do better than that. I already talked to Lori. They were together."

He shrugged, realizing he'd been caught and considered what to say next. "Yeah, yeah, okay. I remember her. Why're you lookin' for her?"

"Mr. Geisler's worried about her. Hasn't seen her since that night."

He shook his head. "Wish I could help you." He jumped into his pickup, a little too anxious to leave.

"Have you heard anything? Has anyone mentioned her around campus?"

He opened a can of wintergreen-flavored snuff and packed the left side of his lower lip with a marble-sized wad of tobacco. "Nope. Nothing." Another lie. He spit a stream of brown juice into an empty water bottle.

I handed him my business card. "If you hear from her, or think of anything you wanna tell me, give me a call."

He glanced at the crossed swords and Marine Corps motto on my card. "You're an ex-Marine?"

"There are no ex-Marines."

He looked puzzled.

"Once a Marine, always a Marine. You have to have served to understand."

He nodded his head, but he didn't get it. "Is that where you got the..." He gestured to my forehead scars.

"Yep. Ended my enlistment." The explosion that took out my team and almost took my life was not something I wanted to discuss with this kid. Not today. He wouldn't understand, and in a lot of ways, I was still dealing with the aftereffects of being the lone survivor. The facial scars were healed, but that dark abyss of emotion was always just a short step away from wherever I was standing.

"I'll let you know if I think of anything. I promise."

"I just wanna be sure she's safe." I held his gaze. His cocky bluster had faded. "I'm not tryin' to get anyone in trouble."

He nodded and spit again. "Were you any good? In high school, I mean. When you played football with Coach V."

I smiled. "Who do you think caught all those passes he threw?"

"Where'd you play college ball?"

"Afghanistan."

He flashed a clueless smile and started his pickup.

CHAPTER SIX

Owen Bauer's tires spit gravel getting out of the parking lot. He could have been rushing to a hot date—it was Friday night on Oktoberfest weekend, and the Battlin' Billies had a bye week, but I suspected that something I said touched a nerve. I wondered how much of her past Maya had shared with her classmates. Had she hidden the fact that she was born in Fredericksburg? Was she ashamed of her roots? Did Lori and Owen know where she was? The answer to all those questions seemed to be yes.

I thought about my high school years. By the time my senior year rolled around, I knew everybody in my class. There were different cliques like in any school—the rich kids like Bauer, the jocks, the band kids, and the nerds, which included any kid who didn't fit into the first three categories. We also had kids from transient families, mostly Mexicans moving through the area working on local farms and ranches. Sometimes the families stayed and blended in with the community, but most of the time the families moved on, looking for better opportunities. There were a few disagreements between groups, but for the most part, we all got along. And there weren't any secrets.

I followed Owen down a side street parallel to Main. Did he have a secret? Where was he going in such a hurry? He sped down South Milam Street, then turned right onto San Antonio. All the locals knew to avoid Main Street through downtown during Oktoberfest weekend. I slowed to let him get a block ahead of me, but I didn't think he would be expecting a tail. He was a high school jock, after all, not a CIA agent or a hardened criminal. I'd tracked a few nasty characters who wouldn't have thought twice about throwing lead in my direction, but underneath the bravado, Owen seemed more like a scared kid than a gangster. Something I'd said spooked him.

He pulled into the parking lot behind the German Bakery and left his new F-250 in the loading zone beside the rear entrance. I checked my watch. It was after two thirty. The restaurant closed at three. Maybe he was hungry after practice, but I guessed he was anxious to talk with Lori. I found an empty spot on the street behind a row of newly planted oak trees.

He hurried to the back door and let himself in. I waited. I was supposed to meet Kelly at the motel by six o'clock. That still gave me three hours. I still had time to take a shower and shave before she arrived. All wasn't lost. I'd planned an evening of sausage, sauerkraut, and large quantities of German beer. Kelly added polka dancing to the list of activities. She'd told me about attending an Oktoberfest celebration in Lubbock, but it sounded more like a church social compared to the party in Fredericksburg.

Letting work interfere with our relationship probably wasn't the best way to start things off. Either Kelly would understand, or she wouldn't. She'd been a Marine officer, and now she worked for the police crime lab. Two jobs that required more than just nine to five. She'd volunteered to help me on my last case. First by running a rapid DNA analysis in her department's advanced lab. Then she'd dropped everything and brought supplies and weapons when I briefly hit the state's most wanted list after killing a corrupt SAPD homicide detective for murdering my grandpa. I wondered what she'd say now when I told her I was on an active case.

Five minutes later, Owen pulled Lori out the back door. The first angry words carried over the traffic sounds and the open parking lot.

"What the hell were you thinkin'?" he yelled.

Lori stopped a few feet out the door and jerked her hand away. "What was I supposed to say? He's a private detective. He knows my family, and yours too."

"So?"

"So, he's working for Mr. Geisler."

"Keep it down. You never told me that." His voice was hard. He lowered his volume so that I couldn't hear the rest of the conversation. Lori stared down at her shoes and played with a strand of her blond hair. If I confronted them now, they would both feign innocence and clam up for good. If they were covering for Maya, it seemed likely that one of them would finish the argument and pick up a cell phone, or even better, go talk to Maya in person. Maybe warn her that someone was looking for her.

My phone rang. The caller ID said Kelly. "Hey, gorgeous," I answered. Ever the charmer.

"Why aren't you home in bed?" She made it sound like I'd escaped from the hospital.

"That's TV noise in the background. I'm flat on my back, saving all my energy for you."

"Liar. Your ranch house doesn't have a TV. I hear traffic. You're supposed to be recuperating."

"Okay, you caught me. I'm in town getting the keys to our love nest for the weekend."

"You promised me a night of polka dancing."

"I was thinking we could limit ourselves to beer and brats. I'm still really sore."

"Oh, no. Put on those lederhosen, Mr. Fischer. Don't play the wounded warrior with me." I'd made the mistake of telling her I had a pair of leather shorts that I wore once in middle school. "I bought a dirndl online. We're going to make a cute couple."

Before I could explain that I was proud of my heritage, but even if they fit, I had no intention of ever putting the lederhosen on again, Owen slapped Lori hard across the mouth. It was all I could do to stay in my pickup and not rush across the street and put the teen quarterback on his ass. Lori covered her face with her costume apron. Both fell silent. Owen took a step back. Lori sat down on a metal bench.

"Nick, what's happening?" Kelly asked.

"I'll tell you about it when you get here."

She could tell I was distracted. "You're working on something, aren't you? You're supposed to be resting. You promised me a relaxing weekend."

Owen sat down beside Lori and put his arm around her. She stood abruptly, shouted, "No, Owen. I can't do that," and stomped back inside the restaurant. Owen watched her go, then walked back to his pickup.

"Nick, are you still there?" Kelly asked.

"I gotta go. Call me when you get to town," I said and disconnected. I had to make a choice—confront Lori while she was reeling from a slap in the face or squeeze the truth out of her boyfriend. My whole morning had been one choice after another.

This one was easier than the others. Dealing with tearful females wasn't my specialty. When Owen jumped back in his pickup and raced out of the parking lot, I put my pickup in gear and followed him east out of town. The road paralleled the Pedernales River through prime farmland and dozens of new businesses. The area drew wineries, produce stands, antique shops, and an upscale brewery because it was the main road from Austin, Houston, and Dallas, where most of the weekend tourists came from.

He turned north on a gravel road, kicking up a cloud of white, limestone dust. I fell back a few miles to avoid the airborne debris. The cloud was easy to follow, like chasing a tornado across Kansas.

The road wound through rocky pastures full of whitetail deer, sheep, goats, and a few cattle. The grass had turned from green to shades of brown in the late summer, and many of the stock tanks were reduced to mud holes. When the column of dust began to settle, signaling Owen had slowed down, I pulled to the side of the road and looked at my watch. Five fifteen.

Meeting Kelly was going to have to wait. Owen's pickup turned off the road, went over a cattle guard, and disappeared into the thick scrub brush. We'd climbed out of the river valley and the terrain was steep, rocky, and covered with cedar and live oak trees. I turned off the motor, unrolled the windows, and listened to the hot engine tick. Two turkey vultures floated in leisurely circles on an afternoon thermal, searching for their evening meal. Five minutes turned to ten. Ten to fifteen. Kelly would be getting into town soon after her five-hour drive from Lubbock. Her reaction to my absence would determine the future of our relationship.

I thought of another girl who disappeared near this same remote area of Gillespie County. She was younger than Maya, and unlike Maya, her disappearance wasn't forgotten. It created a firestorm that turned up the heat on the sheriff to find her. It took three days, but the sheriff, my dad, found her in a trailer house about a quarter mile from where I was now parked. He was working on a hunch, and he didn't have probable cause to search the property. So, he waited for a warrant. He frequently complained about it, but he always followed the letter of the law. The long wait gave the kidnappers time to prepare. When he finally went in after her, he was shot and killed. The deputy who brought Grandpa and me the news had said not to visit the area because there was nothing to see but the burned remains of a trailer—some melted aluminum siding and a dozen or so blackened cedar trees. I was a teenager full of curiosity, so naturally, I had to see it for myself. The ashes were still smoking when I arrived on the scene. Crime tape and a deputy kept me from sifting through the ashes, but I remembered feeling the heat and wanting to break down and cry. I held back my tears because the deputy was there watching. I didn't break down until after his funeral, and I was alone in the horse pasture.

Since the incident involved the murder of the county sheriff, the Texas Rangers conducted a follow-up investigation. They said the fire was probably sparked by gunfire from one of the suspects and accelerated by volatile chemicals they were using to cook meth. It was when the meth epidemic was new to rural Texas, and the cooks could still buy all the necessary ingredients at the local drug store.

The Rangers found the remains of five bodies. One was the fourteen-year-old girl who was missing, and one was my dad. The fire burned so hot that it melted his 1911 .45 pistol down to the ivory handles. The other weapon he carried was a Mossberg tactical shotgun. There was nothing left of it but a twisted piece of the barrel. I wondered if he regretted waiting for a warrant and if going in sooner would have made any difference.

My cell phone rang and snapped me back to the present. It was Kelly. I checked my watch. Five forty-five.

"Are you ready to polka?" she asked.

"Always," I lied. Here was the crucial moment. Would she blow a gasket, or would she understand?

"Where are you?" Her voice was still friendly.

I could lie, or shade the truth, but I wasn't very good at that. "On a dirt road about ten miles out of town." A flash of sunlight reflected off a piece of glass or metal about five hundred yards from the road. "Hold on one sec." I dug my binoculars from the console and put the phone on speaker.

"What are you doing?"

"Following a lead." I glassed the brush-covered hillside and could just make out the outline of a double-wide trailer that I hadn't noticed before. The flash of sunlight must have come from the front door swinging open. Most of the yard was invisible to the road. With the ten-power Bushnells, I saw two figures standing by the door. One was Owen, and the other was a big guy with a blond ponytail that hung down to the middle of his bare back. His muscles were cut like a body builder's and covered with tattoos. When he turned, I saw the head of a red-and-green dragon decorating his right breast. He was laughing at something Owen said. The butt of a pistol protruded from his tight jeans.

"You still there?" Kelly asked. "I'm on Main Street now. Wow, it's like downtown Lubbock on game day. You weren't kidding about Fredericksburg's Oktoberfest being popular."

Ponytail stepped back into the trailer and shut the door. Owen had already stepped behind a tree. I could hear a pickup engine start.

"Nick, are you still there? You better not stand me up, Mr. Fischer. I might have to kick your ass." Her voice was still playful. That was a good sign.

"I'll explain when I see you. Keep going through town. The motel's on the east side. The Best Western on Main Street. I'll meet you there," I said and disconnected.

The haunting memory of what happened to my dad and the girl he was after when he waited to rush the trailer swept over me. I knew it was irrational to link the two events together. I had no reason to believe Maya was being held against her will or that she was even in the trailer. I just had a hunch that something wasn't right. The only difference was that the occupants of this trailer didn't know I was coming. To keep the element of surprise, I would have to leave now, or Owen would pass right by me.

If Maya was in that trailer, I would find her.

CHAPTER SEVEN

The bevy of German-themed motels in Fredericksburg complete with Bavarian murals on the outside walls, as well as the dozens of bed-and-breakfast rentals catering to Oktoberfest visitors were all booked several months in advance. When Kelly said she was coming, I'd put my name on a waiting list for several of those and been lucky that the Best Western had a cancelation.

The alternative would have been for Kelly to stay at the ranch. Having her and Helen under the same roof didn't appeal to me. I'd learned at an early age that sound travels too well in a stone house with wood floors. I could never sneak out, talk on the phone, or do anything private that escaped my grandparents' attention. The last thing I wanted was for Helen to hear our conversations or something more intimate. And I was really hoping for something more intimate. I also didn't want Helen to make friends with Kelly. When she wanted to, Helen could turn on the charm. I'd watched her do it at the funeral. She knew that the more friends she made, the easier it would be for her to play the victim when I tossed her out of the house. I overheard her telling several mourners that she'd lost her husband and her father, and I was the only one left in her life. Boohoo.

Inching through downtown traffic, I thought of when we'd first met in the Marine Corps when we were both stationed in Afghanistan. We were attracted to each other then, but she was an officer, and I was enlisted, so regulations kept us apart. We had a brief conversation outside the chow hall at Camp Leatherneck. She overheard someone call me "Tex" and asked me what part of Texas I was from. A year later, we met for beer at the VFW along the San Antonio River Walk. She'd called me out of the blue when she landed in San Antonio. She told me she was mustering out and wanted to catch up. At the time, I'd just started dating my law school classmate. When I told her, she seemed disappointed. I gushed over Sylvia like a charmed schoolboy, which at the time, I was. Sylvia was a knockout, and I was blinded to our glaring differences. I was a poor country boy, and she was a rich city girl. Fast forward two years, and I called Kelly to help me with a murder case. She'd taken a job at a crime lab in her hometown of Lubbock. The DNA test she ran helped me track down the killer. In the final showdown, she'd covered me with a tactical shotgun when Sylvia tried to distract me with a kiss while her new boyfriend fired his .38 revolver. That was three months ago. This weekend was going to be our first reunion since my release from the hospital.

Kelly's Dodge Ram sat in the shade of a giant pecan tree near the entrance. She was leaning against the front bumper. I glanced at my watch. Six twenty. Only twenty minutes late. The moment of truth. She wore her short blond hair loose and had on a tight, V-neck Texas Tech T-shirt tucked into khaki shorts that showed off her athletic legs. She had a healthy tan and reddish cheeks that came from spending time outdoors on her father's farm. Seeing her gave me a warm feeling, and not just because of her shapely legs.

I glanced at myself in the rearview mirror. My snap shirt was sweat-stained and dusty from an afternoon on a dirt road, and I hadn't picked up a razor in a couple of days. "Use your cowboy charm," I said, and stepped out of my pickup. "You look amazing." I hoped I sounded suave and debonair. I tipped my cowboy hat back on my head and waited for her reaction. This could be a very short reunion.

She smiled, wrapped her arms around me, and kissed me hard on the lips. The charm was working. My lateness and sweat-soaked shirt didn't faze her at all. "Sorry I'm late. I—" She stopped me with another kiss.

"I've missed you, Mr. Fischer," she murmured. I took her hand and led her toward the front office.

The franchise owner had tastefully painted the lobby wall with edelweiss blooming in an alpine meadow. The other decorations were the usual Texas kitsch, a wagon wheel chandelier, a "come and take it" flag, and several black-and-white photos of cowboys on main street taken in the early 1900s. The décor contrasted with the strong pungent odor of curry wafting from the back room. A young dark-skinned clerk entered, smiled, and asked for my driver's license and credit card in a thick Indian accent. He showed no reaction when Kelly wrapped her arm around me and kissed my neck.

I took the keycard and Kelly giggled a thank you. We raced to our second-story room and stumbled through the door like two high school kids on prom night. Absence did make the heart grow fonder.

• • •

Two hours later, she snuggled against me under the thin sheet and informed me it was time to polka. I couldn't say no since I was the one who'd proposed she visit on the festival weekend. She modeled the dress she'd found for the occasion. It was a modern, sexy version of the traditional dirndl that fit her like a glove.

"I can't believe you didn't bring your lederhosen. You're all into your German heritage."

She seemed a little disappointed.

"I said I had a pair. I never said they still fit. I grew out of them. I put on a little weight since high school."

"Liar. You haven't gained an ounce since I saw you at Camp Leatherneck."

I didn't know she remembered our first conversation. "Okay, you got me. The truth is I'm not exactly comfortable in leather shorts."

"Since when are you shy?" She went into the bathroom to put the finishing touches on her makeup and hair. "Next year, we're going to go in costume together," she called from the open door. "We have eleven months to find you a pair that fits." She said *next year*, as if our being together until next year was a given. I hated making predictions when it came to romance, but I liked where this one was going.

CHAPTER EIGHT

I parked on a side street near the Marktplatz, and Kelly and I followed a line of people around the temporary fencing that circled the park to the ticket booth. The city park was in the center of town and across the street from the new county courthouse and the old county courthouse that now housed the library. The sun was a large orange ball on the western horizon resembling an oversized pumpkin appropriate to the harvest season, and the temperature hovered in the low seventies. The smell of sausage and beer, and the sounds of Oompah music, laughter, and murmured conversations emanated from the open-air festival and permeated the town, giving every visitor a festive energy.

We stood in line behind a family that included four generations who'd probably never missed a festival. Even though the event had grown into a full-blown tourist attraction, with attendees from around the state and the country, all the locals also showed up. You were just as likely to run into a fifth-generation rancher in line at the beer tent as you were a banker from Houston or a student from Dallas. I only remember missing twice and both times I'd been stationed overseas.

I admired Kelly's formfitting blue-and-white dirndl that accented her curves and left her tan thighs exposed. She caught me looking.

"Don't you wish you'd worn your leather shorts to match me?" she said.

"Then I would take all the attention off your lovely figure."

Her laughter made me glad she came. Maybe it was because I'd had to deal with Helen in the interim, but I'd missed Kelly's presence by my hospital bedside that dragged on into weeks and became more intimate as my muscles finally allowed for a full range of motion. I was always leery of things that seemed too good to be true. But her being here with me now was a step in the right direction.

"Are any of the parties involved in your missing persons case going to be here tonight?" Kelly asked.

"Everybody shows up at the Oktoberfest," I said.

She looked a little disappointed. "Does that mean you're working?"

"I may be able to gather some intel."

"You're not getting out of dancing."

I slipped my hand in hers and smiled. "I won't let it interfere with our fun."

Her smile reappeared. "It better not," she said, and spit between her fingers.

"What was that?"

"What?"

"You just spit through your fingers."

"To ward off bad luck." She smiled mischievously.

I paid for a couple of tickets, and we shuffled through the crowd to the beat of tuba and accordion music. We passed the octagon-shaped Vereins Kirche Museum—a replica of the original community church—and a giant-sized beer stein that served as a welcome sign and photo opp. I led the way to the food court, where several local restaurants maintained booths. We bought a German sausage sampler plate to share, then we moved on to the *biergarten* for a couple of souvenir cups filled with German beer. I pulled my cowboy hat down low over my eyes, hoping not to have to talk to too many hometown people I knew in order to focus on Kelly. So far it was working. I'd passed a dozen people I grew up with who didn't seem to recognize me. When we reached the main tent, my hope of anonymity ended. Every table was full, and every table held someone who knew me and wanted to shake my hand. They weren't fooled by the new cowboy hat.

I obliged them all and made the rounds of the tables. They remembered

Kelly from Grandpa's funeral. The old-timers reiterated their condolences for Grandpa's passing. What I dreaded most was having to retell the story of Grandpa's murder and my shootout with Marcus Lopez, the corrupt San Antonio attorney who was running for governor without regard to ethics or legality. Everyone knew that for a twenty-four-hour period I'd been the state's most wanted fugitive. They peppered me with questions like "How did you know it was Marcus Lopez?" and "What happened to Patrick Allison?" The San Antonio newspaper had left out a number of juicy details given that both men, though guilty of murder and corruption, were still part of the ultra-rich Texas good ol' boy club.

Telling the story was easier because Kelly wasn't shy about filling in the details. I started with the young woman in the river, linked it to Danny Allison, then described walking into a trap at the ranch where I'd found Grandpa's body. The best part for Kelly seemed to be explaining how my ex-girlfriend's white shirt was left covered in Marcus Lopez's blood. She was a police officer and had been a Marine MP, so she was very good at giving the facts. At the end of the story, most of the listeners would shake their heads and say something like "It's a wonder y'all 're still alive." I wondered at that too.

Thankfully, the band was loud enough under the tent to restrict conversations to short periods when they were on a break. Kelly was serious about dancing, and we did our best imitation of a polka dance along with the throngs of college kids, locals, and tourists.

When they started the "chicken dance," I pulled Kelly off the dance floor. The warm October night had us both sweating. I led Kelly to the grassy picnic area between the dance floor and the biergarten. A kid wearing a Battlin' Billies T-shirt was trying to sneak a beer cup from the bar. His mom caught him and made him put it back. I remembered sneaking a few when I was in high school. Just when I thought we had a quiet moment to ourselves, I heard a high-pitched, nasal voice.

"Fischer, you ol' scallywag!"

I was immediately transported back to high school.

"Rocky V," I said and raised my beer. "*Prost*. You remember Kelly." They'd met during Grandpa's funeral.

He wore a red cap with the Battlin' Billies logo, red polyester shorts that stretched over a beer belly, and a white polo shirt with Coach V stitched above the breast pocket.

"Sure do." His eyes were glassy. "You look prettier than a Munich barmaid." I knew he'd never seen a Munich barmaid in person, but I let it go. He had a constant smile because his lips couldn't close over his two prominent front teeth.

Kelly held out her hand, but he went in for the hug. It was awkward. He planted a wet one on her cheek, then grabbed my free hand and shook it like a workout rope at the gym.

"Easy," I said. "I'm still in recovery." I knew I'd be sore in more places than one when the sun came up.

"Sorry. Keep forgettin' you're Wyatt Earp."

His wife followed a step behind him. She hadn't been to the funeral because she was the head volleyball coach and had been with the team on an out-of-town game. This was wife number four for Rocky. I was best man at his first wedding because it had come the week after high school graduation. The bride, his high school flame, was three months pregnant at the time. Wife number four was younger than Rocky by ten years, which would put her in her early twenties. Rocky had met her when she transferred from Round Rock as a senior in high school. A year after graduation, they were married. She had a matching polo shirt that was a size too small.

"This is my wife, Gwen," Rocky said. "She just got her boobs done."

Gwen stuck out her chest for us to admire. "Nice, huh? Rocky says I should go bigger. What do you think?"

I didn't comment. "Nice to finally meet you." I held out my hand, trying to avoid eye contact with her implants.

Gwen skipped the handshake and went in for the hug. I gritted my teeth. She pushed her enhanced boobs into my chest. "Hi, handsome," she whispered in my ear.

I glanced at Kelly over her shoulder and saw her eyes roll.

Gwen turned to her. "I just love your outfit, honey." She tugged a handful of Kelly's dress like she was examining a mannequin at Walmart. "Aren't you a tiny little thing?"

"What'd ya think of our little celebration?" Rocky asked Kelly.

Gwen didn't wait for her to answer. "I saw you two cuttin' a rug out there. Are y'all takin' lessons?"

They fired questions from both sides, not sober enough to care about the answers.

Kelly smiled and took my hand. "This is the first time we've danced together."

"Well, aren't you just the cutest couple?"

Kelly's smile got a little bigger. The skin on her neck turned red, but she didn't say anything.

"Have you seen Jimmy or Castro? They're around somewhere. Allison's here too. Three sheets to the wind. She's lettin' it all hang out, if you know what I mean." Rocky winked at me.

Gwen slapped him on the shoulder. "You stop that, now."

"It's true," he said.

A group of high school kids passed us, giggling a little too loudly. "Hey, Coach V," they said in unison. Rocky and Gwen both turned to them and flashed a thumbs-up. Owen Bauer was in the group. He had his head down, trying to go unnoticed. Lori wasn't with him. Neither was Maya. They must have just arrived.

"Saw you in the parking lot after practice," Rocky said to me. "Why didn't you stop by the locker room?"

Gwen grabbed Kelly's arm and pulled her away. "Let the men catch up for a minute. Follow me to the little girl's room," she said to Kelly.

Kelly's eyes pleaded with me to intervene, but I wanted to quiz Rocky about Owen, so I just smiled with pretend innocence.

"Here's some tickets. Bring us a round of beers when you come back," Rocky yelled over the crowd noise. He thrust a roll of concession tickets at his young wife. She took it and Kelly's hand and marched toward the row of porta-potties.

"I heard about your little interrogation," Rocky said. He sounded irritated. "Why're you pickin' on my star quarterback?"

"I just asked him a few questions about—"

He cut me off. "Maya Chavez. I know. Word gets around fast, or did you forget what small-town life was like?" He never missed a chance to chastise me over my move to San Antonio. "Owen didn't know she was old man Geisler's granddaughter."

"What difference does that make?"

"Just for the record. Did you talk to Zeller? He was around asking the same questions when Helmut reported her missing. He didn't find nothin' then. What're you lookin' for?"

Les Zeller had been a Battlin' Billy a couple of years ahead of us in school. I remembered him as a bully, and now he was a town cop. "I will talk to Zeller. I'm not real confident in his abilities. I followed the Bauer kid after I talked to him. He went to see Lori Kostoch. They argued, and he belted her in the face."

Rocky forced his lips over his teeth in a moment of concentrated thought. "Doesn't mean nothin'. You know how these kids are. It's high school. Tomorrow they'll be partying at Lori's mom's house."

"I'd just talked to her about Maya. She's the one who sent me to Owen. She wrote his name on my lunch receipt."

"Doesn't mean he knows anything," Rocky said defensively.

"Then he hauled ass out the creek road past his old man's place. He talked to a tatted-up dude in a trailer stuck out in the brush."

"So what? The guy probably works for Mike. Most of that part of the county is Bauer land. There's a bunch of cousins scattered around out there."

"Come on, Rocky. That ain't normal behavior. Owen knows something. If not where Maya went, he knows what happened."

"Things have changed since we went to school."

"What's that mean?"

"There's a lot of new folks moving into the county. Twenty years ago, we knew everybody that came through that gate." He pointed to the ticket booth. "Now, I don't recognize half of them."

"I still saw a lot of folks I know," I said.

"That's 'cause you're a famous gunslinger now. Everybody wants to shake your hand."

"What's this have to do with Maya?" I asked.

"Things have changed is all I'm saying. In the old days, our families ran the place. It's not like that anymore. There's new money in town. There's private jets at the airport almost every weekend."

"So what?"

"If you're thinking of staying in town, you need to know that."

"I haven't decided whether I'm gonna stay or not. Right now, I wanna find Maya."

Rocky drank the last of his beer. I could see him searching for the right words to tell me something. He closed his lips over his buckteeth again. I knew him too well. That was a sign he was serious.

"Owen Bauer is my star player. The kid's a natural. Reminds me of you before you threw it all away to go shoot terrorists." He put his hand on my shoulder and leaned in close. I got a strong whiff of hops and German sausage on his breath. "I don't want anything to happen to him. We got a good chance of gettin' to regionals this year, if not further."

There it was. A girl was missing, and he was worried about the Battlin' Billies football season. "Congratulations," I said. "Tell him to come clean about Maya, and I'll leave him alone."

"Damn it, Nick. I'm askin' as a favor. The kid's sensitive. If he's worried about you followin' him around, he'll fuck up in the game next week. I can't have that. We're playin' Boerne. They're tough this year."

"All I want is the truth," I said.

"Still the hardheaded German. I swear to god, I never met anyone as stubborn as you."

"I'm talking about a missing girl. Helmut's granddaughter. You're talking about your football season."

On some level he seemed to get it. "All right. Let me talk to him. Will you do that? You come on like Rambo. Hell, the kid's shittin' bricks."

"He's got nothin' to worry about if he tells the truth."

The girls elbowed their way through the crowd. Both held a cup of beer in each hand.

"I didn't think we'd ever get through the line. It gets more crowded every year." Gwen said, handing a beer to Rocky.

He quickly exposed his buckteeth and slipped back into happy-go-lucky coach mode. "Thanks for the beer, baby," he said and planted a sloppy kiss on her lips.

Kelly handed me a beer.

"To old friends," I said.

"*Prost!*" we said and tapped our plastic cups together.

"The band's playing again," Kelly said. She pulled my hand toward the dance floor.

"Don't take too long with Owen," I said to Rocky. "I need some answers." I waved at Gwen. "Nice to meet you, Gwen."

Rocky closed his lips over his buckteeth. "I'll talk to him."

The full moon guided our walk in the warm fall night from the Marktplatz back to my pickup. Kelly took my hand. The move felt natural, and I smiled as we made our way through groups of tired couples carrying sleepy kids and grandparents searching for their own parked vehicles. Kelly's fingers were strong from working out and bucking eighty-pound alfalfa hay bales at her daddy's farm. She was a natural athlete. Teaching her to polka took only a few minutes, then she quickly surpassed my rudimentary moves. I followed her lead for the rest of the night. We'd spent the last thirty minutes watching a grandmother teach her four grandchildren how to polka. They were all under ten years old, wearing traditional German costumes, and didn't seem the least bit self-conscious. I'd learned to dance the same way, holding Grandma's hands while she spun me around, counting *eins, zwei, drei, eins, zwei, drei*, over and over. Grandpa would occasionally cut in and show me how it was done. The two would swing around the concrete dancefloor with a practiced familiarity made possible from fifty years of marriage. Grandma's dirndl would twirl in the air, and grandpa's silver Stetson would be pushed back on his head. I glanced at the pregnant moon, trying to relax and live in the moment. I wanted to enjoy Kelly's company, but the polka and Oktoberfest brought back Grandpa's ghost and the guilt I felt for leading a murderer to his doorstep.

Kelly slipped her arm around my waist when we reached my pickup.

"You're thinking about your grandfather," she said.

"How'd you know?"

"Because there's a full moon, your belly's full of German beer, and there's a beautiful woman who can't keep her arms off you, but you're still pensive."

"I'm thinking of a new technique to try in our Best Western love nest."

She smiled and kissed me. "Liar."

"Okay, you caught me. This was his one social event of the year, besides going to church on Christmas and Easter."

"I'm sorry I didn't get to meet him," she said.

We drove in silence back to the motel. The wounds on my chest and arm were sore from dancing and shaking hands. It would be another few months before I was a hundred percent, and I resolved to step up my exercise program. It would be much longer before I could forgive myself for not getting to the ranch in time to save Grandpa's life.

I parked in the back of the full motel parking lot and went around to open Kelly's door. We walked to the front of the pickup and stood leaning against the fender, looking at the moon filtering through the oak trees. I pulled her close. Her hair smelled like lavender, and I felt her heartbeat against my chest.

"You gonna be all right?" she asked.

"Yeah. It'll take a while. He was my father, mother, and grandpa for a long time."

"Wouldn't hurt you to let it all out. I promise I won't tell anyone."

She tilted her face up and kissed me on the lips. Would it hurt me? I didn't know. I remembered breaking down in the hospital bed after spending three unconscious days recovering from the shootout. I'd killed the dirty cop who'd shot my grandpa, and I'd ended the life and political ambitions of a corrupt politician who put him up to it. Kelly was there in the hospital when I woke up. So was Skeeter. It was the first time I'd ever let anyone see my tears. When my mother left, I was fourteen. I took my tent and camped out on the backside of the ranch. I spent three days out there by myself until Dad finally came and got me. He said he knew how I felt and that we would just have to make the best of it. We never talked about it after that. When Dad was murdered, I was sixteen. I held it together until after the funeral, then walked out into the pasture and let loose where only the horses and cattle could see me. The skin on my neck and face turned hot remembering, and I felt vulnerable.

"It's okay," she said. "I understand."

I pulled her closer, partly to feel her warmth and partly so that she wouldn't see my tears. She was raised on a farm. Her ancestors were from pioneer stock like mine. Maybe she did understand. My last girlfriend couldn't grasp how anyone could remain silent and gloss over traumatic events with a joke. Long periods without speaking made her panic, and she interpreted my emotional detachment as a personality flaw instead of strength of character.

Kelly was different. When I let the silence stretch for a long minute, she kissed me. "Remember the first time we kissed?"

"Of course. In Lubbock while we were waiting for the DNA test on my suspect."

"Uh-huh. Were you surprised?"

"You caught me off guard."

"Then you left me. Did you really go back to San Antonio that night because of the case?" she asked.

I wasn't sure which answer would get me in more trouble. If I said I left her in the parking lot so I could pursue the case, she might think I would always choose work over her. On the other hand, if I told her I left her because at the time I still thought I could work things out with my girlfriend, she might be insulted that I chose Sylvia over her. I had never been very good at negotiating the dating world, which was why I spent most of my time between girlfriends.

"It took all my willpower to walk away from you that night," I said.

She smiled. "Good answer."

Maybe I was learning.

"There's something else holding you back tonight," she said, and kissed me again.

There was one other thing. Feeling guilty and sorry for myself about losing Grandpa was a reminder that Maya was still out there, and my gut feeling told me she was in danger. "What makes you say that?"

"I'm telepathic. Besides, I'm practically throwing myself at you, and you still haven't ripped my clothes off and taken advantage of me."

A family of four with two pre-teenage boys pulled into the empty parking space beside us. The two young boys in the back seat of the minivan pointed at us and giggled. Their mother said something to calm them down, but it didn't help. The product of too much cotton candy at the festival. It would be a while before they went to sleep. Unfortunately, they trudged up the stairs and went into the room next to ours.

"You only think you're complicated. You miss your grandpa and you're feeling guilty about his murder, and now you have a missing girl to look for. You forget I watched you in action on your last case. Once you start something, you don't back down and don't give up."

I started to explain that I was worried about Maya, but she cut me off with a finger on my lips. "You don't have to explain. Besides, I like that about you. If I didn't, I wouldn't be here." She slipped out of my grasp and walked to the passenger side door.

"What are you doing?" I asked.

"You think Maya's in that trailer you staked out this afternoon. If I don't go out there with you, you'll go on your own." She was right. If Maya was in that trailer house and something happened to her, it was on me. Kelly not only knew what I was thinking, she was willing to go along.

CHAPTER NINE

I cut the headlights and slowed to thirty miles an hour. The white caliche road to the trailer house glowed in the moonlight and was easy to follow. The dangerous part was avoiding the herds of deer and feral hogs grazing along the dark fencerow. If the animals spooked, they could easily flash across our path. At two hundred pounds or more, a full-grown boar hog could put a pickup out of commission even at slow speeds.

Kelly held my hand across the console. It was an odd sensation. I'd never held hands in the pickup with Sylvia, even after two years of dating. It wasn't something we'd discussed. Holding hands just seemed unnatural. With Kelly it was different. She caught me glancing at our linked hands.

"What? You don't like holding hands?" She tried to pull away, but I held firm.

"No. I like it." I smiled back. "I was just thinking that I'm not used to PDA."

"Well, get over it." She leaned over and kissed me on the cheek. "Besides, we're in the middle of nowhere on a gravel road without headlights. Whatever we do out here wouldn't be considered a public display of affection."

"I see your point."

She searched the dark pastures beyond the barbed-wire fences lining the road. "Where is this place? I'm starting to think you brought me out here to take advantage of me."

"If I wanted to do that, I'd have kept you in the motel room."

"If we don't find what we're looking for, can we get naked in the back seat?" She glanced at the loose tarp I used to protect the seat from Sam.

"Deal," I said. "Don't worry, the dog cover comes off."

"Don't make promises you can't keep, Mr. Fischer."

"That's something I never do."

I pulled to the side of the road at the cattle guard where Owen Bauer had crossed that afternoon. We saw lights about fifty yards back in the brush and heard muffled music. The night was still and warm, and I unrolled the windows to try to catch the faint breeze. A barn owl called from his perch in a live oak tree along the fence line. The pulsing music didn't seem to bother him. I pulled out my binoculars and swept the small clearing where the trailer stood. I made out the outline of two pickups.

"I don't hear any polka music," Kelly said.

"Not much dancing going on either." Two bodies emerged from behind the trailer. They both had shaved heads and wore sleeveless jean jackets. I checked for weapons. Each wore a holstered pistol on his belt. There was a fire burning in a fifty-five-gallon drum about twenty feet in front of the trailer. The barrel was cut in half and lying on its side. The two men walked closer to the fire and inspected the contents. "I see two thugs watching a barbecue pit. The brush is too thick to see anything else."

"Let me take a look."

I handed her the binoculars. She studied the layout for several minutes. "It's a stash house," she said.

"You're sure?"

"It's hidden out in the brush. The windows are masked over. Couple of guards outside. Couldn't be a better place to hide a shipment of drugs."

"I forgot you were a policewoman."

"What was Owen Bauer, star quarterback for the Battlin' Billies, doing here?"

"Exactly." She handed back the binoculars. Despite the warmth of the October night, a chill ran down my spine. Something in the back of my memory was tapping at the front door of my brain. The sensation gave me an uneasy feeling. That afternoon I remembered the shootout near here that had killed my dad, but there was something else that happened here. Something older. Something that reminded me of Maya. I search the horizon above the line of brush that hid the trailer. Only the brightest stars shown through the moonlight. Then it hit me. It was on bright nights like this that Comanches and Kiowas raided settlers along the Texas frontier. And one kidnapping happened very near this spot.

"What is it?" Kelly asked. A shaft of moonlight lit her worried facial features.

"Something happened here that reminded me of Maya. It's been bugging me since we crossed Palo Alto Creek." I finally realized what it was. "We're hunting a missing girl within a few miles of where Anna Metzger was abducted, and her sister was murdered by a Comanche raiding party."

"I didn't think there were any natives left in Central Texas."

"It happened in 1864."

"Ahh, ghosts of the pioneers."

"This area was the frontier. A lot of bloody history here. Anna survived nine months in captivity. Her fourteen-year-old sister was murdered on the spot. The Comanches forced Anna to watch as they raped and scalped her sister, then tossed her naked body on the snow and filled it full of arrows."

"That's hideous. I thought the Fredericksburg folks had a treaty with the Indians. There's that statue in the park of a pioneer and the Indian smoking a peace pipe. Wasn't that from 1840-something?"

"The Meusebach Treaty. It was a good effort. The Comanches trusted him and considered the German settlers around Fredericksburg a different tribe than other Anglos invading their hunting grounds. The problem was that any Comanche brave was free to rape, pillage, and plunder at will. All he needed to do was convince enough of his buddies to go on a raiding party with him. They didn't have a central government, so no other band was obligated to follow the treaty. Besides that, after a few years, the Indians couldn't tell the difference between Germans or any other Anglo group."

She shivered and crossed herself.

"What was that for?"

"Keeps the ghosts away." She smiled.

"You're afraid of ghosts?"

"There are some things a pistol won't protect you from."

"Like evil spirits?"

She nodded. "What happened to Anna?"

"The girls had been visiting their older sister who worked at the Nimitz Hotel on Main Street. It was February, and there was snow on the ground. They were walking the three miles back home when riders appeared on the road. It was dusk, and they thought it was someone they knew. They waved, then realized too late that it was a raiding party. Before they could run, one grabbed Anna and strapped her on the front of his horse. The older sister, Emma, resisted. She screamed that she would never be taken alive."

Kelly chewed her bottom lip. A crease I hadn't notice before formed between her blond eyebrows. "That's terrible."

"The Indians didn't want to be bothered with a captive who put up a fight. While Anna watched, the Comanche stripped her sister's clothes and scalped her. Her family found her body the next morning lying in the snow bloody, beaten, and full of arrows."

"Oh my god. And they took Anna?"

"They rode north toward the Red River and Oklahoma territory. It took twelve days, with only brief stops for river crossings. The only food they gave her was raw liver. She said her tongue got so swollen from lack of water she couldn't speak. A story came out in the Austin newspaper, and years later, she wrote her own book about the ordeal."

"How long was she gone?"

"She spent nine months in captivity. When she returned, she married and moved up the road to Mason. The first settlers were a very tough bunch. She lived to be eighty-one years old."

Kelly crossed herself again. We both sat quietly in the dark thinking of the horrors Anna must have faced. Finally, she said, "You think Maya was kidnapped?"

"The thought did cross my mind. I'm starting to think she didn't leave on her own."

I pulled my Springfield XD .45 pistol from the glove box, checked the magazine, and strapped on the shoulder holster.

"You're not gonna break into that trailer."

"No, I'm gonna do a little recon. No one will know I'm there. Unless I see Maya."

She pulled a SIG Sauer P226 pistol from her purse and clipped it on her belt. "Dating you is going to be interesting."

"So... We're dating? Is it official?" I asked.

"Are you kidding? We already danced the polka and made love in a Best Western. It doesn't get any more official." She leaned over the console and kissed me. "Let's go see what's going on in that trailer."

We hopped the barbed-wire fence and made our way through the thick brush toward the lights. The moon was still bright enough for us to avoid major rocks and the lethal cactus spines. A coyote yipped, followed by a dozen or more. They were on the hunt, and so were we.

We crept to within fifty feet of the trailer. Two skinhead guards were outside. One was tending to a large piece of meat on the barbecue pit. The other sat in a folding chair drinking a Coors Light. There were two tricked-out Super Duty pickups fitted with chrome roll bars and a new black Jeep Grand Cherokee with oversized mud tires parked in the clearing.

"What do you think?" she whispered.

"This is Bauer property, but those vehicles are way too fancy for Bauer's field hands."

All the curtains were closed. A diesel generator hummed, creating the power for the lights and the AC unit mounted on the roof.

While we listened to the heavy metal noise and watched the skinhead turn the meat, the tattooed guy stepped out of the trailer. He had his shirt off and his hair in a ponytail. The distinctive dragon tattoo decorated his chest. "That's the guy I saw with Owen."

"Looks like a gangbanger," Kelly said.

A young girl stepped out of the trailer and onto the wooden pallet used for a porch. Her cutoff jean shorts were tight, and she wore a black tank top. I guessed she was in her late teens or early twenties. Her hair was dark and stringy and clung to her head like she hadn't washed it in a week. She lit a cigarette and stood looking down at the meat on the barbecue pit.

"Is that Maya," Kelly whispered.

I studied the girl while she turned her face into the light. "No. Her eyes are dark. Maya has green eyes."

"What d'ya think you're doin'?" The guy with the tattoo said loud enough for us to hear.

"I just came out for a smoke," the girl answered defensively.

"Get your ass back in the trailer and finish business," he said.

"He stinks. Besides, he passed out."

The guy with the tattoo laughed at her. He was six two or three and probably tipped the scales at around two thirty without an ounce of fat. He was definitely the man in charge.

"You stink," he said, grabbing the lit cigarette from her lips and tossing it into the barrel. "I don't want you seen out here."

"Who's gonna see me?" the girl whined. "We're in the middle of fuckin' nowhere."

"Get, girl." Tattoo raised his hand as if to strike her.

I took a step forward. I wasn't gonna stand by and let the big guy smack the girl around. I'd already let that happen once with Lori.

Kelly grabbed my arm. "Wait," she whispered.

The girl cringed as if she expected to be hit, but Tattoo didn't swing. The girl quickly retreated into the trailer.

"If you go over there, somebody's gonna get hurt."

"That's the idea," I said. "If there's one girl, there may be others in the trailer. Maya could be one of them."

"You're forgetting about the hole in your chest. You know you're not one hundred percent, and that tattooed guy looks like a handful."

"Thanks for the vote of confidence."

"Just being practical."

She smiled and I smiled back. She was tough. I knew that much. There was no doubt she would take on the guy with the dragon tattoo if she had to.

"I need to look in that trailer." My first instinct was to slap some sense into Dragon Tatt after watching the girl's reaction, but I understood Kelly's point.

"I'll create a diversion. Work your way around back and see what you can see through the windows."

I nodded. She stood up without another word and walked directly toward the circle of light surrounding the trailer.

I didn't like what she was about to do, but I couldn't stop her. I knew she was armed and could take care of herself. She made it to the edge of the brush before the man with the dragon tatt saw her.

"Well, well, well," he said in a loud voice.

"Easy, big boy," Kelly's voice carried over the music. "I'm looking for Mike Bauer."

While she had their attention, I ducked behind the trailer and searched the edge of the first window. There was a small tear in the white plastic that gave me a view inside. The room was small with warped wood paneling and no furniture except a bare double mattress that rested on the floor. The young woman I'd seen outside was lying on the bed staring at the screen of her smartphone. A naked man in his forties with a pumpkin-shaped beer belly and a farmer tan sprawled on the bed beside her, unmoving. Sleeping or passed out.

I crept to the next window. The plastic shade was raised a couple of inches, and I could see a sink full of dirty dishes and a built-in table against the opposite wall. Two women sat smoking. Each had shorts and tank tops exposing a cluster of tattoos. A half-empty bottle of tequila sat in front of them. They were older and neither looked like Maya. I peered around the small space. The TV blared a reality show I didn't recognize. Dirty clothes littered the floor, along with black plastic trash bags stacked to the ceiling against one wall.

I moved to the rear window. It was covered with white plastic that was taped down to the edge of the frame on the inside. The light caused the white plastic to glow. I heard muffled voices but couldn't make out words. The metal window frame buzzed from the loud music and the diesel generator. I couldn't leave without knowing if one of the voices belonged to Maya.

I took out my folding knife and slowly lifted the edge of the window frame. The metal was old and oxidized, and easily opened half an inch. I grabbed a mesquite branch and wedged it under the glass to hold it open. The voices were loud enough to hear now. They were young female voices speaking in Spanish. I didn't know if Maya knew the language, but her father was Hispanic, and she'd spent eight years in Southern California. It was possible.

I risked lifting the white plastic covering. Two young women Maya's age sat on a double mattress resting on the cracked linoleum floor. They were dressed like the older women in shorts and tank tops. I smelled the distinct odor of marijuana. The women had long shoulder-length dark hair. Both wore heavy makeup accented with dark red lipstick, and each had brown eyes. I wondered what they were doing there and what they were talking about.

One turned to the window. Their conversation stopped. I ducked. They sensed a presence watching them. I took the twig from the window and slipped into the surrounding brush.

Kelly was waiting for me when I got back to the pickup.

"What'd you find out?" she asked.

"No Maya, but there're four other women in the trailer. The one we saw talking to Mr. Tattoo was on the bed with a fat naked guy in his forties. He looked passed out."

"Any drugs?"

I told her about the plastic bags stacked against the wall and the smell of marijuana. "It might be enough to get the sheriff department to take a look." We got in the pickup, and I made a U-turn in the road and headed back toward town.

"What'd you say to the tattooed guy?" I asked.

"Told him I was looking for Mike Bauer. I showed him my campus police badge. He didn't seem impressed. The two skinheads were stoned. They looked like ex-cons who definitely shouldn't have drugs or weapons, but the big guy didn't seem shy about showing off."

"What'd he say about Bauer?"

"Said he works for him. Mike would be back in the morning. He offered me some barbecue and a joint if I wanted to wait."

"How generous."

"The guy's evil. I do know that."

"Because of the dragon tatt?"

"That and his eyes. Cold. Dead. No empathy. A prison stare. The kind of guy that makes my skin crawl." She crossed herself. "Don't go up against him alone. Not now. Not with holes in your chest and your arm."

"Not planning on it," I said, but something told me I wouldn't have that option.

CHAPTER TEN

Detective Les Zeller had been a couple of years ahead of me at Fredericksburg high school, and the kind of sweet lovable bully that everybody avoided like the middle seat on a bus. My best memory of him was the day he threatened to beat up a kid name Julian Gonzalez. I was in ninth grade and Les was a senior. It happened in the parking lot before school. Les called Julian a wetback, meaning an illegal alien who'd recently crossed the Rio Grande River border from Mexico. Julian was born in Texas but lived in Mexico for part of each year. His parents came north to work following the harvest seasons. Everybody knew it, and nobody bothered them because the farmers needed labor. Everybody except Les. He told Julian that if he didn't go back to where he came from, meaning Mexico, he'd beat him within an inch of his life and turn his family in to the Border Patrol. At the time, Les weighed close to two twenty and everybody on the football team suspected him of using steroids because his muscles were too clean and cut for an eighteen-year-old. Julian was dark skinned and skinny, not more than a hundred and ten pounds soaking wet. He didn't stand a chance against Les.

Rocky Velosic and I watched the scene play out from my pickup. Julian stepped out of a rusted-out minivan, said goodbye to his mother in Spanish, and walked toward the front door of the school. Les stood with his hands on his hips, blocking the door, wearing an undersized Battlin' Billies T-shirt that showed off his enhanced muscles.

Whether it was because my father had been sheriff or because he'd been murdered on the job, I had a keenly formed instinct to protect the weak or innocent. It sometimes got me into fights I didn't win, but that never stopped me from trying. I got out of my pickup and stood next to Julian. Rocky joined me. Not because he had the same instinct but because he was my friend.

"You two faggots sticking up for a wetback?" Les sneered.

"No, we're sticking up for Julian," I said.

Les sauntered toward us. Rocky and I stepped in front of Julian and prepared to do battle with a charging bull. Just as he was about to throw a roundhouse punch in my direction, the head football coach walked out the front door. Les was a senior and football season was in full swing. Coach yelled at Les to stop. Then ordered him to report to the locker room. We never heard what coach told him, but he didn't bother us or Julian for the rest of the school year. We saw Les that day after football practice doing bear crawls alone on the practice field.

"And now he's a police detective?" Kelly said when we'd parked beside the county law enforcement center.

"And probably hasn't changed a bit."

We found Detective Les Zeller eating a blueberry kolache and talking on his desk phone. He'd lost the cut muscle definition. The bulk of his weight had shifted from his chest to his belly. No doubt kolaches had replaced his steroid injections. And he sported facial hair. A dark woolly caterpillar covered his upper lip and I wondered how he kept it from crawling down his chin. He'd instantly recognized my name when I called to make an appointment and agreed to give me a few minutes of his time on the busy Oktoberfest weekend without any hint of animosity. Maybe the bully had softened along with his muscles.

He motioned us into a couple of metal folding chairs and held up two fingers, which I took to mean give him two minutes to finish his phone call. The other party seemed to be doing all the talking. Les was nodding as if the caller could see him and grunting responses through blueberry-stained teeth. He pointed at a large white pastry box on the desk and gestured for us to help ourselves. I recognized the box as coming from the German Bakery and couldn't resist selecting a pastry filled with cream cheese.

Kelly declined, making me feel guilty for indulging.

"Well, you two look like newlyweds," Les said, when he hung up the phone.

Kelly blushed and offered a bright smile.

"This is Kelly Hoffman. She's a police officer in Lubbock."

He wiped the blueberry off his mouth with a paper napkin and stood to offer Kelly his hand. "Miss Hoffman." He pasted on a smile that he must have thought looked genuine.

"Pleased to meet you," Kelly said.

"A fellow officer." He sized her up a little too closely for me, but I held my tongue. He sat back in his chair and rested his folded arms across the natural shelf of his protruding belly.

"We were all sorry to hear about your granddaddy. Otto was a real fixture around here."

"Thanks, Les," I said. Most of the town had come to the funeral. At least, everyone that had lived there more than twenty years. Les's father had been there. He'd been a deputy in the sheriff department under my father and recently retired and moved to Rockport on the Gulf Coast. I hadn't seen Les.

"That was a crazy thing you were involved in. Some folks are even callin' you a hero for killing that Lopez character."

"I didn't have a choice. I was returning fire." He was talking about my encounter with Marcus Lopez, the shootout that left me with a hole in my chest.

"All the same, the way I heard it, you made a hell of a shot. Lopez had his pistol out and aimed, but you managed to draw and blow his head off."

"He did get off a shot. Nailed me in the chest."

"Ouch, that's gotta hurt."

"Only when I breathe," I deadpanned. He didn't get the reference.

"I heard you took out a half dozen of his bodyguards too."

"Kelly helped with that. She was there. Wouldn't have survived without her."

He let out a long whistle of admiration, which made the caterpillar on his lip wiggle. "Too bad about that SAPD detective you killed."

I wasn't quite sure what he meant. The caterpillar went back to sleep, and his face was a stone mask. Was he sorry the detective was a dirty scumbag, or was he sorry I'd killed him? The SAPD detective killed my grandpa, put a bullet in my partner, and shot my dog. I wasn't sorry he was gone, and I felt zero guilt for killing him. The detective was on Marcus Lopez's payroll. Since I found out Lopez was blackmailing a very rich family to finance his run for governor, the detective drew a bullseye on me and my family.

"Yeah, the bastard was dirty." My blood pressure rose, and the bullet wounds throbbed. Les Zeller hadn't changed. His methods for baiting a fight were more subtle, but I was more sophisticated too. I wasn't gonna bite. "We came to ask about Maya."

Zeller's desk phone rang before he could respond. He picked it up and listened to the caller, then held up his hand, signaling for me to wait again while he took the call.

I stared at Les and considered his comment about the SAPD detective while he chatted on the phone. The fact that I'd killed an officer during the course of the investigation, regardless of his obvious criminal conduct, rubbed some in law enforcement the wrong way. Cops didn't like dirty cops, but they didn't like anybody outside the fraternity doing anything about it. They wanted to punish their own. Les seemed to think that way.

"Give me five minutes," Les said into the phone and hung up.

I figured that was the time he was giving us, so I let the SAPD remark slide for now and plunged in with my story. "Like I said on the phone, I'm here about Maya Chavez. Helmut Geisler told me she went missing in August. He's worried. I told him I'd look into it."

He nodded. "You're officially workin' the case?"

"He hasn't seen her in two months, Les. I'd say there's reason for concern."

He put his elbows on the desk and thoughtfully tapped his fingertips together, putting on a show of concern. "Helmut's been in here to talk to me a couple of times. I like Helmut. He's a good man. But he's gettin' long in the tooth if you know what I mean. I think he's way off base with Maya."

"What makes you say that?" Kelly asked. She didn't like the way this was going, and neither did I.

"Here's the deal with Maya," he said. "She's what you might call a wild child. I spoke with my counterparts in San Bernardino and Riverside County. Maya had a history. Picked up for truancy. She had gang ties. Her father's side of the family."

"She was born here, Les."

"She spent eight years in Southern California," he said, as if that explained everything.

"We both spent time in Iraq and Afghanistan," Kelly said. "We're still Texans."

He sighed. "You were adults. Maya left when she was an impressionable kid."

"Doesn't matter. She's still missing," I said.

"She's eighteen. It matters. There's no law against her leaving home. You did it."

"I joined the Marine Corps. It wasn't a secret. Everybody knew where I was going. And I packed my suitcase. Maya left without anything."

"The thing is, as much as I'd like to help, we don't have the manpower to chase down every runaway case we get. We notify the hotline and wait for a tip. If she committed a crime or she was a victim, and we knew she was still in the area, we could go after her. We can't just go breakin' down doors. We gotta have probable cause." He said this last part like he was explaining it to a third grader. "That means we would—"

"I know what it means, Les." My face felt hot and that meant my forehead scars had turned red. He was enjoying goading me into taking a swing at him.

"The rules have changed, Nick," he said. "We follow the law."

"What the hell's that supposed to mean?"

"I got the call the day you killed that SAPD detective. You played fast and loose with the law." He fixed me with a practiced cop stare.

I suppressed the urge to put a right jab into his smug face. "It was an ambush, Les. I didn't pick a fight, and I didn't fire first. When I got there, my grandpa was already dead and San Antonio's finest was waiting for me in the hayloft with a department-issued .308."

Kelly put a hand on my forearm, reminding me why we were here. "We just wanna know who you talked to about Maya." Her calm voice tossed cold water on the escalating tension. "You called the runaway hotline, but did you track her phone or put anything out on social media? That kind of thing?"

Zeller wiped sweat from his face with a paper towel. "We opened a file." He held a manila folder up as proof. "The phone number Helmut gave me was a burner. I talked to a couple of her classmates over at the high school and to her mother. She hadn't made many friends, and nobody'd seen her. We don't have the time or the resources to do social media."

"Was one of the friends Lori Kostoch?" I asked.

"Yeah, one of them was Lori," he said, reading from the file.

"What about Owen Bauer?" I asked.

He didn't look back down at the file. He didn't need to. "Yeah, him too."

"I saw him yesterday. After we talked, he got into a fight with Lori Kostoch, then drove out to a trailer house past Palo Alto Creek."

"The trailer looks like a stash house," Kelly said.

"Now, wait a minute." Les laid his chubby hands flat on the desk and leaned forward. "That's all Bauer property in that part of the county. You can't be out there without Mike's permission."

"Is Mike Bauer dealing drugs these days?" I asked.

"You saw drugs in the trailer?"

"I saw plastic bags stacked to the ceiling. The windows are closed. Get a warrant and go check it out. I smelled marijuana, and they had firearms."

"No law against havin' guns," he said.

"Unless you're a felon," Kelly reminded him.

"There were also some females in the trailer. You can take a wild guess why they were there," I said.

Les's face turned red. It was my turn to get under his skin. He stood up. "I need more than that to get a warrant to search Mike Bauer's property. This ain't your daddy's county no more. You can't run around here like you own the place."

"Who owns it now, Les? You? Mike Bauer?"

Lester painted on a smile. "Still the same hot-headed Nick wantin' to save the world."

"I guess we never change, do we, Les." I matched his fake smile.

"I got work to do, Nick. Nice to meet you, Miss Hoffman. Enjoy yourself at the Oktoberfest." He stood and put on his dark blue FPD cap. "I understand you have a legal license to investigate, and Helmut can retain your services. But don't bother Mr. Bauer or his son again. And stay off his property and away from his employees or I'll have to haul you in."

"And what about Maya?" I asked. I stood in the doorway blocking his exit. We were the same height, but he still outweighed me by thirty pounds. He cocked his right arm slightly behind his hip, and I wondered if he was thinking of the punch he never got to throw in the parking lot of Fredericksburg high school.

"Sometimes kids just run off. My guess is, she'll get tired of partying and come home."

"Thanks for the kolache, Les. Say hi to your daddy for me. He was a good man and a good deputy."

Kelly stepped between us. She took my hand and led me down the hall and out of the building. I had a feeling I would square off with Detective Les Zeller again.

Outside, in the cool October morning, my blood pressure returned to normal.

"You handled that well," Kelly said, meaning the opposite.

"Like I said, he hasn't changed."

"You haven't either."

CHAPTER ELEVEN

I'd promised Kelly schnitzel and red cabbage for lunch but the two best German eateries on Main Street, The Ausländer and Rathskeller Bistro, had wait times over forty-five minutes. Every year, the Oktoberfest celebration attracted more tourists. Grandpa said that was a bad thing. He preferred the older, smaller version of the town that he wistfully remembered from his youth, before LBJ's ascent to the White House brought worldwide attention. On the other hand, to the pro-growth developers like Mike Bauer and his family, the more the merrier. Mike's grandpa had seen the writing on the wall in the seventies and helped Hondo Crouch purchase and promote the nearby ghost town of Luckenbach, the same one celebrated in the Waylon Jennings song, as a destination bar and music venue. Grandpa never forgave him for that because the "town," which consisted of a single building in 1970 and a population of three, was located about four miles from our ranch, and when Willie Nelson, Waylon, or Jerry Jeff Walker played there, the original population of three swelled to five thousand, snarling traffic to a standstill and prompting Grandpa to put up *No Trespassing* signs and patrol our property on horseback.

I drove slowly past the dozens of people loitering outside The Ausländer restaurant, wondering how to tell Kelly that I didn't want to wait in line. She saw my concern and took my hand. Said, "I'll settle for a hamburger. Didn't Germans invent that too?"

"Probably. It's got the three things we love best, bread, meat, and cheese."

"Throw on a potato and you'd be in Valhalla."

"Now you're talking dirty."

She laughed. She got my jokes. I took that as another sign of our compatibility. I couldn't wait to tell the Fischer ancestors when I returned to the ranch. It may not cause a smile, but it might assuage the tension. I pulled into the drive-through line at Whataburger, a Texas based fast-food tradition, a few blocks from the motel. There were half a dozen pickups ahead of us, but it wasn't called "fast food" for nothing.

"Sure you don't wanna wait for the good stuff?"

"I don't mind fast food. Just promise me we won't make this a habit."

"Done. I'll even cook for you at the ranch."

"I know that means grilled meat, so I'll accept."

"You don't think I can cook anything else?"

"I was raised on a farm. I know what men mean when they say they'll cook dinner."

I laughed and pulled forward in line. She knew exactly what I had in mind. All the things I liked to cook centered around the main course. Deer, beef, pork, and chicken, in that order. Unless it was bird season. Then I would include turkey, duck, or dove. I remembered that Helen was cooking deer roast at the ranch, but I had enough to worry about without opening a war on the domestic front by introducing her to Kelly. Helen would try to use her to gain sympathy, and I'd have to explain why forgiving my mother was out of the question. The roast would keep.

"Why do you think Les got defensive when you mentioned Bauer?" Kelly asked.

"He's a city cop. Bauer's on the council. He knows who signs the checks."

"What about Owen?"

"Everybody supports the football team. If they're winning, the coach and all the players are royalty. There may be a population boom, but it's still a small Texas town. You can bet Les will have a conversation with Mike about our visit."

The drive-through intercom squawked, and a high-pitched female voice asked for our order. I cut the ignition switch so I could hear over the engine noise. My ten-year-old pickup was pushing 200K and sounded like a gas-powered leaf blower at idle. I wanted to trade it in on something newer but needed a paying gig to afford it.

"The people who run this town are a close-knit group. They all talk to each other. They may not all like each other, but they all talk."

"I always thought of Lubbock as a small town."

"Compared to San Antonio. Not compared to Fredericksburg."

A tap on the glass startled us both. I turned to see Lori Kostoch standing outside my door.

"Mr. Fischer, can I talk to you?" She glanced nervously over her shoulder and spoke in a low, frail whisper. Her blond hair hung loose, and she wore a blue T-shirt with the German Bakery name stenciled in white gothic letters over Wrangler jeans.

"Sure, Lori. Get in."

She glanced at Kelly. "I'd rather it was private."

"It's okay. This is Kelly Hoffman. You can talk in front of her. She's working with me. She's a police officer. I told her about Maya, and she agreed to help."

Lori opened the rear door and hopped in the back seat.

"Is everything okay?" I asked, studying her in the rearview mirror. She didn't answer. I could see the fresh cut on her lip where Owen had slapped her. She'd made an effort to cover it with red lipstick, but it was still swollen.

Lori stared at her hands uneasily.

"Would you like something to eat?" I asked.

She shook her head.

I pulled forward to the second drive-through window. Lori ducked down on the floorboard, hiding from the young cashier. She would know every teenager in town, and she was obviously concerned about being seen with me.

I took our bag of burgers and fries and drove around the city block to see if we were being followed, then pulled into the parking lot of Fort Martin Scott, a restored US Army outpost built in the mid-nineteenth century. The location was on the edge of town and had just enough tourists in the parking lot to keep us from looking conspicuous.

I took a cheeseburger from the Whataburger sack and offered it to her. "You sure you don't want something?"

"No, sir. Thank you." She still spoke in hushed tones and sat low in the seat to make herself less visible.

I was starving but wanted to give Lori my full attention, so I reluctantly put the burger back in the sack. "Did you think of something else?" I studied her from the front seat. Lori's eyes were wide and obviously scared.

"I lied about Maya," she finally said, looking down at her hands again. "The night she—The night she left. I was with her. I drove her to the party on the river."

Kelly raised her eyebrows, shot a glance at me.

"I'm sorry I didn't tell you before, but I was scared."

"Scared of what?" I asked.

"I—I don't know. Just scared."

She did know, but she didn't wanna tell me yet. "It's okay. Tell me about it now."

"I picked Maya up on the road outside the Geisler ranch and drove to a party on the river. It was the weekend before school started."

I waited without speaking. Lori glanced out the windows at the other cars in the parking lot, then scanned the faces of a family of tourists reading the historical marker. She seemed to be expecting someone to jump out and approach the pickup at any moment.

"You're safe here," I said. "Don't worry. Do the seniors still make the freshmen stay on the rocky end of the beach?"

Lori flashed a brief smile. "Yeah. The seniors always get the best spots."

"What do you remember?"

The smile vanished. "It was different this time." She glanced at me, then Kelly, deciding how much to tell us, and if she should trust us.

"There were guys there I didn't recognize. Older men. They wanted us to, like, dance for them. There were a couple of older women too. Maybe in their twenties. They danced, you know, like strippers. They wanted us to dance. It was disgusting. One of them grabbed Maya and pulled her top off." The words tumbled out of her mouth and left her short of breath.

"Slow down. Who were they?" I asked.

"Owen's friends. One of them told Owen to bring Maya. He—He asked me to help him convince her to go. Owen said not to worry. Everything was cool, you know?"

"And you were tryin' to impress Owen?" I asked.

She nodded. "Yeah. I told him I'd talk to her. Get her to go to the river."

"Did they hurt her?" Kelly asked.

"They were all over her. Us. Then this guy stopped them. I'd seen him before. He works for Owen's dad. Owen called him "Dragon." He has this big, like, tattoo of a dragon on his chest. It's, like, green with red flames. Weird, you know? He punched the man who took Maya's top. The rest just backed away like they were afraid of him."

"You were afraid of him," I said.

"Yeah. The guy was creepy, you know?"

"What happened to Maya?"

"I don't know. That's what I wanted to tell you. When Dragon stepped in, I took off. I ran back to my car. I was scared. I waited for like an hour. When Maya didn't come, I left. My mom called and said I had to come home. I thought she would be okay, you know? But that was the last time I saw her." She looked down at her hands, then out the pickup window. "I wanted to tell you earlier, but Owen said to keep my mouth shut."

"Is that why you fought with Owen behind the bakery?"

She touched her swollen lip and nodded.

"And Dragon. Is he the one who asked Owen to bring Maya?"

She nodded.

My skin felt hot, and I knew my facial scars were red and throbbing. I thought about the women in the trailer and the thug with the tattoo. The idea that Maya was somehow mixed up with the same crowd and that Owen Bauer knew about it made my blood boil. I pursed my lips and let out a slow breath. Showing my anger might put Lori over the edge. She was freaked out enough. I needed to keep her calm and on my side. "You did the right thing coming to me. I'll find Maya. Don't worry."

Kelly reached over the seat and put her hand on Lori's shoulder. "We're here to help you and get Maya home safely."

Lori took a deep ragged breath. A weight seemed to lift from her shoulders, and her eyes suddenly flooded with tears.

Kelly found a paper towel in the console and handed it to her.

I waited while she blew her nose and dried her eyes. "We need to know everything. If I'm gonna find Maya, you can't hold back."

She put her shaking hands on the back of the seat and looked me in the eyes for the first time. "Do you really think you can find her?"

"I'll find her." I hoped I sounded confident, but deep down the situation scared me for different reasons. Too much time had passed. If Maya was a victim of trafficking, she could be in a different state or country by now. I needed a lead to point me in the right direction, and I needed it fast.

CHAPTER TWELVE

We drove Lori back to the Whataburger, and I stopped in the parking lot beside her Honda SUV. It was two o'clock in the afternoon, and traffic was tight. The Marktplatz gates were open for Oktoberfest, and tourists flooded the German-themed streets looking for that small-town, family-friendly experience that Fredericksburg had perfected.

Lori seemed reluctant to get out, as if she had more to say.

"You have my card. Call me if you think of anything else."

"Okay," Lori said and fished it out of her back pocket.

Kelly took it and wrote her name and cell phone number below mine along with our motel room number.

"This has both our cell phone numbers and our room at the Best Western," she said. "We're here to help you." She handed the card to Lori with a smile. "Stay away from Owen. If he touches you again, I will personally kick his ass."

Lori smiled at that. She knew Kelly wasn't kidding.

I drove east out of town on Highway 290, toward Austin. All the traffic was going the other way, so I stepped on the gas and raced a little faster than the speed limit.

"Do you think she's holding out?" Kelly asked.

"I do."

"Any theories, or are you gonna keep everything to yourself?"

"Fear. That's my theory. The guy with the dragon tattoo scares the hell out of them and I wanna know why."

"Zeller warned you to stay off Bauer property and away from his employees."

"Yep."

"And you're gonna completely ignore the law." It was a statement, not a question. Her lips were pursed, and she wore a serious frown. She operated strictly by the book, and even the hint of impropriety made her nervous. She'd volunteered to help me on my last case because I was the victim of corruption, and the very idea made her blood boil. She didn't see the similarity with this case, but I did. Zeller may not be corrupt, but he was inept. That amounted to the same thing as far as I was concerned.

I laughed. "Of course not. I wouldn't dream of breaking the law. I'm going to ask Mike Bauer for permission."

She let out of sigh of relief. "Thank you," she said and put her hand on my shoulder.

I didn't tell her that talking to Mike Bauer wasn't really about getting permission. It was about rattling his cage. There was a connection between him and the source of Lori's fear, and I wanted to know what it was. Besides, I was good at rattling cages, and the technique, while admittedly dangerous, could produce the quick results I was after.

We passed a dozen new wineries en route that had sprouted over the last five years, adding to the more than sixty in Gillespie County. A few had an acre or two of token grapevines, but the Central Texas heat posed a challenge. Most of the grapes came from the High Plains north of Lubbock in the Texas Panhandle. It was still hot, but farther from the coast. The elevation and lower humidity produced cooler nights which was supposed to be good for grapes. I was never a wine enthusiast or connoisseur. I was a beer guy who occasionally tossed back some Jack Daniels when the mood arose or memories threatened my sleep, so I never paid much attention to the growth of the local wine industry. Farmers like Bauer were building tasting rooms and cashing in on thirsty tourists.

"Ever been to Napa Valley?" Kelly asked, spotting another sign offering wine tasting.

"No, but I have always wanted to visit the nearby Jack London state park."

"You'd love the Wolf House. I saw it when I did a wine tour. A few from my unit drove up while we were stationed at Pendleton."

"I'd rather go to a brewery."

"You're a beer snob. Don't Germans make wine?"

"Sure, but just to make money off the French."

"Funny guy."

Fertile farmland and pastures stretched out on both sides of the highway in the wide Pedernales River valley. Beyond that, to the north and south, the rough outline of limestone hills covered with evergreen cedars and brown grass. The only sure signs of fall were cut and cleared hayfields and pumpkin stands on the side of the road.

"Did you grow up with Bauer?"

"Mike went to school with my dad. I've known the family all my life. His family's been here as long as the Fischers. His great-great-granddad's log cabin is in the pioneer museum on Main Street. Mike paid to have it dismantled and reassembled at the park. If Grandpa were around, he could tell us the full history. I know Mike's involved with the city council and is big in the Catholic Church. His ancestors were town folk."

"And yours lived in the country?"

"That's right. Most of the immigrants who were part of the church settled in or close to town. Lutherans and Catholics. German intellectuals who'd escaped the political fallout from the failed 1848 revolution set up ranches and communities further south."

"So, the Fischers were intellectuals?" She sounded skeptical.

"Why is that so hard to believe?"

"Isn't that an oxymoron?"

"What?"

"German intellectuals?"

I grinned. She could take it and dish it out. "Now who's being funny? Ever hear of Martin Luther, Nietzsche, or Kant?"

"Did they play for the Astros?" she said with a straight face.

"You're on a roll."

She smiled. "I've also heard of Hitler, Kaiser Wilhelm, and Karl Marx."

"Every country has its demons and angels."

"Seems like both are concentrated in Germany."

"You're gonna mock my heritage?"

She laughed again. "Don't be so sensitive."

"I can't help it. It's part of my natural charm."

She laughed. I pulled into the Bauer winery parking lot. The tasting room was built like an oversized nineteenth-century barn complete with an exterior of distressed wood and a roof made of faux rusted metal. The newly paved parking lot and the tasteful landscaping reminded me of Knott's Berry Farm in California.

"Feels like I've been here before," Kelly said.

"I think that's the general idea. All the tasting rooms seem to be either going for the old-world Italian look or a retro farm style."

Inside, there were shelves full of namesake wine, along with caps and T-shirts and other Bauer wine-oriented merchandise featuring a Gothic B created out of grapevines. The room had high ceilings complete with exposed wooden rafter beams. In the center was a square open bar where three gray-haired couples sat listening to a young hipster with a trimmed beard and round glasses deliver the vintner's speech. Something about temperature and the acidity, how long to let it breathe, and which part of the tongue tingled when you drank it—all over my head.

One of the women, wearing a new Fredericksburg T-shirt, dutifully swirled a half inch of red wine, then stuck her nose in the glass. "Oh, yes, young man. I can smell the cherries and maybe a hint of chocolate." Her husband rolled his eyes.

A younger couple at one of the tables had skipped the tasting and gone straight for a full glass of wine, getting a head start on the Oktoberfest that evening. We stopped at the bar and a woman in her early twenties wearing jeans and a western shirt approached.

"Here for a tasting?" she asked, flashing a big country-girl smile. "I'm Brenda. Y'all from out of town?"

"Actually, I'm looking for Mike Bauer. I'm an old friend of the family. Is he in today?" I took off my cowboy hat and set it crown down on the bar.

She frowned. "Mr. Bauer usually doesn't come out until noon." Her eyes lingered on the scars across my forehead, trying to judge the likelihood of me buying a case of wine. She probably got paid in tips and commissions.

I checked my watch. Eleven forty-five. "We can wait. While we're here, can we try your Texas Tempranillo?" I said and winked. "I heard it's good."

This brought her smile back with a slight blush.

Kelly arched an eyebrow in my direction so Brenda couldn't see.

"I'll have to get another case out of the back. It's one of our most popular," Brenda said, and hurried down the hallway.

"Were you flirting with her?" Kelly asked.

"Working on my people skills."

"Ahh… Well, just a little warning. I'm the jealous type," she deadpanned. "I thought you didn't know anything about wine."

"I don't," I said, pointing to the flyer for Tempranillo wine on the counter.

Before we could take a seat, Mike Bauer followed Brenda out of the back office. He was a big bear of a man in his late fifties with a dark beard streaked with gray and a full head of frizzy hair that reached to his shoulders. He wore khaki pants over orange Crocs and a tie-dyed shirt with the Gothic B winery logo.

"Nick Fischer," he said, striding down the hallway. His voice was loud and booming and he held out a large paw for me to shake.

"Mike, it's been a long time."

"Sorry about your grandpa. I wish I could have made the funeral, but I was out of town. Wine business. This place keeps me busy."

"This is Kelly Hoffman, my girlfriend from Lubbock."

Kelly held out her hand, and Mike took it between his thumb and index finger and kissed her knuckles. Kelly stiffened but didn't pull back or smack him.

"Pleasure to meet you. Lubbock, eh? I'm up there at least three or four times a year buying grapes. The Llano Estacado is an ideal region for growers. The vines aren't as susceptible to fungus." His eyes lingered on Kelly's formfitting jeans and white Oxford shirt that she left untucked to cover the butt of the SIG Sauer 9mm tucked behind her belt.

"I know you're busy, Mike—"

"Not at all." He cut me off and held up both hands, gesturing around the mostly empty room. "In fact, I've been meaning to call you. Do you have a card or something?"

I produced one of my private investigator cards and handed it to him.

He looked it over and smiled. "Semper fi. Nice. I heard you saw some action."

"We both did," I said, putting my arm around Kelly's shoulders.

"A lady Marine. Impressive."

Kelly didn't respond. Even fellow Marines sometimes teased her about being a female in the service, and she'd learned to let it go.

"Come into my office, will ya?" He turned without waiting for my answer and gestured to Brenda. "Bring us a bottle of reserva, Brenda," he called to her. He put his arm around Kelly's shoulders. "You're gonna love this wine. Gold medal at the livestock show in Fort Worth last year."

I followed him down the hall, curious about why Mike wanted to talk to me and wondering if it had something to do with my visit to the trailer parked on his land or my talk with his son. Maybe my plan to rattle his cage was already paying off. The office looked just like the showroom, only smaller and with a lower ceiling. It had an oak desk cluttered with papers and a wall dedicated to wine awards and pictures of Mike receiving them. The opposite wall was dedicated to his son, Owen. He seemed to match his father trophy for trophy, only his were for baseball, basketball, and football. The kid was a hometown hero judging by the framed headlines from the local paper.

Brenda brought the wine and three glasses. I knew I wasn't gonna like it, but I decided to go with the flow. Brenda poured a couple of inches in each glass and left the bottle on the table. Mike handed us each a glass, then held up his own.

"To Oktoberfest."

We clicked our glasses and drank. "*Prost!*" I said, trying to match his enthusiasm.

"What'd you think?" he was anxious for a compliment.

"Wonderful," Kelly indulged him.

"Yeah, best I've had in a long time," I said. I wasn't kidding. It was the only wine I'd had since I'd been forced to share a bottle over dinner with my last girlfriend.

Mike refilled our glasses. He made a point of touching Kelly's hand while handing her a full glass. He was definitely flirting with her.

"I knew you'd like it. I can't keep it on the shelf. Wait till this afternoon. All those folks headed to the Marktplatz will stop by when they see the weekend promotion—free tasting. They buy it by the case. You know, we should have Oktoberfest once a month."

"Then it wouldn't be Oktoberfest," I said.

"Hey, we have Christmas in July." He talked like a used car salesman with a new lot full of lemons to unload. "People don't care. Give it a German name, and they'll come. Why do you think they invented Oktoberfest?"

He looked at us, waiting for an answer. I let him fill in his own punch line.

"To sell more beer," he said, and laughed at his own joke. It was a big bearish laugh that exposed a jumble of stained teeth. I knew there was a sales pitch coming next, so I waited for him to finish before moving on to ask about his trailer tenants.

"Listen, if I'm being too forward in asking, just tell me. Sometimes I get so caught up in a deal I can't help myself." He paused to take a breath and finish his glass of wine. "I wanted to ask you about your grandpa's ranch. I know you're a private detective and all. Hell, who doesn't? Hell of a thing, you shootin' that politician. What was his name?"

"Marcus Lopez," I said, hoping he wasn't going to ask me for any details. I was tired of talking about it and had told the story so many times it was starting to sound like an episode from *Gunsmoke*.

"That's right. Man, he could have been our governor. Hell of a thing. Goes to show, you never know about people. I didn't like him anyway. Everybody knew he was gonna push for a state income tax. I liked his highspeed rail idea, though. That might have brought in more customers from Dallas. Lot of folks thought he should have gone to trial."

There it was. Mike was one of the crowd who thought I'd used excessive force. "Yeah, I thought the same thing, Mike. But he pointed a pistol at me and pulled the trigger. Wanna see the scar?" I felt my neck flush, and I smiled to mask my irritation.

He laughed nervously. "No, that's okay, Nick. I'll take your word for it." He held up the reserva bottle. "Have some more wine?"

I looked at Kelly. She shrugged.

"No thanks, Mike," we said together.

He ignored us and filled our glasses. "Anyway, I know you're getting your grandpa's affairs in order..." He poured the rest of the wine into his glass, twirled the red liquid in the sunlight, and said: "I'd like to buy your family's ranch."

There it was. A bottle of wine and twenty minutes later, he finally got to the point. I was here to rattle his cage and now he was rattling mine.

"I know you're thinkin' it's not worth much since it's pretty far away from town, but I'm prepared to offer you a fair market price."

He was lying through his teeth about the value. Grandpa had turned down several generous offers. "It's not for sale, Mike." I hadn't made up my mind about what to do with the family land, but I wasn't ready to negotiate a price while Grandpa was still warm in his grave.

"Your mother said you were finishing the paperwork. I thought that meant you were getting' ready to put it on the market."

"You talked to Helen?" The thought of her talking to Mike Bauer about the family ranch turned my stomach.

"I drove out yesterday to talk to you, but you weren't home. Isn't that why you're here? Helen thought you'd sell out as soon as you recovered from your injuries. I told her y'all could stay in the old house as long as you wanted."

"Helen Jarvis doesn't have anything to do with my family ranch," I said a little louder than I should have. Kelly reached out and put her hand on my arm.

"Hey, I figured since she was livin' there..."

"She's not living there. She came for the funeral and is leaving soon." I checked my own emotions. His interest in the ranch'd caught me off guard.

"Well, I figured you'd be anxious to get back to San Antonio. You know, to work."

I set the remainder of my glass of Bauer Reserva wine on Mike's oak desk. Everybody I talked to seemed to think I was anxious to get back to San Antonio. Maybe I was. First, I had to find Maya Chavez.

"I am workin', Mike. Matter of fact, Helmut Geisler asked me to find his granddaughter, Maya." If there was any recognition in his eyes, I didn't notice it. "That's why I'm here. I wanna ask you a few questions."

"His granddaughter's missin'? First I heard of it."

"The last time anybody saw her was at a party on the river. You know the place."

He nodded. "Damn kids. I own that property. I've been trying to keep them out of there for two years."

"You own it?" I asked. This was news to me.

"New business venture. Can't talk about it now. It's gonna be huge. The original owners moved to Houston in the sixties. Never came back. Hell, that's why everybody in high school parties out there. My class partied out there. I know yours did too. Now, I'm trying to keep the kids out of there. It's an insurance thing. You know?"

"Your son was at the river along with one of your employees. I already talked to Owen. I'd like to talk to the employee. Big guy. Dragon tattoo on his chest."

He stroked his beard and studied me for a moment. "That'd be Russell Stevens. He's head of my security team."

Finally, I was getting somewhere. "Security? In Fredericksburg?"

"Lot's changed since you lived here, Nick. New folks in town. We got big city problems here now."

"He lives in a trailer house near Palo Alto Creek?"

"Well, he don't exactly live there. I gave him permission to use it."

"I want your permission to access your property and talk to him."

He hesitated slightly. "Sure, but what for?"

"He may have seen Maya at the party."

He held my gaze without expression. Finally, he nodded. "Okay, sure. I'll call him." He pulled a cell phone from his shirt pocket.

"That won't be necessary. If you don't mind, Kelly and I will just swing by."

He put the phone away. "Be my guest."

I extended my hand, and Mike shook it a little too vigorously. I tried not to show the pain from the sourness in my chest. He pulled Kelly close with his big right arm and gave her a full-frontal hug. He held her for an extra awkward moment.

"I can see that the climate in Lubbock is good for more than just grapes," he said.

I thought Kelly might slap him this time. Instead, she twisted away from his bear grasp and slipped her hand into mine.

"Thank you," she said. "I've never been compared to a wine grape before."

Mike unleashed a forced laugh and slapped his thigh. Mercifully, before he could think of a comeback, his cell phone rang. Mike pulled it from his pocket and looked at the caller ID. "Gotta take this. Good seein' y'all. Let me know if you change your mind about the ranch. I know how much trouble a piece of land can be."

CHAPTER THIRTEEN

"I should've worn boots. The BS was starting to pile up," Kelly said when we climbed back in my pickup. I got in beside her and started the engine.

"The rest of the family's the same way," I said, waiting for the cars to clear so I could make a left turn back onto the highway. "If Mike wasn't the first born in the family, he'd be selling used pickups in San Antonio."

"Mike and Zeller both made it clear that you're no longer a part of the Fredericksburg good ol' boys club."

"What do you mean?"

"I got the impression they were sending you a message that things have changed. The Fischers, meaning you, are no longer one of the movers and shakers. Maybe more to point, they were in charge. Now that your grandfather is gone, they don't consider you a member of the elite, even though you were born and raised here. I guess you've been out of town too long."

"I got the same impression. Kinda like Maya. She was born here but lost her native card when she moved to California." I pulled out behind a dually pickup hitched to a massive forty-eight-foot travel trailer going too fast, probably headed to the Lady Bird Johnson RV park near the county fairgrounds.

"You stir up a lot of tension around here, and not just because you're after a missing girl. Zeller, Mike Bauer, and most of the locals you shook hands with last night acted like they were afraid of you."

"Seriously?"

"They aren't veterans. Those guys are civilians who've never seen another person killed in a firefight, let alone someone like Marcus Lopez. They may sound impressed, but did you notice they all kept their distance?"

"I guess I didn't."

"The women were different. The looks you were getting made me jealous."

"I guess I didn't see that either."

"If I wasn't with you, a dozen of the local ladies would have given you their number. And at least half of those would have gone home with you, including Rocky's new wife."

"What're you talkin' about?"

"Ha! I swear, for a man who has a college degree, four years in the Marines, and two years of law school, you don't know squat about women."

I glanced at her and smiled. "My secret's out. I do know a good one when I find one."

She took my hand. "There's something about a dangerous man women find attractive."

"Does that include you?" I stopped at the light, lifted her hand, and kissed her fingertips.

"No. I just drove four hours from Lubbock to drink German beer and dance the polka."

"You're gonna hurt my feelings again," I said, trying to keep a straight face.

"I like the sensitive types," she said, leaning over and kissing me.

A honk behind me cut the moment short. The light had turned green and I was holding up traffic. I drove north out of town toward the trailer and Russell Stevens, aka "Dragon."

"Where to now?" she asked.

"Back to the trailer."

"You romantic devil."

"I promise to focus on you after we question Russell Stevens. Mike said he was supposed to be keeping the kids off that river property, but Lori said he asked Owen to take Maya out there that night. One of them is lying. If we wait till tomorrow, Mike will have warned him we're coming."

I drove past the point where Kelly and I'd jumped the fence. This time we would go through the front gate and knock on the door. The gravel road wound through a thick cedar break. Kelly pointed out a surveillance camera mounted on a limb beside the road.

"Looks like they're monitoring our approach."

I stopped and pulled the .45 from my shoulder holster, then jacked a cartridge in the chamber just in case the Dragon didn't fall for my overwhelming charm.

"Just remember that you're injured. If it comes to the rough stuff, let me do it." She smiled sweetly. Kelly wasn't what I would call petite. She had a strong jaw and an athletic figure. Anyone could tell she worked out on a regular basis. The charming smile was what fooled people. As a Marine Corps police officer, it was her best asset. Her smile could disarm even the most belligerent jarhead. She used it like a stun gun. While the perp's brain was registering gorgeous lady, her boot was traveling at the speed of sound toward a vulnerable part of his body.

We broke out of the trees and spotted a thug with a shaved head standing near the trailer door. Light sparkled off the sweat beading on his smooth scalp. I scanned the perimeter but didn't see any other bodies. Only one of the Super Duty pickups was there alongside the black Jeep Cherokee with oversized tires. I parked beside the Jeep. Kelly and I got out.

"Howdy," I called to the skinhead. He sauntered toward us with a sneer on his face and what looked like a Glock 19 clipped to his belt.

"Remember me?" Kelly asked.

"This is private property," he said. "Y'all are trespassin'." He stopped about ten feet away and put his right hand on the Glock. He was my height, six-two, and stocky. A week-old beard covered an angry purple scar running from his chin down his neck.

"We've got permission from Mike Bauer. We came to talk to Russell Stevens."

Kelly smiled and took a step sideways, giving her a better angle in case things got western. I liked the way she thought. Spreading out forced baldy to split his focus between the two of us.

His eyes narrowed as if trying to think. It didn't look easy for him. "I didn't hear nothin' about it," he said.

I took a step closer to him. "That's 'cause it was need-to-know information. You didn't need to know."

His muscles tensed, and he spread his legs, preparing to draw the Glock. "Listen, smartass. Get back in that pickup and get the fuck out of here. Take the bitch with you."

"Watch the language around the lady. Where's Russell?"

"Ain't nobody named Russell here," he said.

"Maybe you know him as Dragon."

The trailer door opened, and Russell Stevens stepped out wearing tight jeans and square-toe cowboy boots with a sleeveless T-shirt that covered the dragon tatt but showed off his bulky prison-yard muscles.

"What's this about?" he asked. He was an inch taller than me and every cut muscle in his body was coiled and ready to spring.

"Mike said you're head of security for Bauer Farms. You a local?"

"What's that got to do with anything?" He walked toward me with his arms spread like he was stepping into the cage for an MMA match, his movements fluid and menacing.

"Just curious," I said.

He sized me up and seemed to dismiss me as an unworthy opponent, then focused his attention on Kelly. His whole demeanor shifted like the surface of a lake on a windy day. "You came back. Why don't you ditch this asshole and party with me?" he asked like he was accustomed to getting his way with women.

Kelly flashed her Lubbock police badge. "We're here on business."

"We're looking for a girl named Maya Chavez." I held up the school picture of Maya Helmut had given me.

Russell crossed his arms and made no effort to look. "Never seen her before."

"She's a senior at the high school. Just turned eighteen. Dark hair about shoulder length. Green eyes. Five three or four. Her grandpa's a local, Helmut Geisler."

Russell kept his attention on Kelly. Said, "Don't know her."

"She was last seen at a party on the Pedernales River in August. Owen Bauer was there. Maya was there with another girl, Lori Kostoch. She's a blonde. Same age. A little shorter. Lori said she saw you there."

This caught Russell's attention. His demeanor shifted back to cage fighter. He looked at the skinhead thug, then back at me.

"Part of my job is to keep the kids away from that place," Russell said.

"So, you were out there when the party was going on?"

"The land is private property. It's well posted. Mike don't want nobody out there. For insurance purposes. It's a liability. You should know that."

"Yeah, I get it," I said. "You went out there and told them to leave, is that it? You were just doing your job?"

He blew a sharp blast of air through his nose that sounded something like a snort from a buffalo. Russell was losing his patience. That was good. I wanted him a little off balance.

"You want answers, talk to Mike." He closed the gap between us and stuck his chest out like a silverback gorilla in the wild.

"We're just trying to find out what happened to the girl," I said.

He didn't speak. The expression on his face was blank. His eyes dead. I held my ground. He was a big guy. If he started swinging, I wanted to be inside his wheelhouse where he couldn't get a full windup. On a good day, I knew I could land two punches to his one. My first would be to his throat. If that didn't connect, I'd go for the balls. Anything soft and vulnerable. I'd spent a lot of time in the gym trading punches with some pretty good heavyweights and the Marine Corps made sure every jarhead could hold his own in a fight against a bigger opponent. The problem was, this wasn't one of my good days. I was still recovering from the bullet wounds to my chest and upper arm. Both were sore as hell.

"Time for you to go," Russell said.

Kelly was closing on his right shoulder. She had her hand behind her back, no doubt resting on the P226. If Russell did take a swing at me, she would press the barrel into his temple.

"Sure, Russell, sure. No problem." I held up the yearbook picture again. "Just to be certain. This is her. This is Maya. You're positive you've never seen her before?" I watched his dead eyes take in the picture without showing a hint of recognition. This was what Kelly had seen last night—his eyes were cold and unflinching. Evil. He said nothing.

I put the picture away. "Thanks for your time, Russell. Good luck with the security job." I turned and opened my pickup door.

Kelly jumped in the other side. "That went well," she said as I backed up and made a three-point turn.

"Yeah, we know he saw Maya at the party. The question is, why did he lie?"

"Why is everybody lying about her?" Kelly said.

"And where is Maya now?"

CHAPTER FOURTEEN

Helen's car was parked by the barn when Kelly and I rounded the edge of the spring-fed pond and drove to the ranch house. There was something unsettling about knowing she was inside using things that belonged to a family she'd abandoned twenty years ago. That, and her talking to Mike Bauer about selling the property without telling me put me in a foul mood.

"Maybe we should skip the ranch visit till Helen's gone," I said.

"Don't worry about it."

"She's gettin' on my nerves."

"Have you considered that she doesn't have any place to go?"

"She smells a payday."

"That's cynical."

"It's true."

Helen came out on the porch and waved at us. "I made some venison roast sandwiches," she called in a singsong voice. Sam followed her out and stood wagging his tail.

"Sam seems to like her," Kelly said.

"My dog's a turncoat." Labradors liked everybody, especially those bearing food. He'd let the SAPD detective who shot him in the head into my house through the front door because he was holding a cheeseburger. He hadn't taken an instant liking to Helen. After his recovery from the head wound, he'd developed a healthy distrust of strangers, even those bearing food. It took Helen a week to break through his newly acquired defenses. She fed him scraps from each meal and scratched his belly every time he rolled over. A Labrador can only resist so much. Now, they were pals for life.

"Y'all come on inside," Helen called sweetly.

Sam sniffed my jeans when I opened the pickup door. "So, you've gone over to the dark side," I told him. He ignored my admonishment and playfully circled between my legs, then paused to lick my outstretched hand. I noticed his nails were trimmed and he smelled of oatmeal soap. "Don't get used to all that extra treatment," I said, scratching the still-pink scar behind his left ear.

We went inside and sat at the kitchen table. Sam stood beside Helen's chair, anticipating his portion. She'd laid out roast deer meat sandwiches cut into diagonal portions along with sliced sweet-and-sour pickles, coleslaw, and German potato salad made from Grandma's recipe.

"You didn't have to go to all this trouble," Kelly said.

"Oh, it wasn't any trouble."

She handed me one of my own Shiner Bocks in a longneck bottle and sat down in Grandma's place as if she were entertaining guests.

"Thank you for lunch." I tried to be nice for Kelly's sake. She didn't know the whole history and I didn't wanna come off as a jerk.

Helen waved her hand, dismissing the compliment. "I knew y'all'd be hungry."

Kelly took a bite of potato salad. "This is wonderful."

Again, Helen waved her hand. "I had some time when I got back from town. I know how much Nicky likes Grandma's recipe."

I finished my sandwich and washed it down with Shiner. "Why didn't you tell me Mike Bauer stopped by?"

She folded her hands on the table in front of her. "We haven't had a chance to talk. I know you've been busy with Kelly here and the Oktoberfest going on."

"You told him I was going to sell out." I took another drink of beer.

Her eyes got wide. "I didn't say that. You know how Mike is. He's always trying to make a deal. He means well. He's done a lot of good things for the town." She stood up quickly and grabbed a pitcher of sun tea from the counter. "Would you like some tea?" she asked Kelly. "If you'll excuse me, I want to get started on the bedroom. I bought the paint this morning, and I have everything covered."

"You're going to paint the bedroom?"

"Those rooms haven't been touched up in years," she said. "If we do decide to sell, the house will be ready. If we stay, it'll be fixed up."

She hustled out of the kitchen before I could respond. She'd said *we*, putting herself into the decision-making process.

Kelly saw my expression and covered her mouth to stifle a laugh. "Look at it this way. You don't have to worry about doing housework while she's here."

"I'm glad you find this amusing."

"Oh, come on," she said sotto voce. "I don't see why you're threatened by her."

"First my dog, and now my girlfriend."

"Suck it up, Marine." She leaned across the table and kissed me. She tasted like Grandma's potato salad. Delicious. I pulled her closer. Sam stuck his head on my lap.

Helen walked back into the kitchen. "Sorry," she said. "Came to get my paint rag. Don't mind me." She grabbed a rag from under the sink and hurried out.

"If I'm such a dangerous man, how come I can't get any respect in my own house?"

Sam wagged his bulky tail, dismissing my comment.

Kelly handed him a slice of deer meat, which he wolfed down. "Because we know you're only dangerous outside the family."

After we'd cleaned the lunch dishes, I took Kelly outside for a tour of the barn and the rest of the property. Sam followed us, but not before he mooched another slice of roast. When Kelly'd been to the ranch the first time, it was during grandpa's funeral. A steady stream of family friends filled the house with food and flowers, and the old-timers stayed to share stories about Grandpa's exploits. Since I'd lived away most of the last fifteen years, I didn't know how much he'd done for the community. He and Helmut organized the junior livestock show and provided animals for the high school FFA program. He was never one to brag about what he was doing.

"What's next in our investigation?"

"Our investigation?"

"I'm hooked. I wanna help you find Maya."

"Don't you have to go back to work on Monday?"

"Maybe. I wanna see the cowboy detective in action." She laced her arm through mine. "The last time, you didn't call me until the final showdown. I wanna get in on the investigation."

"Have you been talkin' to Skeeter?"

"Why do you ask?"

"'Cause he made the same crack about cowboy detective."

"Great minds think alike."

I wasn't sure I liked the nickname, but it sounded like I was stuck with it. When we reached the barn, and were out of Helen's ear shot, I pulled out my cell phone. "Time to put that other great big mind to work." I speed-dialed Skeeter's number.

"How's rehab coming?" he asked as a greeting.

"I was just going to ask you the same thing."

"I'm enjoying the peace and quiet." Normally, he lived with his mother on the south side.

"Great. I have two houses, and I have to rent a motel room to be alone with my girlfriend." I put the phone on speaker so that Kelly could hear both sides of the conversation.

Skeeter let out a baritone chuckle that erupted from deep within his six-foot-seven, three-hundred-pound frame. The resulting sound was like the prelude to a thunderstorm. I imagined him in my living room with his feet propped up on *my* desk, staring out at *my* front yard.

"Did you at least mow the grass?" I asked.

More chuckling. "I'm not supposed to do any strenuous work. I let the neighborhood kid do it. I told him you'd pay him when you came back to town."

"Thanks. Run up the bill."

"I haven't gotten a paycheck in a while."

"Have you done any work?"

"I been burning up the internet while you been spooning your new girlfriend."

"That's not all I've been doing. And she's here on speaker."

"Hi, Clarence. I tried to get him to let me stay at the ranch, but he's afraid of his mother." Kelly was the only one besides his mother who he let use his real name.

"Our boy's got mommy issues," Skeeter said.

"Tell me about it."

"You two are supposed to be on my side." They were ganging up on me, so I changed the subject. "What have you got, Mr. internet sleuth?"

After a short pause, no doubt to suppress his laughter, he got down to business. "The burner phone was a dead end. Your buddy Officer Zeller did put her name in the missing persons system. No hits so far. I posted her up on Facebook, but no leads yet. I checked her account. No activity since August. Same for her Instagram and Snapchat."

"Dropped off the grid?"

"Apparently."

"I don't like that. I don't like that at all. Check out Lori Kostoch and Owen Bauer. See what's happening in their social media world. They're both seniors at the high school. They were with Maya the night she went missing. Also, I want you to do a background check on a thug named Russell Stevens, aka "Dragon." He's supposedly head of security for Bauer Farms here in Gillespie County. See if he has a record anywhere."

"Dragon, huh?"

"Yeah, he's got a really cute tattoo of one on his chest. Likes to show it off."

"Sounds like an outstanding citizen," he rumbled.

"Oh, he's got the personality to back it up. Kind of a deadeye, prison stare, along with cut steroid muscles. Also, check the Greyhound records for the week following the tenth of August. I know the bus stops in town. There's no terminal, but she could have bought tickets online."

"Already checked. Nothing. No tickets in her name from any Greyhound bus station in Central Texas. If she went back to California, she caught a ride with someone else."

"That could mean she's still in the area," Kelly said.

"What's your gut feeling on this?" Skeeter asked.

"Somethin' ain't right. Too many people are lyin'."

Skeeter cleared his throat.

"What?" I asked.

"It's good to be working again," he said, and disconnected.

I put the phone in my pocket. "Now we wait while he works his magic."

"That's how the cowboy detective investigates?" She raised her eyebrow but couldn't suppress a smile.

"You were expecting a stakeout and more interviews?"

"Uh-huh."

"Don't worry. There'll be plenty of that. Usually, Skeeter can narrow down the search and save a boatload of time."

The old barn door was mounted on a metal roller, which gave a rusty squeal when I shoved it open—a sound it never made when Grandpa was alive. I felt a sudden pang of guilt for neglecting my duties. Kelly followed me inside.

"This is where you killed the detective?" she asked. The temperature was ten degrees cooler inside the two-foot-thick stone walls.

"Yeah, the son of a bitch was wearing Grandpa's shirt and hiding in plain sight, leaning with his back against that support beam. That's how he got the drop on me. Turns out, Grandpa was already dead. Shot through the heart that morning. Detective Peterson had been waiting for me to show up. I sent Skeeter through the front gate to create a diversion while I slipped over the fence and approached on foot through the brush. Peterson was waiting in the loft. When Skeeter stepped out of his pickup, Peterson shot him in the chest. The way Skeeter hit the ground, I thought he was dead."

We walked up the steps to the hayloft. I pointed out the smudge marks on the wall where a fire had scorched the inside timbers the year after the Civil War and showed her the "new" steps Great-Grandpa had built because he got too fat to climb the original narrower planks.

"He shot Skeeter from this window." We peered out the hayloft at the front yard. The spring-fed pond and the hundred yards of gravel road that led to the front gate spread out in front of us. I pointed to the line of cedar trees to the north of the house about fifty yards away. "I crawled to the edge of those trees and waited for Skeeter. When he got out, he left the shotgun I'd given him on the front seat. I saw Peterson's rifle barrel poke from the window and fired, but I was too late. Skeeter never saw it coming."

I pointed to the bullet holes in the window frame. "These are from my pistol."

She studied the layout—the view of the hills to the north, the line of brush, and the bullet holes in the window frame. "You're both lucky to be alive," she said.

We walked back to the ground floor. Grandpa's John Deere tractor was in the corner with the hay baler attached. He'd left me a hundred head of cattle, fifty or so goats, and a couple of horses that were both past their prime. I would have to decide what to do with them. Being a rancher was a full-time job that didn't pay full-time wages.

"Where did you find your grandpa?"

"In the last horse stall."

I suddenly smelled the sharp, pungent odor of dried blood, but I knew it was only my memory playing cruel tricks. It had been six weeks since Grandpa's murder. The air inside the barn felt heavy, as if the barometric pressure had suddenly dropped. I turned and walked outside. Kelly followed. I leaned against the stone walls and took in a deep breath. White puffy mares' tails galloped across the pale blue sky. Sam'd had enough of the tour and took off running toward the cool water of the spring-fed pond. Kelly pressed against me.

"Not an easy thing to get over," she said, putting her arms around me.

I looked up at the sky. "Grandpa used to say mares' tails meant rain was on its way," I said. I couldn't look at her for fear of letting her see my eyes fill with tears. I didn't need to say I missed him. She understood.

"You gonna be okay?" she asked.

I watched Sam swim laps in the pond, chasing a turtle that kept dunking underwater just out of his reach. Honestly, I couldn't answer. Grandpa had been the one stabilizing force in my life. He'd helped me transition back to civilian life after my last deployment left me wounded, angry with the world, and feeling guilty for coming home alive. He had his own special recipe for rehabilitation consisting of work and reading history.

He said work kept your mind off your problems, and history reminded you that you aren't the only poor son of a bitch suffering in the world. It had worked once, and I was counting on it working again to help me ease the pain of losing him.

"If Grandpa were here, he'd tell me to get to work. That was his answer to pretty much everything."

"Good advice, and I wanna help you."

I took her hand. "You have a job in Lubbock."

"I wanna find Maya as much as you do. I can take a leave of absence. I haven't taken a vacation since I started."

"I might have to put you on the payroll."

"I'll start with room and board."

"Fair enough."

I wiped my eyes on the back of my shirt sleeve. Just the thought of getting back to work lifted my spirits. I held Kelly close and kissed her.

"There you are," Helen called from the front porch, interrupting another moment between us. "Would you help me move the furniture while you're here?" She was talking to Kelly. "I didn't want Nicky to do it. He's not supposed to lift anything heavy."

"Sure," Kelly said, unfolding herself from my arms.

I reluctantly let her go. "Go ahead, I need some work on the range," I said.

"Don't open that wound again. You sure you should be doing shooting practice so soon?"

"If I don't keep my edge, next time I might not be so lucky."

She shook her head. "Don't even talk about things like that." She turned away and followed Helen into the house.

I stepped out behind the barn where I'd set up a pistol range. Like any other athletic movement, shooting required hours of repetitive practice. It was a perishable skill that I couldn't afford to let atrophy. My last case had taught me that. I'd had a split second to drop, draw, and fire. Had I missed or hesitated, the .38 from Lopez's revolver would have hit a vital organ and I would no longer be standing.

I'd set up seven combat shooting stations outside the corral using a variety of practical targets consisting of man-sized silhouettes and rotating metal. The course had straw bales and wooden crates for obstacles with different groupings at each station for single and multiple targets.

After fitting my Springfield .45 into its shoulder holster and attaching an extra magazine to my belt, I strapped the .38 revolver around my ankle. My goal was to move through the stations, first forward, then backward, expending both .45 magazines first and then switching to my backup .38 to finish.

I started slowly, walking through the stations and deliberately taking down each target. Standing and firing at a single target had its uses, but training for when the shit hit the fan, when the target was shooting back, required movement. Before my injury, I could complete the circuit in under two minutes. For now, I wanted to make sure all my body parts worked.

After forty-five minutes, I stopped to catch my breath and check the targets. The groupings were close, but not perfect, not up to my usual standards. Getting up to speed would take another two weeks, at least. Against a trained adversary, I'd need luck and a prayer to survive. I checked the bandages under my shirt. What I thought was sweat from the exertion turned out to be blood from the re-opened wound. It needed more time. Trouble was, I didn't think Maya had any more time. She was somewhere out there and needed my help.

CHAPTER FIFTEEN

The Geisler ranch was ten miles north of Fredericksburg, tucked into the rolling limestone and dolomite hills, punctuated with granite outcroppings. The biggest and most famous of these was Enchanted Rock, which rose eighteen hundred feet above sea level and stood out like the pink crown of a giant's bald head. The surrounding sixteen hundred acres was turned into a state park but had been a private ranch and its startling appearance on the skyline provided a source of Indian legends for thousands of years. The Tonkawa, Lipan Apache, and Comanche tribes considered the rock to be sacred. There is a story of a cowboy who climbed the rock and escaped an Indian raiding party who declined to pursue him, presumably because of the rock's great spiritual power. And in 1841, Captain Jack Hays of the Texas Rangers further established his fearless reputation by fighting off a band of Comanches while hunkered down in a depression on the summit. The incident is celebrated by a historical marker in the park.

I recited both incidents to Kelly as we drove in the shadow of the outcropping. She seemed interested, if not overly impressed. "You love this country, don't you?" she said, staring out the open window.

I nodded at the semi-arid landscape dotted with live oaks, mesquite, hackberry, juniper, and prickly pear cactus. "This is my backyard. I love every inch of it. The buffalo herds are gone, along with the Comanche, but there's still plenty of white-tailed deer, feral hogs, and turkey. Along with coyotes, mountain lions, and the occasional black bear."

"Black bear?" she said skeptically.

"They're making a comeback."

"And don't you mean 'bison'?"

I shook my head. "Don't get me started on that. I don't have to use the word 'bison' just because an eighteenth-century Swedish biologist published a book about it. Do you want to change the name of the 'Buffalo Soldier' to 'Bison Soldier'? I think you'd get a lot of pushback."

She laughed. "Okay, don't be so touchy."

I smiled and squeezed her hand. "Sorry." The sky was impossibly blue, and the air was dry and smelled of fall. Kelly's presence was an added bonus. She was dressed in jeans and a black Texas Tech T-shirt and had her short blond hair pulled back in a tight ponytail. I shouldn't have felt uneasy, but I did. We were on the way to pay a visit to Helmut Geisler and see if there was more information he might be able to share. I knew there were some details he'd left out.

When we crossed the bridge at Palo Alto Creek, I realized the cause of my uneasiness was Anna Metzger, the kidnapped child from the nineteenth century. The road we were on followed the same route the Comanches took with the young girl tied to a horse. I thought about the horror she must have felt and the extreme hardship she endured. Had Maya Chavez been kidnapped? Lori was obviously frightened but said she hadn't seen anything happen. Owen denied even knowing Maya at first, then claimed he hadn't seen her at the party on the river. Russell Stevens had openly lied. Something happened that night on the river. Maya couldn't have vanished into thin air. Without realizing it, I was tapping on the steering wheel as I drove.

"You're getting antsy," Kelly said, nodding at my nervous hands.

I stopped tapping. "This situation surrounding Maya gives me a bad feeling."

"You think Helmut knows something he's not telling you?"

"He said Maya didn't take anything from the house, but there may be something she left behind that could shed some light on where she went."

"So, you don't know what you're looking for."

"When I take Sam bird hunting, he doesn't ask for a list of clues. He searches every brush pile and clump of grass until the quarry appears."

"I get it. The cowboy detective has to be part birddog."

I laughed. "It works for me."

I stopped in front of Helmut's ranch road. Most of his family's original stone fences had been replace with goat wire years ago. In the last five years, he'd added a metal gate decorated with a life-sized iron silhouette of a cowboy kneeling in front of a large cross. I wondered if the new Christian theme had something to do with his wife's failing health.

Kelly opened the gate, and we drove across a hayfield that was cut and plowed under, awaiting rain and next year's crop. A herd of white-and-brown goats anticipating a meal followed my pickup to the single-story, limestone house. The design was a smaller version of my grandpa's house and built around the same time, a hundred and seventy years ago.

Everything about the ranch was squared away—fence wire tight, cross braces straight, nothing out of place. A small patch of Bermuda-grass lawn was freshly mowed, and a row of peach trees stood at attention beside the stone barn. Like Grandpa's property while he was alive, all the farm implements were in their proper places, repaired, oiled, and ready for use.

I slowed to let the dust cloud kicked up by our approach settle before it engulfed the house, then coasted forward to a stop. Helmut appeared in the open barn door, holding a welding torch. The heeler that gave Sam fits joined two border collies and a Labrador mix to quickly disperse the goats and returned to surround my pickup.

"No one could ever sneak up on him," Kelly said.

"Every rancher I know has a pack of ranch dogs."

"*Platz!*" Helmut shouted at his barking dogs. They instantly quieted down and retreated behind him. "*Guten tag. Wie gehts?*" he greeted us in German.

"*Sehr gut, danke,*" I said.

The Lab mix snuck past Helmut and sniffed the cuff of Kelly's jeans. When she rewarded him with a scratch behind the ears, the others rushed her. She laughed and tried to give them all some ranch-dog love. "They must smell Sam."

"*Wer ist deine schöne Freundin—*" He started to say more, but I stopped him with my upheld hand. I understood the word "girlfriend" because Grandpa used to tease me as a kid. The basics of the language were in my wheelhouse—greetings, prayers, and commands, but I quickly got lost in the details.

"Helmut Geisler, meet Kelly Hoffman."

"Sitzen!" Helmut growled at the dogs. They quickly ran back to his heels and sat down wagging their tails. He took Kelly's hand. "Glad to know you, Kelly," he said. "I remember you from the funeral."

"Yes, of course. Good to see you again, Mr. Geisler."

"Call me Helmut."

"Okay, Helmut."

He looked up at the mare's tail clouds. "Rain's coming soon."

"We need it. Grandpa's pasture is burnt to a crisp," I said. I'd never talked to a farmer or rancher who didn't mention the weather to start a conversation.

We both studied his dry pasture scattered with goats. Anyone else with a missing granddaughter would have peppered me with questions before I'd gotten out of my pickup, but the rural code of conduct dictated we cover pleasantries first to avoid appearing anxious. I didn't keep him waiting any longer.

"I asked around town about Maya. No luck yet. I need some more information from you. And maybe we could take a look in Maya's room. It might give us a clue about where she went."

Helmut studied me for a moment and rubbed his leathery fingers against the stubble on his chin. "Not much there in her room," he said after careful consideration. "She didn't have a lot of stuff of her own. You're welcome to look. What other questions do you have?"

"I talked to her mother. She said you took her to court," I said.

A mixture of anger and regret flickered across his craggy face. "It was the only way to get her to act. Her brain is addled." He turned to Kelly. "I'm sorry," he said. "But my daughter's a drunk."

"Kelly is a police officer in Lubbock," I said helpfully.

He gave her an approving nod. "This is *gut*," he said. "We'll go into the house." He abruptly led the way. "I have cold beer."

The house was warm with no air conditioning but had been designed with rows of windows to catch as much of the breeze as possible. An older woman with her gray hair pulled into a tight bun, wearing a blue cotton dress and a yellow apron, met us in the front room. The skin on her face and arms was translucent and stretch paper-thin around delicate bones.

"We have company, Mother," Helmut said to the woman. "He came to ask about Maya and look in her room."

She looked puzzled. "Well, there's not much there, but he's welcome to look if it'll help get our girl back."

"That's what I told him."

"Mrs. Geisler, it's good to see you up and around. This is Kelly Hoffman." I offered my hand. She stepped past my hand and gave me a full hug. She felt as if she might shatter if I squeezed too hard.

"Oh, goodness gracious," she said. "Just terrible what happened to your grandpa. How are you holding up?" She had survived her fourth heart attack, and yet she wanted to know how I was doing.

"I'm fine, thank you," I said. "How are you feelin'?"

She shrugged and crossed herself. "The Lord has given me one more life to live," she said, and held out her hand to Kelly. "I'm Elena, honey. Nice to meet you. Can I get you anything to drink? Supper's not quite ready."

Kelly glanced around the perfectly preserved room. The furnishings were Victorian style and hadn't changed since I'd first been here as a child. "I'm fine, thank you. You have a lovely home," Kelly said.

"We won't bother you for supper," I said.

"Oh, nonsense. I'll set two extra plates. There's plenty of food. Maya's room's this way."

We followed her down a narrow hall and into a small bedroom that faced the barn.

"That poor girl's been through a lot," she said with a sigh.

"Moving back to Texas must have been a shock," I said, looking around at the sparsely furnished room.

"That and her mother. She'll be a strong woman one day, if she ever gets the chance. She's hardheaded, that one. She gets that from her grandfather."

"Which bathroom did she use?" I asked.

"The one at the end of the hall," she said, pointing. "I'll check on dinner while you look." Elena walked back toward the kitchen and left us alone. I went into the small bathroom. There was an old-fashioned tub with legs and a simple cabinet and sink. Judging by the dark tinted age marks around the bottom edge of the mirror and the octagon brass hardware on the cabinets, I'd guess everything in the room was early nineteen hundred vintage, like the furniture in the living room. I found a toothbrush in the medicine cabinet along with a bottle of Tylenol and a tube of extra-whitening toothpaste. Helmut was right about her not taking her toothbrush. The room was clean, and the old-fashioned tub seemed recently scrubbed. I doubted whether Mrs. Geisler would have had the strength or the energy to clean the bathroom. Helmut might have done it, but I had a feeling that it was Maya's handiwork.

I walked back to the bedroom. Kelly was standing on a multicolor throw rug in the center of a small ten-by-ten room with hardwood floors.

"She left her toothbrush. What'd you find in here?" I asked.

"Not much."

There was a twin bed with a neat patchwork quilt in one corner and a small desk with a vanity mirror in the other. A matching dresser stood beside the door. There were no boy band posters on the walls or anything that gave the appearance of a teen girl's room, except the plastic appaloosa horse on the dresser.

"This was probably once her mom's room," I said, examining the horse.

Kelly opened the top drawer of the dresser and looked at a collection of underwear and socks. The next drawer contained jeans and shorts, all neatly folded and put in place.

I opened the drawer on the desk and found a small diary with a tiny lock.

"Here's something," I said.

We looked at the diary.

"It's locked."

Kelly smirked and quickly extracted a pin from her hair and jimmied the lock open. "I had one just like it," she said.

We sat on the bed and thumbed through the pages. The handwriting was easy to read. She had a looping style filled with hearts and exclamation points.

"Dear diary, I hate my life!!!!!!!!!" the first line read. I flipped to the last page and read the date. It was more than thirty years old. It was Maya's mother's diary. She probably still felt the same way.

The closet wasn't any more helpful. There were two pairs of Justin Roper boots and three pairs of tennis shoes that looked well used. There were a few modest dresses on hangers and a straw cowboy hat crown down on the shelf. I also found a pink-camo backpack and a large red duffel bag.

"Why would she run away without taking her toothbrush or packing her suitcase or her backpack? You came for the weekend and you brought a suitcase and a backpack. And you're a Marine."

"I knew I'd be hanging out with you and likely get shot at or chased through the brush."

"Good point," I said, hoping she was teasing me. "Can you imagine a teen girl out here by herself?"

"I didn't see a TV. Did you?"

"No. It reminds me of growing up with my grandma and grandpa."

"How did you survive?"

"I got a job and bought a used pickup. They couldn't argue with work. That gave me the money to buy the things I thought I needed to keep up with the crowd. After high school came the Marine Corps. I heard they were looking for a few good men."

"And women." She laughed.

Footsteps clopped down the hallway. Helmut opened the door.

"Find anything useful?"

"Are these clothes Maya's?" Kelly asked.

"Everything in the dresser is hers. I didn't keep any of my daughter's clothes."

We followed Helmut back to the front room, where he offered us both a beer. We took them and went outside to the porch. Kelly and I sat on the double-seat swing, and Helmut sat in a wooden rocking chair.

"Dinner will be ready soon," Elena called. The herd of dogs joined us and resumed their flirtation with Kelly.

"We don't have a lot of the things young people want out here. We never bothered with TV, and I wouldn't know what to do with a computer," Helmut told us.

"Was Maya upset about that?" Kelly asked.

"I gave her a horse to ride, and she had plenty of chores to do. She liked to help me feed the goats and the cattle."

"Did she have any of her friends come out?" I asked.

"She said she hadn't been in town long enough to make friends."

We were getting a bleak picture of Maya's home life with her grandparents.

"Did she talk about going back to California?" Kelly asked.

"Never mentioned anything to us," Helmut said.

I drank some beer and thought about Maya. She had spent most of her life in California. Then she was suddenly forced to come back to rural Central Texas for her last year of high school. Maybe Les Zeller was right. Maybe Maya had decided she would rather be in California. Still, it didn't explain her checking out of social media altogether or how she got there.

"You know, Helmut," I said. "Maybe Maya decided Fredericksburg wasn't for her."

Helmut cleared his throat. I waited a long time for him to speak. I figured he was coming to grips with the idea that I might be right, and that Maya simply chose California over him and Central Texas.

"She was taken," he insisted.

"I know you've had a hard time with your daughter. I get that. She's an alcoholic. But is there anything else you're not telling me? I have to know everything if I'm going to find her."

Helmut stopped his rocking chair and stared out at his goat herd. "I'm an old fart, but by god if you won't go after her, I will." He turned to challenged me. His eyes were clear and penetrating. "In the old days, when a girl went missing, all the neighbors would form a posse to go after her. The local law was just as useless as it is today. We had to take care of our own."

I met his gaze. "I'll find her," I said. "Elena needs you around the house. Let me do the heavy lifting."

He nodded. I went to my pickup and got the standard contract for him to sign that would cover my ass in case I had to explain why I was asking questions and requesting information. Helmut agreed to work out the fee later.

"Call me if you think of anything else or if she gets in touch with you," I said.

"You're a good man, Nick," Helmut said, shaking my hand.

"Come in and eat," Elena called from inside the house.

We did as we were told, knowing she wouldn't take no for an answer.

CHAPTER SIXTEEN

Kelly and I drove in silence for the first few miles back to Fredericksburg. The sun was going down. The air was dry, and the temperature had dropped ten degrees. I cut the a/c and rolled down the windows. The smell of cedars and fresh-mown hay filled the cab. We passed a fruit stand advertising fresh tomatoes and apples. Kelly's blond hair fluttered under her Texas Tech baseball cap. I appreciated the fact that she didn't feel the need to fill every moment we had together with conversation. When the silence stretched longer than sixty seconds, Sylvia would accuse me of torture.

I was thinking about Maya and wondered if she was watching the sunset and enjoying the same smells or if she was somewhere nature couldn't reach her. That she had problems at home was obvious. Her mother couldn't or wouldn't provide for her. Helmut was trying his best. His heart was in the right place, but he had to take care of his wife. Elena put up a good front but didn't have the energy to raise a teenage girl. Maybe this wasn't a simple case of Maya running away or a direct kidnapping, but a combination of the two.

Kelly broke the silence. "Why didn't you tell Helmut about Russell Stevens?"

"Didn't want him to get worked up about it," I said.

"You think he'd do something?"

"Folks like Helmut and my grandpa are used to taking care of things on their own. It's in their blood. If he thought Mike Bauer or Owen had anything to do with Maya's disappearance, he'd likely show up at Mike's house with a shotgun in his hand. He'd either shoot someone or get shot. Zeller be damned."

"You think he'd take on a gangster like the Dragon?"

"In a heartbeat. He'd face the devil himself without battin' an eye. Helmut's great-grandpa was fending off Comanche raiding parties during the Civil War. The army abandoned the frontier forts after Texas seceded, and the Indians took that as an open invitation to raise hell and push back at the white settlers encroaching on their hunting grounds." I stopped at a streetlight on Main Street. Traffic was still heavy. Oktoberfest was in full swing until midnight.

"So, this is a full-scale investigation?"

"As full as it gets. I'm gonna find Maya and bring her home."

"What's next?"

"We need background info on Russell Stevens. That's Skeeter's job. We'll wait for his call. I also wanna talk to Owen again. I have a feeling our conversation with his dad and Russell will shake things up. He may even spill his guts to Coach V before we get to him."

She smiled. "Do we have an hour to kill? It's my last night in town."

I took a deep breath and turned my attention back to her. "We do. I can either turn right and go back to Oktoberfest and dance the polka—or I can turn left and go back to the motel room where we could get naked, drink more beer, and make out to a polka band on YouTube."

"Why are Germans so romantic?" She twisted out of her seatbelt and sat in my lap.

"It's the hops in the beer. Brings out our animal passion," I said with a straight face.

The light turned green. Someone behind me honked. My lips were glued to hers. They honked again.

"Turn left," she whispered.

I found the gas pedal and pulled into traffic with her in my lap. Probably not the safest driving maneuver, but we were cruising at under ten miles per hour. Main Street was crowded with tourists and locals on their way to and from the Marktplatz. All the shops and restaurants along Main

Street were open for business, sponging the tourists for every dollar they could get. It was all I could do to keep my attention on the slow-moving vehicles in front of me and off Kelly's roving hand.

"I'm gonna miss you when you leave," I said.

"Liar. You'll be working the case. You won't even notice I'm gone." She moved her hand a little farther down the front of my shirt. "You're married to the job, and I feel like the mistress."

"Yeah, but you're a hot and sexy mistress."

"You really think so?" She traced the scars on my forehead with her other hand.

"Without a doubt."

She smiled without speaking. By the time I parked in the only open space in the back row of the motel parking lot, I'd managed to work her shirt up, revealing a good portion of her red lace bra. We both jumped out of the pickup and ran for the staircase. I caught her on the bottom step and wrapped my arms around her. Our lips locked together. I heard footsteps on the stairs. A couple in their late sixties dressed alike in white shorts, tennis shoes, and Hawaiian shirts passed us. The woman frowned at Kelly. The man eyed her exposed red bra.

We giggled all the way to the top of the stairs. I dug the keycard out of my wallet and opened the door.

Inside, I pulled her shirt over her head.

She let it drop to the floor. The red lace bra went without protest. I pulled at her belt, and she pulled at mine. Her bare skin glowed in the ambient light shining through the window. I lifted her from below the waist and shuffled toward the bed with my Wranglers around my boots. I felt the sharp pinch in my chest from the bullet wound, but I ignored it. No pain, no gain.

I looked over her shoulder for a clear landing place on the bed and came face-to-face with a naked body lying face up and spread eagle across the mattress. It was a young woman, and her pale skin took on the bluish tint of the moonlight.

"Oh shit," I said, thinking we had somehow stumbled into the wrong room.

"What? What is it?" Kelly scrambled out of my grasp.

"It's a little crowded in here," I said.

Kelly turned and saw the body. "Oh my god!"

I pulled my jeans up so I could shuffle to the light switch without falling over.

"It's that girl, Lori."

The harsh light from the motel lamps only amplified the starkness of Lori's naked body. I felt a lump in my throat. I'd seen many bodies in my time but finding a dead young girl in my motel bed was a first. Kelly looked away and finished getting dressed. I took a deep breath and looked closer. Red marks on her throat indicated she'd been strangled. There were rough abrasions on her upper arms and trauma to her wrists and ankles as if she'd been tied with rope at some point, but the pieces were missing. I put my finger on her neck, checking for a pulse. Nothing. Her skin was cold and chalky, her lips blue from lack of oxygen. The bed cover and the top sheet were on the floor, as were the pillows. Kelly joined me beside the bed. As a Marine MP, she'd seen her share of death. It's not something you ever get used to, but she was trained to deal with it.

"Who would do this to a young girl?" Kelly asked.

I shook my head. "A cold-blooded killer."

"A dragon?"

My business card was on the nightstand. I picked it up by the edges and turned it over. Kelly's handwritten name and number were on the back along with the motel and room number.

"You think she came here on her own?" Kelly asked.

"Maybe she had more to tell us." I checked my phone for messages, remembering I'd turned off the ringer on our way to Helmut's. There were two missed calls and two voice messages. I put the phone on speaker.

"Mr. Fischer?" Lori's voice sounded thin and scared and came in quick bursts. "This is Lori Kostoch. I thought of something else..." Then a pause and a sharp intake of breath. "Please, call me back." I could hear traffic noise in the background. The message had come at two thirty, thirty minutes after we'd dropped her off.

"She sounded desperate. Like someone was watching her," Kelly said.

"There's another message. This one came twenty minutes later. Almost three o'clock." I pressed play.

"Mr. Fischer, this is Lori again." Her voice came in a whisper, the phone pressed against her lips. "Can you please call me as soon as you get this?" There was a five-second pause. "You're probably at Oktoberfest," Lori continued. "There's something I need to tell you. I'll wait for you at your motel." She disconnected.

"You think someone followed her here?"

I stepped to the center of the room and scanned the small space. The window was locked from the inside and on the second floor. The front door had not been tampered with. I stepped closer to the door that connected the two rooms. The frame was cracked, and the door was ajar. I pushed it open with my boot. Both connecting doors were open.

"He got in from the next room," I said. "Check the front desk. See if they saw anything or if they have surveillance cameras. Ask who checked in next door."

Kelly went out quickly.

I checked my watch. It was six thirty. I searched the small room again, careful not to disturb anything, although our prints and DNA were all over the room anyway. Nothing under the bed or in the open closet. In the bathroom I found Lori's clothes in a pile by the tub. They were the same items she'd worn that afternoon. I also found three lengths of rope. It was cheap yellow-nylon cord, the kind sold at every convenience store in Texas.

I walked through the broken door. The adjacent room was trashed. Clothes everywhere. Bathroom stuff scattered around the sink. Both queen beds had been slept in. I remembered hearing the two boys bouncing off the walls the night before. The occupants hadn't checked out. This room hadn't been robbed. It had barely contained two teen boys full of cotton candy.

I went back to our room and studied Lori's body. There were no bullet holes or knife wounds. There was no blood on the white sheet. I checked her fingernails and hands for signs of a struggle. There were no abrasions. She hadn't put up a fight. There was a lump on her forehead. Someone had put her lights out with a single powerful blow to the head. Someone with prison muscles and maybe a dragon tattoo or maybe a young football star.

Kelly met me in the parking lot. "The surveillance system was offline. Something about vandals. It won't be fixed until next week. The girl on duty in the lobby had talked to Lori. They were school friends. Lori told her she was going to wait for us to return."

"Did you tell her Lori was dead?" I asked.

Kelly nodded. "She didn't take it very well."

"What about the room next door?"

"Still occupied by the family with the teen boys. They went to the festival early this afternoon. Haven't been back. Someone could have stolen their key." She pulled a scrap of paper from her back pocket with the motel name and logo. "Lori left this note for you at the front desk."

I took the paper. Lori had folded it in half and written my name on the back. I opened it. The name "Club Forty-Four" was written inside. "That's all she left?"

"Yep. You know Club Forty-Four?"

"Yeah, it's a strip club in San Antonio."

Kelly raised her eyebrows. "Hangout of yours?"

"Do you know a Marine who hasn't been to a strip club?"

She shook her head. "You're right. What do you think it means?"

"I don't know. But Lori risked her life to tell us."

I found Les Zeller's number and hit dial. He picked up on the second ring. "Hey, Les," I said. "Sorry to bother you, but there's a dead body in my motel room. Her name's Lori Kostoch." I paused for him to respond. He didn't say anything. He probably didn't get too many calls like that working on a small-town police force. "Les, can you hear me? This is Nick Fischer. Lori Kostoch is dead. I found her in my motel room about ten minutes ago."

"Don't touch anything," he insisted, regaining his composure. "I'll be right there." He hung up without saying goodbye.

"Is the cavalry on the way?" Kelly asked.

"Yep. Just like in the old days, a day late to save the victim."

CHAPTER SEVENTEEN

Before I could pocket my phone and walk back to my pickup, four FPD cruisers lit up the parking lot like a Fourth of July carnival. The cavalry had arrived. It was a good response time, but as usual, it was too late to prevent the crime. The ostentatious display of police force fit Les Zeller's personal style.

Les was the first one to hit the blacktop. For a big, well-fed guy in his late thirties who hadn't seen the inside of a gym since high school, he was surprisingly quick on his feet. Six other officers followed, while he shouted orders for them to spread out and secure the scene. He was reading from the active shooter playbook and didn't display overwhelming confidence. The men took up positions behind open car doors and drew their weapons. Kelly and I walked back to the second-story landing with our hands up to avoid an accidental shooting.

"You'd think we were giving away free kolaches," I said to Kelly.

She flashed me a stern look. "It *is* a murder scene."

"But the murderer is long gone. We need an evidence tech and the JP. Not Colonel Mackenzie and the Fourth Cavalry."

"I'm sure he doesn't get many murder calls."

"He's just showing off."

"Cut him some slack. You intimidate him."

"He's supposed to be a professional." When it looked like the troops might open fire, I yelled at Zeller. "We're friendly. Put the damn weapons down. The scene's secure."

Zeller hesitated, scanned the parking lot, then called out: "All clear." The officers holstered their weapons reluctantly, and Zeller hustled toward us with two of his men in tow. The sun was already down, but they all still had on wraparound mirror sunglasses as if they didn't trust the sun to stay beyond the horizon. They also had matching high-and-tight haircuts that would look good on a recruiting poster.

Kelly and I put our hands down and watched Zeller approach.

"Is this your motel?" he asked. He was as sharp as a razor.

"I think it belongs to Best Western."

"You gonna start shit, Fischer?"

"I called you, Les. There's a dead girl upstairs. The killer's long gone. Lori's body's in my room. Number two thirty-six. Top of the stairs. It's open."

Zeller scowled, telegraphing his intent to throw me in jail, but he couldn't think of a reason yet, so he pushed past us and stomped up the stairs. "Don't go anywhere," he said over his shoulder.

"The adjoining room door was jimmied. Looks like somebody used a screwdriver or a crowbar," I called to him.

Zeller kept walking. "We'll do the investigating, Fischer. I'll need an official statement from both of you." Zeller yelled at one of the high-and-tight officers. "Secure the premises. No one in or out of the parking lot." He turned to the younger one, who stood next to me. He looked all of eighteen with a slim build and a flaming case of acne. "Get their IDs and log their information." Zeller disappeared into my motel room.

"Were y'all at the festival?" I said to the young cop, trying to be friendly. He removed his sunglasses. His eyes were small and set close together, and he made an earnest effort to stare us both down.

"Could I see some identification?" he said.

"Relax. I'm the guy who called you, Officer Markey," I said, reading his name from his name tag.

"Sorry, sir. It's part of the procedure."

I sighed and handed over my driver's license along with my private eye creds and my concealed carry permit, hoping the kid wouldn't freak out.

"I am armed, Officer," I said.

Kelly showed her ID, which included her police badge from Lubbock. "We're both armed," she said.

He stiffened and looked at our IDs as if he was not sure what to do next.

"Markey, get up here!" Zeller yelled down from the second floor.

Markey jumped. "Yes, sir!" He handed us our IDs and ran up the stairs two at a time.

Zeller ordered him to secure the room, then stomped back down the stairs.

"All right, Nick. Why don't you start at the beginning?" Zeller pulled out his notebook.

I went over my meeting with Lori, starting at the beginning and including the fight with Owen. I added the part about my interview with Mike Bauer and Russell. Zeller seemed to dismiss all of them as suspects before I'd even finished, but he did take notes.

"I told you not to harass them."

"I asked Mike's permission. He was okay with it. You can talk to him."

"I will. When did you last see the victim?" Zeller asked.

"You mean Lori. This afternoon. She tapped on my window while I was going through the drive-through at Whataburger. She said she drove Maya to the party on the river. Owen was there and so was Russell Stevens, Mike Bauer's security guard."

"She never said anything to me," he said.

"Too scared, probably. She called again this afternoon. I didn't get the call because I'd turned my ringer off."

"Turned off your ringer," he repeated and made a note.

"We went to visit Helmut, and I didn't want to be disturbed."

He made another note. "Any other reason?"

"You think I'm a suspect?"

"Everyone she came in contact with is a suspect. Did she leave a message?"

I sighed and got out my phone. "She left two." I hit play. Lori sounded even more desperate than I remembered. "The last message came at two fifty-five. We got here at about six."

"And y'all were with Helmut all afternoon?"

"Call him if you want. Elena fixed dinner for us. We went to talk to him about Maya."

He looked at his watch. "I'll call him in the morning. It's past his bedtime. I don't wanna piss him off. Busiest weekend of the year..." Zeller let his sentence trail off.

"You have two obvious suspects," Kelly said.

He looked at her, still annoyed. "I get that you're a police officer in Lubbock and all, but we have our own procedure here."

"Just trying to help," she said, meeting his snarky response with a cold seriousness perfected from her years as a Marine MP.

"This has everything to do with Maya's disappearance," I said.

Zeller bristled. "This isn't your case. I know you're working for old man Geisler, but this is a murder investigation. We haven't established a connection between the murder and Maya's disappearance."

"You're kidding me, right?"

"We're professionals," he said, implying that I wasn't. "We follow the evidence. So far, we don't have any."

"Lori had information about Maya. That's why she was killed."

He ignored me. "I'll need you both to come down to the station to sign a statement tonight."

"Set up an appointment," I said. "Right now, we're tired, and our room is double-booked, so we need to find another place to stay on Oktoberfest weekend." I took out a business card and handed it to him. "Here's my number. I'm not hard to track down."

Zeller's jaw muscles clenched. "Goddamnit, Fischer. Don't be such an asshole."

His cheeks turned red. He was flustered, but I didn't care. "Lori's dead because she had information about Maya that she wanted to share with me. Right now, I'm more concerned with preventing another murder than retelling my story of finding Lori."

"How about our suitcases? Can we get those out of the room?" Kelly asked.

"Everything stays where it is until after the crime tech finishes."

"My toothbrush and your underwear are important pieces of evidence. We better let FPD have them." I took Kelly's hand, and we walked back to my pickup. Zeller seemed like he wanted to protest, but I didn't give him a chance.

"I told you he was intimidated," Kelly said after we'd climbed into the cab.

"I think your wrong. He's givin' me shit because he never got the chance to finish the fight he started in high school."

"With that hole in your chest, he might get the upper hand."

"I could tie one hand behind my back and still kick his ass."

"That's good to know."

I put my pickup in gear and sped out of the parking lot before Zeller could order our arrest and make us spend the next several hours at the station repeating the awkward circumstances that led to our discovery of the body. Lori's murder left no doubt in my mind that Maya was in grave danger. Someone was willing to kill to keep me from finding her. I headed east on Main Street out of town and speed-dialed Skeeter.

"What're you thinkin'?" Kelly asked.

I put the cell phone on speaker, and we listened to it ring. "This case just got a lot more dangerous and a lot more complicated."

"You think Maya's involved in the murder?"

"I don't know. I think she's in over her head. Whoever killed Lori won't hesitate to do it again to preserve whatever kind of illegal operation is going on."

"What if she's already dead?"

"Then it's not a missing person case anymore."

Skeeter finally answered. "Tell me you've been working," I said.

"Nonstop," he said.

"Good. 'Cause the shit just hit the fan." I filled him in on what we'd learned about Maya's homelife from visiting Helmut's ranch and our visit with Lori from the time she came to see us in the Whataburger parking lot until we found her strangled in the motel room. "So far, we've got Russell Stevens, Owen Bauer, and maybe his daddy on the short list. What does your research tell us?"

"Well, if we're looking for someone with the means to do it, Dragon is our man. He took a baseball bat to his stepdad when he was in high school. His defense team argued he and his mother were abused one too many times. The judge had sympathy for him and reduced the murder charge to manslaughter. He did five years."

"What's he been up too lately?"

"For ten years, he's kept his nose clean."

"That or he learned how to stay under the radar in prison," I said.

"He has some scary known associates," Skeeter added.

"Do any of them work for Club Forty-Four? Lori left a note with my name on it at the motel. She wrote Club Forty-Four and gave it to the clerk."

"That joint has a nasty reputation."

"Tell me about it."

"I'll see if there's a link. Where are you headed?"

"First, I wanna check out the trailer house on Bauer's property to see if Dragon's home. If we don't find anything there, we need to check out the strip club."

"Be careful."

"Always." I hung up and turned north out of town. "It might be a late night," I said.

Kelly shrugged. "You sure know how to show a girl a good time."

"What can I say?"

"How do you know about Club Forty-Four?"

"I had a few run-ins with the staff and a particular dancer at Club Forty-Four when I first mustered out of the Corps. It wasn't my proudest moment. I was battling demons with the aid of Jack Daniels and wallowing in self-pity. Grandpa staged an intervention."

"You've never talked about it."

I was silent for a moment. "Like I said. It wasn't my proudest moment."

"Survivor's guilt?"

I stiffened and felt the muscles in my shoulders and jaw tighten. She knew most of my story because she'd heard me screaming in my sleep when I was out cold in the hospital after taking a bullet from Marcus Lopez's snub-nose .38. Stress and hospital beds always seemed to unleash the demons in a swirling round of nightmares. Tonight, I had work to do and didn't want to stare into the abyss. Thankfully, Kelly sensed my mood.

"I get it. Let it go. Let's focus on finding Maya."

Dragon's trailer was abandoned. The front door was unlocked, the lights were off, and the driveway was empty. I grabbed my Maglite and searched the perimeter. Nothing. Inside, the trailer smelled like marijuana and sour milk. The only thing left was a half package of bologna in the refrigerator and an open quart of milk on the counter. The plastic garbage sacks I'd seen through the back window were gone. Russell Stevens and his entourage had moved out.

My phone rang. Skeeter's name popped up on the caller ID.

"Anything at the trailer?" he asked.

"Nope. It's cleaned out." I put the phone on speaker and held it up for Kelly to hear.

"Russell's on the payroll at Club Forty-Four. Looks like he started when he got out of prison. Someone gave him a fresh start. Doesn't give a job description, but I'm guessing he wasn't a dancer."

"I'll meet you there in two hours," I said and disconnected.

"And if we find him there?" Kelly asked.

"I'll ask him a few questions."

"Like, did you murder Lori Kostoch?"

"Exactly."

"You think he's gonna tell you if he did?"

"No, but I wanna rattle his chain, let him know killing Lori's not gonna save his ass. If he's there we'll sit on him for a while. He might get careless."

We got back in my pickup and drove toward town. "There won't be any rooms left in the county tonight. You can stay at the ranch. Sorry your last night in town has to—"

She raised her hand to cut me off. "Don't even think about dropping me off. I'm coming with you."

"What about work tomorrow in Lubbock? I don't know how long this will take."

"I'm calling in sick. Besides, you and Skeeter are recovering from gunshot wounds. I'm the only one any good in a fight."

"You keep this up, I'm gonna have to put you on the payroll."

"I was thinking more like a partner. *Hoffman, Davis, and Fischer – Private Investigations.* I saw you interact with Detective Zeller. You need someone to keep you on the right side of the law."

"Why does your name come first? I'm the company founder."

"Obviously, because ladies come first, and I'll be the brains of the operation," she said.

CHAPTER EIGHTEEN

Club Forty-Four was located northwest of downtown on Loop 410. The pink neon sign featured the silhouette of a well-endowed female with her head tilted back, seductively holding the large revolver that gave the club its name. I drove around the crowded parking lot until I found Skeeter's Dodge Ram 4x4 pickup. He was in the driver's seat with the crown of his head leaning against the window glass.

"Looks like he's taking a nap," Kelly said.

"He's out past his bedtime." I got out and tapped on the glass. He was wearing headphones and his mouth was slightly open. A string of drool leaked from his lips to the black interior door panel. I tapped a little harder. Finally, he opened his eyes and lifted his head. The window rolled down, and he wiped the droll from his lips.

"Took you long enough." He pulled off his headphones. Old-school rap music was pumping through the tiny speakers. His bulk filled the open window.

"We had to stop for gas. What's on the iPod?"

"The Fat Boys," he said.

I had no idea who that was and didn't care to ask because I knew the question would lead to a lecture about how rap was once great and how the new generation had ruined it. He could go on for hours.

"Hey, Clarence," Kelly called.

Skeeter smiled and unfolded himself out of his pickup. At six-foot-seven and three hundred pounds, he made Kelly and me look like sixth graders on a fieldtrip. His size and the metal hook he wore as a prosthesis presented a fearsome figure. It was easy to imagine him in his former life as an All-American defensive tackle for the University of Texas football team. If it hadn't been for the accident that took part of his arm on the night he was drafted, he'd probably still be terrorizing quarterbacks.

"Kelly!" His big baritone voice vibrated from somewhere deep inside his chest. "Did he drag you into this?" He leaned down and folded her in a bear hug, and she kissed him on the cheek. It felt like a family reunion.

"Nick put me on the payroll," she said playfully.

Skeeter raised his eyebrow at me. "Sounds like we need to have a business meetin'."

"What business meetin'? I'm the boss. It's Fischer Investigations. I'm Fischer."

"You're resisting the expansion?" Kelly said, taking my arm. "Think of the volume we could do with three employees instead of two."

"This is more like a hostile takeover. And technically you two would be employees. I'm the boss."

"Make it equal partners. I want my name on the business cards," Kelly said.

"Yeah, Hoffman, Davis, and Fischer," Skeeter said. His baritone chuckle rumbled from deep down in his massive chest like a volcano before an eruption.

Kelly tapped her finger on her lips thoughtfully. "Has a nice ring to it."

"So, now my name's last." I wasn't sure what had just happened.

"Does that mean I get a raise?" Skeeter asked.

"Sure, you can have half of my salary. Helmut agreed to pay with hog and goat meat."

"You kiddin' me?"

"Actually, we didn't talk numbers, but he's a rancher. He's got more livestock than ready cash."

"You should have talked that over with your partners," Skeeter said.

"When he signed the contract, I didn't have any partners," I argued.

"Maybe we can renegotiate our fee," Kelly said.

"Let's find his granddaughter first. That will give us some leverage," I said. "Now, if you two are finished reorganizing my company, let's see if Russell Stevens is on duty."

The three of us walked through the busy parking lot toward the entrance. The music pulsed louder as we approached. It was a few degrees warmer in San Antonio, but still a pleasant sixty-five degrees. Not bad for fall in South Texas. The air smelled like exhaust fumes and fried tortillas from the Taco Cabana next door, a local Mexican fast-food chain that featured a signature pink building. The sky reflected city lights instead of stars, one of the things I missed most when I wasn't living in the country.

Two chunky bouncers wearing too-tight black T-shirts sat on barstools by the door. They were checking the IDs of two boys who looked like they were in high school. A row of Harley choppers lined the north wall of the building. The rest of the parking lot overflowed with pickups and utility trucks. The dress code was casual, and the two teens wore T-shirts and baggy jeans.

"You think Maya's here?" Kelly asked.

"Lori said that crowd on the river expected them to dance," I said. "That made me wonder if there might be a connection between them and this place."

"You plannin' on goin' all Afghanistan and shit if we find Russell?" Skeeter asked.

"I wasn't planning on keeping a low profile. Whoever murdered Lori upped the ante. It's time to go all in. Maya might not have much time left."

"You ever been in one of these places before?" Skeeter asked Kelly.

"You forget my background," Kelly answered.

Skeeter shrugged and glanced at me. I had no doubt she'd been in a strip club before, but I guessed it was with her pistol drawn to collar a drunk Marine and not for pleasure.

We waited behind the high school boys while the musclemen pretended to study their fake IDs. One of the boys passed a greenback to the bouncer. I couldn't see the denomination. The kid nudged his friend with his elbow. A moment later, the friend produced a bill that the bouncer quickly palmed. This time I saw it was a fifty. I checked the entrance for surveillance cameras and saw two on the corner of the building. One facing the parking lot and the other trained on the entrance. Either the cameras weren't working, or the two clowns in tight T-shirts didn't care they were being filmed. Several moments later, they let the two teens walk through the entrance.

Kelly had her phone out, video-recording everything. I stepped forward. Skeeter stayed a step behind us. Both bouncers focused on him, his bulk, and his metal prosthetic hook. Even though their muscles strained their T-shirts, they were no match for Skeeter.

"You really take bribes when the surveillance cameras are rollin'?" I asked. I was there to shake things up. That's what I did best. The bouncer to my left smiled nervously, exposing crooked yellow teeth. His focus stayed on Skeeter. "He's with me," I added.

"What're you talkin', dude?" Crooked Teeth said.

"Those two boys were probably sixteen or seventeen. You let 'em go in. I saw them slip you a fifty-dollar bill. Does that make them legal?"

"You a cop?" the other bouncer said. They were both standing now.

"Private investigator," I said. "These are my associates." I nodded toward Kelly and Skeeter and held up my credentials. "Do those work?" I pointed to the surveillance cameras.

"You ain't no cop," Crooked Teeth said. "We ain't gotta talk to you."

"Is that the way you wanna play it?"

"Yeah, fuck off," his partner said and reached behind his back.

Kelly saw the move. She grabbed his thumb and twisted it behind his back, then she pulled a Glock from his waistband and pointed it at the other bouncer. Her swift action surprised me as much as the two bouncers. Skeeter let out a deep rumbling chuckle.

"What the fuck do you want, man?"

"We wanna talk to the manager," I said.

"Fuck you," he said.

Kelly gave his arm a twist.

"Okay, bitch. Back off, Jesus."

"Watch your language around the lady. You don't wanna piss her off. Let's go inside."

Kelly pocketed his pistol, and we followed Crooked Teeth and his partner inside the club. The music was throbbing loud enough to feel against my skin, limiting conversation to hand signals and facial expressions. The lighting was minimal except over the three mirrored dance stages. When my eyes adjusted, I could see the place was packed with a cross section of bikers, college students, and businessmen. A trio of topless girls gyrated on the main stage, each with a collection of bills tucked in her G-string. The place hadn't changed. It smelled of alcohol, body sweat, and cigarette smoke. The memory and the stink turned my stomach. I'd promised Grandpa I wouldn't set foot in this place again, but this was business. I was working. That's something he would understand.

We followed the bouncer to a door behind the bar. I stopped Skeeter before we went inside. "Wait for us here," I shouted. "Don't let anybody else in." I chinned toward the door.

He smiled and held up his thumb.

Inside the office, a slight-built man in his early forties with hipster glasses and a shaved head sat behind a metal desk. He wore a blue velvet suit without a tie, and he had a tattoo of a cross on the back of his left hand.

"You the manager?" I asked, pushing past the two thugs. Kelly followed me inside and shut the door. She stood with her back against the wall.

"That's right. I'm Arnold Garza. What's this about?" His voice sounded like sandpaper being pulled over a stick of wood.

"I'm Nick Fischer, and this is my partner Kelly. We're private investigators looking for this girl." I showed him the photo of Maya. His eyes flicked to the picture but quickly went back to me. "Her name's Maya Chavez. She went missing from Fredericksburg on August tenth."

"Never seen her before, man." His eyes showed no sign of recognition.

"Is Russell here?"

"Who's that?"

"Russell Stevens. Big guy, blond hair. Beautiful smile. Likes to wear tight jeans. He's got a cute dragon tattooed on his chest. We talked to him in Fredericksburg yesterday."

Garza's eyes narrowed. "Don't know him."

"Sure you do. He started working here after he got out of prison."

"Lot of guys have worked here. So what?"

"Fair enough. That's the way you wanna play it."

"What'd ya want? We're busy."

"We wanna see your surveillance tapes," I said. "Starting with August tenth."

Garza laughed. It was forced and awkward. His eyes were dull and dilated like he'd been high for most of the day. "You're not cops. Get the fuck outta here."

"Here's what we already have," Kelly said and pulled out her cell phone. "Your bouncers on video taking a bribe from two underage kids. Let us look at the tapes, and we won't tell the cops what happened outside. We wanna see if Maya Chavez stopped by here after she disappeared from Fredericksburg."

Garza stood up. He was about my height, six-one, but skinny with a sunken chest. He stepped in front of Crooked Teeth. "You stupid fuck!" He slapped him with an open hand. The bouncer outweighed him by fifty pounds, but he didn't make a move against the manager. "Did you take a bribe at the door?"

The bouncer shook his head. "No, boss. I swear."

The manager slapped him again. "Asshole! Get the fuck out of my sight."

"How about showing us the surveillance tapes?" I asked when both bouncers were gone.

"I'll have to check with the owners," Garza said and picked up his cell phone. I walked to the door marked Private. "You can't go in there." Garza moved to cut me off.

I opened the door. The room held a stack of electronic equipment and a back door.

"Did you hear me, asshole?" Garza shouted.

I shut the door and stepped back. "Take it easy, Arnold," I said. "Call the owner. We'll have a drink out front while we wait. Kelly followed me to the door. "Give 'em my name, Nick Fischer, private investigator." I handed him one of my cards. "Tell them I already talked to Russell."

We found a young dancer sitting at the bar beside Skeeter. She wore a sheer top over a gold G-string and had her tiny hand on Skeeter's huge forearm. His eyes were glued to her enhanced boobs.

"Enjoying yourself?" I shouted.

His head whipped in my direction. He grinned. "This's Candy," he said.

"I'll bet she is," I said.

The girl had heavy green eye makeup that sparkled in the dim light and skin as smooth as a baby's butt. If she graduated from high school, it wasn't long ago. She stared at my forehead scars and sucked her bottom lip between her teeth.

I flashed her what I hoped was a paternal smile. "Hi, Candy. It's okay, we're friendly."

She glanced at Kelly, then back at me. "Y'all cops?"

"Private investigators," I said, leaning close to her ear. "Is there someplace we can talk?" I held a fifty folded to show the denomination. It had worked for the teens; it might work for me.

Candy looked nervous but nodded and jumped down from the barstool. We followed her to a curtain that led to a private area behind the main stage. Another bored bouncer with a diamond stud in his ear slouched on a barstool beside the curtain. He looked up from his cell phone when he saw Candy. She said something to him I couldn't hear. He nodded. She rubbed her fingertips together in the universal sign for money. Everyone gets a cut. My expense account was getting low. Helmut's livestock wouldn't pay the bills. I still had a mortgage on my fixer-upper in King William. Last time I checked, the bank didn't accept meat as payment.

I pulled out another fifty. "Got change for a fifty?"

The bouncer smiled and tucked the bill in his tight sequined jeans. I turned back to Skeeter. He shrugged his massive shoulders. I pointed to the main stage where the three dancers were doing a pole routine.

"Enjoy the show," I said. "Don't let any surprises through the curtain."

He nodded and then pulled a barstool from the edge of the stage and sat down opposite the bouncer. The bouncer didn't object. When you're six-foot-seven and weigh three hundred pounds, you sat wherever you wanted to.

I followed Candy and Kelly to a private booth set up for close encounters. I'd been here before too. The queasy feeling returned to the pit of my stomach, as if my personal demons could smell a relapse and were planning an escape. The only lights were from fake candles flickering on the tables and a line of guide lights embedded in the floor so the servers could keep the overpriced drinks flowing. The music still vibrated off the walls, but it was quiet enough for conversation. I could hear a man in the opposite booth ask for another beer. I slid in beside Candy and held out the picture of Maya.

"Ever seen this girl?"

Candy glanced at the photo, then quickly covered it with her hand. "You're gonna get me in trouble."

"For answering a few questions?" Kelly asked.

"I thought you wanted a dance, you know."

"Do you often dance for couples?" Kelly asked.

"Yeah, all the time."

Kelly raised her eyebrow, confirming my suspicion that she'd never entered one of these places without the intent to arrest or detain.

I shrugged.

"You swear you're not cops?" Candy asked. "'Cause if you are, you gotta tell me."

"I swear I'm not a cop." Technically, Kelly was, but she was off duty. "The girl's grandpa hired us to find her. Her name's Maya Chavez."

Candy chewed her bottom lip. A waitress wearing purple pasties and a matching G-string stopped at our table. I wasn't going to get out of here for less than five hundred dollars. Kelly and I ordered two ten-dollar Shiner Bocks. Candy ordered something called a Mad Mako and waited until the waitress was gone before she continued.

"I seen her last week. Dragon brought her in with two other new girls."

My pulse quickened. Finally, a break. "What happened to her?" I asked, squeezing the edge of the table. I fought the urge to grab her tiny shoulders and shake her enhanced boobs.

"I don't know. Some girls only stay for one night. Some girls"—she gestured to herself—"stay and work."

"Where do they go?" Kelly said.

Candy squirmed. "I said too much already."

"What's Dragon's connection here?"

There was a commotion at the door. Diamond Stud was suddenly beside us along with Garza. "It's time for y'all to leave," he said. "I talked to the owner. He don't care what you have on video. He wants you gone."

"No surveillance tapes?" I asked.

"Get the fuck out of here."

We all stood up. Diamond Stud closed his hand around Kelly's elbow. Big mistake.

She twisted out of his grip, grabbed his thumb, and forced it behind his back. Round two for her. Garza held his purple jacket open and showed me the butt of a Glock stuck in his waistband. He expected me to step back and raise my hands. Instead, I stepped forward, grabbed the pistol, and shoved the barrel into his crotch. "Do you keep one in the chamber?"

His brown skin turned gray, and he licked his lips. I took that as a yes.

"Bad habit to get into. You never know what might cause it to go off."

He held up his hands. "Okay, man. Fuck."

The waitress arrived with our drinks on a tray.

"Rain check. We were just leaving. Candy's a great dancer. We enjoyed her company." I tried to sound convincing so Candy wouldn't take the heat for talking to us.

"That's right. She showed us a great time." Kelly handed Candy a twenty and I tossed another on the table.

"I'll leave your Glock at the front door," I said.

Skeeter's eyes were glued to a well-endowed dancer shaking her sequined pasties an inch from his nose. He lived with his mother and didn't get out much.

I tapped him on the shoulder. "What happened to guarding the door?"

"I didn't know I was *guarding* the door. Besides, there were only two of them."

"Come on, let's get out of here."

"Ah, man. Just when the show's gettin' interestin'." He sighed.

CHAPTER NINETEEN

Kelly and I sat in my pickup and Skeeter stood by the window. We were still in the Club Forty-Four parking lot. I kept my eye on the door, expecting one of the bouncer thugs to remind us we weren't welcome. My ears were still ringing from the over-cranked music, and the smell of the place stuck to my clothing like barbecue sauce without the pleasant aftertaste. I tried to see the stars, but the lights created a glowing dome over the city, reminding me how far we were from Fredericksburg. The two places in Texas had always been clear and distinct in my mind. Rural versus urban. Farm and ranch land filled with friendly families versus ghettos, gangbangers, and strip clubs. I was intimate with both worlds and had always prided myself on my rural roots. Now the distinctions were fading. The bad actors moved freely between urban and rural. Maybe it had always been that way. My dad's murder at the hands of a meth dealer should have shattered my idyllic notion of rural life in Gillespie County, but when I left to join the Marine Corps and witnessed big cities and war-torn countries firsthand, the family ranch became my bucolic center of the universe, a place where God still existed and heroes like my grandpa still sat on the front porch and smoked cigars. Now, the only difference seemed to be the light pollution and the population densities.

Candy hinted that Russell Stevens trafficked girls. Had he brought Maya here from Fredericksburg? Where was she now? Was she safe? I refused to think she'd already met the same fate as Lori. I also refused to believe she would have come here of her own free will.

I started the engine. "You handled yourself pretty well in there," I said to Kelly.

"You keep forgetting I'm a Marine MP."

"Seeing you out of uniform plays tricks with my memory and gets me all worked up."

Skeeter rolled his eyes. "You two love birds get any info in there, or were you too busy makin' out in the dark?"

"Candy said she saw Maya. She didn't say where she went, but I'll bet she knows more than she let on. We were cut off before she could finish."

"She wanted to talk, but she was scared," Kelly said.

"We need to catch her away from work." I raised my eyebrows in Skeeter's direction.

"I know that look," he said. "You're gonna asked me to do something illegal like break in and steal the surveillance tapes, aren't you?"

"Nope." I'd asked him to break into a downtown nightclub on our last case because he'd installed the security system and I wanted the footage to connect my suspect to a murder victim. We had gotten away with it, but just barely avoided capture when the building's backup security alarm had gone off. Skeeter didn't like running from the police.

"You two boys work this out. I've gotta call my boss and let him know I'm contagious and can't risk infecting the whole department on Monday morning."

We watched her jump out of my pickup and activate her cell phone.

"Really? No breakin' and entering? Kelly got you on the straight and narrow?"

"Maybe she does, but we don't need the surveillance tapes now. We have an eyewitness."

He nodded. "Candy."

"You got promoted to partner and all of the sudden you started using your brain."

"I figure I own a piece of the company now, so I'm invested in its success."

"That's good, 'cause we need to find Maya fast. I've got a feeling that if she's alive, she won't be for long. Either that or she'll be trafficked out of the city or the state."

Skeeter nodded agreement.

"When Candy comes out, follow her. If we're lucky, she'll lead us to Maya."

"Where you goin'?"

"To get some sleep. I'll take the second watch. If you see anything interesting, call me. I'll leave my cell phone on."

"Get some sleep, huh?" He smiled. "I see how this is goin'. I do all the work and you have fun with your new girlfriend."

"You mean partner."

"Yeah, right. I'm gonna give this romance one week."

"What're you talkin' about?"

"You remember that *Seinfeld* episode when Jerry starts dating a girl who's exactly like himself?"

"You're comparing my life to a nineties sitcom that was about nothing?"

He flashed his pearly white teeth. "You missin' the point."

"Whatever. What's the point?"

"She a Marine. She can fight, drink, and shoot…" He let the sentence trail off.

"All right, I get it. You think she's my female doppelganger."

"Damn straight. But without the cynicism, and one other crucial difference. She's a straight arrow. You, my friend, like to play fast and loose with the rules."

"You of all people know evidence sometimes leads to an innocent man."

"Hey, I'm all in with you. I'm just sayin' that might cause friction between y'all."

I nodded. "Point taken."

Kelly tapped on the windshield and held up her cell phone and a thumbs-up. Her boss must have bought her story. She opened the passenger door and got in. "He gave me three days."

• • •

We pulled into my driveway in the King William neighborhood beside the giant pecan tree. The front of the house had a porch on the right half supported by ornate Victorian columns. The left half held a large bay window that showcased a parlor I'd turned into an office. Two windows with detailed trim looked down from the second story. The colorful red with white trim paint was fading, and it needed a new roof, but it was livable. The house was on the edge of one of the oldest neighborhoods in the city that in recent years was getting a makeover. I bought it hoping to cash in on the gentrification. When I actually got around to fixing it up, I was sure it would pay off.

Kelly climbed in my lap and unhooked the top buttons of my shirt. I leaned back in the seat and saw my next-door neighbor, Rose Gustafson, peering through her front room window.

"We've got an audience," I said.

"Rose?"

I nodded. Kelly had met Mrs. Gustafson the week I was in the hospital. I'd sent her to pick up extra clothes and a box of books. After the break-in that led to Sam getting shot, Rose kept a sharp eye out when I wasn't home.

"She might think you're attacking me," I said.

"I am," she purred, and continued working my shirt off.

"Let's take this inside. I don't wanna make an old woman blush."

Kelly kissed me, then led me inside the house. We dropped our clothes on the way up the stairs. I grabbed her around the waist and lifted her over the bed.

"Wait," she said quickly. "Turn on the light. I don't want any more surprises."

I flipped on the lights. The bed was empty.

CHAPTER TWENTY

My buzzing cell phone shattered a rare, pleasant dream that involved me and Kelly on a deserted Gulf Coast beach. I opened my eyes and checked my watch. It was a quarter to seven. I grabbed the phone and sat up. I'd overslept. Skeeter, Candy, and the events of last night flooded my mind. The caller ID said Ochoa. What the hell did she want? That would be Detective Diana Ochoa from the SAPD homicide division. Why the hell was she calling, and what happened to Skeeter? I'd expected him to call when the club shut down or when he'd followed Cindy to her car. I let the phone ring and thought of the last thing I remembered from last night. It was the pleasant image of Kelly's face on the pillow smiling up at me. After our athletic lovemaking, I must have passed out and slept like a mummy. I put a hand on Kelly's side of the bed. It was warm, smelled like lavender, but empty. Before my head could clear, the phone stopped ringing, then it beeped to show a voicemail message.

Ochoa'd been involved with my last case. She was a rookie homicide detective who'd worked her way up the ladder to her dream job by being smart and tough enough not to be intimidated by the good ol' boys club. It wasn't her fault she'd been assigned a corrupt detective for a mentor. He was the same asshole that killed my grandpa and covered up the murder of a young girl at the request of that slimeball candidate for governor, Marcus Lopez. In the messy aftermath of the case, I'd spent days telling and retelling the details to her, the sheriff department, and the Texas Rangers from my hospital bed because the killing involved a state politician. That was almost two months ago. I didn't wanna rehash the details. I was on a new case. Ochoa could wait.

I smelled coffee and the warm scent of eggs and fresh pie crust. Two female voices drifted up from downstairs, a murmured conversation punctuated by a familiar shrill laugh. My neighbor Rose was here and had probably brought breakfast as an excuse to satisfy her curiosity about Kelly's sudden reappearance in the middle of the night. So much for my hope of a morning quickie before I went to check on Skeeter and Candy.

Before I could call Skeeter to get an update, my cell phone rang again. Ochoa. She wasn't going to be put off. "Detective Ochoa. Didn't expect to hear from you so soon."

"I thought you were gonna take some time off," she said, sounding irritated.

"I am taking time off," I said. "And *trying* to sleep in."

She ignored the jab. "Are you back in San Antonio?"

I didn't like where this was going. Why was she checking up on me? "I'm looking for a missing girl from Fredericksburg. A friend of the family contacted me about his granddaughter. I followed a lead to San Antonio last night."

There was a long pause. I could hear her measured breathing. "Thanks for being honest."

"No reason to lie to you. I gotta make a living."

"Your job seems to be making my job a lot harder."

"Why? What's this about?"

"A nightshift clerk at Walmart took the trash out this morning. He found a naked female corpse in the dumpster. Your business card was on top of the body."

Whatever grogginess remained from my restful sleep quickly vanished, leaving a lump in my chest. My first thought was of Maya. Was I too late? I took a slow breath to steady my nerves and ease the sudden urge to panic. "Do you have an ID?"

"Nothing on her, literally. That is, except for your card. Somebody wanted to send a message. The girl got the shit beat out of her and was apparently strangled to death. You wanna tell me what's going on?"

Anger quickly replaced the fear and panic. If it was Maya, someone was going to pay. Dragon was on the top of my list. I took in another slow breath and pushed the emotion down to a deep internal locker and twisted the key. I needed to focus on the objective, which meant I needed information first.

"Which Walmart?" I said. She gave me the address. "I'll meet you there in twenty minutes." I recognized the address as being less than a mile from Club Forty-Four. Had I been too wrapped up with Kelly and let Maya down? Was she Dragon's second victim? And what the hell had happened to Skeeter?

I slipped on a pair of clean Wranglers and a T-shirt and made my way downstairs.

Kelly and Rose sat at the kitchen table sipping coffee. A half-eaten egg pie cooled on the table in front of them. They both smiled like two teenagers caught spreading juicy rumors.

"Good morning," I said. "Y'all are up early."

"Oh, we've been cackling like two hens since dawn," Rose said. "I saw her go out jogging early, so I invited myself over."

"What's wrong?" Kelly asked, seeing the strain on my face.

"That was Detective Ochoa on the phone. A young woman turned up..." I hesitated, glancing at Rose.

"Don't mind me," she said, sensing the gravity of the situation.

It would be in the news later anyway, and Rose soaked up gossip and the local crime report like a dry sponge. "A young woman was found dead in a Walmart dumpster. Ochoa said she was carrying my business card, like it was some kind of warning."

"Oh my god. You think it's Maya?"

I didn't answer. I didn't want to face that possibility.

CHAPTER TWENTY-ONE

The tranquil Sunday morning in the Alamo City felt like the eye of a hurricane that I'd once experienced while visiting my aunt in Rockport. My dad and grandpa had taken me with them to the Gulf Coast to help Grandpa's sister sandbag her property and evacuate before a category four storm hit and stayed when she refused to leave her herd of wild cats that lived in the thicket behind her house. Needless to say, Dad and Grandpa weren't happy, but I was at the age when riding out a category four storm in a clapboard house built in the 1930s was a Tom Sawyer style adventure. There was no danger while my dad and grandpa were there, or so I thought. The first indication that I had misjudged the situation came when I saw a twelve-foot sign from the nearby Whataburger fast-food restaurant fly through the front yard and slam into my aunt's garage. Trees bent at a forty-five-degree angle with the wind. The thing that stuck with me the most was standing in her flooded front yard when the eye of the storm passed over the house. The sun was out, and the light wind felt cool on my face. There was an eerie orange tint illuminating the mass destruction of her neighborhood. Buildings and houses were scattered like a giant game of pick-up sticks. My aunt's house had survived, but I could feel the dread oozing from the three adults as they pointed at the eyewall quickly approaching from the west. It signaled the return of the hurricane-force winds and the possibility that the remaining structures, including my aunt's house, would be destroyed.

We survived and so did my aunt's house and her cats. But most of the town was leveled. My most vivid memory of the experience was that feeling I had standing in her front yard in the eye of the storm. It was the first time I'd ever felt a chink in my dad's or grandpa's indestructible armor. I felt their vulnerability as they both went to work frantically reattaching the plywood that had come loose from the windows and clearing an oak tree that threatened to crash through the second-story roof.

This Sunday morning, I felt as vulnerable as if I was in the eye of a category four hurricane again. I glanced at Kelly in the passenger seat. We hadn't spoken since leaving the house. I briefly wondered if she regretted taking a leave of absence. Two young women had been murdered and there were more to come unless I could go to work and prevent further loss of life.

The traffic was light as I accessed the Interstate 10 on-ramp and gazed out at the quiet city. The bulk of San Antonio rested on the eastern side of the Balcones Fault Zone, which meant it was pan flat and covered with a sea of green trees punctuated by scattered tall buildings that resembled ships floating in the Gulf. The seven-hundred-and-fifty-foot needle-point Tower of the Americas built for the 1968 World's Fair dominated the skyline and served as a compass point for navigation around the city. I was headed north to a Walmart dumpster and a dead body that I hoped wasn't Maya Chavez.

Skeeter's number was on speed dial. I punched it in and put the cell phone on speaker for Kelly to listen in. He answered on the third ring.

His voice sounded more awake than I expected. "Davis, Hoffman, and Fischer Private Investigation. This is Davis. How can I be of assistance?"

"That depends, Mr. Davis. Anything to report?"

"Yeah, I'm hungry and tired, and after a night of watching a strip club parking lot, I'm more convinced that the world is full of degenerates. Do you have any idea what goes on in a strip club parking lot?"

"I have some idea."

"You would. Did you enjoy your night off?" He tried to sound sarcastic, but he didn't have enough practice to pull it off.

"He slept like a baby," Kelly chimed in.

"Good morning, Kelly. I'm sure you had something to do with that."

Kelly's cheeks turned red.

"Did you follow Candy?" I asked.

"I lost her," he said.

I tried not to show my anger. "How's that possible?"

"Russell showed up with six young girls. I could have sworn one of them was Maya. Same dark hair and facial features. He took the girls inside. Candy slipped away while I was taking a closer look. It wasn't Maya. When I came back out, Candy was gone."

"Well, shit." I started to chew him out, but I couldn't fault him for following a possible lead on Maya. After all, she was the primary target.

I told him about Ochoa's call and that we were in route to Walmart to check it out.

"Holy shit," he said. "I'll be right there."

"No. Take the morning off and get breakfast. I'm gonna need your computer sleuth skills later, and I want you rested. I'll let you know what we find."

I disconnected and slowly approached the scramble of emergency vehicles, curious bystanders, and SAPD officers congregated in the Walmart parking lot.

"You think it's her, don't you?" Kelly asked.

"I'm worried. Skeeter saw Russell at Club Forty-Four. That puts him near the scene."

"And now you feel guilty."

It was true. Despite my best efforts, I couldn't hide anything from her. "I should have taken the first shift."

"Instead, you were entertaining me." She reached out with her left hand and touched my arm. "What would you have done differently? You would have taken a closer look at the girl who looked like Maya, just like Skeeter did. Candy would have gotten away from you too."

"It's still my responsibility." I parked behind an SAPD cruiser.

"There's more to it than that," she said when I climbed out of the pickup.

"Maybe, but it's too early for psychoanalysis. Wait here. Let me deal with Ochoa."

She stayed in the pickup, and I approached the ribbon of yellow crime scene tape and a burly beat cop. He immediately told me to get back in my vehicle. My PI creds didn't change his mind. He had a job to do. I spotted Detective Ochoa standing by the dumpster and shouted her name. She waved and walked toward us.

Detective Diana Ochoa was short and athletic, like a gymnast. She wore dark slacks and practical shoes with a cream-colored blouse that accentuated her lithe figure. She wasn't afraid of being feminine. With her shoulder-length raven hair stylishly curled, she looked like an actor stepping off the set of a cop show. Something about her had changed. In the short couple of months since our last encounter, she seemed more comfortable in her role as detective. Maybe it was the walk or the way she held her chin up and took in her surroundings. When we'd met last, she was a rookie and I'd just killed her mentor and partner.

"It's okay, Manny," Ochoa said to the beat cop. "He's with me." I ducked under the yellow tape. "Good to see you're up and around. How're you feelin'?" She studied my face, looking for signs of distress.

"Never better." I flashed my charming smile.

She shook my hand but didn't buy it. "Liar." Her deep brown eyes sparkled like we'd shared an inside joke. What was it about these women who seemed to be able to read me like an open book?

Kelly ignored my suggestion and got out of the pickup and crossed toward us. Ochoa's expression hardened. It wasn't like Kelly to dismiss a direct request, but I held my tongue. She'd met Ochoa in the aftermath of my last case. Maybe she just wanted to say hello.

"Thought you were still in Lubbock," Ochoa said when Kelly reached us. The two women shook hands, sizing each other up. They were both strong, athletic and in their thirties. Kelly had that scrubbed-clean cheerleader look with an easy smile and confidence gained from leading Marines as an officer. Ochoa's beauty was more refined, something I couldn't put my finger on, but she matched Kelly's self-confidence.

"I came down for the Fredericksburg Oktoberfest."

Ochoa's smile vanished. "You knew Nick was involved in a case?"

Kelly held up her hands. "I'm just an observer. He didn't tell me anything about it until after I arrived."

"Look, Detective. I'll tell you whatever you wanna know. Just show me the body," I said.

She studied my face. "Follow me. Don't touch anything. We don't have an ID yet, and CSI isn't finished." She led us to the dumpster, where two ladders had been set up to form a scaffolding. "Take a look." She pointed to the ladder.

I took a deep breath and let it out through my nose. My heart pounded so hard that I was afraid Ochoa and Kelly would hear beating against my chest. I climbed the ladder and peeked over the lip of the dumpster. A blast of rotten garbage mixed with the distinct pungent odor of dried blood and decomposing flesh hit me in the face like a wet towel. The streets of Afghanistan immediately flashed through my mind. The smell of garbage and human waste permeated every backroad my team patrolled. I chased the memory away and held my nose. A frail, naked body rested in the filthy metal container. It looked more like a discarded mannequin from a display window than a young human female. I controlled my reaction and considered my next move.

"I've never seen her before," I lied, still examining the body. It wasn't that I didn't trust Ochoa, but I didn't want police exposure to jeopardize my effort to find the killer. I had a good idea Russell Stevens was behind this, and I didn't want him to bolt before I nailed him.

Ochoa turned to Kelly. "Does he pass his cards out on the street corner?" she asked, raising her eyebrows.

I glanced down at them from the top of the dumpster. "It's not illegal, and it's free advertising," I deadpanned.

Ochoa frowned, sharpening the tiny wrinkles around her eyes. "Don't bullshit me, Fischer. You said you'd tell me what you knew."

I turned back to the body. There were bruises on her thighs that had a yellowish tint like they'd been made days before. Her wrists and ankles also showed signs of trauma, but those were fresh, and there were contusions on her neck. Same MO. It was the same markings I'd found on Lori's body. It couldn't be a coincidence.

"You wanna tell me what's going on?" Ochoa met me at the bottom of the ladder.

"You're the detective," I said. "I can tell you that the card is definitely mine. How she got it, beats me."

She put her hands on her shapely hips. "That's not good enough, Fischer. People seem to drop dead when you're on a case. This has all the earmarks of something you're working on. The card seems placed here on purpose, as a warning. Any comment?"

"If I think of anything, you'll be the first to know," I said and left her standing by the dumpster. Kelly followed be back my pickup.

CHAPTER TWENTY-TWO

I accelerated onto Interstate 10 and headed south, back toward the Tower of the Americas. The sun was out, and the Sunday traffic was still light. The sea of green over the Alamo City covered something evil lurking just below the surface, and I could feel it sucking me under. Kelly stared at my profile and chewed her bottom lip until she couldn't stand it any longer. Finally, she blurted out, "Damn it, Nick. Are you gonna tell me?"

"What?" I said.

"You know what. Was it Maya?"

"No."

"Oh, thank god. Did you recognize her?"

"It was Candy."

"But why didn't—"

I cut her off. "Why not tell the detective? Because she had the same marks on her neck and wrists as Lori Kostoch, and the card had to be a warning to me to stay away from Maya."

"Yeah. So, you're gonna withhold information from SAPD?"

"I'm gonna tell Detective Ochoa everything. But I wanna find Maya first, before she ends up like Lori and Candy."

"You don't trust her?"

"I'm not doubting her commitment. She has her priorities, and I have mine."

"Meaning?"

"Police priorities are set by the bureaucracy. Ochoa has to have a crime to investigate, which means she'll focus on Candy and work her way backward. The system's not set up to prevent crime. Meanwhile, Maya's life is on the line. I can't wait to go through official channels when the killer just upped the ante."

"Thank you for clearing that up." She turned away and looked out the window at the thick green canopy of trees. She wasn't happy with my answer. "I'm a cop, and I'm a Marine," she finally said.

I didn't reply. I knew what she meant. Her sense of duty and adherence to the letter of the law had been imprinted on her DNA. The thought of operating on the fringe made her extremely uncomfortable. I saw the law as a gray area that sometimes helped and sometimes hindered me from gaining access to truth and seeking justice.

Skeeter's assessment was correct, as usual. And the fissure he foresaw was opening much sooner than I expected. The question was, did we have enough of a connection to bridge the gap. Only time would tell.

"I'm working for Helmut. My priority is to find Maya. Hopefully, alive."

"I get it," she said. "I understand why you didn't make a career out of the military. You have a real problem with authority."

"Authority has its place. I respect the law and the Marine Corps. I'd rather rely on myself. I know I can move fast and get western when I need to."

"I'm not disputing that. I've seen you work up close. If anyone else would have challenged Marcus Lopez, he'd have ended up dead. I volunteered to help you on that case because there was no other choice. This case is different. A girl is missing, and the prime suspect is operating in two different counties. He's also involved in other crimes. This is bigger than Maya's disappearance. We need to involve law enforcement and move slowly to build a case that will put that evil degenerate away for good."

"I'm not law enforcement, and I'm not breaking any laws by going after Maya. This is not about building a case. My job is to find a missing girl and take her home. That's it."

She looked out the window and chewed her bottom lip. The

uncomfortable silence stretched to a minute and then two. Finally, my cell phone buzzed. The screen said Skeeter. I put it on speaker.

"Well," he asked. "Was it her?"

"It was Candy." I filled him in on what I'd found and told him we were on our way to his mother's house. I needed his special skill set. A plan was slowly forming in the back of my mind that involved a deep dive below the city's cozy green urban façade where Russell Stevens lived and breathed. A plan that would take weeks of pounding the streets if it weren't for that modern phenomenon called the internet. Besides, my gut instinct told me I didn't have days, let alone weeks, to find Maya. Russell had upped the ante. It was time to call his bet.

• • •

Lola Davis lived on the far south side of San Antonio near Brooks City Base and Mission Espada, the southernmost of the five Spanish missions built along the San Antonio River in the eighteenth century. As I drove south past the Alamo and downtown, I thought about the city's long history of gentlemen's clubs and their relationships to outlaws. The Sporting District was a well-publicized gambling and prostitution zone established by the city council in the late nineteenth century to contain the seamy activity to one ten-block area where the city fathers thought it could be controlled. There was even a pamphlet called the *Blue Book* published as a guide for out-of-town tourists. "Seeking a good time while in San Antonio, Texas?" the cover asked. Inside was a detailed list of must-see attractions. It operated aboveboard starting about 1889 and became the largest red-light district in the state, and one of the largest in the country, until San Antonio Police Commissioner P. L. Anderson shut it down at the breakout of World War II. During its heyday, the Sporting District attracted some of the era's most notorious outlaws like Butch Cassidy and the Sundance Kid along with the rest of the Hole in the Wall gang, as well as some famous lawmen, like William Pinkerton from the National Detective Agency. Russell Stevens would have fit right in playing cards with Butch and the gang in Fannie Porter's brothel and easy to find. Today, he was underground, and I had to dive in and find him.

"Hello, Mr. Fischer," Kelly said from the passenger seat, jolting me out of my rumination in time to recognize the turn to Skeeter's house. "You gonna share our strategy or leave me in the dark?"

"Sorry, I zoned out." I made a quick turn into Skeeter's neighborhood. "I was thinking about San Antonio's outlaw past and how Russell Stevens would have fit right in."

She put a hand on my arm. "This isn't the nineteenth century. I was hoping you were thinking of a legal plan to find him."

"Maybe it's better that I don't tell you about it."

She chewed her lip some more. I drove through a row of modest-sized single-story houses, each with a lawn and a collection of oak trees and ornamental laurel. Skeeter's pickup was in the driveway, and I parked beside it. His mother didn't drive, and I didn't see any other cars parked near the house, which was a good sign. It meant Skeeter hadn't told his mother in advance we were coming. Had she known, family members from all over town would gather as if it were a Christmas party or a homecoming for a long-lost relative. It was Lola who first came to me when I launched my private investigation business. Skeeter was accused of setting an apartment fire on the east side that killed more than a dozen people. She insisted he was framed and hired me to find the real killer. The search nearly killed me, but I found the true guilty party and convinced the DA Skeeter was innocent.

Kelly and I got out and made our way to the door. I saw movement from the front window and heard Lola's shrill voice. Before I could touch the bell, the door flew open and Lola Davis filled the frame from top to bottom in a flower-print muumuu and pink fuzzy slippers. It was easy to see where Skeeter got his size.

"Lord have mercy. Look at you. Skinny as a rail. Come in this house." She stepped back for us to enter. Her arms were thick and looked and felt like they could squeeze a man in half. "Clarence!" she yelled toward the basement, then turned back to me. "Where've you been, child?" She wrapped her man-killer arms around me. "I can tell right now, you ain't gettin' enough to eat. Land's sakes, how you gonna recover from that bullet wound if you don't eat?"

"Good to see you, Miz Davis. How're you?"

"Takin' care of Clarence takes all my strength. Lordy, don't get me started on that boy's bad habits."

"I heard that, Momma," Skeeter called from the basement.

"And this must be Kelly. Clarence told me about you." Lola swept me aside and studied Kelly. "You're a pretty little thing." Lola's gaze peeled back the normal layers of social armor that people put on when they met someone for the first time. She took Kelly's hands and held them at chest level.

Kelly chewed her bottom lip. "I hope they were good things." She stood erect, accepting the inspection, as she had throughout her military career, but this wasn't like a Marine inspection focused on polished shoes and sharp creases. Lola Davis looked into her soul.

An awkward minute ticked by. Then Lola suddenly swept Kelly up in her big arms and squeezed her like a rag doll. "My, my, my," she said. "This one's got a mind of her own. Mr. Fischer, you've got your hands full." She cocked an eyebrow in my direction. I had no idea what she meant. "She needs some meat on her bones, but I'll fix y'all up right now."

"Don't go to any trouble," I said. "We just came by to say hello and visit with your son."

As if on cue, Skeeter stepped out of the stairwell. He saw Kelly smothered in his mother's arms and nodded knowingly toward me.

"Nick Fischer, you know better than that," Lola said. "You come with me, suga," she said to Kelly. "You can help me put together some lunch, and I'll tell you a few things about Nick you need to know." She took Kelly's arm and led her into the kitchen.

"Step into my office," Skeeter said.

Whatever Lola Davis was going to tell Kelly was out of my hands, so I followed Skeeter down the stairs and into the basement he used as a combination computer research laboratory and bedroom. The space was twenty by thirty feet long and stuffed with electronic gear hooked together with bundles of wires and power cords that emitted a constant electric hum. One corner held an extra-long double bed covered with a quilt that he also used as a couch. I followed him to a large display monitor mounted on the back wall.

We sat in the two worn office chairs. Skeeter hit a key on the remote and the screen sprang to life showing a mug shot of Russell Stevens as a younger man. He was smiling for the camera as if he had a secret he was dying to tell.

"This is one bad dude," Skeeter said. "A poster boy for prison reform. Turned eighteen in Huntsville doing time for beating his stepfather to death with a bat. The judge reduced the charge to manslaughter because the defense attorney claimed years of abuse. When he got out, he went underground. No convictions, but he's linked to drugs, prostitution, and auto theft. Must have learned how to stay under the radar from Convict U."

"Outstanding citizen."

"His name came up in a case against a cartel member prosecuted in Houston, but the case was dropped."

"What was the charge?"

"Trafficking underage women."

"The question is, how did this character get mixed up with Mark Bauer in Fredericksburg?"

"No direct connection that I've found, but everything Dragon does is under the table. Mr. Bauer has some interesting plans. His company has been buying up a lot of land in Gillespie County."

"Yeah, he wants to buy my grandpa's place. Said he's gonna put in grapevines on the hayfield and make the house into a bed-and-breakfast."

"The biggest purchase was a section along the Pedernales River. Some kind of convention center."

"That would include the beach where we used to party, the one Lori went to with Maya the night she vanished." The image on screen shifted to a map of Gillespie County, highlighting a section of land along the river. "Looks like a half mile of riverfront."

"Oh, this is a big plan." He switched the picture to an architectural rendering showing a huge convention center complete with a thirty-six-hole golf course and condos facing the fairways. In the center was a luxury six-story hotel.

"Mike thinks big," I said, marveling at the intricate design.

"Fists full of cash changing hands, which may explain what Russell is doing there. Could be he's looking for legit businesses to launder gangster money."

"It doesn't get us any closer to finding Maya."

He showed me the Facebook missing persons posting and the several dozen comments it had received—none offered more than moral support. The state and national hotlines were no better. It was frustrating, and unfortunately, all too familiar. We needed to locate her soon because the chances of ever finding her diminished daily.

"What about Russell's network here in San Antonio? If he's branching out to Fredericksburg, my guess is he's got other connections besides Club Forty-Four."

"Nothing yet. The only explanation I can come up with is that he's got some powerful friends covering his ass. Money buys a lot of protection."

"There's got to be some other business connection, something we can use."

He smiled and emitted a low, rumbling chuckle. "I know what that means. You wanna hit him where it hurts."

"Right in the nuts."

"Lunchtime," Kelly said, sticking her head into Skeeter's basement lair. The smell of fried chicken and cornbread followed her into the room. She studied the architectural rendering on the screen next to Russell's mug shot. "Who's the kid?"

"That's Russell Stevens before he became the Dragon."

"Wow, talk about contrast. He into real estate?" she asked.

"This is what Mike Bauer's building in Fredericksburg," I said.

"Clarence!" Lola Davis called from the top of the stairs in a voice that could have been heard downtown.

Skeeter immediately got to his feet. A lifetime of conditioning. "She don't like to call twice. Let's go eat," he said and ducked through the door.

Kelly and I followed him up the stairs to the kitchen, where there was enough food laid out to feed a platoon from the local Army base.

"You didn't have to go to all this trouble," I said.

Lola kissed me on the cheek and pointed to the place of honor at the head of the table. "Bless your soul. You know better than to tell me that."

When we all sat down, Lola held out her hands and bowed her head. We joined hands around the table.

"Bless us, oh Lord, and these Thy gifts, which we are about to receive from Thy bounty," she chanted in a strong contralto voice. "And bless your son Nick Fischer. Guide him in all he do. Without him my son would not be with us today..."

As she continued to sing my praises to the Lord, Kelly squeezed my hand. Maybe talking to Lola Davis had bolstered my cause. Getting so much attention and praise made me nervous. Two girls had lost their lives. Would I still be a hero if Maya died before I found her?

CHAPTER TWENTY-THREE

There was no reason to sit in Skeeter's basement and watch him surf the internet for links between Russell Stevens and area businesses. He needed time to work and sitting around doing nothing wasn't one of my favorite pastimes. Maya was out there somewhere. The only good news was that no one had found her body. She'd gone missing from a party on the Pedernales River. No one disappears without a trace. I thought about Owen Bauer. Whatever Lori knew and wanted to tell me besides Russell's connection to Club Forty-Four, Owen also knew.

"You thinking about Owen?" Kelly touched my arm. I snapped back down to earth and realized she'd once again successfully read my thoughts.

"Yeah, how'd you—"

"Because he's the only other link we have to Maya."

I glanced at her and smiled as I got back on Interstate 10. "Right."

"You thought there was something more to it?"

"Maybe."

She laughed, still holding my arm. "Mrs. Davis thinks you walk on water."

"True, but only because I don't like getting my boots wet."

"What I know is, you're persistent. Once you sink your teeth into a case, you don't let go. I could strip naked and sit on your lap, and you'd be calculating how to get the drop on Russell Stevens."

I smiled. "You could try it and see."

She crossed her arms and flashed a playful frown. "Forget it. I can wait till I have your full attention. Let's talk about Owen. You think he's in danger?"

"Unless he killed Lori, I think he has a bullseye on his back."

Traffic slowed to a crawl and forced my attention to the road. No matter the time or the day, Interstate 10 into or out of San Antonio was clogged with traffic due to the perennial road construction. The Texas Department of Transportation started road projects to alleviate traffic based on population density data from twenty years ago. When they finished, the improvements were already out of date and due for more construction. It was a vicious cycle.

"What makes you think the Bauer kid will have more to say?"

"Lori's dead, and he's probably scared shitless of Russell Stevens. That's enough to loosen his tongue."

"You gonna call Zeller?" Her expression turned serious.

I searched for an answer she might like or at least one that would satisfy her finely tuned sense of adherence to law and order. I couldn't think of one. It was against my nature to shade the truth or beat around the bush. "Time's running out for Maya. I'm not gonna waste an afternoon talking to Zeller."

She pursed her lips, then tucked a loose strand of blond hair behind her ear before she spoke. "Owen's a seventeen-year-old high school kid. If he won't talk, you can't touch him. You do know that."

"The only thing I'll hurt are his feelings."

She studied me for another minute. I expected her to ask me to take her back to the ranch and her pickup so she could be on her way to Lubbock and her safe and orderly police career. Instead, she said, "If I was missing, I'd want someone like you looking for me."

"So, you share Mrs. Davis's opinion?"

"I think you earned her respect, but I pity the cops that have to put up with you."

I didn't have an answer to that or a snappy comeback that wouldn't result in a sock in the arm. I knew I was on thin ice with her, so I kept my mouth shut. It was an October Sunday afternoon. During the night, a northwest wind had snuck over the border and chased the humidity back to the Gulf. The sky was clear, and the air felt crisp and dry. The fall season brought a mood change to Central and South Texas. There was a scent of expectations in the air. A successful hunt, winning the game. Hunting season was in full swing, Friday night lights illuminated the gridiron in every town, fans flocked to university stadiums on Saturday afternoons to cheer on their team. Everyone celebrated surviving the brutal Texas summer heat. Under normal circumstances, this was my favorite time of year.

Back in my high school days, October Sunday afternoons meant a trip to the river for a swim and a cold beer before the new school week started. Football practice took a day off, deer season wouldn't start until November first, and the hay was in the barn. It'd been sixteen years since I smuggled a cooler full of longnecks down the Pedernales trail, but I knew traditions died hard in rural Texas. Unless Mike Bauer really did build a resort on the river bend, the parties would continue for another generation.

A dozen pickups filled the gravel turnout near the trailhead. Owen's pickup stood closest to the fence, which meant he'd been the first one to arrive.

"Looks like our boy's here," I said, pointing to Owen's jacked-up 4x4. I pulled in close to his bumper to block his exit in case he tried to run, and Kelly and I got out. "Where did you hang out when you were in high school?" I asked her.

"On Sunday afternoon, we'd go to the softball field behind the Catholic church. That is, when I finished doing chores. My dad was strict about me doing my share of the farm work with my brothers. We tried to get everything done early, right after we got home from church."

"I had the same problem. My grandpa didn't believe in kids having free time. Idle hands are the devil's workshop."

"Sounds like he and my father would have gotten along beautifully."

We followed a couple of teenage boys toting an ice chest no doubt full of beer. They glanced over their shoulders at us and picked up their pace. Both wore sunglasses, board shorts, and farmer tans. Their suspicious look suddenly made me feel old, like a principal catching kids smoking behind the gym. We let them get ahead of us. No doubt they would spread the word of our arrival. We stopped at the bluff overlooking the beach.

"So, this is where Mike Bauer's gonna build his resort?" Kelly asked.

"So it seems. The Battlin' Billies will have to find a new place to party when he does."

A couple dozen young people congregated along the riverbank. Some soaked in the shallow water, others stretched out on beach towels. Owen Bauer sat in a folding lawn chair wearing red-and-white board shorts and sipping a longneck beer. Two teens his age stood flanking his chair with their arms folded over bare chests like hired security. A half dozen girls lounged on beach towels near his feet, all focused on their cell phones. A boom box blared one of those generic electric-guitar-heavy country songs driven by a hard bass line and a rapid-fire singing style. Not the kind of country music I'd grown up with.

"That's Owen in the lawn chair," I said.

"The one with the mirror shades and bushy hair?" Kelly asked.

"He's a stud, isn't he?"

The two boys standing beside Owen uncrossed their arms when we approached. Both were tall and filled out with steroid-enhanced muscles. They wore peach-fuzz beards that would have scrubbed off with a washcloth and were identical except one had dark hair and the other was strawberry blond. I guessed they were linemen or maybe linebackers and very protective of their quarterback. Both stepped forward to intercept our path to Owen.

"Private party, man," the darker one said.

"Coach V know you're drinking during the season?" I asked.

They both stood up a little straighter, not expecting to hear their coach's name. "He gave us the beer," the blond said, making a quick recovery.

His buddy laughed. I got the feeling the blond was used to covering for his friend. The girls around Owen stopped looking at their phones and paid us closer attention. Owen tried his best to look nonchalant behind the mirror shades.

"No shit?" I said. I knew he was lying. "In that case, give an old man a cold one."

Kelly shot me a curious sideways glance.

I turned my head and winked so the boys couldn't see it.

"Y'all defense or offense?" I asked.

They looked at each other as if they weren't sure.

"I'll bet you're both linebackers."

"That's right. We're linebackers, man," the blond answered.

"That's what I played. Tight end too. We played both sides of the ball in my day. I was on Coach V's team."

Both quickly lost the chip on their shoulders and relaxed.

"You're Nick Fischer," the blond said, taking a closer look.

"That's right, son."

"I seen your picture in the locker room," the dark-haired one said.

"You boys gonna take care of business this year?"

"Yes, sir," they replied in unison. It was the question every high school player in the state got asked when they met anyone in public during the season.

"How 'bout that beer?"

The dark-haired one beat feet over to the cooler and brought me a Shiner Bock longneck. Kelly cracked a smile but didn't say anything.

"Hey, Owen," I yelled over the music. "We need to talk."

The linebackers looked at each other, then back at Owen as if waiting for instructions.

Owen stood up and reluctantly walked over to me.

"We already talked, man," Owen said.

"But we left so much unsaid." I smiled and took a drink of beer. It was cold and tasted too good to be wasted on teenagers.

Owen stared at me like he had probably stared at most of his teachers during his academic career. I could relate. I'd been just as clueless until I joined the Marine Corps.

I leaned close to his ear so I wouldn't have to shout. "I'll make this easy for you. We'll go stand in the shade. I don't wanna get sunburned. We'll be far enough away that your friends don't have to listen."

"My dad's gonna nail you for this," Owen said.

"Whatever. Let's go. We just wanna talk."

He studied my scarred forehead for a moment, then started walking toward the large cottonwood tree about fifty yards upstream. Kelly and I followed.

Owen leaned against the wide trunk and crossed his arms, determined to keep up the tough guy act and not to tell us anything we wanted to know. I handed my beer to Kelly and snatched the mirror shades from his face.

"I like to see who I'm talking to," I said.

Owen blinked in the bright sunlight. "Coach V's gonna hear about this. So—So's my father," he stuttered, shooting a look over his shoulder at his entourage.

I turned to Kelly and raised my palms in mock surrender. "Wow, he's got us now."

Kelly cocked her eyebrow as a warning to me.

I leaned into Owen's personal space. I knew my temper made the scars on my forehead turn purple and more pronounced. In these situations, that was an advantage. "I remember when I was a high school football stud, I thought the sun rose and set in my asshole. When I left town, it didn't take long to figure out I'd been a big fish in a very small pond."

"Are you threatening me?"

"I don't make threats. I tell it like it is. I want answers. Starting with Lori Kostoch."

"What about her?"

"I noticed you're not in mourning."

"Why should I be?"

"Because she's dead."

His lips parted, and his tan skin turned a shade lighter. He hadn't known. News usually travels fast in a small town. Somehow, news of her death hadn't hit his radar. Maybe Zeller had kept it quiet until after he'd made the call to Lori's mother. If he did, I'd have to give him credit for being a nice guy.

Owen unfolded his arms and looked at the river water churning downstream thirty yards away. His eyes filled with tears.

"Did you see her or talk to her yesterday?" Kelly asked.

"I—I don't know nothin'," he stuttered.

"That's not what she asked," I said. "She was strangled and left naked in my motel room. Tell me if you talked to her."

"I don't know nothin'," he whispered.

"Oh, you know something. I followed you after our last conversation. You went straight to Lori. You met her behind the café. I watched you smack her around."

"It—it wasn't like that."

"Bullshit!" I raised my voice. "I followed you after you left the restaurant. You went to a trailer house on your dad's ranch and talked to Russell Stevens."

Owen looked away, hiding his tears.

"The police will get around to questioning you before long. You better have a better story to tell them, or you just might find yourself in jail. I don't care who your daddy is or how much pull he has. Murder is murder."

His teary eyes bugged out. "You got it wrong. I didn't have nothin' to do with her murder."

"Why'd you slap her around? And don't tell me you didn't do it. I was there."

Owen stared at his group of friends, who had all lost interest in him and were enjoying the cool river water and drinking beer. He wished he was with them.

"Whatever you're into, I can help, Owen," I said, lowering my voice to a friendly level.

"We know about the kegger in August," Kelly said. "Lori told us you asked her to bring Maya."

"You don't know this guy," Owen said, his voice slipping into a raspy whisper, as if someone might be listening. "He's fuckin' crazy."

"Who? Russell?"

Owen wiped his eyes with his fingertips. "He likes to be called Dragon."

"I'll keep that in mind. Did he take Maya?"

Owen nodded. "I don't know. I swear. I was just supposed to bring a girl to the party. I told him about Maya. She was from Cali and acted like a party girl, you know."

"What did you get out of it?"

"Dragon let us party here, man. He said he wouldn't tell my dad."

"You paid for the party by bringing Maya? Have you done it before? Did you bring him other girls?"

"No, man. Only Maya."

"You picked her 'cause you didn't think anybody would miss her?"

"Yeah, that's right. I—I didn't know she was Mr. Geisler's granddaughter. Everyone called her the Cali Girl."

"So, you used Lori to help you get Maya?" Kelly asked.

Owen nodded.

"What did you argue about behind the bakery?"

"After you showed up, she got worried about Maya. She said we should both tell you everything we knew. I tried to warn her that he—that Dragon was dangerous. She didn't understand."

"She understands now," I said.

The tears flowed down his suntanned cheeks. "I'm sorry, man… I…"

"Where's Maya now?" I asked.

He clenched his jaw and shook his head. "I don't know."

Kelly grabbed my arm before I could crush his pathetic face with a stiff right hand. The kid deserved to get the shit kicked out of him, then to get thrown in jail. He was at the center of a murder and a kidnapping, but if he showed up with a shiner at the public school, I would be arrested or tarred and feathered and thrown out of town before lunchtime.

"Talk, Owen, or I'll turn him loose," Kelly said. "Tell us what you know."

"That's all I know. I swear."

I slammed my open hand against the cottonwood tree, inches from his face. "You little pissant! You're supposed to be the captain of the football team."

"I do my job on the field. I'm talkin' to college coaches. I got a career lined up."

The kid really didn't get it. It had only been sixteen years since I'd left the high school gridiron, and the whole concept of high school sports had changed. Owen used the game to give himself celebrity status. My faith in the idyllic rural life took another hit.

"Forget about the football season—it's over for you. Forget the college coaches too. My advice—join the Marine Corps. I did. Best move I ever made." I fished a business card from my wallet and handed it to him. "And stay away from Russell Stevens or you'll end up like Lori. I'm serious. If he calls or wants to meet, call me. Maybe I can help. If he has Maya, I will find her and take him down."

He clenched his teeth and wiped his eyes again with his fingertips. For a moment, he looked like he understood.

CHAPTER TWENTY-FOUR

We left Owen drying his tears in the October sun and walked back to my pickup. The teen crowd kept their distance. Both linebackers were picking up their empty beer bottles. Maybe there was still hope for their generation. I finished my beer and tossed the empty to the blond linebacker.

"Thanks for the beer. Take care of business this season."

He glanced to his sidekick, and both nodded with pride as if accepting the awesome responsibility of guiding the team. It brought back warm memories of my high school football days. In the larger scheme of things, it didn't matter that much, I thought, but didn't tell them. That's something they would have to learn on their own.

We climbed the bluff and took one last look at the teens splashing in the river. The slow-moving water was clear and peaceful. The dry west wind sucked the moisture out of the air and created an azure-blue sky unique to the drier, cooler months. Had it not been for the circumstances, this would have been a pleasant trip down memory lane. I watched a boy and a girl jump in the water and swim to the opposite bank. It reminded me of when Allison Offenbach pulled me into the river and gave me a kiss underwater, and when her boyfriend Brady sucker-punched me as I grabbed a towel to dry off. It was a scandal the next week at school. Brady played left guard, and by Monday's practice, coach had heard the story. First, he made us both run extra wind sprints. When Brady still wouldn't calm down, he had the team circle around us while I squared off with Brady in a tackle drill. He outweighed me by twenty pounds, but we came out even. When it was over, we shook hands and ran to the locker room. Neither one of us dated Allison after that. Too bad adults can't settle their differences on the gridiron. Life would be much simpler.

Kelly cleared her throat and ended my reverie. "So, Owen sacrificed Maya for a party on the river?"

"That's what it sounds like. An offering to the devil."

"Do you think the kid knew what would happen to her?"

"I don't think he's that smart. In fact, I think he'll contact Russell and tell him I paid him a visit."

"You told him to stay away from Russell Stevens."

"Reverse psychology. Owen's never eaten humble pie and still thinks he's the smartest kid in school."

"What if he ends up like Lori and Candy?"

"I warned him."

"Whatever gets you the results you want. Is that how it is?"

She waited for an answer, but I didn't have a snappy comeback. I kept walking ahead of her down the trail and back to my pickup. She wanted to argue about ethics and morality. I was dealing with evil people who had none. They sold drugs and girls and had no regard for human life. I'd seen firsthand the limitations of law enforcement. My dad had worked as a Texas DPS officer before getting elected sheriff of Gillespie County. I'd worked as a reserve deputy in Travis County while I was in college. Law enforcement came with a layer of bureaucracy that could interfere with justice. When Skeeter was framed for the murder of multiple people trapped in an apartment fire, the lead detective followed a string of evidence, built a solid legal case, and put an innocent man behind bars. SAPD didn't care as long as they followed procedure and someone paid for the crime. Law school had left me equally uncomfortable. After two years, I realized that the courtroom was all about making an argument that could be proven, not finding the truth. The only thing I could think of to say was, "I believe in justice and helping those who can't help themselves, like Maya Chavez."

Kelly didn't respond. She wasn't comfortable with the gray area that existed between justice and police procedure. Her time as a Marine Corps MP shaped her view of the law and the clear line between right and wrong. She'd stepped outside of her comfort zone when she'd helped me evade the manhunt on my last case long enough for me to prove my innocence and take out the man responsible for more than one murder. Why she was back for more was a mystery.

When we reached my pickup, I turned and took a last look at the dark-green canopy of cottonwood trees that marked the river's meandering path. Mike Bauer's convention center may be good for the local economy, but it would sure as hell mess up a nice retreat in the country.

When we were in the cab and headed back to Fredericksburg, Kelly said, "Skeeter says you're an adrenaline junky, that you like to fight and that's why you do what you do."

"What do you think?"

"I think he's right. At least, that's part of it. You don't back down and you don't compromise. You have an edge that's intimidating. Men like Zeller take it as a challenge. Others tend to back away. Obviously, Russell Stevens sees you as a threat."

"You're saying I should back off because he killed Lori and Candy? You think if I throw in the towel, he'll stop what he's doin' and give up Maya?"

"No, he won't stop. But does it have to be you that goes after him? Can't you let someone else take him down? You're operating without backup. You took a bullet last time that nearly killed you. What if your luck runs out?"

"I'll deal with that when it happens."

She put her hand on my arm. I glanced at her and saw her eyes were filled with tears. "Women like dangerous men. It's true. I fell for you. But I don't wanna see you die. I couldn't take that."

I understood. It was the argument my mother made for leaving my dad when he was elected sheriff, and I never forgave her for it. When we passed the quaint *Willkommen* to Fredericksburg sign, a police cruiser lit us up and abruptly changed the subject. Officer Zeller was on my bumper with his lights on and siren blaring. I pulled over in front of the liquor store and reached for the door handle. Les's tenor voice broke through my closed window.

"Stay put, Fischer! Hands on the wheel. Ten and two." He was out of breath by the time he jogged to my door.

"Les, what the hell's wrong with you? Was I speeding?" I asked.

"Roll down the window," he barked.

"I can't do that with my hands at ten and two."

"Unroll it, smartass."

I reached for the power window button. As the glass receded into the doorframe, Les poked his Pillsbury Doughboy face through the opening. I smelled the cheeseburger with onions he'd eaten for lunch.

"I just got a call from a very angry parent who said you assaulted his son."

I could see my own pissed off reflection in his mirror shades. I took a slow breath and moved my hands back to the steering wheel to keep myself from smacking him across the face.

"Did Mike call you?"

"You were trespassing on private property and his kid is seventeen."

"Come on, Les. Half the high school football team's down there drinking beer."

"I'm a witness," Kelly chimed in. "Nick only talked to him."

"That may be, but I'm gonna have to take Mr. Fischer down to the station."

"That's bullshit, Les. You know what goes on at the river, and you don't do anything."

"Mike hired private security to handle that."

"Sure, a gangster that calls himself Dragon. He wasn't on duty this afternoon. You know damn well what the football team is doing down there because you and I did the same thing when we were Battlin' Billies."

"Just doing my job, Nick," he said, a flicker of a smile on his lips. "If a citizen calls in a complaint about an assault to a minor, I gotta follow procedure." He was enjoying this a little too much. "Step out of the car, please."

I glanced in the passenger side mirror and saw Officer Crowley approaching at a crouch with his hand on the butt of his weapon. "Crowley, if you pull that Glock, I'll come over there and beat you over the head with it," I called out.

Crowley stood up by the passenger window and put his hands on his hips. "Shoot, Nick. I'm just followin' procedure."

"Procedure for what? I'm not Billy the Kid." I took my phone from the console.

"No phone calls till after booking," Les said.

"You're really gonna do it?"

"Damn straight, Fischer. Out of the car."

I handed the phone to Kelly and whispered so Les couldn't hear. "Call Rocky Velosic. He's in my contacts."

"What can he do?" she asked.

"Tell him what we found on the river and what we know about Owen's involvement. If nothing else, he'll want to protect his quarterback. If he doesn't answer the phone, drive over to the stadium. It's Sunday. He'll be watching game film in the field house."

"Never a dull moment with you."

"I'm stepping out, Les. I'm not armed, so don't shoot me." I reached for the door handle and slipped off my ankle holster at the same time. As long as Kelly was in the pickup, he wouldn't search under the seat. My .45 was in the console, and I didn't want either to end up in a police storage locker.

"Okay, Fischer. Let's go," Les barked.

A dozen lookie-loos slowed down to stare at Fredericksburg's finest making an arrest.

"Hands on the hood," Les barked.

"You're gonna cuff me, Les? What the fuck's wrong with you?"

"Look, Nick. I know you, and I knew your family. But this is my job." He motioned Crowley forward while he stood with his hands on his hips, posing for the slowing traffic.

I put my hands on the hood and looked through the windshield at Kelly. She bit her lip to avoid laughing. At least she was enjoying herself. I probably should have kept my mouth shut, but just because you've known someone for a long time doesn't make them a good person. Les was an asshole in high school, and age hadn't changed him.

"Do you give blowjobs to all the city council members or just Mike Bauer?"

Crowley snickered under his breath and slipped on a pair of blue plastic gloves.

Les's face flushed. "You're such a nice guy, Nick," he said.

Crowley was nervous and started to pat me down a little harder than necessary.

"There's a bandage on my chest. It's a bullet wound, and it's sore as hell. If you cause me any pain, I'll kick your ass," I said.

Crowley eased off on the pressure, unclipped my pocketknife from my back pocket and tossed it on the hood.

"He's clean," Crowley said.

I put my hands behind my back and let him slip the handcuffs on. It wasn't the first time and probably wouldn't be the last time I felt cold steel on my wrists. My face felt hot, and the scars on my forehead throbbed. Being humiliated in front of my hometown, even though most of the traffic was tourists, turned my stomach. I fought down my anger, knowing Les hoped I would resist arrest and give him an excuse to brain me. Crowley opened the rear door of the cruiser and guided me into the back seat.

I'd been to the local police station many times as a kid when my dad was still alive. The last four years of his life he had been the county sheriff and the two departments shared the county building. I used to stop by the station on my way home from football practice. Dad even locked me in a holding cell once to show me what it was like. The closest I'd ever come to actually getting arrested was the summer after he was murdered. Rocky and I thought it'd be fun to tie one of his uncle's rodeo bulls to the front door of the courthouse. Les's father had taken over the sheriff duties until there was a new election and instead of arresting us, he made us both work all summer to pay for the new door.

We drove the short distance back down Highway 290 to the station. When Zeller pulled into the parking lot, Rocky was already there, leaning against his pickup.

"Lester, have you lost your marbles?" Rocky shouted.

Les used the open door to pull his bulky frame out of the cruiser. "Rocky, you stay out of this. I'm takin' Nick inside. You can talk to him later if you want."

"We need to talk, Les," Rocky said.

Crowley left the door closed and me locked inside while Rocky led Les toward the opposite side of his pickup. I could hear some sharp exchanges but couldn't make out what they were saying. Rocky was doing most of the talking. Les's chubby cheeks were getting redder and redder. Rocky took out his cell phone. I saw him dial a number and hand the phone to Les. After a minute, Les handed the phone back to Rocky.

"Let him out," Zeller said. "Turn him loose."

"But—" Crowley started to protest.

"Get out of here, Fischer," Les said. "This is my town now. I don't care if you're a private dick. I don't need help solvin' crime. You got that?"

Crowley opened the door and took the cuffs off.

"Sure, anything you say, Lester," I said. "Have a nice day."

Les took a step toward me, both fists clenched. If he could get momentum and put even half his weight behind a punch, he could take out a good-sized bull. His trouble was, he was slow and telegraphed his moves like the trailer for a blockbuster movie.

"Drop it, Les," Rocky said.

Les's forward motion stopped. His eyes said he wanted to hit me. He thought he had what it took to take me out. With the wound in my chest, maybe he did. We wouldn't find out today.

"Good choice, Les. I'll take my pocketknife," I said.

He held my gaze for a full minute before he spoke. "Watch your step, Nick," he finally said and walked to the station door.

Crowley handed me my knife and followed his boss inside.

Rocky waited until they were gone before he spoke. "You're still the same cocky bastard you were in high school. Les was itching to take a swing at you."

I followed him to his pickup. "Why'd you stop him?"

"'Cause he was lookin' for an excuse to lock you up. You almost gave him one."

We got in and he cranked the engine.

"What'd you tell him to get him to let me go?"

Rocky chuckled. "I called Mike. Told him I would suspend Owen for drinking and put him on the bench for the rest of the season if he didn't make Les turn you loose."

"Your linebackers said you bought them the beer."

He sighed. "Those little bastards'll pay for that. Didn't I ask you not to harass my star quarterback?"

"Come on, Rocky. I gave you a chance. A girl's missin' and now two are dead. Owen Bauer is involved. I don't give a shit about your football season."

Rocky turned off the engine, irritated. "Goddamnit!"

"Owen's not just involved in some prank. He may be involved in kidnapping Maya and Lori's murder. I'm not the bad guy in all this. I'm trying to find Maya and bring her home."

His top lip closed over his buckteeth. "You're right, you son of a bitch. I don't know what I was thinkin'. I guess I was too caught up in the damn season to see it." He slammed his open palm on the steering wheel. "Shee-it!" He looked out the window at the row of oak trees lining the parking lot. "We'd have had a hell of a year. The kid's gifted on the field anyway." He shook his head as if he'd just lost his mother.

"It's just football, Rocky."

He let out a humorless laugh. "You've been away too long. It ain't a big deal if you're a Marine overseas, or a private detective livin' in San Antonio, but this is small-town Texas."

"Fair enough." He was right. I'd left to join the Marines and stayed away to finish college. Now, I lived in San Antonio along with two million other people who didn't all have small-town values. "Do you think Mike's mixed up in something illegal?"

"Come on, Nick. The Bauer family's loaded. Owen's just a dumbass kid makin' a stupid mistake. Mike wouldn't throw everything away like that."

"Unless he was forced to, or he thought he could get away with it," I said.

My phone rang. The caller ID said Kelly. "Come and get me, darlin'. I'm at the station."

"Am I breaking you out?"

"They let me go. Something to do with my being German."

She laughed. "In this town, it wouldn't surprise me."

CHAPTER TWENTY-FIVE

Kelly pulled into the station parking lot driving my pickup. She waved to Rocky, and I jumped in the passenger seat, still angry and embarrassed from the public showdown in my own hometown.

"Hey, jailbird," Kelly said, and giggled. She wasn't gonna let me live it down.

"I didn't technically go to jail. Rocky intervened. But thank you." Hearing her laugh took the edge off my desire to kick Lester's ass and reminded me of the bubbly personality that had attracted me to her, and that if I didn't pay more attention to her, I was gonna lose her.

"This guy Zeller really doesn't like you."

"The feeling is mutual." I told her about my conversation with Rocky and how he convinced Officer Zeller to let me go.

"You think Mike Bauer's protecting his son and Russell Stevens?" she asked.

"Mike's a businessman and a shrewd operator. He donates a lot of time and money to local events every year. One of the beneficiaries is the Battlin' Billies sports program. I don't know why he'd jeopardize all of that to go into business with a gangster."

"Maybe Dragon made him an offer he couldn't refuse."

"Blackmail?"

"It would explain the relationship."

"Yeah, but for what? What could a lowlife like Russell Stevens have on Mike Bauer?"

When I got out to open the ranch gate, the porch light was on and there was movement in the house. In all the excitement, I'd forgotten Helen was still in residence. So much for getting a good night's sleep. The temperature had dropped into the low fifties, and the north wind was blowing. That should have put me in a good mood. The norther would bring flocks of mallard and teal ducks following the central flyway. They would rest for a day or two, or longer if no one bothered them, in the lakes and small ponds or stock tanks on ranch land throughout Central Texas. Sam sensed it too. He joined me at the gate and ran circles around my legs. He was ready to go hunting.

"I know what you're thinkin'," I said, scratching his ears. "There'll be ducks on the pond in the mornin'." Two things I needed to do before I could enjoy the weather and the upcoming hunting season—find Maya and chase Helen back to Colorado where she belonged.

Sam studied the pond out the rear window as Kelly drove past. He whined anxiously, letting me know the ducks were already there. When we approached the house, there were two vehicles instead of one parked in the yard. Beside Helen's white Chevy Tahoe was a black Suburban with Bauer Farms stenciled on the door.

"Looks like your mom's got company," Kelly said.

"What the hell is Mike Bauer doing here?"

We got out and heard laughter emerge from the old stone house. My muscles immediately tensed. Kelly took my hand. "Take it easy. Maybe he came to discuss Owen."

"Maybe. At least he saved us a trip to Bauer Farms."

We found Mike and Helen seated side by side at the kitchen table. Helen stood, obviously surprised. Empty dinner plates held the remains of spaghetti and red sauce. Two bottles of Bauer's reserva wine, one empty, revealed the party was in full swing. Mike wore a blue polo shirt with his company logo that stretched tight over his belly. Helen wore a western style dress over black cowboy boots and a turquoise neckless. Her makeup was perfect. Her blond hair stylishly curled. It pained me to think she looked stunning and not a day over forty, fifteen years younger than her actual age.

"Entertaining guests?" I asked Helen. Her cheeks flushed red, and she produced an innocent smile.

"We were just finishing dinner. I didn't expect you."

"Nick, come on in. We saved y'all some wine," Mike said. He grabbed the full bottle and a corkscrew. Helen hustled to the cupboard for two more glasses.

"I didn't think you'd be back tonight, Nicky," Helen said, retrieving two of my grandmother's long-stem wineglasses that ever since I could remember had been reserved only for Christmas, Easter, and Thanksgiving.

"Where else would I go? It's my damn house."

Mike popped the cork and filled the two glasses. "Now, Nick. Your mother and I were just having a little dinner. Nothing wrong with that."

Both acted like two teens caught making out under the bleachers.

"I wanted to talk to her about the property." Mike regained his composure and handed Kelly a glass of wine.

"Helen has nothing to do with my family ranch," I said.

"I was looking out for your interests," Helen said. "Mike has made a very generous offer that I think we should consider." She stood behind Mike and put a hand on his shoulder.

"There is no *we*," I said. "What *I* do with this ranch is none of your damn business."

"Nicky, don't get all worked up," she cooed like I was throwing a third-grade tantrum.

Kelly sat in the chair by the front window holding the delicate wineglass and wearing a neutral expression like a family counseling therapist.

"Helen might have a legitimate claim to the ranch. I've been checking the county records," Mike said.

"Helen has no rights to the Fischer family ranch. If she ever had any, she gave them up twenty years ago. When she walked out on her family." I paused to let that sink in. "And what the hell were you doing digging into the county records?"

"Nicky, he was just—"

I cut her off and pointed at Mike. "You were trying to find a way around me to get your hands on the ranch."

"Now, it's not like that. I was going over the land records to establish a fair price."

"Skip the crap, Mike. I'll let you know my answer right now. The Fischer ranch is not for sale. Not now. Not ever. Not at any price. It stays in the family." I turned to Helen. "And by that, I mean it stays with me."

Helen opened her mouth to speak, then closed it. For once she was at a loss for words.

"You have worn out your welcome. I asked you to leave nicely. Now, let me put it more bluntly. You're out. Pack your stuff and go."

Her eyes suddenly brimmed with tears. "You don't have to be cruel." She wiped her eyes with the back of her hand. "I thought we could have this conversation in private." She glanced at Kelly for support.

"We did have this conversation in private, several times. It didn't do any good."

"I only want what's best for you," she said.

"Bullshit. If you wanna stay in Fredericksburg, I can't stop you. But I want you gone from the ranch. Now. Tonight. In the next five minutes. Get your stuff and go."

"You can't mean now."

I pointed up the stairs. "Now."

Helen slowly backed away and retreated up the stairs.

"You didn't have to do that," Mike said. "She's your mother."

I turned my attention on Bauer. He was a big bear of a man with a full beard and at least forty pounds heavier than my two hundred. He was accustomed to using his size and position to bully anyone who opposed him. It was easy to see where Owen got his attitude. He put his hands on his hips, a practiced gesture intended to intimidate his opponent.

I stepped forward into his personal space. "This is personal, Mike. None of your damn business. Helen is not a victim. She's responsible for her own actions. We all are. She left twenty years ago. There's nothing here for her."

"Everyone deserves a second chance, Nick."

The conversation was over as far as I was concerned. I stared him down until he took a step back and reached for his wineglass. "Why did you sic Zeller on me this afternoon?" I asked.

He choked on his mouthful of reserva, not expecting the shift in topics. "Now, hold on—"

I poked a finger toward his pudgy chest, sensing I'd caught him off guard. "Were you afraid of what information I might find talking to Owen?"

A trace of fear flickered over his face, quickly replaced by belligerence. "You slapped my boy around at the river. Owen came home whining about you pickin' on him. That's not appropriate."

"So you told Zeller to arrest me?"

Mike looked genuinely surprised. "What? No. I just asked him to find out what happened. That's all, Nick. I swear it. The other stuff was all on his own."

"Why didn't you just call me? I would have told you what happened. Your employee, Russell Stevens, is a degenerate of the first order involved in murder and kidnapping. He's dragging Owen down with him. Did you know about it? Are you protecting Owen?"

Mike's chubby cheeks turned a darker shade of red. "That's preposterous."

I couldn't tell if he was showing legitimate outrage or if it was all an act. Kelly was standing now, slightly behind him and to his right. The wineglass was on the lamp table. She was a practiced interrogator and the move put Mike on the defensive.

"If you're protecting him, that makes you an accessory to the murder of Lori Kostoch and the kidnaping of Maya Chavez," I said.

"He's right, Mike. If you know something about your son's involvement, you better come clean," Kelly said.

Mike glanced at Kelly, then back at me. "Kidnapping? Murder? What the hell are you talking about?" A tiny bead of sweat broke out on his forehead. "You're a piece of work, Nick. The whole town knows you've got a screw loose. Ever since you came back from Afghanistan you've had a tenuous grip on reality and you're always itching to start a fight."

"You're wrong, Mike. Afghanistan taught me the value of life and true justice. If anything happens to Maya, Russell's a dead man. And if I find out you knew what Russell was doing, I will bury you right beside him."

"Now wait just a goddamn minute! You can't threaten me."

"I don't threaten, Mike."

"Watch your step."

"What's he got on you?" I asked.

"What're you talkin' about? Russell Stevens is legitimate. He works for me. There's nothing illegal going on," Mike insisted.

"He's got a record. You gonna tell me you didn't know that?"

Mike let out a deep breath and seemed to get himself under control. "You can't hold that against him. I run a farm business. I've helped out a lot of ex-cons. If I didn't, I wouldn't have a workforce. You can't pay high school kids enough to work anymore, and the state's cracking down on hiring wetbacks."

I held Mike's gaze for a full minute. He blinked his eyes rapidly and shifted his position so he could see Kelly and me. He was lying about something, but I didn't know what.

Helen interrupted the moment by dragging her suitcase to the top of the stairs. "Can I come back for my other things later, Nicky?" she asked sweetly.

I shifted my attention to Helen. "Fine. I'll put everything by the front gate," I said.

"Oh, be serious!" she huffed.

Mike climbed the stairs, retrieved her suitcase, and carried it to the front door.

I stepped to within a few inches of Mike's face when he set the case down. "You better not be hiding anything from me, Mike, 'cause I might just lose my grip on reality and go Afghanistan on your ass. I wanna find Maya, before your friend with the dragon tattoo ties a rope around her neck."

His smile disappeared, and he formed a fist with his free hand. Fully recovered, I knew I could take him, even though he outweighed me. But with the bullet wound in my chest, he had a distinct advantage. I prepared to swing for soft targets, the throat and the groin. Kelly stepped beside me. She knew what was happening. Her presence brought the smile back to Mike's face. His fists relaxed and he stepped back.

Helen stomped down the stairs. "I hope Nicky listens to you," she said to Kelly.

Kelly tactfully kept her mouth shut.

Helen hesitated at the door, waiting for a nod or a gesture of reconciliation—a sign that I would change my mind and let her stay. I didn't give her one.

PART TWO

Lost and Found

"Wer nicht hören will, muss fühlen."
If you don't want to listen, you have to feel.

German Proverb

CHAPTER TWENTY-SIX

A muffled cell phone woke me from a restless sleep. The Fischer ancestors, shrouded in darkness on the stone walls, reminded me where I was. Maybe it was the dim light, but they seemed more cordial this morning. I wondered if they'd overheard my shouted commitment to keep the ranch in the family or if they approved of Kelly sleeping beside me. I couldn't remember anything after Helen left. Had I passed out from exhaustion? Kelly wore one of my T-shirts. I was down to my skivvies with a clean bandage on my chest and arm. She must have cleaned the wound and rewrapped it. I sat up and rubbed my face. The muffled ringing stopped. I heard a distant beep signaling a voicemail. I put my feet on the cold floor and glanced back at the photos. "Y'all wanna tell me what happened last night?"

Kelly shifted on the bed, still sleeping. She was naked under the T-shirt. "On second thought, don't answer that."

The phone began ringing again. I searched the empty bedside table. When I didn't see the phone, I padded across the cold floor and followed the ringing noise downstairs and into the front room. The cell phone was in my jeans pocket on the floor. The digital clock read two thirty. The caller ID said Skeeter. I accepted the call and stifled a yawn.

"What is it?" I said.

"I found Maya."

I was suddenly wide awake. "Where?"

"A house on the west side, south of Commerce Street. I followed one of the bouncers from Club Forty-Four."

I punched the phone on speaker, tossed it on the floor, and pulled on my jeans. "She's in the house? You got a visual?"

"Confirmed. He had two of the dancers when he left the club. They didn't look happy. I followed him to an old two-story house. More like a shack. You know what that neighborhood's like. The dude took the girls upstairs. That's where I saw Maya. She came to the window and looked out at the street. It was definitely her."

"Did you see Russell?"

"Nope. Just her."

"How many people in the house?"

"I counted three thugs downstairs and one dude upstairs. I'm guessing the one upstairs be a customer. Know what I mean?"

"Yeah, I was afraid of that. Stay on the house. I'll be there in an hour." I stuffed the phone into my back pocket.

Kelly leaned over the upstairs railing. "Everything all right?" The T-shirt hung like a robe to her mid-thighs. She held her SIG Sauer pistol up and ready for action.

"Skeeter found Maya."

She lowered the pistol. "Oh, thank god. Is she safe?"

"She's alive."

Sam scratched on the front door, and I let him in. He stared up at me with his Labrador eyes. It was fall, and it was early morning. That usually meant we were going hunting.

I scratched his neck. "Sorry, ol' boy. I know you wanna check the pond for ducks, but we gotta find Maya first." He licked my hand like he understood.

"What're you gonna do with him?"

"I'll call Helmut and ask him to take him for a few days."

"If you hadn't kicked your mother out, you wouldn't have that problem."

Sam barked as if he understood that too. I didn't have an answer for either one of them, so I stayed silent.

• • •

By the time we hit the San Antonio city limits, early morning commuters crowded the I-10 freeway. At four a.m. on Monday morning, the area military bases were open for business, which meant coffee shops, taco trucks, and drive-through breakfast stops were open too. I followed the directions Skeeter texted me. I knew the area well. The house was located near Lucky's boxing gym, where I spent long hours trading shots with Lucky's stable of fighters.

I took the Vance Jackson Road exit off Interstate 10 and cut over to Zarzamora Street. The plan was to meet Skeeter at the gas station a block from the location, then work out the details. The street was lined with car repair shops and Hispanic markets. The only new businesses in the neighborhood in the last twenty years seemed to be the Dollar General stores.

A taco truck open for business caught my attention, and I pulled in to grab some breakfast. I didn't want to take on three thugs with an empty stomach.

"You hungry?" I asked.

Kelly studied the food truck and the string of Christmas lights illuminating two graffiti-covered picnic tables. A customer in a black silk shirt and sequined jeans leaned heavily against the window as if he was about to throw up. I guessed he'd partied most of the night away.

"Too early for me," Kelly said.

"Suit yourself." I stepped out and closed the door. The sizzling aroma of grilled meat mixed with onions, cilantro, and freshly scorched flour tortillas hung above the colored lights. This was my kind of place. I waited for the party animal to take his bag of tacos to the picnic table, then approached the window. An older woman stood on a wooden box behind the grill, her face a roadmap for the many places she'd cooked early morning breakfasts. A younger man appeared with a bright smile.

"*Buenos días*," he said.

"*Tengo hambre*," I said. He smiled. My accent was a little too white, but he understood.

"You came to the right place, *amigo. Qué quieres?*" The older woman was watching and listening.

"*Dos huevos y barbacoa*," I told him, holding up two fingers. "*Y dos huevos y papas.*"

She checked with him for clarification. Evidently my Spanish wasn't clear enough for her to understand. He repeated my order in a rapid-fire version. She nodded understanding.

"*Bueno*," she said and laughed at my expense.

While she cooked my breakfast, I called Skeeter. The status hadn't changed. The customer had exited, and another one had taken his place. Business was steady. I told him to meet me at the taco stand.

Kelly got out to stretch her legs, the SIG clipped to her belt.

Skeeter and my bag of tacos arrived at the same time.

"You're takin' your life in your hands eatin' here," he said through his open window.

Kelly laughed. "That's what I was thinking."

"I met the cook. It's safe." I handed him two over-stuffed tacos.

"In that case, I'm starving."

"What have you got?" Kelly asked. She was cool and confident, reminding me of the day not long ago that she insisted on backing my play in a shootout with Marcus Lopez and his gang of security thugs.

Skeeter stuffed an egg and potato taco in his mouth and chewed while he talked. "It's a two story with a front porch. Kind of like your place, but better maintained."

"Thanks a lot," I said. I didn't think my San Antonio fixer-upper was in that bad of shape, but Skeeter was always encouraging me to get started with the fix and repair part.

"You have a leak in the upstairs bathroom, and the kitchen sink is backed up," he said.

"I haven't been home in a month."

"Can we talk about home improvement later?" Kelly was impatient.

I bit into an egg and barbacoa taco. The meat mixed with grilled onions and cilantro were in perfect proportion, with just enough jalapeños to make my tongue tingle and my eyes water.

"This is what breakfast tacos are supposed to taste like," I gushed.

She rolled her eyes, turned to Skeeter. "What about the house? Is there a door upstairs?"

"There're steps leading to an upstairs deck off the side of the house. I wouldn't trust them, but they would probably hold you."

"That's the plan then," I said and pointed at Skeeter. "Load your 870 and take the front door. If anyone's awake, you detain them long enough for us to slip up the stairs and get Maya."

I finished my second glorious taco and tipped grandma an extra five. The young man nodded and smiled. I glanced at the old woman and patted my belly in what I hoped would indicate my satisfaction with her cooking.

"*Cuidado. Vaya con Dios*," she said and crossed herself. Be careful. Go with God. I wondered if she had a premonition or if she said that to everyone.

CHAPTER TWENTY-SEVEN

The ramshackle two-story house slouched on a corner lot in a row of cookie-cutter houses built during the housing boom following World War II and neglected ever since. Some showed signs of renovation—a fresh coat of paint, new shingles, a potted plant, but most were dilapidated, beyond repair, or simply abandoned. Hurricane fencing contained yards guarded by mongrel dogs and filled with plastic toys and car parts. I parked two houses down and across the street. There were no signs of movement through the lit upstairs or downstairs windows. A hard-edged rap beat escaped from the downstairs area. It was loud enough to mask any noise we'd make approaching the house.

Skeeter unrolled his window and listened. "That's the kind of crap that ruined rap."

"Whatever," I said. I didn't share his taste in music and didn't understand the nuances of the different styles. To me it all sounded the same. "If we're lucky, they're all passed out."

Skeeter checked the loads in his shotgun. It was a model 870 with a pistol grip. The pump action was a challenge to operate with his metal hook, but after getting shot in the shoulder, he'd worked out a system that made it look easy and natural. I offered to swap it for a semiauto, but he said he liked the sound it made when he racked a shell in the chamber. When he stepped into the street, he looked like an overweight cyborg soldier sent from the future to kill John Connor.

"Give us two minutes to clear the top floor," I said to Skeeter. "If you have any trouble, use that shotgun." I checked my watch. Four twenty. With any luck, we'd get Maya and be gone by four thirty.

The streetlight on the corner had long since been shot out, and the yard was dark except for the light bleeding through the windows. Several dogs barked from the neighbor's yard, announcing our arrival.

Kelly followed me to the back staircase. Light poured through gaps in the rotten house boards, and nails protruded through the wooden steps. I pulled my .45 and pointed out the flaws in the stairs to Kelly before leading the way. The wooden frame squawked and pulled away from the house several inches with our combined weight but held firm. When we passed a side window, I heard electronic gunshots blasting from a video game mixed with the rap music. Somebody was awake in the front room. I hoped Skeeter was ready for them.

We stopped at the second-story landing. I flashed a thumbs-up, signaling Skeeter in the front yard, then tried to indicate I'd heard the video game by pointing to my ear then miming holding a controller. He flashed an okay signal as if he understood, then pointed the 870 toward the front door and climb the porch steps.

The back door on the second story was locked. The deadbolt above the knob was completely rusted, and the wooden doorframe suffered from years of neglect. Obviously, no one had used it in the past decade.

I stepped back and lifted my leg, preparing to give the lock a blast from my boot heel. The small three-by-three wooden landing wobbled like a three-legged chair, forcing me to put my foot down to keep from launching both of us into the yard.

Kelly put a hand on my shoulder and produced a Marine Corps issue Ka-Bar knife, known in the military's distinct parlance as, *Knife, Fighting Utility*—a lethal weapon with a sturdy seven-inch fixed blade honed to a needle point. She slipped the blade between the door and the jamb and gently popped the door open like she did it every day of her life.

We found ourselves in a dark hallway that ran the length of the second story. There were three doors on the right facing open windows. The air smelled like cheap perfume and marijuana smoke and clung to my skin like a damp paper towel. At the end of the hall, a staircase descended to the first floor.

The music abruptly stopped, replaced by Skeeter's baritone voice barking orders. "Keep your hands up where I can see them." So far so good. No gunshots and no running feet. The six-foot-seven, three-hundred-pound cyborg had a chilling effect on most people.

Kelly and I flattened out on either side of the first door. I reached for the knob. Locked. Kelly held up her Ka-Bar knife. I held up my hand for her to wait. We heard a shuffling of feet and a female voice shout, "Stop it." It sounded scared and desperate. I heard the distinct smack of a hand hitting skin, then a muffled cry. No time for the Ka-Bar. I stepped back and kicked the door, fracturing the frame and scattering splinters on the floor.

A man in his late twenties with no shirt and a collection of random tattoos held a naked girl by her long dark hair. The girl was on her knees facing him. It was too dark to see her facial features, but judging by her slight build, she couldn't have been more than sixteen.

Tatts kept his hand on the girl and turned to me. "What the fuck, man. I ain't finished."

I took two quick strides across the dark room and hit him across the temple with the barrel of my .45. He dropped like a wet bath towel. "You are now."

Kelly pulled the soiled sheet from the mattress on the ground and wrapped it around the naked girl. I flipped on the lights. The room was bare except for the mattress and a powder-blue Hello Kitty backpack.

"It's okay," Kelly assured the girl. "We're here to help you."

The girl's eyes were dull and her pupils dilated. There was a discarded syringe on the floor, and I guessed the contents was responsible for her lethargic state. I produced Maya's yearbook picture from my pocket and showed it to her.

"Have you seen this girl?"

She blinked her eyes slowly as if she didn't hear me. Tears streamed down her face.

The john came to with a red face and an angry attitude. "You fucking hit me," he said, touching his temple and gazing at the blood on his fingertips. The guy was a genius. "I paid for that shit." He pointed at the girl. "You fucking hit me."

I shoved my pistol under his chin and flipped open my private investigator license. "What do ya think's goin' on here, Ace? The girl's underage. Look at her. You know what that means?"

His eyes swiveled toward the girl. In the harsh glare of the single 60-watt bulb dangling from the broken ceiling fixture, she looked even younger. The heavy makeup around her eyes and dark red lipstick couldn't mask her youth.

"I didn't know, man," he said. Reality was starting to sink in.

"Bullshit." I kept my pistol jammed under his chin while I yanked the chain that was hooked to his belt. A black leather wallet appeared from his pocket. I opened it and found a stack of bills with a hundred on top. I didn't count it.

"Here," I said, handing the money to the girl. "Find some clothes and get out of here."

"You can't do that," he protested.

"Just did. The only reason I don't shoot you is I don't wanna traumatize this girl any more than she already is by splattering your brains all over the wall." I leaned close to his face. "Take a good look. If you ever see my face again, you better be running the other way. Understand?"

"Yeah, man. Got it." He zipped his pants, then stumbled backward toward the door.

"Get out of my sight. Take the back stairs at the end of the hall."

"You're letting him go?" Kelly asked, still kneeling beside the girl.

"I'll call the police. Leave the girl. Let's find Maya."

Kelly's look said she didn't like it. "Help is on the way," she told the girl and followed me back to the hallway.

The next door was open. I flipped on the light. Empty except for a half dozen cockroaches scurrying out of the glare. It had the same drab layout. A dirty mattress on the floor, bare walls with mildew around the edges of the window. There was a worn carry-on suitcase with wheels and an extension handle. Whoever parked it there hadn't been here long or was planning a trip.

The last room was locked. I paused to listen. I heard voices behind the door. The video game still played downstairs. I hoped Skeeter had it under control. The neighborhood was quiet. No police on the way. The dogs next door were silent. I checked my watch. Four thirty. If Skeeter was right, one of the voices behind the door belonged to Maya.

I kicked it in.

Two girls gasped as I stepped into the room with my .45 held at the ready. One sat on the dirty mattress. The other sat on the floor with her back against the wall. Both had dark shoulder-length hair, and both dressed alike in jean shorts and T-shirts. The girls didn't move. The air was damp and sticky and smelled like weed and sugary candy. I quickly stashed the weapon in my shoulder holster.

"It's okay. I'm Nick Fischer." The girl on the floor matched my picture of Maya. Her hair wasn't combed, and she looked like she'd skipped a few meals, but the green eyes told me it was definitely her. I knelt and breathed a sigh of relief.

"Maya Chavez?" I asked.

She nodded. "What d'you want?" She was instantly on the defensive. Something I didn't expect.

"You a cop?" the girl on the bed asked. "We ain't done nothin'."

"I'm a private investigator. Maya's grandpa hired me to find her and bring her home."

Maya pushed herself up from the floor and sat down next to the girl on the bed.

"What if I don't wanna go?" She took the other girl's hand and dared me to respond.

I didn't know what to say. I glanced at Kelly, hoping she had an answer.

"Do you understand what's goin' on here?" Kelly asked the girls.

"I'm not going back. Nobody in F-burg gives a fuck about me." Maya sounded bitter.

"That's not true. Your grandfather loves you," Kelly said.

My disbelief morphed into anger. "Two people have died already. Your friend Lori, and Candy from the strip club. I think you better come with us before that happens to you."

"Lori's dead?" Maya stared at me in disbelief. She tried to focus her eyes and wrap her brain around the new information.

"That's right. She was trying to get to me. To tell me about what happened at the river. Somebody got to her first. She told me about Club Forty-Four. I went to the club and found Candy. She told me she'd seen you there. She was gonna tell me what was going on, but Russell Stevens murdered her and tossed her in a Walmart dumpster."

Tears swelled up in Maya's eyes and flooded down her cheeks. "You're lying. Russell wouldn't do that. He—he wouldn't do that to me."

"Maya, you're not safe here. None of the girls are safe here," Kelly said.

"But Russell loves me."

A loud explosion shook the old house. A shotgun blast from Skeeter's 870. No more time for conversation. I threw Maya over my shoulder and ran for the door. She weighed maybe a hundred pounds, all knees and elbows.

"Put me down," Maya protested.

Kelly grabbed a small white backpack from the floor. "This yours?" she asked Maya.

Maya didn't respond, but the girl on the bed nodded. Kelly took it. "Police are on their way," she told the girl, then followed me down the stairs.

Maya pounded my back with her fists, but there was little strength behind the blows. Three thugs in their twenties wearing T-shirts and baggy shorts sat rigid on a threadbare front room couch. On a widescreen TV, cartoon thugs chased cops down a generic urban street. A glass bong rested on the scarred coffee table in front of them.

Skeeter stood to the side of the screen with his shotgun leveled toward the couch. His eyes didn't move from the thugs. "That our girl?"

"Yep. Meet Maya Chavez," I said.

"She don't look too happy."

"Let me go!" Maya shouted.

I put her down but kept a firm grip on her thin upper arm. "Can you talk some sense into her?" I asked Kelly.

"Take it easy," Kelly said, taking Maya's hand. "We wanna help you."

"I don't need no fucking help." Maya tried to jerk her hand away, but Kelly was too strong and adept at keeping perps under control.

"Put her in the pickup. We'll sort it out when we get her away from here," I said.

Kelly led Maya out the front door. I turned my attention back to the game on the big screen. "What is that?" I asked. "*Grand Theft* four or five?"

The thug on the right with a flame neck tatt acknowledged my presence. "One," he said, reaching under the couch cushion.

"Wow, that's old-school." I hit him in the temple with the barrel of my .45, then caught his head and pushed it back against the armrest. I found the Glock 9mm he'd been reaching for under the cushion and stuck it behind my belt.

The thug in the middle made a move to stand.

"Sit tight, pardner," I said, raising my pistol.

He sat back down.

"We don't want any trouble. We came for the girl. I'm taking her home."

The third thug squirmed in his seat. He was older than the other two and had probably been left in charge. "You fucked up, dude," he said.

"I know, I know. You're the baddest of the bad and you're gonna fuck me up."

"You know it, motherfucker. This house belongs to Dragon, man. The girls are his property." He said it like a threat.

"Last time I checked, owning another human was against the law. Am I missing something, Skeeter?"

"You be correct, boss. The Thirteenth Amendment outlawed slavery."

"Y'all remember that from your US History class or did you skip school that day?"

"Fuck you. You dead, man."

"I'm shakin' in my boots." I picked up a cell phone from the coffee table. "This your phone?" The thugs didn't respond.

During my time in the sandbox, cell phones were a gold mine of intel. I tossed it to Skeeter. "This might come in handy." The phone bounced off his chest and hit the floor. He picked it up with his prosthetic hook and shoved it in his back pocket.

"You can't take that," Neck Tatt said.

I held up my .45. "This pistol and the big guy with a metal hook give me the right to do whatever the hell I want. The fact that you were pimping out little girls means you lose your right to disagree." I pulled a handful of zip ties from my back pocket. "Show me your hands. I don't wanna get followed, and you better pray to god I don't ever have to come back here."

"That's fucked up, man."

"File a complaint with SAPD."

CHAPTER TWENTY-EIGHT

Skeeter and I hustled across the dirt lawn under the thick canopy of oak and pecan trees that seemed to close their branches to protect the neighborhood secrets. The dogs next door woke and barked a warning of our pending departure. A few houses down, an engine cranked and didn't start. Cranked again and stopped. Somebody was gonna be late for work. I checked my watch. Four forty. We were only ten minutes behind schedule.

"Mr. Dragon will be pissed off," Skeeter said.

We crossed the street. The cab light was on in my pickup, and Kelly was sitting in the back seat beside Maya.

I opened my door. "We got what we came for. I don't care what he does." I climbed in and turned the key. Luckily, my engine started.

Skeeter got in the passenger side and stared at my profile.

"What?" I asked.

"You don't think he'll come after us?"

"One thing at a time."

"We have a problem," Kelly said.

"You're kidnapping me!" Maya shouted from the back seat.

I put the pickup in gear, made a U-turn, and drove back toward Commerce Street. The first stop was going to be my house in King William. I figured we could all use some rest. Tomorrow, I'd finish the job and take her back to Fredericksburg.

"Did you hear me?" Maya shouted again.

"Maya, calm down," I said in the most soothing voice I could muster. "Everybody on the west side heard you."

"Don't tell me to calm down! Let me out." She reached for the door handle.

Kelly grabbed her wrist. "We're trying to help you, Maya."

"I don't need your help," she protested.

I sped up to avoid a red light. "Just keep her in the truck till we get home," I said.

"I know my rights. I'm eighteen. I can do what I want." Maya spat the words across the seat. "You can't hold me against my will."

"She has a point," Skeeter said.

"You're not helping." I focused on Maya's image in the rearview mirror. "Talk to your grandpa first, then you can do whatever you want. He's worried sick about you. If you still wanna go off on your own, I won't stop you. I'll even give you a ride wherever you wanna go."

"I wanna talk to Russell," she insisted.

"That's not gonna happen." I was expecting a grateful, happy reunion. Instead, I felt like I'd just snatched a first grader from her birthday party before the cake and presents. There wasn't any point in arguing. I had to hold her till morning, then get her back to Helmut and hope for the best.

Rose was at her kitchen window when I pulled into the driveway. She never seemed to sleep. She waved. There would be plenty of gossip to spread tomorrow. I hoped she wouldn't come over for breakfast. Kelly helped Maya out of the back seat while Skeeter stood beside the door. Both expected her to bolt at any minute.

"You're gonna keep me here?" Maya said.

"It's not that bad. The shower works, and it's got furniture."

"You can't do that."

"Only for tonight," I said, feeling like I'd just stepped off the trail and walked into a prickly pear cactus.

Kelly and Skeeter escorted Maya into the house and sat her down on the leather chair in my office. I went to the kitchen and put on a pot of coffee. None of this was making any sense. I was hoping a jolt of caffeine would help.

While the coffee brewed, I confronted Maya. She sat with her arms crossed and a scowl on her face. Her hair wasn't shiny or curled like in the school photo and it completely obscured her left eye. She made no attempt to brush it out of the way.

"Are you hungry?" I asked.

She didn't speak.

I glanced at Kelly and Skeeter. They both shrugged.

"How about something to drink?"

She let out an exaggerated sigh. I'd delt with uncooperative detainees before, on patrol in Afghanistan and as a deputy in Travis County, but I'd never faced a belligerent teenager. I couldn't imagine being a teacher with a classroom full of them. Kelly motioned me into the kitchen. I poured two cups of coffee. We both took a sip.

"What do you think?" I whispered.

"She's scared right now and probably still high. Try to be a little less intimidating."

I nodded, not sure I knew how to do that. We walked out of the kitchen. Maya's position hadn't changed. She sat with her arms crossed and her jaw clenched, challenging me. I saw her nose was running and handed her a tissue, a peace offering. Then I knelt beside her so that we were both on the same level.

"Your granddad asked me to find you. He's worried sick. We all were. Why don't you want to go home?"

She took the tissue and blew her nose. Her eyes were red and still brimming with tears. "That's n-not my home," she stammered.

Kelly stood beside her. Maya let her brush the hair from her eyes. "Tell us what happened." She took Maya's hand.

"He doesn't want me," she said.

"Did you have an argument?" Kelly asked.

"Y-yes," she stuttered.

Helmut could be a little rough around the edges. He was a tough-as-boot-leather Central Texas rancher whose track record with young female family members wasn't exactly stellar. His daughter had turned to drink in high school and had run off with her boyfriend the day after high school graduation.

"What about your mother? She's worried about you too," Kelly said.

She let out an angry laugh. "Have you met my mother? She's a drunk. She don't give a shit about me."

"What about school?" I said. "Don't you want to finish your senior year?"

"Not in F-burg. The people suck. They're all rednecks. The town's a joke."

I thought about bringing up the two girls who died in the aftermath of her disappearance, but I didn't want to argue with her or upset her even more. Her mind was made up. I wasn't a counselor, and I got the feeling that the more I talked, the worse I made it. I knew a little something about being stubborn because it was my MO. I checked my watch. Five o'clock in the morning. Not the best time for a therapy session.

"Let's get some sleep," I said. "I promised your granddad I'd find you and bring you home. That's what I'm gonna do. What you do after that is your own business. I know Helmut. He's a good man. Maybe you can work out your differences. If you give him a chance, he's got a lot to offer."

Maya's jaw clenched shut again at the mention of her grandpa. She'd said all she was going to say tonight.

"Maya, you can sleep in the spare bedroom upstairs," I said. "Skeeter, take the couch."

Kelly escorted Maya upstairs, and I followed. The spare room had a bed and a separate bathroom. I used it for storage, but the bed was made, and the sheets were clean. I let Kelly take Maya in and get her settled. Hopefully, she would go to sleep so that we could all get some rest. I thought about cuffing her to the bed, but there was only a small window and that opened to a twenty-foot drop. To get downstairs, she would have to pass my open bedroom door and get past Skeeter at the front door.

When Kelly came into my room, she looked exhausted. "What do you think?"

"I think Helmut's gonna have his hands full."

"She's eighteen. Legally, she can do whatever she wants."

"You sound like Les Zeller. You want me to leave her with Dragon?"

"I'm just sayin', you can't force her to go back to Fredericksburg. The law is the law."

"What about what's right and wrong? You saw what was going on in that house. Are we supposed to sit back and let that happen? She's a scared little kid. I don't care if she's eighteen. She's obviously under the influence, and she doesn't know what she wants. I promised Helmut I'd bring her back, and that's what I'm gonna do."

She stripped to her bra and panties and lay down beside me. I took a deep breath, aware that I'd let my emotions overheat.

She put a hand on my chest and kissed my cheek. "What happens when an unstoppable force meets an immovable object?"

I rolled on top of her. "We'll have to work that out tomorrow."

CHAPTER TWENTY-NINE

"She's gone!" Kelly yelled as she flashed by the open bedroom door and ran down the stairs.

I sat up instantly. Sunlight streamed through the open curtains, and I squinted against the glare. "Gone?" Remnants of a dream that had reunited me with my dead grandpa evaporated like steam from a cup of coffee. My head cleared, and I reached for my Wranglers. "How the hell did she get out? I didn't hear anything," I shouted.

Kelly appeared at the open door. "She's not downstairs."

I pushed past her into the spare bedroom.

"She went out the window. We were both out of it. Your snoring woke me up. I felt a cold breeze and found the window open in her room. Her bed doesn't look slept in."

I inspected the open window. She would have had to creep along a rusty two-inch gutter to the porch roof, then jump down twenty feet onto hard-packed dirt.

"What the hell was she thinkin'?" I shook my head in disbelief.

"I checked everywhere, downstairs, the backyard."

"Outsmarted by a teenager," I said. "Now we know?"

"Now we know what?"

"What happens when an unstoppable force meets an immovable object?"

"The immovable object jumps out the window?"

"Apparently."

There was a knock on the front door. For a brief instant, I thought it might be Maya wanting back in. Kelly and I hustled downstairs. Skeeter was still sleeping on the couch.

"Reveille, reveille, reveille," I said, smacking the lamp table near his head.

Skeeter lifted his head. "What's up?"

"Maya flew the coop," I said on my way to the door.

He shot bolt upright. "What the hell?"

"Exactly."

The knocking got more insistent. I peered through the peephole. It wasn't Maya. It was my neighbor, Rose, bearing breakfast. She smiled at the door and held up a pie pan covered with tinfoil. She had on a canvas barn coat over pressed jeans tucked into white rubber shrimper boots she wore to work in her garden. Her hair, as usual, was curled in tight braids on top of her head. I opened the door.

"I saw you had company and several extra mouths to feed." Her voice was high and reedy with a distinct Texas accent.

"Hi, Rose. Now's not a good time," I said.

She took that as an invitation and pushed passed me to Kelly. "Well, hello, sweetie. I thought you could use some breakfast." She walked to the kitchen, uncovered a steaming dish, and began setting the table. Rose had retired from teaching and spent her time gardening, raising cats, and keeping track of the neighbors. She treated everybody like her first-year bio students. I probably should have invited her over last night to deal with Maya.

"Do I smell quiche?" Skeeter said. He was sitting in my office chair tying his size sixteen Adidas cross trainers.

"*Västerbotten*," she corrected him. "And there's plenty for everyone. That was quite a racket y'all put up last night." She found a carton of orange juice in the fridge, put it on the table, then searched my cupboards for appropriate glasses. The only ones I had were plastic beer cups marked with the Fredericksburg Oktoberfest logo.

"Sorry if we woke you," I said.

"You know I sleep like a hummingbird. And my hip's been bothering me lately something fierce." She looked around the room. "Where's the young girl you brought home?" She hadn't missed anything.

Kelly and I shared a look. I wasn't sure how much I wanted to tell her. Kelly shrugged. "That's what we're trying to figure out. She ran off last night," I said. She would find out anyway, and maybe she could help us. "Did you see anything unusual?"

Rose kept a journal on a lamp table near the front window where she noted the people who came and went in the neighborhood. She kept several, in fact, one notebook at each window in case she spied something unusual. She said it occupied her time on nights she couldn't sleep. "I saw a black Jeep parked on the corner about an hour ago. The windows were tinted, and I couldn't see the occupant clearly. The motor was running. I made a note of that. I watched it for about ten minutes, then it was time to feed Astrid, Ivar, and Freya. When I came back to the window, it was gone."

I knew those were the names of three of her cats because I'd fed them, much to Sam's dismay, when Rose had gone to visit her sister. She had three more that ate in the evening, but I didn't remember their names.

"Russell Stevens drives a black Jeep Grand Cherokee," Kelly said.

"That's right. That son of a bitch," I said. "Excuse my language, Rose."

"I'm almost eighty. I've heard every cuss word there is. I'm not easily offended."

"Did you get the license plate number?" Kelly asked.

"Of course. I wrote it down in my journal."

I found my socks and boots and put them on. "She must have had a cell phone in her pocket. I should have searched her."

"You think she called him to come get her?" Skeeter asked.

"Or he called her and demanded to know where she was," I said.

We all stood in silence. I was trying to think of a scenario that didn't end in tragedy but couldn't come up with anything.

Rose filled the momentary silence with her teacher voice. "Come into the kitchen. You'll need a full stomach to go after that young lady."

We all shrugged and moved toward the kitchen table, conditioned by years of public education. She sliced the Swedish quiche and served us all a large portion. I poured coffee for all of us and sat down. Skeeter pinched a fork in his metal hook and held it like a tiny trident.

"Thank you, Rose," he said. "This is wonderful."

While I ate, I tried to think of a plan that didn't involve getting Maya hurt or worse and dreaded calling Helmut to tell him that I'd found his granddaughter only to have her slip through my fingers.

Skeeter finished this quiche and washed it down with a big slurp of coffee. "Why not call him?" he said. He held up a cell phone with a smug look. It was the same phone I'd taken off the thug. "You were right. It had a wealth of intel, including our boy's number."

Kelly and I stared at him, not believing he'd already analyzed the phone.

"What?" he said. "You wanted intel. I got intel. Here's the number."

"You had this all along? Why the hell didn't you say something?"

"I figured it out last night after everyone went to bed."

Skeeter dialed the number and put the phone on speaker.

We listened to the phone ring several times. Finally, a tired, raspy voice came on the line.

"Yeah." It was the Dragon's voice.

"Where you at, dog?" I said, trying to sound like a thug. Skeeter rolled his eyes.

"Who's this?"

"Who you think, Dragon?"

"Nick fucking Fischer," he said, sounding fully awake now. The ruse hadn't worked.

"My middle name's Lee, after my dad, but close enough. Should I call you Russell, or do you prefer Dragon?"

"I don't want you callin' me at all. I want you to disappear, along with that cute bitch from Lubbock and that big fuckin' one-armed nigger."

"Now, don't get personal. Mr. Davis is my partner, and he doesn't like the N-word."

"Like I care. How'd you get this number?"

"It was in the phone book. Listen, Russell. Let's cut the bullshit. I'll leave you alone if you give me Maya."

"She's with me. Don't you get that? She made her choice."

"She's a kid. She doesn't know what she wants. Turn her loose or I'll take you apart."

"Fuck off. You don't know who you're dealin' with. I can crush you anytime I want. You can't do jack. You ain't the police."

"Let me talk to Maya," I said, but the line went dead. I hit redial and got the *not-in-service* message.

"We know who has Maya," Skeeter said.

"What do we do now?" Rose asked. She'd listened in fascination to the whole conversation and spoke as if she was now part of the team. "I've got my shotgun."

"Leave it in the closet," I told her. She looked disappointed. I'd seen her shotgun. The weapon was handed down from her father. I had no doubt she could and would use it if she had to. I also knew her reaction time wasn't what it used to be, and her cataracts limited her vision.

"We're gonna need some lunch," I said. "And Maya may come back here on her own. I don't want the house to be empty."

That got her attention. "I'll watch the house and get started on lunch," she said and hurried off to start cooking. "Leave the plates. I'll tend to them later."

I turned to Skeeter. "It's time for the backup plan. Did you find Russell's underground connections?"

"Working it," he said, already pulling his laptop from his backpack.

Kelly ignored Rose and cleared the table. "What's the plan?"

"You heard the Dragon. He's not gonna give up Maya. He's got her brainwashed."

"So, you're gonna target Russell Stevens?"

"Got a better idea?"

"Yeah. Go to the police. Call Detective Ochoa and tell her what's going on."

"And she'll do what? Maya's eighteen, remember. We can't link Russell to any crime yet. Her hands are tied."

Kelly chewed on her bottom lip. She didn't like my answer or my plan.

"He's behind two murders, besides the drugs, and trafficking girls. If I were a cop, I'd build a case to put him away for good. But that's not what I do. I was hired to find Helmut's granddaughter. I'm gonna get Maya back before it's too late."

"Targeting Russell Stevens makes you a vigilante."

"Should I wait and let her end up like Lori and Candy?"

She put her hands on her hips. "What happens when you find him? Are you gonna shoot him in the head?"

"I'll do what's necessary to get Maya home safe."

She crossed her arms and glared at me, then turned and walked out of the house.

Skeeter grunted something low and guttural that I couldn't understand.

"What?"

"You know what."

"You're taking her side?"

"No, I'm with you, boss. But you could have handled that a little better."

"You're the one who warned me it wouldn't work out between us. Remember the *Seinfeld* episode?"

"She is a cop. It wouldn't hurt to hear her out."

"All right, all right." I shrugged and walked toward the front door. "I'll listen, but I already know what Ochoa's gonna say. Get me that intel on Russell's local connections ASAP."

CHAPTER THIRTY

The San Antonio Public Safety Headquarters was a six-story building flanked by a taller parking garage west of the San Antonio River and less than a mile from the Alamo. It combined the city fire and police departments in what the city planners claimed would result in integrated technology, increased efficiency, and better protection for the public. It was a lofty goal, but in the end, a new building couldn't overcome the old bureaucracy.

I parked in the public garage across the street. Kelly zipped up the fleece-lined coat she'd borrowed from me. The few clothes she packed for the weekend hadn't included winter gear. The next heaviest thing I owned that wasn't at the ranch was a jean jacket, which I buttoned over a gray hoodie and prepared to be cold the rest of the day.

I'd agreed to meet with Detective Ochoa to appease Kelly and Skeeter and, I had to admit, to calm my own self-doubts. I was willing to listen to all sides as long as the end result was the same. My first instinct urged me to go scorched earth on Russell and all known associates until he handed over Maya of his own free will. There were risks involved in my methods—it was dangerous—but there were also risks in waiting. Maya could die or be sent out of state. Hitting fast and unexpectedly had worked for me in the past. The thug who framed Skeeter never saw me coming. He had an armed crew and an expensive lawyer. He anticipated a courtroom battle, but I'd hit him where it hurt—his drug business.

My self-doubt came from not being fully recovered from my bullet wounds. Mentally and physically, I wasn't at my peak performance level. Russell Stevens was prison hard and connected to a Mexican cartel. Even with the element of surprise, I knew I would be walking into a shitstorm of the highest caliber.

Kelly and I walked past the odd public art display that consisted of a handful of thirty-foot-tall metal beams painted white and standing on end like unstable teepee poles in a gale-force wind. It was one of those things that made you scratch your head and wonder how much of your tax bill they wasted, and how exactly the art would increase the efficiency of public safety. We went through the glass door and found Sergeant Hugo Vera on duty at the front desk. He nodded at me and smiled at Kelly.

"I see you're keepin' better company these days," he said, winking at Kelly.

"What's the good word?" I asked. We shook hands over the desk.

Vera was an old-timer who'd retired from SAPD once but came back to work part-time because his wife got tired of seeing him around the house all day. We also had a long history. He'd worked as a deputy for my dad when he was sheriff of Gillespie County and was on duty the day he was murdered. I'd known him since I was a kid when he would let me use his desk at the station to finish my homework after school.

"Every day above ground is a good day," he said, his smile big and genuine. "I see the PI business is attracting some very beautiful company." He'd always been a shameless flirt.

Kelly held out her hand. "Kelly Hoffman," she said, returning his smile.

Vera stood and shook her hand. "I hope you can keep this cowboy in line," he said, nodding toward me.

"That's a full-time job," she said.

"You look up to the task." He sat back in his chair and turned his attention to me. "Who'd you come to harass today?"

"Detective Ochoa," I said. "She's expecting us."

Vera shook his head. "That explains why she's on the war path. Have anything to do with Helmut's granddaughter?" I wasn't surprised he knew what I was working on. He knew Helmut and was still plugged into the good ol' boys network in Gillespie County.

"It does indeed," I said, not wanting to get into the details. In addition to being a flirt, Vera liked to gossip, and I didn't want to take the chance that word about Maya's escape would get back to Helmut before I told him in person.

He shrugged when he saw I wasn't going to share anything more. "She brings me donuts when she's havin' a good day. I haven't had any in a week."

"Then you ought to thank me for helping you manage your weight."

He stifled a chuckle and turned to Kelly. "Good luck with this guy. He's stubborn as a barn-sour mule." Vera made the call upstairs, and I heard Ochoa say to send him up.

"Will you agree to do what she says?" Kelly said when the elevator door closed.

"I agreed to share information with her to prove I can keep an open mind. I'm not a cop, and unless I'm breaking the law, I don't have to follow her advice."

"So you keep reminding me."

We got off the elevator and found Detective Ochoa standing by her corner desk. She didn't look happy to see us, but she motioned us to join her.

"Lone Wolf Fischer. I didn't expect to hear from you," she said with thick sarcasm. She raised one dark, carefully trimmed eyebrow and folded her arms under her breasts. She wore low heels, dark slacks, and a light blue blouse that was just tight enough to accentuate her ample curves. Her hair was pulled into a tight ponytail, exposing an oval face and a high, olive-skinned forehead. I couldn't help picturing her in front of a camera on that cop show, *Blue Bloods*. That she'd made detective in a male-dominated profession told me she was tough and could hold her own. She sized me up, then studied Kelly, as if they were wearing four-ounce gloves and about to get it on in an MMA cage match. If that happened, I wasn't sure who would win.

"Truce," I said. "Mind if we sit down?"

Ochoa shrugged and slumped into a worn swivel chair behind her desk. A five- or six-year-old boy with shaggy dark hair smiled from a framed photo on the metal cabinet behind her. It was a new picture. The last time I was in her office, the boy's hair was purple.

"How's your son?" I asked, trying to thaw her chilly mood and establish a rapport.

A flicker of a smile crossed her face, but she quickly pursed her lips. "He's fine. With his father this weekend. He gets him one weekend a month. We're both SAPD, so sometimes the schedule is hectic."

"Nice he can spend time with his father," Kelly said.

Ochoa's expression turned sour. "One day Aaron will realize on his own what an A-hole his father really is. Until then, I won't interfere with their relationship." She composed herself and checked our reactions, embarrassed she'd let slip so much information.

I cleared my throat. "Candy."

Ochoa frowned. "I'm fresh out. Aaron steals it from my desk whenever he's here."

"No. Candy was the name of the dead girl in the dumpster."

"You suddenly remembered that obscure name while eating your breakfast taco?"

"Actually, I had *Västerbotten*, but yes that's what happened."

"What's that?" She smirked.

"Swedish quiche. My neighbor makes it. Very tasty. I'm working a missing person case. An eighteen-year-old girl from Fredericksburg. Her grandpa asked me to find her. He's an old friend of the family."

"Why tell me now? It was a secret two days ago."

I started at the beginning and explained how I'd gotten involved with Maya's case and what we'd found so far. Ochoa jotted notes on a legal pad and nodded for me to continue, her expression neutral. "I only withheld the name because I was certain that Maya was going to be the next victim and I didn't want you to interfere."

She made one last note and looked up, waiting for more. "Usually, people come to the police for help, but I understand how you operate. What's changed now?"

"We found Maya," I said. "But she ran away again."

"When was this?"

"Last night. I took her to my house in King William. Sometime during the night, she jumped out the window. Russell Stevens came and got her."

"How do you know it was Stevens?"

"Because I called him this morning and asked him."

"You have a phone number for Russell Stevens? How did you get that?"

I shrugged. "I had a number. I'm sure it's out of service now."

"Russell Stevens is already on our radar. He's into more than prostitution. He's a big-time dealer supplied by the alpha dogs across the border. Runs distribution in Bexar County."

"He must have branched out to Gillespie County."

"What makes you say that?"

"A girl in Fredericksburg was murdered. Before she died, she tipped me off about Club Forty-Four."

"She stood up and walked around the front of her desk. "Are you sure you're not leaving out any of the details?"

I shrugged and tried to look innocent.

She leaned back against the edge of her desk and crossed her arms under her breasts again. Her eyes bored into me. She'd perfected the deadeye cop stare. I met her gaze with a hard look of my own. "Where did you find the girl last night?" she said.

Something told me she already knew about our clandestine raid to retrieve Maya and had been waiting to see if I would supply the details. "West side. I'll have to find the address."

She leaned forward and narrowed her eyes. "A group of vigilantes broke into a house on the west side and rousted the inhabitants last night, including the girls we suspected of being trafficked by Russell Stevens. Now, we can't finish our investigation or make an arrest. In fact, citizen Stevens called 911 last night and claimed his girlfriend Maya Chavez was kidnapped by someone named Nick Fischer."

"That piece of shit," I said.

"Technically, he's right. It was a kidnapping."

"Maya was there against her will."

"Then why did she run away from you?"

"You know that happens all the time," I said. "The victim gets attached—"

Ochoa cut me off, annoyed. "I know that. The problem here is you ruined my chance of linking a crime to Mr. Stevens. I don't have a money trail. I don't have shit. You helped him give me and the SAPD the royal shaft."

"What about Candy?" I asked. "She was gonna tell us about Maya."

"We already ID'd the girl. Kim Lucey, from Portland, Texas. Ex-cheerleader. We also have the time of death. The Dragon has an alibi. The strip club surveillance cameras put him at the club at the time she was killed."

"What about Maya?" I said. "She's in danger now."

"I know he's a thug. I know he's dealing drugs and pimping out underage girls. But until I have evidence, my hands are tied," she said. "Even if I knew where he was, I couldn't arrest him. I have to follow the law."

"Thanks for your time." I got up and walked to the opening of her cubical.

Ochoa put her hands on her hips. "Give me one good reason I shouldn't arrest you for that vigilante move you pulled last night?"

I turned and faced her. "My charming and charismatic personality."

She almost smiled but checked herself. Said, "Stay away from Russell Stevens, or I will arrest you." Her expression was firm, but there was something in her tone that was softer. I couldn't explain it.

Ochoa put a hand on Kelly's arm. "You're a cop. You know what I'm talking about. Do him a favor and convince him to let us handle it or this may be his last job as a private investigator. I'm building a case against Russell Stevens, and I don't want him screwing it up."

CHAPTER THIRTY-ONE

Kelly picked up her pace and caught me as I entered the parking garage. "I know you're worried about Maya, but Ochoa's right. You should let her handle it. Besides, she did you a favor."

"What do you mean?"

"She gave you a pass. She likes you."

"She 'likes' me?"

She gripped my arm, and I stopped and turned to her. She studied my face. "If I were her, I'd have arrested you for your own safety."

"That's good to know."

"You're a focused operator, as good as any RECON Ranger I've ever seen. And you have a knack for self-preservation and getting to the truth. But you really don't understand women." She turned abruptly and walked to my pickup.

I stared after her, not knowing what to say. Part of that was a compliment, especially coming from a fellow Marine. The part about women had hit the mark. I had no idea what she was talking about. Was she jealous of Detective Ochoa? I thought back to my interactions with the detective. She was a looker, there was no doubt about it, but had my gaze lingered on her too long? And had she noticed? The answer to both questions was probably yes.

I sped out the parking garage and turned north on Santa Rosa. Kelly stared at my profile.

"I stayed here to help you find Maya. I didn't sign up to fight a gangster linked to a Mexican cartel. Your wound isn't completely healed. Go after him now, and you'll get yourself killed. If that's your plan, I won't wait around to see you die if you don't mind." She wasn't angry, but emphatic.

"Thanks for the vote of confidence," I said. I couldn't help it. I was hardwired to deflect with a joke. But she also had a valid point. My own self-doubt was eating away at my confidence.

She punched me on the arm. "Damn you, Nick Fischer."

"Okay, I'm sorry. I'm pissed at myself for losing Maya and that I have to face Helmut and tell him what happened. I'm also pissed at Maya. What does she see in a thug with a dragon tattoo? Why would she go back to him?"

She thought for a moment while I maneuvered my pickup onto the 410 freeway. "She was obviously angry at the world. Her mom's a drunk. Her grandpa lives on an isolated ranch, which for me would be cool, but she spent most of her life in urban Southern California where the pace is a little bit faster than in Fredericksburg, Texas. Maybe a guy with a dragon tattoo was more like the kind of people she's used to hanging out with. Or maybe she was showing off for the locals. Being in high school, especially a new high school your senior year, can be really awkward for a young girl."

"Were you like that in high school?" I asked.

"I remember wanting to get away from the farm. But my situation was different. I had a mom and dad and three brothers who would have never let me take off with someone like Russell. The only daring thing I ever did in high school was take the bus to Fort Worth with my girlfriend. We wanted to go to the rodeo, but Dad said I was too young to go by myself."

"What happened?"

"We snuck out and went anyway. My older brother was there and caught me. He made me get in his car so he could drive me home. I was grounded for two weeks, and I had to do my brother's chores for a month."

"Sounds reasonable."

"Ha! He wasn't supposed to be there either, but because he drove me home, Mom and Dad thought he was a saint."

"What I'm wondering is, when I do bring her home, what's gonna keep her there without handcuffing her to the bed?"

"Maya said she had a fight with her grandfather."

"Yeah, I know. He can be a crusty old fart. I've known him all my life."

"Why don't we ask him what the fight was about? Maybe we can get him to reach out to Maya. It could change her mind about returning home."

She had a point. I knew she was also grasping at anything that would prevent me from launching a direct assault on Russell Stevens. I would go along with her, at least until I heard from Skeeter.

I stopped at Chris Madrid's for burgers and fries. It was a San Antonio landmark that I tried to hit once a month, but my extended recovery at the ranch had changed my routine. It was early, so we avoided the usually long lunchtime line. Kelly ordered the regular house favorite cheddar cheesy, and I had the same, but upgraded to "macho" which doubled the quarter pound of beef. At some point in the near future, I would have to get back to Lucky's gym and work off the few extra pounds that threatened to expand over my belt, but for now I justified the extra calories in the name of rehabilitation. We sat inside with a half dozen businessmen in suits, a street crew in uniform, and a handful of students from nearby Trinity University. The courtyard sat empty, too cold and windy for patrons.

I tried calling ahead to see if I could catch Helmut at home and tell him we were on our way, but like my grandpa, Helmut didn't have a cell phone and didn't have an answering machine. Calling him was like sending a sound wave message into space—you know the aliens are out there somewhere, but it could take centuries for them to receive and return the message.

The drive after lunch to Fredericksburg was quiet. Once I negotiated the perennial road construction on Interstate 10 west, the afternoon traffic was light. Kelly and I were both absorbed in our own thoughts. I needed Skeeter's intel to form a plan. Deep down, I knew what I would have to do, but for the first time in my life, I had second thoughts.

I took Highway 87 north out of Comfort. Signs of fall increased as we drove north. Central Texas didn't get the dense fall colors like New England. Here the signs were more subtle—barns full of hay, crops harvested, fields plowed under, and farmers selling pumpkins and gourds of all shapes and sizes along the highway. When we reached the turn to Helmut's ranch, I unrolled my window. The smell of damp fresh-cut hay helped clear my head. The air felt cold and crisp like it always does after a norther blows through Central Texas, as if Mother Nature was apologizing for the damage created by the storm.

"You think he's home?" Kelly asked when I stopped at the ranch gate. We both studied the large metal design over the gate featuring a cowboy holding his horse's reins and kneeling with his hat in his hand before an iron cross.

"Monday afternoon. If he's not here, I don't expect he's gone very far. The livestock auction's on Thursday. Sunday is church. Friday nights he goes to the football game and the fish fry at the VFW. He might be at the grocery store, but other than that, where's he gonna go?"

Kelly got out and opened the gate. Helmut's pack of dogs started barking as soon as she rattled the chain. They gathered near the porch when we drove into the yard and waited at the passenger door wagging their tails. Kelly met them, offering the uneaten half of her huge Chris Madrid cheeseburger wrapped in a napkin. The Lab mix took charge and pushed the other dogs out of the way.

"Sit," she commanded. They all obeyed immediately, eyes glued to the greasy napkin. She tore the burger into equal parts and gave each dog a portion.

Helmut stepped out on the porch. "You made friends for life."

I held out my hand. "*Guten tag*, Helmut."

He shook hands with me, then Kelly. There was apprehension on his grizzled face.

"What news of Maya?" he said, uncharacteristically skipping the customary chat about the weather.

"We found her."

The corners of his mouth turned up with a hint of a smile.

"But she ran away again."

He scratched the gray stubble on his chin with a leathery hand. The hint of a smile faded. The silence stretched into a minute. The dog pack remained still, sensing tension and anticipating their master's mood. Helmut was like my grandpa and most of the Central Texas ranchers I knew. They took the good news and the bad with a stoic acceptance. It was something bred into the people in this part of the country, especially those families who had been here since the beginning when death and misfortune were constant companions.

"You'd better come inside," he finally said. The dog pack relaxed and resumed wagging their tails and shamelessly begging Kelly for attention. "Elena's gone to town with her sister. Won't be back till suppertime. She does the grocery shopping on Monday and catches up on the gossip. Takes her six days to recover."

We followed him inside and sat down at the hundred-year-old kitchen table while Helmut lit the gas burner with a kitchen match and slid the metal coffee percolator over the flame.

"Just made this fresh for lunch," he said.

I waited until the coffee had heated and Helmut had poured three cups full and sat down. "She was staying at a house in San Antonio. We believe she was coerced into going there by a man named Russell Stevens, who she met at a party on the river." I explained Russell's connection with Mike Bauer and the events that had taken place so far.

Helmut absorbed the information without speaking. When I paused, he held my gaze, waiting for me to continue.

"She said y'all had a fight," I said. "She doesn't think you want her to come home." I waited for him to respond. When he didn't, I kept going. "Why would she say that, Helmut?"

Kelly took a sip of the ink-black coffee and made an involuntary grimace.

"There's milk in the icebox," Helmut said. He still called the refrigerator an "icebox," referring to the original cooler, before refrigeration, that worked by placing a fifty-pound block of ice in the lower compartment. "Don't use it myself. Never got the taste for it. Elena uses it because she says I make the coffee too strong." After sixty years of marriage, they had worked out their differences. It was the same way when I was growing up. Grandpa made the coffee because he didn't trust Grandma to make it strong enough. Grandma compromised and drank her coffee with canned milk.

Kelly found the small can of condensed milk in the refrigerator. She filled her cup to the brim and stirred until the color resembled chocolate milk.

"So, you found her and took her home, but she run off again," Helmut said.

"She's eighteen, Helmut. If she doesn't want to come home, there's not much anybody can do about it," I said.

The old man took a sip of coffee. His chair faced the front window, which looked out over the freshly mowed hayfield that stretched for three hundred yards to the county road. He seemed to be looking beyond that, to Cross Mountain or the pink granite dome of Enchanted Rock. The country surrounding his ranch was as unchanging as he was. I let the silence extend for a full two minutes and was grateful that Kelly didn't get antsy and fill the void.

Helmut took another sip of coffee and spoke without looking at me. "I told Maya that if she was going to live with us, she'd need to abide by our rules. No smoking or drinking. No staying out after ten. And she had to go to church every Sunday. She also had a suitcase full of clothes that made her look like a two-bit hussy. I told her we'd buy her some new clothes, but that California stuff had to go."

Kelly suppressed a smile. She couldn't hold back any longer. "She is a teenaged girl. The dress codes are different in California, Helmut."

"That don't mean she needs to show off her skin. Every young billy goat in the county will be chasin' her around."

Helmut lived in the nineteenth century untouched by a modern world that obsessed over the sex lives of the Kardashians. Maya had grown up in Southern California, where nothing seemed real unless it showed up on Facebook or Instagram and young girls were sexualized by the time they got out of elementary school.

"Did you tell her that?" I asked, starting to understand the problem.

Helmut nodded. "Yep. For her own good." Helmut took another sip of coffee and turned his attention to me. "I raised one drunken daughter. I'll not do it again."

"You told her to shape up or ship out?"

"That's about the size of it."

Kelly shook her head but stayed silent. I had known and respected Helmut all my life. I grew up listening to him and Grandpa swap tall tales and discuss the history of Gillespie County. But his tough love approach with Maya had backfired just as it had with his own daughter.

"Goddamnit, Helmut. What did you expect? She spent most of her life in Southern California doing whatever the hell she wanted. Did you think she was gonna settle down and live on a ranch ten miles from town without any compromise just because you said so? You might as well have asked her to join a convent."

Helmut raised both bushy eyebrows. He wasn't expecting my response. I was keenly aware that twenty years ago if Grandpa or Helmut had heard me swear or talk back, meaning disagree with their opinions, they would've beat me with a stout switch. "Rules are rules," he said.

Being a Marine had cured my fear of authority, so I plunged ahead. "No, they ain't. Not when it comes to your own family. Maya's not a cowhand. You can't toss her out of the bunkhouse because she don't pull her own weight. Now she's living with a damn drug dealer in San Antonio. Is that what you want?"

Helmut stood up and walked to the stove. His back was to us. I figured he would turn and point at the front door and tell us to leave. I wondered if I'd wasted my breath, if it was too late for the old man to change or accept any advice. He reminded me of the iron cowboy on his front gate, only his head wasn't bowed, and he wasn't kneeling.

He took the percolator from the burner, refilled his cup, and tested the temperature. Satisfied, he turned back to the kitchen table.

"Y'all want more coffee?" he asked.

"I'm fine, thanks," Kelly said.

I shook my head and waited.

A shaft of sunlight shot through the kitchen window, and dust filtered through the yellow light. One of the dogs barked. The pot in Helmut's hand began to shake. He set it on the stove.

"What have I done?" he asked. For the first time in his life he was completely unsure of his next move.

"Do you want her back?" I asked. "Even if it's on her terms?"

Helmut steadied himself with a hand on the back of the kitchen chair. Then he said something I never expected him to say: "I'd give anything to have her back." His shoulders shook. "I was wrong to tell her that." I resisted the urge to put a hand on his shoulder. He wouldn't want pity or sympathy.

Kelly stood and took a step toward him, but I waved her off. Then, as quickly as the emotion had come over him, it was gone.

He let out a slow breath. "Bring Maya home. I'll make it right with her."

CHAPTER THIRTY-TWO

When we crossed the Palo Alto Creek south of Helmut's ranch, I thought of another kidnapped girl, not Maya or Anna Metzger, but Cynthia Ann Parker, the most famous of the Texas frontier captives and the story that inspired the movie *The Searchers*, John Wayne's iconic western. She was captured by Comanches when she was nine years old and spent the next twenty-four years with the Indians. When she was finally returned to her family, she had three children with the tribal chief and wanted nothing more to do with white civilization. She spent the rest of her short life trying to reunite with her native family. In the movie, John Wayne's character, Ethan, spent five years looking for his niece. When he finally caught up with her, he feared she'd been violated by the Indians and threatened to kill her, but he finally brings her back to her family for a Hollywood ending. I wondered which ending Maya would have, and if I was destined to play out the John Wayne character for the next five to twenty years. The thought sent a cold chill down my spine.

Kelly saw me shiver. "What is it?"

"I was thinking about Cynthia Ann Parker and the movie *The Searchers*. Parker spent twenty-four years with the Indians. In the movie, John Wayne searched five years for his niece."

"You think it will take that long to find Maya?"

"I'm worried the window of opportunity is closing fast."

"Would Helmut really go after her himself?"

"Yep."

"You can't let him do that. Russell Stevens would tear him apart."

"What can I do? He's over eighteen."

"Be serious."

"Oh, I'm serious."

"What're the chances of convincing Maya to go home and move back in with Helmut?" Kelly asked.

"I don't know, but the longer she's with him, the harder it will be. Cynthia Ann didn't want to return home when they finally found her, even though she'd watched the Indians massacre her family. She'd spent twenty-four years with her captors, married a chief of the tribe, and had three kids. One of them, Quanah Parker, became the last free chief of the Comanche tribe."

"Did it happen near here?"

"It was closer to Dallas and thirty years before Anna Metzger's ordeal. When Cynthia Ann was reunited with her white family, she could barely speak English. She was completely assimilated into the tribe and was never able to make the adjustment back to western civilization. She tried to escape several times, but each time, her family caught her and brought her back."

We both looked out the window at the harsh Hill Country terrain full of cactus, mesquite, and live oak trees. If you avoided looking at the powerlines and barbed wire fences, it was easy to imagine Comanches riding on the horizon or cowboys chasing a herd of cattle up the limestone canyon. Not much had changed in a hundred and fifty years.

"Maybe living with her grandfather isn't the best thing for Maya," Kelly said.

"You'd rather have her stay with Russell Stevens?"

"She did make a choice."

"You really think that?"

I parked in front of the Fredericksburg police station. In the back of my mind, I already knew what Detective Zeller would say. I was putting off the inevitable, but I'd promised Kelly I'd try to enlist his help. Kelly noticed that blood had seeped through the bandage on my chest and formed a red line under my shirt pocket. "You're bleeding," she said, alarmed. She reached across and unbuttoned my shirt. "Why didn't you say something?" She found a paper towel in the console and wiped the blood from my skin.

"I didn't notice," I lied. All the activity the last two days was not good for the healing process and was the prime source of my self-doubt.

"You should be home in bed," she scolded. "When we're finished here, I'm taking you back to the ranch. You can take the rest of the day off."

We found Officer Zeller at his desk, busy with paperwork or at least pretending to be. The remains of a barbecue sandwich rested in his inbox.

"Didn't know we had any good barbecue in town," I said.

"Backwoods Barbecue," he said. "Out on Tivydale Road by the fairgrounds. It's first rate. Lots of new things happening." He said it like I was way out of touch. Maybe I was.

We sat in the folding chairs in front of his desk while Zeller cleaned his sticky hands with a wet wipe. "Hear you been causin' trouble again," he said.

The good ol' boy law enforcement network was working overtime. I suspected Sergeant Vera might have spread the word.

"I like to stir things up, especially when I'm on a case. Maya's still missing."

"I heard you found her and let her go. We may not be as sophisticated as the SAPD, but we still follow the law. Do I need to remind you that Maya's eighteen? She can do whatever she wants. The fact that she don't wanna live with her granddaddy don't surprise me in the least. Helmut's a cranky old bastard."

"We talked to Helmut. He agreed to work out a deal if Maya comes home," Kelly said.

"Ha!" Zeller snorted a fake laugh. "I arrested his daughter Helen last month for public intoxication. She was wandering down Main Street cussin' out the tourists. I called Helmut as a courtesy. You know what he told me?" He looked at us, waiting for an answer.

I shook my head and let him continue.

"He said he didn't have a daughter. The drunk woman I had in jail could stay overnight or for the rest of the year for all he cared. Said that it would probably do her some good."

"He might be right," I said.

"The problem is, he told me the same thing before she left for California."

"You arrested her ten years ago?"

"Several times. Not once did her father ever bail her out."

"Well, I think he realized his mistake with Maya. We just have to find her again and bring her home. That's why I came down here. The person who took her works for Mike Bauer."

"You're talkin' about Russell Stevens?"

"That's right," I said. "Maya was with him the night she disappeared. Lori Kostoch was going to tell me that right before she was killed."

"If you're accusing Russell of murder and kidnapping, you're barking up the wrong tree. We have nothing to link him to the Kostoch girl, or Maya's disappearance for that matter. He's got an alibi for the time of the killing. I can't justify arresting him."

"Who provided the alibi?"

"He's an employee of Bauer Farms. We asked Mike about him. Our detectives interviewed him. Everything checks out."

"Did you do a background check on Russell Stevens? The guy's an ex-con and a thug. Ask yourself why he's in town. Why the hell does Mike need a gangster for head of security?"

"Trespassing's a problem," Zeller said.

"Then what's your theory on Lori's murder?"

"More than likely it was a drifter passing through town. She's a good-lookin' girl. She's walkin' around town by herself and the guy takes advantage of all the traffic. He follows her to the motel. We get our share of crazies. Fredericksburg is high profile now. It's top five on all the tourist websites of places to visit and the number one small town to retire in Texas. Every California yahoo now callin' Austin home comes to visit on the weekends. You'd know that if you came back more often." He let that sink in before continuing. He wanted to make sure I knew I was no longer considered a local.

"What about Maya?"

"Like I said, there's nothing law enforcement can do."

"So, she's on her own?"

"Did you lose your hearing over there in Afghanistan when you got them scars?"

"Just wanted to be clear." I stood up. Kelly was watching me. I wanted to reach across the desk and grab Zeller by his sweat-stained shirt collar, but I didn't want to give him an excuse to toss me in a jail cell.

"Thanks for your help, Les. Keep up the good work."

Les nodded, expecting me to say more. I turned and walked out.

Kelly followed me out to the parking lot. "All right, you made your point," she said.

I opened the passenger side door for her. "What?" I pretended innocence.

"You wanted to cold-cock him. Why'd you let it go?"

"I'm trying to turn over a new leaf. Les isn't a bad guy or a bad cop. He's just a dumbass."

CHAPTER THIRTY-THREE

I drove back to the ranch, mulling over the reality that reaching out to Detective Ochoa and Zeller had been a waste of time. Neither one was going to do Maya any good. The law enforcement arm of the legal system worked great once a crime had been committed. Every cop I knew had his favorite story of tracking down the bad guy and taking him off the streets, but only after a crime had been committed. The heroics always came on the heels of a dead body or stolen property. I admired their hard work and dedication, but Maya needed an intervention.

There was a science fiction movie about a police division called pre-crime. The officers got information about a future crime from a trio of vegetative humans who lived in a pool of water in the basement of the headquarters building. The unit was shut down in the end because there was a flaw in the system. Humans have free will. We can choose to do something else besides commit a crime. That may be true on a theoretical level, and it made a good premise for a sci-fi movie, but the guy called Dragon had committed crimes in the past and was going to commit more crimes in the future. I didn't need three vegetable soothsayers to tell me that. If Maya stayed with Russell Stevens, her life would be over before it had a chance to begin.

Kelly got out and opened the ranch gate. A pair of mallard ducks enjoying the afternoon in the spring-fed pond lifted off and circled the house before continuing their migration south ahead of the next norther.

I thought about Sam and remembered I'd asked Helmut to take him for a few days. Maybe I would regret kicking Helen out. With winter coming on and work in San Antonio seventy miles away, I would need to sell the livestock or hire someone to feed.

Kelly interrupted my train of thought. "You're not completely healed."

She was going to try one last-ditch effort to persuade me to let someone else go after Russell Stevens. "I can't let it go. I tried it your way. You heard what Ochoa and Zeller said. No one is going after Maya."

"I just wish it didn't have to be you."

"If I don't, Helmut will. You said yourself Russell would kill him."

"What if he kills you?"

I didn't have an answer. I didn't want to think about that possibility. We got out and made our way into the house. The evening temperature was already forty-five and dropping quickly. It would get down in the thirties and more than likely freeze before sunrise. I turned on the lights. Blood had soaked through the bandage and the wad of paper towels Kelly had tucked under my shirt.

"Will you at least give this hole in your chest a few more days to heal?" She helped me off with my shirt and guided me to a kitchen chair while she stripped the blood-crusted bandage from my chest.

"There's no time. Russell knows I'm after Maya. He'll have to move her. If he does, I'll never find her. I have to come up with a plan to at least slow him down."

She took a bottle of rubbing alcohol and used a dish towel to clean my wound. The skin was red and felt hot and sore.

"Your mother could land a punch on your chest, and you'd go down." She tapped my chest, and I winced in pain. "See?" she said, satisfied she'd made her point. She put the bloody towel in the sink and washed her hands with dish soap.

"I think you're givin' Helen too much credit."

"You know what I mean. Don't try to joke your way out of this." She applied a new gauze patch.

I got up from the table and admired her handiwork in the round mirror over the coat rack. "You do good work."

She stood behind me and wrapped her arms around my waist. Her hands were warm from the hot water. "It feels like you're being deployed," she said, pressing her face into the center of my back.

"Maya deserves another chance." I felt her breath on my skin.

"Even if she doesn't want one?"

I turned to face her. She knew my answer. A tear formed in the corner of her eye. I kissed her and held her tight against me, wondering if it was for the last time.

"What if—" she started to say, but I cut her off. She didn't have to say it.

"You've been deployed. You've seen combat. You know what happens if you start thinkin' about the bullet that missed. You can't *what if* or you'll go crazy with fear and freeze up so you can't act. Right now, I need to act." I didn't tell her I was fighting my own fear. The bloody bandage only emphasized my self-doubt.

My phone rang. The caller ID showed Skeeter. Kelly read it and turned away. She couldn't hide the disappointment.

"What took you so long?" I said to Skeeter.

"You always underestimate the difficulty of what I do," he said.

"Come on, you're sittin' on your ass hacking computers. How hard could it be?"

"If it was that easy, you'd be doin' it for yourself."

"Fair enough. I made you a full partner. What more do you want?"

"How 'bout an actual paycheck?"

"I told you Helmut's paying in meat. I'll put your portion in my freezer. You can pick it up later. Tell me what you got?"

"Mr. Dragon's an entrepreneur."

"That mean you found his contacts?"

"That's what it mean, boss. Is Kelly there, or did you run her off?"

I put the phone on speaker. "She's right here."

"Hi, Clarence," she said without enthusiasm.

"What's wrong?" he asked.

"I'm going back to Lubbock. You boys are on your own."

"He's a rough one."

She laughed, but there was no joy in it. "He's one of a kind, that's for sure."

"Keep in touch," Skeeter said.

"I will. Good luck. Try to keep him safe. He won't listen to me." She went upstairs to gather her stuff and pack her duffel bag.

I took the phone off speaker and listened to Skeeter's report. As he talked, a plan started to form that I hoped would rattle Russell's chain enough for him to want to give up Maya or at least keep him in town long enough for me to locate her.

Kelly came back downstairs, and I followed her out to her pickup.

"I'm going after—" I started to tell her the plan, but she cut me off.

"I don't want to know the details."

She climbed into her pickup, and I shut the door.

She started the engine and rolled down the window. "When it's over, give me a call. I'd like to know you're safe. I don't wanna read about you online."

CHAPTER THIRTY-FOUR

Lucky's boxing gym was located on the west side of San Antonio in a working-class neighborhood—a mixture of neglected track houses, auto shops, and tiny, one-room restaurants. I stopped at the taco truck I'd visited with Kelly and found Grandma still hard at work, standing on her wooden box behind a sizzling grill. She recognized me and flashed a toothless smile.

"*Buenos días,*" she said.

"*Tengo hambre,*" I said, hoping I'd nailed the accent.

She laughed and rubbed her stomach. At least she understood me. I didn't understand her rapid-fire Spanish reply, but I guessed it was something like, *You've come to the right place.*

"*Donde está su hijo?*" I asked, not seeing the younger man that was there before.

"*No hijo, nieto. La universidad,*" she said proudly. She was putting her grandson through college by dishing out tacos to hungry locals.

"*Muy bien,*" I said. "*Dos huevos y barbacoa.*"

She plopped a scoop of lard on the hot griddle and went to work cracking eggs in a plastic bowl with her right hand while she sliced the barbacoa with her left, movements she could make in her sleep. I gave her a five-dollar tip when she bagged my breakfast. Her eyes lit up. I was becoming a regular customer.

"*Cuidado. Viya con Dios,*" she said and crossed herself when she handed me the bag. A blessing and a meal from a street vendor. Maybe my luck was turning.

The gym was the anchor business for a strip mall that also housed a Mexican restaurant, a tattoo and massage parlor, and a Valero gas station. The two-story building once housed a furniture store. After Caesar Hernandez, aka "Lucky," retired from an impressive welterweight professional career, he invested his winnings in a boxing gym as a way of giving back to the community that had supported him throughout his career.

I found a parking space and tossed my empty taco wrapper and paper bag in the trash on my way through the front door. In the afternoon, after the local schools let out, the ground floor looked like a high school gym. Lucky let the kids work out for free as long as they showed him a report card each semester to prove they were in school and keeping up their grades. If they fell behind two report cards in a row, they were out. No questions asked. They would have to show meaningful progress and a note from the principal, who was one of Lucky's regulars, before he would let them back in. The mornings were reserved for serious training and guys like me who were trying to stay in shape, that is, paying customers. Before I took a bullet in the chest, I worked out three times a week. Lucky let me spar with his prospects when they needed a tune-up. I wasn't a natural boxer, but he liked the fact that I could take a punch.

Lucky's partner, Jerry Muth, aka "Sarge," had taken over the second floor. He was a retired Army Ranger who offered classes in mixed martial arts. The surge in wannabe tough guys who were watching MMA on TV thinking they should get in on the action proved profitable. Sarge was the quiet type who looked like Chuck Norris with a gray ponytail and could kick your ass before you knew he was pissed off. They were both pushing seventy but had stood beside me when four of Marcus Lopez's security thugs tried to take me out on the top steps of the gym. The fight'd lasted less than a minute. When it was over, and the four thugs lay groaning on the steps, Sarge and Lucky grinned like orphans at a Christmas party. I trusted them to have my back.

I found Lucky leaning on the center ring ropes watching two middleweights trade punches. When the bell rang to signal the end of the practice round, Lucky jumped down and shook my hand. "What you doin' here? Figured you was still recuperatin'?" He grinned, exposing his missing front teeth. He had two gold replacements, but he kept them in his pocket when he was at the gym or ready to fight.

"I'm workin'. Gotta pay the mortgage. You know how it is when you're the boss."

"I hear that. I got a sparring partner waitin' for you when you're ready."

"Maybe later. I need a workout."

He eyed me closely, sizing me up as if I were about to step into the ring. He didn't give away his assessment. He just nodded and went back to his middleweights. I changed in the locker room and set out to test my strength and see how close I was to fighting shape. I was going to rattle Russell Stevens's cage, and I didn't expect him to take it lying down. When it came down to a one-on-one fight, I wanted to know the odds. I needed my self-confidence back.

I did three sets of squats with three quarters of my max weight. By the last rep, my leg muscles were complaining loudly. I switched from weights to lunges and let the muscles scream a little louder. I was one of those guys who enjoyed the workout pain. It gave me a little more confidence that the muscles would be there when I needed them. The lower-body work wasn't what I was concerned about. The real question was the bullet wound in my chest. Kelly had proved it wasn't ready. The light tap she gave me caused me to flinch. Any fighter, and especially Mr. Dragon, would exploit that in a heartbeat.

After six rounds with the speedbag, I was feeling a little better about my capabilities. I checked under my shirt. The bandage was still in place and didn't show any sign of leaking. I switched to the heavy bag. I imagined Russell Stevens's face superimposed on the canvas. The more I thought about him, the harder my punches got. I slammed my fists into his mug with everything I had. My head moved with my shoulders and torso. My feet followed the rhythm, but my movements were rusty. I pushed myself harder. Each punch I landed sent reverberations up my arm and into my chest, reminding me how much time off I'd taken.

I tried to use the workout to clear my head and focus on the mission, find Maya and take out Russell Stevens, but my mind wandered to the aftermath. When I found her again and told her what Helmut said, would she still want to escape? I believed she wanted to be free. I believed she wanted a second chance. That's what kept me going. I didn't want this to end like Cynthia Ann Parker, after a twenty-four-year chase.

When Lucky tapped me on the shoulder, it took a full thirty seconds before I noticed he was behind me.

"You trainin' for a fight?" he called to me.

Finally, my head cleared and the image of Russell Stevens on the heavy canvas bag faded. Lucky had been watching me the whole time. He knew fighters and fighting better than most. He knew me and my fighting style and could tell when I was playing around and when I was focused on a specific opponent.

"You need some time in the ring. Let's see if you're ready." He gestured toward the center ring, where a big black guy in his early twenties was stretching and shadowboxing.

As soon as I stopped punching, my body ached all over. I looked at the fighter in the ring, then back at Lucky skeptically.

"I know what you're doin'. I've watched you work out here for three years. You're goin' after somebody and you wanna know if you can take it."

I couldn't hide anything from him. Working a bag was great for stress relief, to clear your head, and build confidence, but nothing took the place of stepping into the ring against an opponent who can punch back.

I nodded. "Let's do it."

Lucky knew fighters and fighting, and he knew me better than I gave him credit for. We didn't need to discuss it. I slipped on the headgear and switched to a pair of sixteen-ounce sparring gloves. The black kid was heavy, almost the same size and weight as Russell Stevens, and quick on his feet. He danced back and forth while I got ready and climbed into the ring. His hands were quick. He showed off a lethal jab/hook combination that had probably taken out a few opponents.

We met Lucky in the center of the ring and touched gloves.

"Nick Fischer, meet Darnell Green. He's trying out for a spot on my team."

We nodded at each other and grunted through our mouthguards.

Lucky turned to Darnell. "Mr. Fischer's got a fight coming up. He needs a little tune-up."

Darnell's face broke into a grin. He thought Lucky was joking. Lucky never joked. Not about fighting or boxing.

The bell rang, and Darnell came on fast. I blocked his first combination and landed a right hand to his left ear guard. It didn't faze him. He could take a punch. We stood toe-to-toe and traded several more combinations. I didn't have what Lucky would call "style." I usually planted my feet, blocked incoming punches, and waited for my opponent to drop his guard.

Darnell had style and footwork. He had more to prove and was definitely trying to show off for Lucky. He landed a good left to my chin that set me back on my heels. I countered with an overhand right that jolted his confidence. Until that punch, he had been thinking of me as an old man getting in a workout—he'd wanted to impress Lucky, but he didn't want to knock me out. After that punch, all bets were off.

By the end of the round, my legs were shaking, and my lungs were on fire—the result of two months of inactivity. I leaned against the ropes and noticed Darnell staring at my chest from across the ring. I looked down and saw blood leaking through my T-shirt. Lucky was beside me before I could grab a towel from the corner and cover it up. The bell rang to start the next round, but Lucky waved Darnell off.

"Enough for today," he said.

Darnell walked over to my corner. "You okay, man?" He looked concerned, like he'd hit me a little too hard.

"I'm good," I told him. "It's from an older wound."

Lucky stripped off my gloves, and I pulled my T-shirt over my head. The bandage had slipped down, and blood streamed from the broken scab. Lucky handed me a clean towel, and I pressed it against the wound to stem the flow.

Jerry Muth stepped into the ring. He'd come down from upstairs to watch my effort.

"You should probably take another month off," he said.

Both Jerry and Lucky helped me out of the ring to the main floor. "Whatever fight you got planned, you ain't ready," Lucky said.

"You know how it goes. Trouble don't wait until you're ready," I said. I checked the clock on the wall. It was almost time for Skeeter to show up. I started for the locker room, but Lucky and Sarge blocked my path.

"What kind of trouble you in?" Lucky asked.

I was reluctant to get them involved with Russell Stevens. They had proved that they were both tough fighters, but things were going to get western, and I didn't want to be responsible for them getting hurt or worse. I wasn't going to play games or give any warnings. The plan I had was strictly an S&D mission—search and destroy.

"Let's have it, jarhead," Sarge said. He was a retired Army master sergeant and had earned the right to call me jarhead.

"All right. Let me get cleaned up."

Lucky and Sarge were waiting for me when I got out of the shower. Lucky handed me a bottle of rubbing alcohol, a fresh gauze pad, and surgical tape. While they helped me dress the wound, I told them Maya's story starting with the party on the Pedernales River. By the time I got to the part about finding her in the trap house and her running away, Skeeter had joined us. He took the story from there while I finished getting dressed. He explained Russell Stevens's connection to the strip club and added his new findings. Russell was running drugs out of two used tire stores on the south side.

"I can't ask y'all to get involved," I said when I'd finished dressing.

"You don't have to," Sarge said. "That young girl's in danger. We're coming with you."

PART THREE

Up the Ante

"Bad men need nothing more to compass their ends, than that good men should look on and do nothing."

John Stuart Mill

CHAPTER THIRTY-FIVE

A persistent north wind kept the Tuesday afternoon sky clear and the temperature a crisp, dry fifty-four degrees. I wore a long sleave T-shirt over Wranglers and a University of Texas baseball cap. Skeeter took up the passenger seat in a sweatshirt large enough to cover a king-size bed. He hated the cold and would be perfectly happy to skip both the fall and winter seasons. Lucky sat behind me wearing his usual navy blue, polyester tracksuit. I'd never seen him wear anything else. He claimed he'd bought two dozen pair in the eighties and each one lasted a couple of years. I calculated he should be close to the last pair and wondered what he would buy for an upgrade. Sarge sat beside him. I usually saw him at the gym wearing his black jiu-jitsu pajamas that he called a "gi." When he stepped outside, he looked like a fit grandpa in jeans and a black T-shirt. What made him standout was his quiet, focused intensity. He'd spent twenty years as a special operator, and he wasn't someone to mess with.

After the near beating in Lucky's practice ring, I was happy to have them along. The hard punches the up and comer landed hadn't boosted my confidence. It only proved my body wasn't ready for what I had to do. For the fight against Russell Stevens, I would need luck and a prayer. And my .45. I would hit him where it hurt and keep going until I found Maya. My plan was simple—rattle Dragon's chain until he made a mistake, then nail him and take Maya back where she belonged.

I glanced at myself in the rearview mirror. Despite the workout, my skin was pale, and dark circles lingered under my eyes from lack of sleep. If death had a face, I thought, it would be mine. My eyes flicked back to the road, and I heard a voice that sounded like my grandpa whisper in my ear. *Faith*, he said. *Keep the faith*. The voice was so real that I glanced in the mirror again, but only Sarge and Lucky stared back at me. Grandpa wasn't there, but I felt his presence.

The first stop was the strip club. I circled the mostly empty parking lot. In the early afternoon, there were only two pickups and a city utility truck parked by the back door, out of sight of the street. I parked beside the black, jacked-up Dodge Ram pickup occupying the reserved space.

"At least there ain't much traffic," Skeeter said.

I nodded and drew my Springfield .45 from the leather shoulder holster, checked the magazine, and jacked a round into the chamber. The S&W .38 backup on my ankle was loaded, strapped on, and ready if I needed it. Skeeter pressed buckshot shells into the pistol-grip 870 shotgun. Of the four of us, he was the least prepared for this kind of operation.

"You can wait in the pickup," I said to him. Skeeter was a gridiron tough guy. He'd tipped the scales at over two hundred and fifty pounds since tenth grade and didn't get into many street fights. Nobody was crazy enough to mess with him. In his first brush with danger working for me, he'd left the shotgun on the pickup seat and stepped into the line of fire. He said he'd learned his lesson.

"I'm in," Skeeter said. "You made me a full partner, remember? Let's find Maya."

Sarge tucked a Glock 9mm in his waistband and he and Lucky followed us to the back door. I knew I didn't have to worry about either one of them. Lucky grew up on the mean streets across the border in Nuevo Laredo. He knew the kind of people we were dealing with. Sarge was like me, a combat veteran, trained to neutralize the enemy. We weren't here to negotiate a surrender or read anybody their rights. The time for negotiations had passed.

I opened the VIP entrance used by local celebrities, and we slipped into the darkness. Crates of wine and cases of beer covered the walls from floor to ceiling. An AC/DC song drifted through a curtain leading to the front room. I held up my hand. We all stopped and waited for our eyes to adjust to the darkness while *Back in Black* rattled the bottles.

"Follow my lead," I said, pulling my Springfield and stepping through the curtain. Only the main stage was occupied. A skinny dancer wearing an orange G-string and a long blond wig worked the chrome dance pole in a drug-fueled haze, trying to keep up with the guitar riffs.

The beefy bouncer with the shaved head slouched against the back wall watching the performance. He turned just in time to see the barrel of my Springfield approaching his left ear. He crumpled into a pile on the floor. The dancer kept humping chrome, oblivious. Her focus was on the greenbacks in the city worker's hand.

There was movement near the front entrance. I pointed in that direction. Sarge and Lucky took off. Skeeter followed me between the tables toward the bar. The bouncer with the neck tattoo glanced up. He dropped the beer he was holding and reached under the counter. I aimed my .45 between his eyes.

"Hands on the bar," I yelled over AC/DC.

Neck Tatt slowly put his hands on the bar. Skeeter sank onto a stool and pointed the 870 at the guy's chest.

"Be cool. Stay put and you won't get hurt," I told him.

His eyes focused on the barrel of the shotgun. A twelve gauge always looks bigger when it's pointing at you at short range.

"You fucked up, man," he said. He wasn't scared, but he respected Skeeter's weapon.

"You're gonna tell me where the Dragon is."

"He'll kill you."

"Maybe, but not before I do some damage. I know he's pimping girls. I know he's dealing drugs in here. He can't do that without your permission. You must have a really cozy relationship. How does it work? You need new meat on stage, you give him a call, and he shows up with the girls and passes out the candy? Is that it?"

Neck Tatt's eyes darted to the office door, like he expected someone to come out. The brass knob turned, and the door moved. I took a step and kicked the door just as Arnold Garza shoved his pistol through the opening. The gun exploded, sending a stab of flame into the dark room, followed by the young dancer's scream. The city workers scrambled for the door.

I brought the Springfield down hard on Arnold's wrist. His pistol dropped to the floor. I grabbed his hand and yanked him out the door. He went to his knees still wearing the blue velvet suit he'd had on when we first met. His hipster glasses flew to the carpet. I kicked him onto his back and fitted the barrel of my pistol over his pointy nose.

"Howdy, Arnold. Long time no see." The music suddenly stopped, and the house lights came on. Sarge and Skeeter had taken care of the other employees.

"What the fuck do you want?" Arnold spat. "I told you I'd never seen that girl."

"You lied. I found the girl I was lookin' for. Puff the Magic Dragon took her back. Where is he?"

"He'll kill you."

"So I've been told. I'm sure he'll want to. But I'm not that easy to kill."

"Fuck you."

I holstered my pistol, grabbed Arnold by the velvet jacket, and hauled him to his feet. The surprise and initial fear on his face turned to anger and contempt.

"I'm sending a message to anybody who does business with Russell Stevens."

"We got rights, man. You can't come in here and jack with us," he said.

He'd either heard that line in a movie or it had worked for him before, because he smiled when he said it like he was holding up a magic shield.

"You want me to honor your rights?" I picked up his glasses and handed them to him. "Put these on. I don't want you to miss anything." I took the 870 from Skeeter, pointed it at the mirror behind the bar, and pulled the trigger. Glass showered down like confetti on Neck Tatt's head and shoulders.

"You're fuckin' crazy, man?" Arnold screamed.

"You gave up your rights when you shook hands with Russell Stevens."

I pumped another shell in the chamber, pointed at the liquor shelf, and pulled the trigger. Another shower of glass mixed with spirits rained down on the bar. I pumped the action again. Boom! The mirror behind the stage shattered.

"Okay, okay! What do you want?" Arnold pleaded.

Sarge and Lucky pushed the two bouncers from the front door into the room. Sarge had them covered with his Glock. The bald guy I'd clocked near the back entrance stirred and started to stand. Lucky stepped in front of him.

"Stay down," Lucky said.

The guy should have listened. Instead, he lunged forward and caught an uppercut from Lucky that put him down for the count. The old boxer still packed a mean punch.

"I want Maya," I shouted, jacking another round in the chamber.

"She ain't here, man. I told you that," Arnold said.

Boom!

I took out the mirror behind the second stage. At the very least, it would take them a couple of days to clean up before they could open again. The owner of the club would get the clear message that dealing with Russell Stevens was bad for business.

Boom!

I put another load in the bar. More screaming came from the dancers' dressing room. There was more than one girl back there. I motioned for Lucky to check it out in case there was another bouncer not accounted for. Arnold hopped from one foot to the other. He wasn't sure what I was going to do next. It was the reaction I was looking for.

"Tell Russell to give up Maya or I'll keep going. I know his business contacts, and I won't stop till they're all shut down."

"He won't listen to me, man," he said.

"In that case, I don't need you anymore." I shoved the barrel of the 870 into his chest. Arnold fell backward on the floor. I called to Skeeter: "How many shells does this model 870 shotgun hold?"

"The model 870 express tactical pump shotgun packs a full seven rounds of three-inch 12-gauge firepower with the factory installed two-shot extension," Skeeter recited. He'd memorized the manual when I gave him the weapon.

I looked at the manager. "Seven rounds. Did you keep count?" I pressed the barrel under his chin.

"Okay, man. Don't do it. I'll talk to him."

There was fear in his eyes. I was getting through to him.

"Russell knows my number. Tell him I'm waiting for his call."

I pointed the 870 at the ceiling and pulled the trigger. The pistol grip jerked in my hand, sending a load of buckshot into the ceiling and showering us both with drywall plaster.

"I must have lost count," I said.

A dark wet stain expanded around the crotch of his velvet suit.

Lucky walked out of the dressing room. "All clear."

"We're done here." I handed Skeeter the 870 and walked toward the VIP entrance.

CHAPTER THIRTY-SIX

I backed across the Club Forty-Four parking lot toward my pickup, keeping my Springfield level with the strip club VIP door. Once the initial fear wore off, Arnold would come after me. He couldn't afford to let someone get away with what I'd done to the club. The repairs would come out of his pocket. He wouldn't call the police. He had too much to lose if law and order took a closer look at his operation. I opened my pickup door, found my cheap sunglasses on the dashboard, and slipped them on to cut the harsh afternoon glare. I waited while Lucky and Sarge climbed into the back and Skeeter settled into the passenger seat.

"Wait," Skeeter said. He opened the small black backpack he was never without and took out a black box about the size of a USB wall adaptor. "GPS tracker. In case they come after us or go visit Russell," he explained.

Skeeter fitted the device under the rear bumper of the 4x4 parked in the reserved space and jumped back into the passenger seat. I checked my watch. It was almost five o'clock.

"You don't mess around," Lucky said.

"Thanks for your help," I said.

"You didn't really need us," Sarge said. "But it was fun."

I checked the rearview mirror. Sarge had a smile on his face. The only other time I'd seen him smile was after he and Lucky kicked ass on the four thugs who were after me in the gym.

Skeeter booted up his laptop and checked the connection to the GPS. "We should have a heads-up if Arnold comes to visit. Maybe he'll lead us to Russell Stevens and Maya."

I drove out of the parking lot. "Now that we got the Dragon's attention, it won't be as easy the next time."

"Next time?" Lucky said. "You're gonna keep going?"

"You don't think he'll hand Maya over?" Skeeter asked.

"He'll do what Low Ball did," I said.

"Come after you?"

"Who's Low Ball?" Lucky asked.

"The dude who framed me for murder," Skeeter said.

"That apartment fire on the east side? I remember that," Sarge said.

"Nick saved my ass."

"What happened to Low Ball?" Lucky asked.

"Things got western, as my brother Nick would say. The dude was dealing, had a cozy setup that his rival was cuttin' in on, which is why he took out the apartment. I was supposed to be the fall guy 'cause I'd played ball with the would-be rival. I knew he was dealing, but the dude had been a pretty good cornerback at Texas, man. We were teammates, so I let it go. Big mistake. The fire started in his apartment, and I was the last one to see him, so the cops nailed me for the crime. Nick started shutting down Low Ball's dealers first, then found his stash house and went after the supplier. It didn't take long for the capo boss to turn on Low Ball. Nick offered him a deal. Low Ball confessed the next day."

"What was the deal?" Lucky asked.

I laughed. "I made him an offer he couldn't refuse."

"Maybe the same guy's pullin' the Dragon's chain?" Sarge said.

"No, the cartel took over supply and distribution in San Antonio. They're harder to negotiate with."

Lucky leaned over the back seat and pointed to the damp spot on my chest. Blood had soaked my T-shirt. In all the excitement, I hadn't noticed that the bandage had come loose, and the scab had broken open again.

"You need more than a different tactic. Maybe you should skip town for a few days," Lucky said. "That Dragon dude knows you mean business. Wait for him to make contact."

Skeeter handed me a paper towel. "That sounds like the voice of reason."

Now that the adrenaline rush was wearing off, the muscles in my chest were on fire, and my head was spinning slightly off balance. "One problem. Russell Stevens already killed Lori and Candy. Nothing is stopping him from finishing off Maya. This time we won't find the body."

I took the towel from Skeeter and pressed it over the wet spot on my T-shirt. I had to keep it together until this was over. I drove under the 410 Loop and went south on San Pedro hoping to avoid rush-hour traffic. No such luck. San Antonio suffered from traffic as much as any big city. It wasn't as bad as Houston or Austin, but that was hardly any consolation.

It was past six when I parked across the street from the two-story house where we'd found Maya. I shut the engine off and checked my phone. No missed calls or messages from Russell. I wasn't surprised. He would expect me to back off now and wait for his call. He'd send his thugs to my house in King William. My only concern was my neighbor Rose. If she happened to see someone on my property, she wouldn't hesitate to confront them. They wouldn't hesitate to kill her.

"Looks like they stepped up security," I said, looking at an overfed gangbanger lounging on the front steps. He had a black silk do-rag and a thin wife-beater T-shirt despite the cooler weather.

"He'll be packing," Lucky said.

"Noted," I said. I knew Wife-Beater would have a pistol stuck in his shorts. I didn't think he could get to it in time to protect himself. Several rolls of fat obscured his waistband. I pointed out the staircase that led to the upstairs and sent Lucky and Sarge through the alley. I hoped the occupants hadn't added another lock. I was counting on the element of surprise.

Skeeter reloaded the 870. I waited until I thought Lucky and Sarge had had enough time to climb the back steps, then stepped into the street. Skeeter followed me across the dirt lawn strewn with fast-food wrappers and cigarette butts. I could hear the staccato rap music coming from inside the house. As far as I could tell, it was the same song that was playing the last time I was here. I was sure Skeeter would disagree, so I didn't ask him. I picked up a three-foot length of galvanized metal pipe lying in the neglected flower garden. There wasn't any point in wasting ammo.

Wife-Beater shifted his massive weight forward but didn't get up. He probably weighed in at three eighty and, like all fat tough guys, expected his size to scare people away. I stopped six inches from his black LeBron Nike basketball shoes. They were new and expensive and had never seen a basketball court.

"I'll take a half pound of crank and a couple of underage girls for me and my friend," I said. "Make it to-go. This place stinks, and I'm in a hurry."

He smiled big, stretching the size of his double chin into a full dewlap. He looked like a bulldog waiting for supper. "I know you, *guero*," he said.

"I'm flattered," I said, and hit him in the head with the metal pipe.

"You are a man of few words," Skeeter said.

Wife-Beater slumped forward, a trickle of blood oozing from the edge of his silk do-rag.

"I love good conversation," I said, walking to the front door.

The same three punks were on the couch, playing the same video game, as we came through the front door. I pulled my Springfield and fired at the fifty-inch screen. The TV exploded in a shower of glass and plastic. They flew off the couch like a covey of quail.

The thug nearest Skeeter pulled a pistol from his waistband. Skeeter hit him in the side of the head with the barrel of the shotgun. He dropped the pistol and collapsed on the floor.

I leveled off on the other two. One of them held a pistol pointed at the floor.

"Drop it," I yelled. He let it fall to the floor. "Cover them," I said to Skeeter, then kicked in the door to the back room. A wafer-thin Hispanic woman wearing a black bra and panties was scooping stacks of money into a plastic garbage bag. She ignored me as if she saw men with guns break in the room every day and kept working while I searched the room. There were four kilo bags of meth or coke on a shelf behind her. She'd been mixing and filling smaller plastic bags for sale. I didn't stop to analyze it.

"*Qué pasa?*" she asked, not the least bit self-conscious of being seen in her underwear. Her eyes were glassy and bloodshot like she'd been sampling the product or just inhaling the fumes.

"Just keep working," I said. "Fill up the sack."

She tossed in the rest of the money.

"Throw in the drugs too," I said.

When she was finished, I motioned her toward the front room. Her face showed contempt, but she complied.

The stairs creaked, and three women hustled down the wooden steps followed by Sarge and Lucky. One was in her mid-forties with dyed-blond hair and a Disney World tank top that didn't quite cover her jelly rolls. I guessed she was the house mother for the younger girls. Her face was twisted into an angry scowl.

"You ain't cops," she shouted at me. "You can't come in here."

"All clear," Sarge said.

"Check the kitchen," I said.

He disappeared through a swinging door.

"You hear me? You don't have a warrant. You can't come up in here. We got rights," the big woman screamed. She'd seen the same movie as the strip club manager.

"What about them?" I pointed to the young girls. "Who's protecting their rights?"

"We do business here. Ain't nobody gettin' hurt. They wanna be here."

"I'll bet they do."

Sarge reappeared. "All clear."

"We're done here. Everybody out." I heard a commotion on the porch. The door burst open, and Wife-Beater came through with a 9mm in his hand.

I fired first, hitting him in the left leg. The .45 slug splattered blood on the wall. Wife-Beater screamed and did an elephant faceplant on the hardwood floor.

"Everybody out," I yelled again. "Take fatso with you."

The thug Skeeter cold-cocked came to and staggered out the front door. His two companions helped Wife-Beater to his feet. I took a closer look. The bullet had grazed his outer thigh, missing the artery. He would live. I didn't want to leave any bodies lying around.

House Mamma screamed. Her whole body shook. No words came from her mouth, just a wail that sounded like a coyote caught in a leg-hold trap.

I found a lighter on the coffee table. The house was a late 1940s vintage wood-frame construction. It would go up in smoke like a stack of last year's hay. I fired the lighter and held it to a couch cushion. When it caught fire, I tossed the cushion into the kitchen and grabbed another. By the time I walked out on the porch, smoke was already billowing from the front windows.

"What're we supposed to do?" House Mamma screamed.

"Find a job that doesn't involve drugs or underage girls," I said. She wasn't going to convince me she was a victim. I dialed 911. The local fire department had a great response time and would have this fire out before it did damage to the neighborhood.

We hustled back to my pickup. The neighbor's dogs barked. An older couple across the street came out on their lawn. "It's about time," the older woman yelled. "Those people are a blight on the neighborhood."

House Mamma held up her middle finger.

"You're a disgrace," the man yelled.

The two younger girls had dark skin and long hair. They both looked dazed and confused, no doubt high on something. I led them and the woman in her underwear across the street to the older neighbor. "I called 911. Help will be here soon. Can you see to them until they get here?"

The woman didn't hesitate. She led the girls inside her house. With as much depravity as I'd witnessed lately, it was refreshing to see an act of kindness directed at complete strangers.

CHAPTER THIRTY-SEVEN

We passed the first firetruck speeding toward the blaze as I turned onto Zarzamora Street. Russell'd get my message. Now he knew how I played the game and what the stakes were. I also had a bargaining chip—a plastic sack with his money and drugs resting in the bed of my pickup.

His next move would be to retaliate. I didn't expect him to give up or turn Maya over. I wanted him pissed off enough to make a mistake, to give up his location or challenge me himself. That's when I would nail him. Thugs like him were used to fighting other thugs in rival gangs whose only tactic was a drive-by or a full-frontal attack. I was adapting my military training in urban warfare, using intel, hitting secondary targets to weaken his ability to fight back, and, maybe most importantly, cause his cartel bosses to doubt his ability to do business. That would be the Dragon's bane. Neither he nor his associates could go to the cops, and I hoped I could stay one step ahead of Detective Ochoa until I had Maya safely back in Fredericksburg.

For my next move, I wanted to be alone. Although I welcomed the backup from Skeeter, Lucky, and Sarge, I could move faster when I didn't have to explain my actions to a larger team. Besides, now that the ball was rolling, I couldn't risk their safety. As I drove, I explained to Sarge and Lucky my plan of attack. They didn't like it, but when I told them that Rose was in danger and that she was an excellent cook, they agreed to stay and guard both our houses.

The setting sun shot streaks of pink and orange over the green canopy covering the city. On a normal day, I would be scouting the ranch for deer in preparation for the season opener. Evenings and early mornings were the perfect time to keep an eye on the game trails for potential trophies. Over the last several years, a small herd of Axis deer had taken up residence in the steep back pasture. They're bigger than the native whitetail with white spots and a large three-point rack of antlers. They were imported from India in the thirties by private game farms, and now, like feral hogs, roamed free over large portions of Central and South Texas. Being non-native, like feral hogs, they could be hunted year-round. But I was old-school and preferred to wait until the weather turned cooler, which created better conditions for processing the meat.

Rose appeared in her kitchen window when I pulled into the driveway. I waved. Involving her in my plan was unavoidable. She wouldn't leave town even if I asked her.

"I'll let Rose know what's going on," I told them. "Skeeter will show you the gun safe. Pick out what you're comfortable with and double the ammo you think you'll need."

"You think he'll hit us here?" Sarge asked.

"He'll want to even the score. It's the only thing he knows how to do."

Sarge smiled again. The second time in two days.

Rose met me in the front yard. Her gray hair, as usual, was braided and wound in tight coils, like a Viking queen welcoming the fleet home from Britain. "I trust you've gotten yourself into a pickle," she said, nodding toward Sarge and Lucky.

"Nothing I can't handle."

"Where's Kelly?"

"She went back to Lubbock."

She waited for me to fill in the details, but I stayed silent.

"I wondered how long that would last. You're a hard man to get along with."

I explained briefly that we'd not been able to find Maya and that I was taking things in a different direction than Kelly was comfortable with. “There may be trouble.”

She pointed a boney finger at me. “You’re the trouble.”

“I do what I do best. I didn’t ask her to leave.”

She pinned my ears back with a withering professor stare. “Of course not. But I don’t blame her for going. You’re about as friendly as a ground hornet when you’re working a case.”

“It’s better that she’s not mixed up in what I have to do.”

“I know you better than you think, Nick Fischer. Once you’re on a case, nothing and no one gets in your way. Girlfriends, friends, the law… nothing. If I wanted answers or justice, I would come to you in a heartbeat. I know you won’t stop till you get one or the other. But if I were looking for a husband, I’d drop you like a red-hot coal.”

“So there’s no hope for us?” I asked.

That brought a twinkle to her eye. “You’ve got issues, Nick Fischer. God help you; you’ve got issues. One of these days, you’re going to have to face that fact. And no. You’re a dog man and I like cats. It would never work out between us.”

“You do know how to break a man’s heart.”

She rewarded me with a smile. She still had her Swedish good looks, and I imagined the freshmen in her classes jostling for a front row seat in her class.

I explained that Sarge and Lucky were going to stay in my house just in case the thugs I was after showed up wanting to wreak havoc. I asked her to help by keeping an eye on the neighborhood from inside her house and by cooking some Swedish quiche.

“I can do more than that. You know I keep my dad’s revolver in the kitchen drawer, and I’ve got my shotgun,” she said.

She loved to mention her weapons. The revolver was a .38 Special police model that her dad purchased in the thirties, and the shotgun was a Stevens model 520 from the same era. She kept them well-oiled and loaded, but she hadn’t fired either in forty years.

“I know you can protect yourself. But let Lucky and Sarge do any shooting if it’s necessary. They have newer weapons and more practice.”

"What about the police?" she asked.

"What about them?"

"Shouldn't they be involved?"

"They will be. But right now, they would slow me down. A young girl's life's at stake."

She clenched her jaw like she was going to protest, before slowly nodding in agreement. "Be careful, Nick. I have a bad feeling about this." She whirled around without waiting for a response and hurried toward her back door. She was excited to be in on the action. I just hoped she'd stay out of the line of fire if Russell Stevens or his gang attacked the house.

Sarge and Lucky took inventory of my arsenal. Skeeter had been living at my place while I was recuperating at the ranch, and I'd given him the combo to my gun safe so he could bring me ammo and a spare pistol. Sarge looked like a kid in a candy store.

"We can hold off a small army with this stuff," Sarge said, inspecting an AR-10. I had a dozen spare twenty-round magazines and enough ammo to fill them all a few times over. I told them Rose would stop by with supper. If she didn't, I asked Sarge to check on her. I didn't want to take any chances.

Skeeter was sitting at the kitchen table, glued to his laptop. "That Dodge Ram from the strip club is on the move."

"Headed our way?"

"Not at the moment."

I popped open a Red Bull and watched Sarge field-strip the AR, wipe it down, then reassemble and load it with a full twenty-round clip in less than two minutes. He was an ex-special operator with a warrior's skill set that hadn't diminished with age.

"You gonna wait for Russell to call?" Skeeter asked.

I took another drink, then checked my phone. No messages. It was eight thirty and full dark outside. "That's what he expects me to do. But he won't call."

"You're goin' after him," Skeeter said. It wasn't a question. He knew me too well.

I nodded. "Send me the addresses for his tire shops. Stevens has friends in low places. Aside from his network in San Antonio, he's got cartel connections. If I wait for him to respond, it'll give him time to call for reinforcements and put a band of nasty players on the ground."

I grabbed an AR-15 from the safe. I had another AR-10, but the 15 was smaller and better suited for close combat work. The AR-15 came with a Surefire suppressor, and the reduction of noise might come in handy. It could also take a thirty-round clip in case I needed more firepower. I loaded the rifle, extra magazines, and two spare boxes of .223 ammo in a black duffel bag. The last thing I tossed in was a Mossberg shotgun.

"Stay in contact. I wanna know if they come to the house." Skeeter, Lucky, and Sarge watched me pull on a Kevlar bulletproof vest, then cover it with a button-down shirt.

"Happy hunting," Sarge said as I walked out the door.

CHAPTER THIRTY-EIGHT

The tire shop Skeeter linked to Russell Stevens's criminal enterprise was located past the Air Force base on I-90 in southwest San Antonio. It wasn't the kind of place you'd take the family minivan to have a flat fixed. There were old tires stacked outside, piles of trash mixed into the weeds, and dead grass along the base of the neglected chain-link fence. The building used to be a gas station, but the pumps had been removed and sealed with metal covers. A new Coke machine guarded the front door and seemed to be the only functioning equipment on the lot.

I parked behind the stack of used tires and looked for signs of life. A vintage Chevy Impala in car-show condition sat in front of the service garage, as if waiting in a time warp for a bow tie attendant to top off the tank and check the tires. It had a deep purple paint job, and the elevated frontend exposed a lowrider hydraulic lift package. Across the parking lot stood an abandoned mom-and-pop Mexican food restaurant that had served its last meal in the nineties. Beyond that was a pawnshop featuring a sign that welcomed active-duty military. They were already advertising a Veteran's Day sale. It was no accident that Mr. Dragon set up near a military installation. Every base I'd ever been stationed at had scum just like him who preyed on young servicemembers looking for an escape from the long duty hours and lonely downtime while they were miles away from home.

A late-model Chevy Tahoe with a base parking sticker pulled in beside the Impala. The driver hit the car horn twice in short staccato fashion. The driver looked young, eighteen or nineteen, with a bootcamp high-and-tight haircut and a baby-smooth face. Two identical young men sat in the back seat.

The front door of the station opened. A man in his mid-twenties appeared. He was not much older than the airmen in the Tahoe. He was white with an array of tatts on his neck and full sleeves on both arms. He wore red high-top basketball shoes and a black silk do-rag that hung to his shoulders. His jean shorts sagged below his waist, cinched there by a white cotton belt. The kid was a *GQ* fashion icon.

He glanced up and down the mostly empty feeder road, then walked to the passenger side of the Tahoe. I couldn't see the exchange, but I didn't have to guess what was going on. Within minutes, the Tahoe sped away, and GQ shuffled back inside the garage with a stiff-legged stride designed to keep his shorts from falling down. I waited a few more minutes to see if there would be any more traffic. The wind blew trash and plastic bags across the parking lot and into the bar ditch beside the highway. I listened to a dog bark from a kennel beside the pawnshop and watched a goliath C-5M Super Galaxy aircraft descend toward a Lackland AFB runway like a giant lazy blimp.

I scanned the roof and light poles for video cameras. Nothing caught my eye. Loud rap music with unintelligible lyrics blared from the garage. I guessed the men inside weren't trained operators, but sometimes those were the most dangerous. They made random moves that didn't make military tactical sense, which in a longer battle would get them killed, but in the short term could be lethal.

I circled the building and searched the plywood-covered windows for an opening and found a hole in the back window large enough to see into the garage. Stacks of boxes took up most of the space. This place hadn't seen a tire customer for a long time. GQ and his twin were lounging in the corner watching a porn video. Both wore the same T-shirt and black-silk do-rag like a uniform. An older thug wearing designer jeans with sequin pockets walked out of the restroom zipping his fly. His skin was dark, and there was a Glock tucked behind his back. He opened a beer and stood behind the younger men staring at a naked woman with impossibly large breasts on the widescreen TV.

I found a length of rusty chain and hooked it gently around the handles of the back double doors, blocking their escape. Then I circled back to the front entrance. It was a shame to trash such a sleek ride, but I knew how they paid for it and didn't feel guilty. I took a gas can from my pickup bed and sloshed fuel on the plastic upholstery. The rush of fumes was overpowering. I jumped back several paces and tossed a lit match. The explosion was instantaneous, hitting me with a blast of superheated air and singeing the hair on the back of my hand. I retreated behind the stack of old tires and pulled out my Mossberg shotgun.

The fire quickly engulfed the Impala. Tongues of flame licked the rusty service station overhang. I waited for the heat or the noise from the fire to get their attention. I didn't have to wait long. In a few minutes, the door sprang open. A hand holding a chrome-plated pistol appeared. Flame spit from the barrel. Shots rang out over the roar of the fire. The pistol bucked four more times, randomly blasting the night air.

A voice shouted: "Who's out there?"

"I'm looking for Russell Stevens!"

The pistol bucked again, this time in my general direction. The bullets made hollow plunking sounds hitting the old steel-belted radials. GQ appeared in the doorway, his pistol level.

I pulled the trigger. The shotgun blast hit him in the chest. Blood spread quickly across his white T-shirt before he collapsed on the driveway.

"Where's Russell?" I shouted.

Two hands grabbed GQ and pulled him back inside.

"Fuck you!" someone shouted. The barrel of a rifle appeared. They were upping the ante. A pistol couldn't penetrate the tires from that distance, but a .223 or a .308 might.

I fired the Mossberg at the door.

"Don't shoot, man. I'm coming out!" a voice shouted.

GQ's twin dove through the open door and landed on his stomach, firing the AR-15 blindly in my direction. The bullets cut through the tires and hit the side of my pickup.

I pulled the trigger on the shotgun.

The twin screamed in pain. He rolled onto his back and put his hands in the air. "You fucking shot me!"

This guy was a genius. "Toss the weapon."

He dropped the AR and rolled away from the fire.

"I'm coming out!" the older voice shouted from behind the door. A hand appeared holding a Glock pistol. "I'm coming out. Don't shoot." The hand tossed the pistol. The weapon clattered on the concrete driveway. The car fire roared like a jet engine.

The man with the designer jeans walked out with his hands up. He had shoulder-length dark hair and enough lines on his face to be in his late thirties or early forties.

"Get down on your knees," I yelled.

"The car's gonna explode, man!"

"I'm hit. Help me," GQ yelled to the older man, but he ignored him.

I walked forward, keeping the shotgun level with the older thug's waist. "Where's Russell Stevens?"

"He don't check in with us, man."

"Down on your knees," I yelled.

He got down on his knees, turning his face away from the flames. "Who're you, *pendejo*? What d'you want?"

Something popped over the roar of the fire. The purple paint bubbled, and the upholstery gave off a thick black smoke. The fire jumped to the plywood covering the garage door. I took another step forward, squinting into the smoke and intense heat.

"There's money inside. Let me go. I'll get you twenty grand," he begged.

"Where does the money go? Who collects it?"

"Come on, man. Dragon will kill me."

"You think I give a shit? I know you sell to the kids on base."

"It's just business. I'm trying to make a living."

I pressed the Mossberg into his forehead. "Who picks up the money?" I repeated. "Tell me and I'll let you go."

He glanced at the burning car. Sweat poured down his face.

"Tell him, Luis," GQ kid yelled. "Get me outta here!" He tried to drag himself away from the flames.

"Leo. Leo the accountant," Luis said.

"Where can I find him?"

"A pawnshop on Culebra."

An explosion rocked the Impala, sending sparks flying in all directions. The man jumped to his feet. His right hand went behind his back.

I pulled the trigger. Boom! The shotgun blast hit him in the legs, forcing him backward into the flames. He screamed and dropped the pistol.

I ran to my pickup. Sirens raced toward the scene. Red flashing emergency lights appeared on the I-90 freeway. I grabbed a blanket from behind the seat and ran back to the flames. I threw the blanket over the man and pulled him out of the fire. I grabbed GQ next and dragged him to safety. They would live but would always remember what happened.

"I'm Nick Fischer," I said. "Tell Russell Stevens what happened here. Tell him I'll keep going until he gives up Maya Chavez."

CHAPTER THIRTY-NINE

I parked on the corner of my street in the King William neighborhood, five houses down from my place. The wind had stopped, and the dormant trees seemed to be anticipating trouble. I spent fifteen minutes studying the street activity, looking for anything out of place. I was under no illusions that Russell Stevens would suddenly do the right thing. He had shaken hands with the devil when he killed his stepfather and never looked back. I suspected he killed Cindy and Lori, and he would kill me in a heartbeat. He didn't play by the same rules as everybody else. To get Maya back, I had to think like him.

I approached my front door with my hands in plain sight. Sarge or Lucky would be waiting and watching. I heard the door lock click open. Sarge greeted me holding the AR-10 at the high ready. He had on a black long-sleeve T-shirt, a black watch cap, and looked like he ate sixteen-penny nails for breakfast.

"Any trouble?" I asked. The aroma of fresh-cooked meat and gravy mixed with gun oil filled the room.

"Skeeter tracked the manager's pickup. It cruised past the house about two hours ago. We had the lights off. He didn't stop," Sarge said.

"How was the pot roast?" I recognized the smell.

Sarge chuckled. "Rose is a good cook. We left you a plate in the fridge, unless Skeeter ate it. He can put away some food."

"He needs a lot of fuel to keep him goin'."

"You smell like smoke."

"I had a bonfire. The tire shop was a front for his drug operation. I shut it down."

"Still no word from the man?"

"Nothing." I walked around the bar and into the light from the kitchen.

"You don't look too good."

"I just need some pot roast and a few hours' sleep." I found the plate of food where Rose had left it in the fridge covered in foil. There was a thick slice of beef smothered in gravy with new potatoes and carrots on the side. The smell reminded me of living with my grandparents on the ranch. Every meal included meat. Grandma served beef from our herd. Wild game like goose, turkey, and duck were part of every holiday, and she served deer throughout the year for variety. Grandpa contributed wild game sausage made from the Fischer family recipe perfected over five generations.

After I polished off the pot roast, I rinsed the plate in the sink and trudged upstairs. I was bone tired, and it felt good to strip off the bloody T-shirt and rinse the wound on my chest. I taped a new gauze pad in place and stumbled onto my mattress. The faint scent of Kelly's lavender shampoo and peppery perfume lingered on the pillow. I missed her. I couldn't deny it. I hadn't wanted her to go. Why couldn't I have stopped her? I played back the events that took place before she left. I realized that she had been waiting for me to ask her to stay. Why didn't I put my arms around her and say the words?

When my phone buzzed, I hoped it was Kelly, but the caller ID showed Detective Ochoa. The wrong woman. I thought of ignoring her but decided she might have word of Maya.

"Tell me again why I shouldn't arrest you?" she asked. Her voice sounded angry.

"Good to hear from you, Detective."

"Don't give me any of your shit, Fischer. I've got calls from all over town about a crazy man that fits your description raising bloody hell."

"I've been home all evening."

"Bullshit. So you're a vigilante now? Where do you get off shooting up strip clubs and burning down gas stations? When I arrest you, your ex-girlfriend will easily convince her boss at the DA's office to have your license revoked."

"All those businesses you mentioned are related to Russell Stevens. If you don't know that, you're not doing your job."

"I am doing my job, which is why I'm calling you in the middle of the night. If you happened to find Mr. Stevens with his hand on a kilo of meth, I couldn't file charges. It wouldn't stand up in court. He would walk free. Even people you think are guilty have rights. Did you forget that?"

"I don't give a damn about your case against Russell Stevens. All I care about is getting Maya Chavez home safe. But I will make a deal with you. Give me forty-eight hours and I'll bring you enough legitimate evidence to put Russell Stevens away."

"You're in a very dangerous place right now. I don't know whether you're my new hero or a vigilante cowboy. Either way, if you keep going, you'll be dead before long. Stevens has powerful lowlife friends. I do know that. Putting you in jail would be for your own safety."

"Not until I find Maya. You know what happens to her if she stays with him."

There was a pause on the other end of the line. Ochoa took a deep breath. Her voice shifted from anger to concern. "If you have something, give it to me now."

"When I have her safe and sound, I'll give you everything."

"No, Fischer. Tell me now. You think I don't want the bad guys off the streets as much as you do?"

"Look, I know you're on the right side, and I trust you. But you can't do what I do because you're a cop. You need warrants and probable cause. I don't. You'd only slow me down."

"*Madre de Dios*, Fischer." She took a long moment to collect herself. I listened to her steady breathing through the phone. "You got twenty-four hours. Get me that evidence or I will arrest you, hero or not."

CHAPTER FORTY

Detective Ochoa had given me enough rope to either get the job done or hang myself. It was unexpected, and I wondered if she'd done it because she felt guilty that her ex-partner, Detective Peterson, had murdered Grandpa and tried to murder me, and he'd done it right under her nose. I'd stopped Peterson. Unfortunately, I'd been too late to prevent the killing, or stop him from putting a bullet in Skeeter. For twenty-four hours after that, I'd been on the state's most wanted list. Every SAPD officer, including Ochoa, wanted to put a bullet through my head. I stayed one step ahead of them until I revealed the depth of Peterson's corruption and his link to the candidate for governor. Everyone in law enforcement, including Detective Ochoa, had to eat crow. Maybe giving me a day to finish the job of finding Maya was her way of apologizing. Then again, maybe she had something else up her sleeve. I wasn't gonna question her motive, as long as she was true to her word.

It was eight thirty in the morning when I arrived at the pawnshop on Culebra belonging to Leo the accountant. The shop opened at nine, and I wanted to be in the parking lot before the owner arrived. Skeeter had done some digging and found a picture of him in an old online advertisement. Everybody had a digital footprint. His included a full name, Leonidas Kostopoulos, and a headshot of a man in his fifties with a trimmed, gray goatee, bushy sideburns, and red designer eyeglasses. His chubby cheeks and double chin gave him the look of someone who spent more time behind a glass counter than in the sunlight. He definitely didn't resemble his namesake warrior from ancient Greek history.

At eight forty-five a new silver Lexus LX pulled into the reserved parking place beside the back door. A man got out wearing a tan leisure suit and a sunflower-yellow button-down shirt. A thick gold chain hung across a chest full of gray hair. He'd put on a few pounds, but it was the same guy from the picture, and he still wore the same designer eyewear.

I reached for my door handle and caught a glimpse of my face in the side mirror. My skin was pale and dark circles hung under my eyes. It didn't look like the face of someone in complete control. "Still with me, Grandpa?" I asked. He didn't respond.

While Leo fumbled with a set of janitor keys hooked to a chain on his belt, I pulled my Springfield and got out of my pickup. He put the key in the lock, and I pressed the barrel of my pistol to the back of his thick neck.

"Good morning, Leonidas."

He raised his hands to shoulder height, giving me a good view of the diamond-studded pinky ring on his left hand. "I don't have any money," he said. His voice had a guttural quality that emphasized a thick Greek accent.

"You're lying, Leo. Let's go inside."

I followed him through the door and into a cluttered back office. There were stacks of papers on a solid metal desk and boxes on the floor covered with dust. I turned on the light and frisked Leo for weapons. He had a S&W .40 stuck inside his elastic waistband.

"Turn around," I said.

Leo kept his hands up and slowly pivoted. His face was pale, and he was sweating despite the morning chill. "You're him."

"Expecting someone?"

"Nick Fischer. You burned down the tire shop. Y-you don't have to do this," he stuttered.

"Do what?"

"Kill me."

I let him sweat while I examined the pictures on his desk. One showed a pretty teen girl in a white school uniform dress, her dark hair tucked behind her ears. She had a shy, intelligent smile. Another showed a boy near the same age, maybe a year older, with ironed khaki pants, a white Oxford shirt, and a dark blue tie.

"Those your kids?" I asked.

Leo nodded nervously.

"They go to private school?"

"St. Mary's Hall."

"Business must be good," I said. SMH was exclusive and expensive.

"I do all right."

I tapped him hard in the chest with the barrel of my .45. He took a quick step back to keep from falling over. "You're the worst kind of scum. You think your hands are clean, but your money is covered in blood."

"I don't know what you're talking about. Why are you doing this?"

"Russell Stevens took a girl your daughter's age from Fredericksburg. She's the granddaughter of an old friend. I want her back."

"I-I don't know anything about that."

"I know. You're just the money man."

"You're gonna kill me?"

"Not unless you get in my way. You're gonna help me get the girl back. I want Russell's money. Where is it?"

Leo glanced at the photos of his children on the desk, then nodded, making a spur-of-the-moment decision. He walked to a closet and opened the door. A metal safe filled the space with a keypad lock. He punched in the combination and turned the handle. Stacks of bills covered the bottom three shelves. Two trays of jewelry occupied the top shelf. I pulled the empty plastic garbage sack from the trash can and handed it to Leo. It was too easy, but I didn't question his motive. "Take the money. All of it."

He filled the sack with more money than I would see in five years of investigation work. The Dragon was doing a very lucrative business. I made Leo carry the sack to his Lexus. The parking lot was still empty when he popped the trunk. He moved a bag of soccer balls and orange cones out of the way and tossed the money into the trunk.

"Your kids play soccer?" I asked.

"Football," he corrected. "My girl plays. I'm the coach."

I raised my eyebrow. He didn't look like the athletic type.

"Back in the day, I played for a club team in Athens," he said, smiling at the memory. "I injured my knee. Tore my ACL. They couldn't fix those back in the day." He patted his plump belly. "I don't get much exercise anymore."

I unhooked the key ring from his beltloop. "You drive," I told him. I opened his door and checked under the seat and the side pocket. I found a pink scrunchy and a plastic squirt bottle of cherry-scented hand sanitizer. There was no doubt Leo had a teenage daughter. The soft leather bucket seats in the Lexus LX fit like a glove, a far cry from the worn cloth seats in my dated F-150. Leo pressed the start button. The engine hummed to life, and the seat automatically adjusted to my weight. A female voice with a British accent said, *Welcome back, Leo. Where would you like to go?*

Leo looked at me. Car and driver were waiting for directions.

"Southcross," I said.

"You're going to hit all my stores?"

"That's the idea. Until Russell turns over the girl."

"It won't work. The money comes from all over. He answers to the higher-ups."

"You mean the cartel boss?"

He glanced out the window and pursed his lips, refusing to confirm a direct connection between Russell and the cartel. "He better make a deal before they find out he's losing money."

"He won't negotiate. That's not what he does. He can't afford to."

"What would you do, Leo? What would you do if someone took your daughter?"

He didn't answer. He twisted the transmission knob to reverse. The rearview camera popped up on the screen. The friendly British woman said, *Use caution backing up. Where should I route the GPS?*

Leo spoke to his car. "Southcross Pawn."

Thank you, Leo. Routing to Southcross Pawn. Head east on Culebra.

"Can we turn that off? You don't need directions to your own shop."

Leo touched a switch on the padded steering wheel. He clicked the transmission knob to drive and pulled into morning traffic. A gold St. Jude medallion dangling from the rearview mirror caught the sunlight. The patron saint of lost causes. I hoped this wasn't one of them.

"I'll never get used to driving without a key and a handle to shift gears," I said. We stopped at a stoplight, and I watched the morning traffic pile up behind us. "I learned how to drive on a stick shift."

"So did I," Leo said. The light turned green, and he pulled into the left lane to get around a slow-moving city bus. "Americans are spoiled. In Greece, everybody drives a stick."

He was still sweating despite the cool air, and he tapped his pinky ring nervously on the dashboard while he drove. My body ached, craving sleep. Ochoa's early morning phone call had ended any hope of rest, and I fought the urge to close my eyes and lean my head on the butter-soft leather seats. She'd also put a ticking time bomb on my mission that meant sleep would have to wait.

Twenty-five minutes later, Leo pulled into the pawnshop and jewelry store on Southcross Boulevard. There were four cars in the parking lot, and the doors were open for business.

"Pull around to the back," I said.

"I'm just the accountant," he said, as if that justified his association with a cutthroat.

"When we get inside, do everything you normally do, and you won't get hurt," I said.

I followed Leo through the back door and holstered my pistol. A narrow hallway led to a small store with six rows of shelves piled with trade goods. A woman in her late forties turned to greet us from behind a glass-top counter. She eyed me suspiciously.

"You're early," she said. Her dress was bright orange and too tight around her bulky figure. The neon-green makeup made her look like a rodeo clown.

"My daughter's game's this afternoon," Leo told her. "I gotta be back on the north side by four."

The woman showed crooked teeth but didn't smile. She stared at me, waiting for an introduction. I didn't offer one. Her eyes lingered on the pistol in my shoulder holster, and she decided to keep her mouth shut. I was grateful.

Leo led the way to the back office. I didn't have to ask this time. There was a similar layout—a closet hiding the money safe. I handed him his janitor key ring and a plastic trash bag. He opened the door and the safe, and I watched him strip the money off the shelves. A lot of money. It was almost too easy. So far, my direct assault had caught Russell flat-footed.

We walked back to the Lexus. Leo opened the trunk and hoisted the money bag into the back. "Where to?" he asked.

"You know where," I said. "Houston Street." Skeeter had found three pawn shops listed for Leo, and I planned to hit them all fast and hard.

"You did your homework." He hit the start button and flipped the transmission indicator to drive. I could feel the dampness under the Kevlar vest and knew that the wound was leaking. Luckily, following Leo the Greek around hadn't been physically taxing, but I was worried about the final stop. Leo'd started tapping his pinky ring on the dashboard again, like he knew something was coming.

When he made the turn onto Houston Street, I told him to keep driving past the pawnshop and to pull into the minimart on the corner. I scanned the street and the nearby buildings for anything suspicious. His employees knew the schedule. They knew who was part of the team and who wasn't. It was their business to know. Their livelihood depended on being aware of who was in charge and who might cause them harm.

Leo tapped a steady beat with his pinky ring. I watched two young women in jeans and sweatshirts enter the front of the pawnshop, each carrying a plastic grocery sack. Fifteen minutes later, the same women came out without the sacks.

"How many employees work here?" I asked.

"Two. A husband and wife. They've been with me for fifteen years. They're good people. Please, don't hurt them."

"Cooperate. No one gets hurt. Your daughter really has a soccer game this afternoon?"

"Football," he corrected me again. "Yes, we play St. Pious. She's the star midfielder."

"I didn't know they had positions in soccer."

"Americans," he said, rolling his eyes. "You probably played American football."

"Yep. In high school."

"American football is not a real sport."

"We're gonna disagree on that point."

He laughed, breaking the tension. I told him to start the car and pull around to the back.

"This girl you're looking for, she's a relative?" he asked while he was waiting for the light to change so he could cross the street to the pawnshop parking lot.

I didn't see any reason to hold back. I told Leo the story of how I'd gotten involved with Maya and her grandfather's relationship to my own grandpa. I also told him how I'd found Maya in a westside trap house and how she'd run away again.

"I'm no saint," Leo confessed. "But I'm just the accountant. I don't get involved in what he does."

"You said that once. That's no excuse. You're keepin' a thug in business."

"You don't understand. I don't have anything to do with his business. I came to this country thirty years ago. My football career was over. I put my life savings into my business. I built it up and opened two more stores. I got married and had two beautiful children. I was living the American dream. Then three years ago, Russell Stevens came to me and said take this money. At first, I refused, but he threatened my family. He's an animal."

"Why didn't you go to the police?"

"I'm Greek. We don't trust police. I knew they couldn't protect me." He pulled the Lexus across the street and around to the back door of the pawnshop. There were two other cars in the lot. Next door, the Jack in the Box restaurant parking lot was overflowing with a lunch crowd. The aroma of sizzling meat and hot grease made my mouth water.

Leo cut the engine and turned to me. He wanted to explain. "I didn't have a choice—" he started to explain, but I cut him off.

"We all have a choice." I didn't want to hear Leo's sad tale. "The only victim here is Maya Chavez and the other girls whose lives Russell ruined." I held up the Springfield. "Last stop. Let's go." I handed him his janitor keys and followed him to the door.

I scanned the stacks of secondhand goods. There was one older guy in a blue mechanic jumper examining a set of used metric hand tools. The husband-and-wife team were behind the counter. The woman looked in her sixties and wore a bright yellow tracksuit. The man was a few years older and sitting at a desk sorting papers. He had a gray polo shirt that matched his hair.

"Everything all right, Mr. Leo?" the man asked.

The woman stayed at the end of the counter. When she looked up at me, she recoiled at my appearance and eyed the bulky Kevlar vest under my shirt suspiciously. I glanced over her shoulder at my reflection in the mirror. My face was still pale and the dark circles had gotten larger. Hello, death.

"It's cool, Buddy," Leo said. "I know I'm early. My daughter has a game today."

The man turned to me, curious. His hands gripped the edge of the desk. The mechanic decided he didn't want the tools and walked out the front door, triggering an electric bell and leaving the store empty of customers. I pulled the Springfield and pointed it at Buddy. "Lock the front door."

Buddy's eyes shifted from me to Leo.

Leo nodded, and the man went to the door and locked it.

I walked behind the counter where his wife stood. There was a small TV monitor that showed three surveillance cameras. One pointed at the front door, one at the counter, and one at the back door and parking lot. They had watched us park and walk inside.

Buddy walked back to the counter and stood beside his wife.

"Both of you, into the back room," I ordered.

Buddy and his wife looked at each other but didn't move.

"It's okay, Buddy. Do what he says," Leo said in a calm voice.

The husband-and-wife team reluctantly walked toward the back office. I motioned Leo to follow. We formed a single-file line. The woman hesitated with her hand on the doorknob. My sixth sense told me the counterattack waited behind the door. She turned the knob and pushed the door open. Buddy followed her inside. Leo went next. He reached for the light switch.

When the lights came on, a shadow slid across the space between the door and the jamb. I kicked the metal door hard, then dropped to my knees. The door hit something solid.

Four quick shots exploded in the small space. Four holes appeared in the door at chest level. I returned fire. The woman screamed. Three more shots rang out. The last one hit me in the chest. The Kevlar held, but the impact thumped me like a mule kick, sending shock waves of hot pain into my chest and down my arms. I dropped the .45, and it clatter to the linoleum floor.

A man stepped out the door wearing wraparound sunglasses, a black, long-sleeve T-shirt, and jeans. His hair was slicked back, and a skull tattoo covered the front of his neck.

"You fucked up, man," he said, with a thick Spanish accent. He aimed his pistol at my head, but paused and shifted his attention to the hole in my shirt. Big mistake.

I rolled quickly to my left and kicked him in the knee. He went down and dropped his pistol. I dove on his chest and grabbed his throat. He tried to counterpunch, but I pinned his arms with my knees. The woman was still screaming. His body bucked, trying to dislodge my grip.

I squeezed harder, cutting off the blood flow to his brain. A minute ticked by, then another. His kicks got less frequent and weaker. Finally, he stopped moving.

I grabbed the door handle and pulled myself up. "Get the money and shut her up." I retrieved my pistol from the floor. Buddy put his arms around his wife, and her screams morphed into whimpering sobs. Leo opened the safe. He found a plastic trash bag and filled it with the money. I noticed a stack of computer disks on the top shelf.

"Take those too," I said to Leo.

He hesitated, calculating his options. He looked from the contents to my .45, then to the unconscious man on the floor. He took the disks and dropped them into the bag.

"You stay inside," I said to Buddy and his wife. "Keep the front door locked until we're gone. Understand?"

They both nodded. I followed Leo to the Lexus, opened the door, and watched him toss the heavy bag in the trunk with the others. I took the handful of computer disks to the front seat for closer inspection and motioned for Leo to get behind the wheel.

Before I could lower myself into the seat, a wave of pain washed over me. The earth seemed to spin off its axis, and I grasp the door to keep from collapsing on the pavement.

"You don't look good," he said.

"I'm fine. Get in."

"Where to?"

I collapsed into the passenger seat and took a deep breath. My eyes focused on the St. Jude medal hanging from the rearview mirror. Maybe it was time for a prayer. "Just drive."

CHAPTER FORTY-ONE

I directed Leo toward Loop 410, and he hit the on-ramp headed south. I wanted to put some distance between us and the pawnshop. Someone would have heard Buddy's wife screaming, and the morning pistol fire would prompt a 911 call even in east San Antonio.

I concentrated on staying focused long enough to call Russell Stevens, then get rid of Leo. The Kevlar had saved my life, but the impact of the bullet had broken my chest wound wide open and maybe broken a rib. I was suffocating, gasping for air, and felt warm sticky blood oozing down my chest and into my jeans.

"Take the next exit," I said through clenched teeth, pointing to the off-ramp for South Presa Street.

He drove a few blocks north to the Mission San Juan Capistrano parking lot and stopped under a shade tree. I opened my door and swung my feet to the pavement. A tour bus had just pulled up. The door opened and a couple dozen blue-haired ladies with their husbands in tow slowly ambled toward the large wooden cross stuck in a huge patch of prickly pear cactus that marked the park entrance. Behind them stood the eighteenth-century church surrounded by the remains of the mission's white limestone wall.

Leo sat behind the wheel, watching me and nervously tapping his pinky ring.

"Ever take the mission district tour?" I asked, chinning toward the senior citizens group.

It took him a minute to digest what I was saying. Finally, he said, "No. I went to the Alamo once."

"You should tour the other missions. Bring your kids. Introduce them to Texas history."

"I'm from Greece. We invented history. The house I grew up in is older than this mission."

I smiled at that, watching a young energetic tour guide herd the blue-hairs toward the entrance. I'd never been to Greece, but I'd been to Germany, France, and England. I knew what he meant. Human history stretched back tens of thousands of years, but the three-hundred-year history of Europeans in Texas was a tiny comma on the page compared to the volumes recorded in Leo's native country.

"There were people here before the missions were built."

"Of course. The Indians. What did they leave behind? Our poet Homer left us the Odyssey three thousand years ago."

"Well, you got us beat on poetry. But we did find some stone tools from about twenty thousand years ago. Just north of Austin."

"I did not know that."

We sat and stared at the white limestone wall of the mission. I waited for my second wind. Maybe it would come after a few hours of sleep, but I didn't have time for that.

"How much money we got?" I asked.

He did a quick calculation in his head. "Two million three hundred and thirty-three thousand."

"You're pretty sure about that?"

"I'm an accountant. I'm always sure about money."

"Call Russell and tell him."

Leo licked his thick lips, then touched a button on the steering wheel. The dashboard lit up. The British female voice spoke: *Good afternoon, Leo. How may I help?*

"Call Russell Stevens," he ordered.

Calling Russell Stevens. After a series of electronic beeps, the phone rang.

A raspy voice answered. "What is it?"

"I'm here with the accountant and a bag of your money, dickhead."

"Who is this?"

"Take a wild guess. You wanna kill me, send a professional."

"Goddamn you, Fischer."

I pointed the Springfield at Leo. "Tell him how much we got."

"Two million three hundred and thirty-three thousand," Leo recited.

"Leo, are you in on this?" Russell spat.

"He's got a gun to my head, Russell. I swear to god."

"You want your money back, hand over Maya," I said.

"You don't have a goddamn clue who you're dealing with, man. That's not my money. These people will kill you and your whole fucking family."

"Too late. I don't have a family. And if it's not your money, you better make a deal."

"I don't negotiate."

"I'll sweeten the pot. You give me Maya, and I'll give you the money and throw in the stack of computer disks you left in Leo's safe."

He didn't speak. The phone went silent as if he'd put his hand over the microphone.

"You still there?" I waited another minute. "Do we have a deal?"

"She made her choice," he said. His voice sounded more confident than it should have, as if he still held an ace in the hole.

"She doesn't know what she wants. She's eighteen. Let her go." I waited for Russell to respond. The silence stretched another thirty seconds.

Russell chuckled. "You're dead, asshole." The phone disconnected.

"Charming guy."

"No one has ever crossed Russell Stevens and lived. He is the devil. An evil spirit."

"Yeah, well I'm the Angel of Justice."

"Raguel himself?"

"I thought you didn't care for history."

"I didn't say that. Your Texas history is covered in newspapers. The history of my people is written on stone tablets."

"Then you know Raguel's function is to take vengeance on transgressors. So, tell me where Russell Stevens is and let me get to work."

"If I knew, I would tell you."

I pressed the Springfield against his forehead. "He's gonna kill you anyway. Maybe I can save you."

He didn't move. "I-I don't know where he is. Please. I don't owe him anything. He killed my wife." He covered his eyes with his left hand and took a ragged breath. "She talked about his money. She mentioned his name. She broke his code of silence, so he killed her." He took another breath to compose himself. "You asked why I didn't go to the police. I have two children. He will kill them unless I do what he asks. My kids are all I have."

"What's on the computer disks?"

He licked his lips as if deciding between me and Russell.

"Come on, Leo. I don't have a lot of time."

"He put them in the safe. I don't know what they are."

"Get out," I said. "Out of the car."

His jaw clenched tight and his double chin shook. "You're gonna kill me."

I gestured toward the parking lot. "Out." The senior tour group was inside the mission. The morning was silent except for the coo of a white-wing dove. The South Texas sun threatened to chase the fall weather back north of the Red River to await reinforcements from Canada's legions of arctic wind. I had to keep it together for a few more hours.

"No, Leo. I'm not gonna kill you. Go home to your kids. Russell's gonna come after you. Get the family and take a little vacation." Another wave of pain shot down both arms. I lost my grip on the pistol, and it dropped into my lap.

"God have mercy," he said and crossed himself, seeing the blood that had soaked into the top of my Wranglers.

"Get out!" I yelled. I didn't want him there if I passed out.

Leo got out, and I climbed behind the wheel. He walked slowly toward the mission.

"Leo," I said.

He turned, expecting a bullet.

I tossed him his cell phone.

He caught it and let out a loud sigh of relief.

I left Leo in the parking lot and drove north on Presa Street. There were extra weapons and ammo in my pickup that I would need before this was over. The traffic was light. I passed the turn for Mission San

José and Mission Concepción, and kept to the backstreets, not wanting to risk exposure on the crosstown freeway. I stopped down the street from the Culebra pawnshop and studied the front of the store where I'd left my pickup. The open sign was on, but no one was going in or out. There were two empty police cars parked across the street. The officers were probably inside. I drove into the parking lot of the minimart next door and saw the two officers searching my pickup. The black duffel bag with my extra weapons and ammo was on the pavement between them. So much for my extra fire power. I was too late.

I called Skeeter and told him what happened. I expected the police would be at my house very soon. I told him to get the weapons and ammo out of the safe and take them to Rose's house in case they got a warrant to search the place.

"Tell Sarge and Lucky to stay with Rose so they aren't on the police radar," I said.

"You don't sound good, man," Skeeter said.

"I'll be all right," I said and disconnected. SAPD had my pickup, and it wouldn't be long before the cops or Russell's gang started looking for Leo's Lexus. I glanced at my reflection in the side mirror. "Don't stop now, cowboy." The face that stared back at me showed determination, but little energy. "Grandpa, if you're still around, I could use a little help."

I hit the Uber app on my phone. A ride was five minutes away. I gathered all my strength and pulled myself out of the Lexus. If I could stay hidden with Russell's money, there was still a chance he would turn Maya loose. I took a step toward the store, and everything went black.

CHAPTER FORTY-TWO

The explosion lifted the Humvee into the air and obscured the blue sky with brown dust. Shards of glass stabbed my forehead. The vehicle came to rest upside down, pinning my legs under the dashboard. Blood flowed from Corporal Lorenzo's mouth and ears. His arms hung lifelessly from the steering wheel toward the roof of the cab. Rifle bullets punctured the frame, hitting like hail on a metal roof. A dozen legs clad in desert boots appeared in the swirling dust outside the broken windshield and circled the vehicle.

"Get down!" I shouted. My legs felt welded to the dashboard.

The boots stood their ground. Protecting me. Faces appeared. Skeeter, Grandpa, Lucky, and Sarge. What were they doing here on patrol?

"Get up!" Grandpa shouted.

I pulled against the dashboard with all my strength. Nothing moved.

The voice shouted again. "Get up! You're not done. You gotta get up."

I felt a hand on my shoulder. The voice shifted in tone. This time it had a Greek accent. "Mr. Fischer, wake up."

I opened my eyes. Leo Kostopoulos stared down at me, eyes bulging and neck skin sagging like the dewlap on a Brahma bull. I blinked in confusion, trying to erase the old nightmare from my memory. For two years after my last deployment, that nightmare of the final moments that ended my Marine Corps career haunted my sleep. The names and faces of my brothers that didn't make it back were seared in my memory. After our Humvee hit an IED, I was trapped in the cab. During the follow-up ambush, my platoon returned cover fire, protecting me from being killed or captured. I survived because they paid the ultimate price. Over ten years later, it still haunted me in times of stress, and as dreams do, distorted the faces of the combatants to include members of my family and friends.

"You were screaming. You okay?" Leo asked. He looked concerned.

I closed my eyes and took physical inventory. There was pain in my chest, but it was manageable. I was lying on a bed with a clean sheet in a sparsely furnished room. I was naked down to my skivvies. The room smelled of rubbing alcohol and detergent. A fresh bandage covered my wound. There was something cold on my chest. I pulled the sheet down. A St. Jude medallion hung around my neck.

"What's this," I asked, holding up the necklace.

"St. Jude. In my Orthodox church he is Thaddaeus, the patron saint of lost causes. You will need his help against the devil."

"Where am I?" I looked around the small, windowless room.

"The basement of my house. I called an Uber to get back to the pawnshop. I found you lying in the street face down beside my Lexus. A homeless guy was trying to use your phone to call 911."

"How long have I been here?"

He looked at his watch. "Six hours. You were out of it. Don't worry, no one knows you're here."

I found my phone and checked for messages. Two texts from Skeeter and a missed call from Detective Ochoa. I called Skeeter and let him know I was all right.

"What's your address," I asked Leo.

"Ogden Lane in the Heights," he said.

I relayed the information to Skeeter. Alamo Heights was an upscale neighborhood north of downtown. There was old money there—businessmen who owned buildings and worked downtown. The perfect place for a mob accountant to hide in plain sight.

Leo crossed to a small table near the door and gave me some privacy.

"How you holdin' up?" Skeeter said.

"As far as I can tell, I'm good to go. I'm here with Leo the accountant."

"Do you trust him?" Skeeter whispered.

"No, but if he wanted to kill me, I'd be dead. I passed out in front of his shop. He brought me home."

"What about Russell Stevens?"

"I rattled his cage. He's gonna hit back, hard. Sit tight at my place and monitor the GPS signal from the manager's pickup."

He chuckled. "We doin' all this for an ungrateful teenage girl and a freezer full of meat."

"What can I say. You wanna get rich, try the stock market."

"I might do that."

There was a knock on the door. "Gotta go," I said and disconnected.

A young female voice said, "Papa?"

"My kids know you're here. I had to explain why we missed the game. They helped me bring you inside."

A teenage girl entered the room. She was seventeen or eighteen years old. Her hair was pulled into a ponytail. She wore soccer-style shorts and a team T-shirt with number eight on the back and knee-high socks with athletic sandals.

"This is my daughter, Penelope."

"The wife of Odysseus. She looks brave enough," I said.

"You're a student of history," Leo said.

"It's Penny," the girl said quickly. "Would you like something to eat?" She carried a bowl of stew and a bottled water to the bedside table.

"Thank you, Penny. I'm starving."

She put a hand on my forehead. "You have a fever. I'll take your temperature. Papa, we should take him to the ER."

"Penelope wants to be a doctor," Leo said proudly.

"I'll be all right after I eat some of that stew. Did you make it?"

"It's a family recipe."

The bowl contained thick chunks of meat in tomato-based sauce mixed with carrots and potatoes and smelled like heaven.

"Would that be deer meat?" I asked, inhaling the pungent, gamey aroma.

She smiled, not scared or intimidated in the least by a half-naked wounded man lying in the basement. "Yes. How did you know?"

"I grew up on deer meat."

"One of my clients has a ranch in Bandera. He lets me take the kids hunting," Leo explained.

I took a bite. It tasted as good as it smelled. It reminded me of my grandma's wild meat stew that always seemed to be cooking on the back-burner during hunting season. Father and daughter watched me devour the food and use the pita bread to clean the bowl.

Penny took away the empty bowl, and I got out of bed.

"What're you doing?" Leo asked. "You need to rest."

"No time for that. You know how Russell operates. Maya's life is in danger. Now, you and your family are in danger."

Leo tried to come up with an excuse to keep me in bed, but there wasn't one that didn't involve putting him and his kids at more risk. He brought me my clothes that had been cleaned and neatly folded. Most of the bloodstains were gone. I got dressed and slipped back on the Kevlar vest. It had already saved my life once. I was sure I would need it again before I found Maya and took her home.

He handed me my Springfield .45 and my S&W .38. I checked the rounds and strapped both in place. "Thank you," I said. "For saving my life."

"Before you came, I was willing to follow orders to protect my children. That monster killed my wife. My kids are the only thing I have left. But you… You are willing to sacrifice your life to rescue the daughter of a family friend."

"I'm gettin' well paid," I said.

"I don't believe you," he said and studied me. I was dressed, my Springfield strapped in a shoulder holster over the Kevlar vest, my ankle bulging with the .38. "If you can do this, I will fight back also."

"Now you sound more like the Leonidas from Greek history," I said.

He nodded but didn't smile. "Also, I opened the files." He pointed to a desk by the door where there was an open laptop. Beside it sat the stack of computer disks we'd taken from the pawnshop safe. "This man is a monster. He must be stopped." He loaded one of the disks. "The girls are my daughter's age. I can no longer be a part of what Russell is doing."

We watched a video cue up on screen. The picture didn't have Hollywood production values. The image was grainy, and the room was too dark, but the people and the actions were clear. My stomach churned, and

I resisted the urge to throw up the game stew. I'd seen men die in combat, and I'd killed men in self-defense, but this made my blood boil. I shut off the tape. The young girls were naked and too young. The men were old and out of shape. Anger quickly replaced my revulsion.

"I need a car," I said. "And I need to know where Russell's hiding." I held up the disk. "I've got to get Maya away from that animal."

"You can take my daughter's Camry." He stroked his salt-and-pepper whiskers, thinking. "I have no idea where he would be. But he will come after his money."

I followed him up the basement steps and into the kitchen. A boy was sitting at the bar doing homework. He looked like Penny's twin, only with his father's chubby cheeks.

"This is Leonidas Junior," Leo said proudly.

The boy stood up from his textbook. He was built stout like his dad and wore his dark hair cut short. He extended his hand and I shook it.

"Pleased to meet you, Mr. Fischer," he said politely. There were no secrets, it seemed, between father and children. They all knew who I was.

I glanced at the textbook. "Math?" I asked.

"Not my favorite subject," he said.

"Junior is my budding artist," Leo said. "My daughter's the scientist."

"The world needs artists, too," I said.

The kid smiled shyly.

I followed Leo out the back door to the garage. He gave me the keys to his daughter's red Toyota Camry and helped me load the money bags and the disks into the trunk.

"You need to leave," I reminded him. "Take the kids. Russell will come after you. He won't believe you had nothing to do with it."

"I know how to take care of myself and my family. I won't run."

I nodded. If he wanted to stay and face the music, I couldn't force him to run. I got in the Camry and started the engine. A mixture of sweet perfume and Skittles permeated the interior. I unrolled all the windows and drove out the winding driveway and into the quiet residential Alamo Heights neighborhood. The lots were big, and the houses set back off the street, hidden by dense live oak mottes and stone fences giving the area an exclusive feel. I didn't blame Leo for wanting to stay.

By the time I got to I-35 south, a cool city mixture of exhaust fumes and fall cedar pollen had replaced the female teen smell inside the car. I felt a tickle in the back of my throat and rolled up the window. On top of everything, I didn't need an attack of cedar fever.

My phone rang. The caller ID showed Skeeter.

"They're coming for you," he said.

"Who?"

"The club manager. I'm still tracking his pickup. Unless he has a house in the Heights, someone tipped him off to your location, or he's paying the accountant a visit. The GPS signal's headed east on Hildebrand. I don't think it's a social call."

"What's their ETA?"

"Fifteen minutes. You want some help?"

"I'm safe. I left ten minutes ago. I just hit I-35 south."

"Sounds like Leo the accountant is about to pay the piper."

I pounded my hand on the steering wheel. "Damn it to hell."

"Nothing you can do for him," Skeeter said. "At least you got out of there."

"Yeah, but I still need to find Russell. I'm gonna need fire power. SAPD impounded my pickup and took my bag."

"Don't come home. They got the street covered. Cruisers on both ends and an unmarked car just pulled up out front. Rose went out to offer them coffee. You're a wanted man."

"Just like old times."

"What're you gonna do?"

"Pray to St. Jude."

"What?"

"I'll call you later."

My phone rang as soon as I disconnected. It was Ochoa. I let it go to voicemail. I didn't wanna talk to her now.

CHAPTER FORTY-THREE

I parked down the street from Leo's house and walked through the oak trees lining his property. The jacked-up Dodge Ram from the strip club was in the driveway. The front door was kicked in, and fresh chunks of wood covered the welcome mat. Was I too late? I pulled my Springfield and jogged to the back of the house. The kitchen light was on. I double-checked that a round was in the chamber, then inched to the window and looked inside. Leo sat at the kitchen table. The club manager stood behind him. Leo wasn't dead yet. I couldn't see the children.

"Where the fuck's he at?" Arnold shouted.

"Gone. Stole my daughter's car," Leo said. His head sagged. "You can look in the garage."

"You brought him home last night."

"He forced me. I told you he stole the money."

The bald-headed bouncer moved into view. He was wearing a Spurs basketball T-shirt and carrying a Glock 9mm. No sign of the other bouncer. I ducked away from the window and put my hand on the back door. Locked.

"If you're lying to me, Leo... I swear to god." Arnold was hopping from foot to foot and bobbing his head up and down, hyper-excited like he was tweaking on meth. The only advantage I had was he and his crew didn't know where I was.

Banging erupted on the interior walls.

"Let me go!" a voice screamed. It was Penny.

I slipped back to the kitchen window. The bouncer with the neck tattoo had Penny in one bear claw and Junior in the other. Junior seemed shell-shocked and ready to piss his pants. Penny was a fighter. She pounded Tattoo with her free hand.

"Take your hand off me!" she shouted.

"We can have some fun with this little bitch," Tattoo sneered. He shoved Junior into a kitchen chair and pressed Penny against the counter. In one swift motion, he ripped Penny's T-shirt off, exposing her black sports bra.

"Stay away from her," Junior yelled, springing from the chair.

Tattoo backhanded him in the face. Junior dropped like a sack of feed, blood spraying from his broken nose.

"Leave them out of this," Leo shouted, lurching out of his chair.

The bald bouncer shoved his Glock into Leo's neck. "Tell me where Nick Fischer is and we'll leave you alone, Leo," he snarled. Things were going downhill fast.

I used my folding knife to pry open the latch. Leo hadn't locked the deadbolt. This time, it might have saved his life.

"Didn't you learn your lesson?" Arnold asked. Sweat rolled down his forehead despite the cool temperature. He wiped his runny nose with his fingers. "Did you tell the kids you watched while we took your wife?"

"I told you, I don't know where Fischer is. He stole the car and took off. He took the money with him. He left twenty minutes ago. You should go after him."

"I think you wanted to help him as payback for your wife," the manager said.

"That's crazy. How could I do anything? He had a gun."

"And now I have a gun. You can watch while we have a little fun with your daughter."

Tattoo smiled and lifted Penny to the counter. She kicked and screamed while he yanked her soccer shorts off and tossed them on the kitchen floor.

She clawed at his face. "Let me go, you bastard!"

Tattoo hit her in the temple. Penny slumped back against the countertop, dazed, but not out. The brute grabbed her black panties. "Let's see what you're hiding."

Boom! I fired through the opening in the back door.

My .45 slug hit Tattoo in the back of the head and splattered his face and brain over the countertop and Penny's half-naked body. She screamed and kicked the dead man to the floor. The sound of the shot reverberated in the small kitchen space.

I dropped to my knees outside the door and yelled. "Put the weapons down!"

They answered with gunfire that ripped through the door and the wall at chest level. I peeked through the opening in the door. The manager grabbed Penny around the neck from behind and jammed his pistol in her ear.

"Who—who's out there?" he stuttered. His gun hand shook. "I'll kill this bitch. Show yourself."

"Let her go!" I yelled.

"Fischer, you motherfucker! Is that you?"

"Let 'em go. Leo didn't have anything to do with it. I have the money. Turn 'em loose."

"Where is it?"

The bald bouncer and the manager pointed their pistols at the back door. Hearing I had the money got their attention, but they were waiting for confirmation before blasting me again.

"It's right here. Come and get it," I yelled and sprinted for the front of the house.

They opened fire, on my voice, but I was already running through the front door and back to the kitchen. Arnold had his arm around Penny's neck with his back to me. Penny squirmed, pulling her head sideways and giving me the clearance I needed for a clear head shot.

Boom!

Arnold dropped his pistol and sank to the floor, the shot missing most of his face. Baldy spun toward me and pulled his trigger, but he was out of ammo. The slide on his Glock was locked back and empty. Somebody was looking out for me.

He went for the backup weapon in his jeans. I fired first, hitting his left leg. He screamed and flopped backward on the kitchen floor, gripping the hole in his upper thigh. I lifted a Glock 43 from behind his belt and stuck it in my back pocket.

Leo and his kids stared in stunned silence. Junior got to his feet, still holding his bleeding nose. I handed him a kitchen towel. Penny grabbed her shorts and slipped them on.

"Is there anyone else in here?" I asked, replacing my empty magazine and jacking a fresh round in the chamber.

"No," Leo said. "Just the three of them. You saved us." He put his arms around both his children. "Thank you."

I turned my attention to the thug on the floor. "Where's the boss?"

"Fuck you!"

"Such a limited vocabulary."

I put my bootheel on his bullet wound and pressed down. He cried out in agony. I knew exactly how he felt. "Where's Russell Stevens?"

"You want that little bitch. Dragon won't give her up. Take another girl. He's got plenty," he said and smiled through clenched teeth.

"Maya's special." I pressed the muzzle of my .45 into his other leg. "You wanna limp out of here or crawl out of here? Tell me where he is."

"Dragon will kill me."

"Not if I kill him first. Tell me where he is."

CHAPTER FORTY-FOUR

I had no reason to believe the thug was telling the truth about Russell's whereabouts, but it was the only information I had to go on. I drove out of the quiet Alamo Heights neighborhood and took the onramp for the 410 Loop. If I moved quickly, the element of surprise might still be on my side. I took inventory of my gear. The .45 in my shoulder holster held the last thirteen-round magazine. The .38 on my ankle held five rounds. The thug's Glock 43 held ten rounds. It wasn't enough to break into a gangster's warehouse. My rifle, the shotgun, and the extra ammo was locked up in the SAPD impound. I had extras at the house, but with SAPD covering the block, they might as well have been in Seattle. I needed a big favor from an old family friend. He might not help me, but it was worth a shot. I fished out my cell phone and made a call.

"What in the Sam Hill's gotten into you? You're fixin' to make the most wanted list, Junior, for the second time this year," Sergeant Vera said when he came on the line. Calling me Junior was his way of saying he disapproved of my behavior. He'd used the same technique since I was in elementary school.

"I don't have time to get into the details. Helmut Geisler's granddaughter's in danger. I need firepower or Helmut will never see her again."

"Helmut's a good man. But if I saw you on the street, I'd have to arrest you."

"I promise to turn myself in when this is over. Right now, I need your help."

I explained my predicament with as few words as possible. When I finished, there was silence on the line.

"You still there? I wouldn't ask unless I was desperate."

He sighed heavily. "Meet me at the annex."

Vera was waiting in his pickup around the corner from the SAPD annex west of downtown. I parked Penny's red Camry on the street and got in the passenger seat of Vera's Chevy 4x4.

"I'll do this on one condition," he said.

"I'll put corn in your deer feeder. You can hunt any day you want."

"I already know that, but thanks. The condition is, you call Detective Ochoa and tell her where you are and what you're up to."

I thought about that while he drove to the guard house. "Do I have a choice?"

"Nope. Nonnegotiable."

"This is my one chance to get Maya. I can't risk getting arrested by Detective Ochoa."

"It's your choice. Call her or go empty-handed."

I weighed my options. This was my one shot. "All right." I didn't want or need the interference, but there was something about Ochoa that made me trust her.

A plump female guard wearing cobalt-blue eyeliner stood under the streetlight by the gate. Vera unrolled his window, gave her a flirty grin. "You're lookin' tight, girl. Did you cut your hair?"

"Don't try getting in my pants, *viejo*," she said with a smirk.

"You can't blame me for tryin'," he said.

"That's sexual harassment."

"I'm an old man. When I see a beautiful woman, I get weak in the knees."

"I could get you fired."

"You can try. I'm already retired. My wife wants me to chase younger women. She says she doesn't like sex anymore."

"That's not what she told me."

The two of them giggled like two bridesmaids at a nail salon. I drummed my fingers on the console of his pickup.

"Can we hurry it up?"

The guard shined her flashlight into my face.

"This is—" Vera started to say.

She cut him off. "I know who he is. Don't say his name. This is all on you, *viejo*. And don't take too long." She opened the gate and went back inside the guard shack.

Vera drove to the back entrance and parked beside the loading dock. I followed him inside to a warehouse-sized room sectioned off by hurricane fencing. He walked to the nearest gate and produced a key for the lock.

"I talked to the officer who found your pickup. He's my cousin. Your bag of goodies is in here. He left it off the inventory."

"You knew I'd come for it?"

"What else would you do?"

"I owe you one."

"This one's for your father." He went to the caged area that was stacked to the ceiling with weapons of every kind—pistols, shotguns, and dozens of AR-15s. Most people had no idea the kind of firepower the bad guys were packing on the streets of the Alamo City. My black duffel bag was on the floor near the gate.

Vera stood calmly and watched me sort through my gear. Everything was still there. My AR-15 with the suppressor, the shotgun, the extra magazines, the ammo. I breathed a sigh of relief, then remembered what I was up against.

"I never told anyone this," Vera said. "When I was young and stupid, looking for a big payday, I decided it would be a good idea to rob a gas station. I took a pistol from my older brother's pickup and walked to the Travel Store on Highway 16 east of Bandera. It was raining and I wore a straw cowboy hat and a raincoat. I hesitated outside the door. I had the pistol out, but I started to lose my nerve. At that exact moment, a DPS cruiser rolled into the parking lot. Your dad got out and clamped on his Stetson hat. He knew me 'cause I'd been in trouble before. 'Hugo,' he said. 'What're you doin' out in the rain?' I froze. I had a pistol in my hand. He could have stepped out and shot me or ordered me to drop the weapon and arrested me. Instead, he said, 'Get in, I'll give you a lift home.' My hands were shaking so bad, I could barely open the door. He took the pistol and handed me a dry towel. He didn't say another word. He drove me home and I got out. He handed me back the pistol and I put it back in my brother's pickup. If he hadn't showed up when he did, I wouldn't be here today. I owe it all to Lee Fischer."

I didn't know what to say to that, so I nodded and repacked the gear in my bag. It was all there, and I would need every bit of it. I stood and walked toward the exit. Vera disappeared for a few minutes. I walked back to his pickup and stood under the blinking fluorescent lights of the building. The sky was clear, and a few dim stars penetrated the Alamo City lights. I tried to keep my mind clear and focused. Find Maya. Take out Russell Stevens. I had to force everything else out of my train of thought if I was going to save her and survive the night.

Vera reappeared and closed and locked the annex gate behind him. He was carrying a black duffel bag about the size of my own.

"I thought you could use a little extra help," he said and grinned. He handed me the bag. Inside I found a tactical flashlight and a pair of night-vision goggles. Very useful.

"Came from a cartel bust last week. Those guys have military-grade weapons directly from the Mexican army. DEA was supposed to pick it up. There must have been a problem with the inventory sheet." He winked at me and started his pickup. "You know, Ochoa called me yesterday. Asked me what I thought about you."

"I hope you gave her the good version."

"Even as a kid, you had a strong sense of right and wrong. You got that from your dad and granddad. I told her that. I also told her that once you got a notion in your head, you wouldn't let it go come hell or high water. She wanted to know if you'd ever cross the line. You know, actively go against the law."

"What'd you tell her?"

"I wouldn't lie to her." He smiled in the dark pickup and winked at me again. "I told her you'd always do the right thing."

"What'd she say?"

He chuckled. "She didn't comment. She's a nice lady and a good cop. She knows her shit," he said. Coming from Vera, that was the highest compliment. "If it hadn't been for her, you'd be in jail by now. She's had your back."

We drove back out the gate, and he parked behind Penny's Camry. I unloaded the two duffel bags and put them in the trunk.

"I'm not gonna try to talk you out of this business because I knew your father and your granddad. Stubbornness is a Fischer family trait. I also think you're doing the right thing. It's what Lee Fischer would have done."

Vera held his hand out the pickup window, and I shook it. "Opening weekend I expect you to have my feeder full of corn and a heater in my deer blind." It was his way of telling me to be careful. He wanted to see me at the ranch when deer season opened on the first of November.

"I'll rope a nice big buck and tie him to a tree."

"Don't forget you promised to call Ochoa." His pickup disappeared around the corner. I cranked the Camry, put it in gear, and focused on the mission. I dreaded that conversation.

CHAPTER FORTY-FIVE

I drove back to Loop 410 and headed south with the speedometer pegged at eight miles an hour over the limit. If I got pulled over now, all bets were off. It took less than fifteen minutes to find the address where the thug said Russell would be. It was a warehouse in an industrial park bookended by an oilfield pipe supplier and a Mexican restaurant guarded by a twelve-foot-tall metal bullfrog wearing a sombrero and playing a guitar.

The warehouse between the two was set back off the road about the length of three semi-trailer trucks. A ten-foot chain link fence topped with razor wire surrounded the compound. The corners had surveillance cameras, and two guards stood inside a shack beside the locked gate. Three rows of bright glowing streetlamps lit the lot like an athletic field. I cruised by on the highway without stopping. The two guards didn't react, so I made a U-Turn and parked behind the bullfrog.

I pulled my AR-15 from the duffel bag, screwed the Surefire suppressor in place, and loaded a thirty-round clip. Two extra mags were already loaded, and I stuck them in the back pockets of my Wranglers. The extra firepower gave me a boost of confidence. The AR felt comfortable and close enough to the military grade that I'd used countless times in Afghanistan.

Things were about to get western, and I was operating at about sixty percent capacity. Even on patrol, there was rarely a time when I faced the enemy at one hundred percent. The physical training and repetitive drills were the keys to survival in the military. I kept the discipline after I mustered out. But since I'd been wounded and recovering, I'd neglected the drills and training. I hoped I had enough muscle memory and stubborn determination to get the job done.

I skirted the light from the floodlamps at the gate and worked my way around the guard shack to the back of the compound. The outside of the fence was neglected and covered with thick brush and trash piled high by the relentless southeast wind. I pushed my way through prickly huisache limbs to the base of the wire.

The loading dock and back parking area were bathed in light. I wasn't going to get within fifty yards without being seen. There was a semi-tractor trailer backed into the landing, and two workers were busy offloading cargo with a forklift. A man with a dark jacket stood near the door holding an AR-style rifle.

I scanned the area with my binoculars. Whatever cargo was coming off the truck was in black plastic bags. They looked like the same size and shape as the packages in the Gillespie County trailer. The warehouse office windows were dark or blacked out, showing no other signs of life. I searched the dozen or so cars in the parking lot and spotted a black Jeep Grand Cherokee near the warehouse door. Bingo.

Russell was there or at least his Jeep was. I hoped Maya was with him.

I worked my way out of the brush and back to the Camry. I needed a way to cut power to the warehouse. I thought of shooting out the transformer. I'd used that ploy on my last case to gain access to the Allison ranch. It had worked then, but only because there was cover between the gate and the ranch house. This time, I'd be exposed for fifty yards, and an easy target.

Then I heard the distinct downshift of a big diesel engine. I ducked as headlights flashed across the Camry. A semi-truck turned off the highway toward the warehouse gate. Opportunity knocked. I pulled the night vision goggles from the duffel bag and slipped them around my neck. I didn't have a clear plan but being able to see in the dark would always come in handy. Thank you, Sergeant Vera. Now, I would have to keep my promise to call Ochoa.

I grabbed my cell phone and scrolled down to Detective Ochoa's number. I didn't want to risk being heard, so I typed out a text message: *Possible 20 for R. S. and Maya. Will confirm.*

As soon as I hit send, my phone vibrated. Ochoa was calling.

The two guards at the gate house approached the cab of the semi-truck. The driver set his air brakes. The phone vibration stopped. I ran to the edge of the Mexican restaurant, closing the distance to the gate and the truck.

My phone vibrated again. Ochoa wasn't giving up. I ducked back behind the building and hit accept.

"It's not confirmed," I whispered.

"Understood. What's your twenty?" Her tone was blunt and serious.

I told her the address of the warehouse and the layout. While we talked, the truck driver opened his cab door and got out.

"Stay where you are," she said. "Do you hear me? Do not attempt to enter that warehouse until I get there with backup and a warrant."

The driver and one of the gate guards turned toward the back of the truck.

"Gotta go," I said and disconnected. I couldn't wait. I'd kept my promise and called Ochoa. She needed probable cause. I didn't. Waiting might cost Maya her life.

I sprinted to the rear of the semi, keeping the trailer between me and the two men, then dove under the truck and wedged myself against the trailer bed and the bumper. If they did a search, it was all over. I only hoped they weren't that careful.

"It's locked, dude," a voice protested.

"Rules are rules," another voice insisted. "Open it up."

"You know what happens if I'm late?"

I heard the driver rattle the lock on the trailer door, his knees inches from my face. If he bent down and peered under the trailer, I was toast. My hands clung to the undercarriage. The exertion caused pain to sweep from my chest to my shoulders and shoot down my arms. I could hold on for two, maybe three minutes. If they delayed any longer, I would drop to the dirt in full view of the guards and driver, and it would all be over.

The retractable trailer door rattled open.

"You see?" the first voice said. "Now can I get back to work?"

"All right, all right. What if you had something else in your trailer, huh? What would Dragon do to me?" I watched the luminous dial on my wristwatch tick past one minute.

Finally, the footsteps receded, a retractable door slammed, and the gate swung open. I kept my body tight against the bumper and the bottom of the trailer, hoping my butt wasn't visible, and that I could hang on until it came to a stop. The truck slowed and made a U-turn. That was my signal to get off. He would be backing into the well-lit loading dock. When the driver hit the brakes, I let go and rolled to the pavement. The wheels immediately reversed. I dove clear and ducked under the nearest pickup.

The semi-truck backed to the loading dock. A man's voice shouted directions. I worked my way toward the side door of the warehouse and slipped inside.

The warehouse was big, probably ten thousand square feet of space and three-quarters of it was filled with pallets stacked with black plastic bags. I could guess what was in them. There were shouts and some laughter as the men unloaded the truck.

I worked my way along the wall to the base of the steps leading to the second-floor offices and found what I was looking for—the main electrical breaker for the warehouse. I'd seen three men, one armed with an AR. Judging from the voices, there were at least four others inside the warehouse. I was outnumbered and needed an advantage.

I opened the breaker box and pulled the main switch. The warehouse went black. I heard a crash that sounded like a forklift slamming into metal. Someone flipped on a flashlight and scanned the warehouse floor with a beam of light. I pulled on the night vision goggles. My view was bathed in shades of green. The men still fumbled around in the dark. I walked up the stairs toward the second floor.

Crouching at the top, I scanned the warehouse floor. There were five men on the ground floor. Three of them had rifles. Only one had a flashlight, and he was holding it so that two of the men could finish unloading the truck.

"Where's the fucking generator?" a raspy voice shouted from the office window less than ten feet away.

It was Russell Stevens. He scanned the darkness below. I didn't move or breathe for fear I'd catch his eye even in the dark.

"We're working on it," a voice responded. Russell disappeared back inside the office.

I felt a warm dampness inside the Kevlar vest. The exertion had broken through the thin scab. No time to change the bandage. I had to reach down deep and gather all my reserve strength. I crept through the office door. The first room was a breakroom with a table in the center and a refrigerator and sink in the corner. I checked my watch. It had been ten minutes since Ochoa called. I checked my phone. There was a text message from her.

Sit tight. SAPD on the way.

Too late. I stepped into the next room. Russell Stevens stood behind a desk scanning the dark warehouse floor through the window. I leveled my pistol at his chest. The lights flicked on. Someone had found the breaker. I slipped the goggles off. Dragon didn't jump or flinch. He turned to me and smiled like he was expecting me.

"You're a real pain in the ass, Fischer," he said.

"Where's Maya?"

"Where's my money?"

"I'll make you a deal."

"I don't negotiate."

Footsteps pounded on the metal stairs. At least two men were racing up the steps. I let out a deep breath, forcing myself to stay in control. "In about nine minutes, San Antonio's finest will be here." I showed him my phone display with Detective Ochoa's message and caller ID. "Give me Maya and I'll tell you where the money is. You can get a head start."

Russell studied my face for signs that I was bluffing. I held his gaze. "Maya!" he yelled. Maya walked out of the back room. Four other girls about her age followed. They looked scared and hesitant. All were dressed like Boys Town hookers with their hair curled and layers of glitter makeup on their faces. Maya's dress was gold, shiny, and skintight. Russell looked them over and flashed a proprietary grin as if admiring his prize broodmares.

I had done it. I'd found her, but something wasn't right. Suddenly, I felt lightheaded. Warm moisture trickled down my skin under my Kevlar vest.

A wave of nausea washed over me. My skin felt cold. I had to keep going. "Maya, your grandpa wants you back," I said. "Helmut told me about the fight you had. He's willing to give you some space."

Maya chewed her bottom lip and looked at Russell, then back at me.

"It's okay, I'll take you out of here," I said, trying to get her to focus on me. The room began to spin, the walls went blurry. I grabbed the back of a chair for support. The Springfield felt like a fifty-pound weight in my hand.

Russell saw blood on my boots and laughed. "You ain't doin' too good, Fischer."

Everything went black.

CHAPTER FORTY-SIX

When I came to, the world was upside down. My first thought was of the Humvee in Afghanistan, but this wasn't a dream. My hands were zip-tied in front of me, and I was hanging from an A-frame engine hoist like a game carcass. The bloody bandage on my chest was still in place, but they had stripped me of my Kevlar vest and shirt. A fresh puddle of blood pooled beneath me on the concrete floor. And Russell's ugly mug was inches from my face, so close I could smell marijuana mixed with tequila on his breath.

"Where's my money, Fischer?"

He wore a self-satisfied smile, like he'd just drawn an inside straight. I glanced down at my wristwatch. Only two minutes had passed, long enough for his men to bind my hands and hoist me in the air.

"You're outta time. No one's comin' for you," he sneered.

"I came here to get Maya. Turn me loose, hand her over, and you can have your money."

He laughed. "You got some big balls."

Maya and the other girls stood near the exit, listening.

"Give him the money, Mr. Fischer," Maya shouted. "He's gonna kill you."

"She's a smart girl. You should listen to her."

The blood pounding in my head made it hard to focus. He thought he had the winning hand, but I remembered my ace in the hole. "I've got more than your money. I found your CD collection in Leo's safe. You want it back, cut me down and hand her over. SAPD's on the way."

His smile faded. He studied me. I knew I'd hit a nerve. "You're lying. You wouldn't call the police. They're after you, man. Cops hate a vigilante."

"You wanna take that chance? Detective Ochoa's on her way here now."

I glanced at my watch again to emphasize the urgency. If Ochoa did actually show up with the cavalry, this might work.

The wheels were turning inside his amoral brain. He backed away and put his hands on his hips. When he did, distant sirens cut through the silent warehouse. Ochoa had come through.

"Last chance. Turn Maya over and let me go," I said.

Russell's jaw tightened. He didn't panic, but he was weighing his options. Still cool and in control. "Kill him. Blow the place," he said to the tall, skinny thug standing guard. He strode to the exit, his bootheels clicking on the concrete floor. He grabbed Maya's arm and shoved the other girls ahead of him through the office door.

Skinny stepped toward me, exposing two missing teeth. He pointed his pistol at my head.

The sirens got louder.

"The money's all yours if you let me go," I said.

The thug lowered his pistol and stepped forward. "Where, asshole?"

"It's in..." I whispered.

He was curious and greedy. He stepped closer.

I swung my head with everything I had and connected with the bridge of his nose. Blood instantly sprayed from his face. He sank to his knees. "You fucker!" he screamed.

An explosion ripped through the building. The room went white, then burst into flame. Pieces of metal roof crashed down around me followed by a wave of superheated air. The explosion rocked the metal A-frame. Dragon was destroying the evidence. Skinny dropped his pistol, jumped to his feet, and sprinted for the exit.

I swung my torso forward and lifted my bound hands to the edge of the A-frame. The plastic tie caught on a metal spur. I jerked my arms down with just enough force to free my hands, then grabbed the top bar and pulled my body up to ease the strain on my legs so I could pull my feet loose and drop to the floor. Pain shot through my chest and down both arms. I had to force myself to go forward and stay focused. Knowing I was close to Maya and the building would soon collapse gave me the shot of adrenaline I needed.

I grabbed Skinny's pistol and ran down the stairs and out into the parking lot. Russell's Jeep Cherokee was gone. The building erupted in flames behind me. Red-and-blue pulsing emergency lights appeared on the horizon along with the surging sound of sirens. The two gate guards jogged toward me, out of breath. I stuck Skinny's pistol behind my back.

"What happened?" one of them shouted.

I didn't respond. I stood still, watching them approach, holding my hands at my sides. The heat felt good on my naked back. The outside temperature had dropped another five degrees. The two guards came closer, eyeing me suspiciously. My torso bandage was covered in blood, and my feet were bare. The one on the left raised his pistol.

"You're Fischer," he said. "Dragon told us to kill you if you came out."

I grabbed his gun hand and hit him in the ear. He went down. His partner was slow to react. I pulled Skinny's pistol and leveled at his chest.

"Put down the weapon," I ordered.

He dropped his pistol.

I picked it up and shoved it in my waistband. "Let's go," I said, waving the pistol toward the guard shack. I followed him inside and made him take off his boots. They were a size too small, but better than bare feet. I took a black leather jacket from the peg on the wall and put it on over my bloody bandage.

"Where's your boss?" I asked the guard.

"I don't know," he said.

I hit him on the side of the head with the pistol. "Where was he going?"

"He'll kill me if I tell you." He put his hand to his bloody face. Russell had put the fear of god in all his employees. I hit him again. He went to his knees, clutching his bleeding ear.

I shoved the pistol into his forehead. "Talk."

The sirens were coming fast. I needed to move. I didn't want to get arrested or have to explain myself to Ochoa until I caught up with Russell and Maya again. I pressed the barrel harder against the guard's skin. "Tell me where he went." I leaned forward, inches from his mouth, and listened. His words were barely audible.

"Airport."

"Thank you," I whispered.

The sirens were less than a mile away, and the emergency lights on the horizon lit up the sky like a weekend carnival. I jogged to the Camry, jumped in, and fired the engine. The flames from the warehouse reflected off the Mexican bullfrog. Another explosion briefly drowned out the sirens. I cleared the front of the building and accelerated toward the highway.

A dark blue Ford Taurus emerged out of nowhere, slammed sideways on the gravel shoulder, and cut me off.

I hit the brakes. The seatbelt cut into my chest, and I slid to a stop inches from the driver's side door.

Detective Diana Ochoa pointed her finger at me through the windshield, as if to tell me not to move.

I flashed an I-give-up grin, hoping she would buy it.

She calmly slid out the passenger door. She wore faded jeans and black tactical boots with a dark blue SAPD windbreaker. The brim of her police ball cap was pulled low, and her tight, jet-black ponytail swished back and forth as she walked.

Now was my chance. I slammed the gearshift in reverse.

Ochoa pulled her 9mm Glock service weapon and pressed the tip against the window.

I paused with my foot poised above the accelerator. I wasn't sure whether she would use it on me or if she was bluffing. I tried to read her expression in the dim light. The cap brim cast a shadow over her eyes and nose. She wasn't smiling. That much was clear.

I decided not to test her. I pressed the gear shift back into park and unrolled the window.

"Your twenty-four hours are up, hotshot."

"I thought you said forty-eight."

"Nice try. Where's Russell Stevens and Maya Chavez?"

"They were in that building, now they're gone. I know where they went. I'm going after them."

"No. You're done, Fischer. Out of the car."

I stepped out. She produced a pair of handcuffs from behind her belt. Keeping the Glock pointed at my head, she reached forward and deftly clipped the cold metal on my wrists.

CHAPTER FORTY-SEVEN

"You wanna nail Russell Stevens, I've got all the evidence you need." I spread my boots to try to maintain my balance, then took two deep breaths. I was still pumped with adrenaline and was afraid if I stood too long with Ochoa, the hormone would dissipate and I would collapse like a wet noodle.

"Don't yank my chain, Fischer."

I squeezed my eyes tight as a new spasm of pain shot through my chest. "I'm bein' straight. Let me go, and I'll guarantee you nail Russell Stevens along with a dozen corrupt local and state big shots. Russell made tapes of a dozen men abusing young girls. The girls he's trafficking. He used it as blackmail. That's how he's been able to operate under the radar."

"What big shots?"

"Gordon Lozano for one."

"The county commissioner?"

I nodded.

"If you're lying to save your ass, I'll make sure you lose your license and do time."

"I don't lie. I may leave out a few details. But I'll never lie."

She studied my face. "You look like death warmed over."

My jaw was clenched and sweat dripped from my temples. "I'll survive," I said, but was beginning to doubt how long I could hold out. I felt the strength that I'd always counted on to carry me through to the end of the mission slowly draining away. The thought irritated me. There was no time for chitchat. "You gotta trust me. Russell didn't blow up his warehouse because he's coming back. He's headed to an airstrip off 1604. The guard told me. If he gets off the ground, we'll never see him or Maya again."

"Damn you, Fischer." She unlocked the cuffs. When she did, she saw the bloody bandage on my chest. "Jesus, you're bleeding."

"I'm fine. Let's go."

"Stand there and don't move." She opened her trunk and got out a first aid kit.

"He's got a ten-minute head start," I said.

"We do this my way, or I'll put the cuffs back on." She peeled off the bloody bandage. "How are you still standing?" She wiped the wound with a paper towel. "You should be in the hospital." She pulled a fresh four-by-four gauze pad from the kit and pressed it over the wound.

I grabbed her hands. I needed her undivided attention. I knew what was at stake, and I needed her to believe me. "I'll get medical help. After I find Maya."

She held my gaze. Her deadeye detective stare faded, and I saw a glimmer of something else. Something softer. "Sergeant Vera was right, you are stubborn. All right, I'll help you. We take my car. I've got a shotgun and an AR in the trunk. If he's flying out of the country on the spur of the moment, it will take time to prep for takeoff. We still have a chance."

• • •

Her Ford was roomier than the Camry and smelled like stale coffee and fried food instead of candy and sweet perfume. Ochoa had her foot on the floor and the all-business expression had returned. I press-checked my AR and loaded a full thirty-round magazine. I also checked her police-issue 870 shotgun. Both were ready to go.

I felt her glance at my profile. "Where's Kelly?"

"She went back to Lubbock."

Ochoa nodded. "Not what she signed up for?"

"Something like that." I wasn't giving up on Kelly or our relationship. This wasn't the time or place to discuss it. I had too much work to do.

Just the idea of talking about my personal relationships with Ochoa made me uneasy.

"You do have a habit of rubbing people the wrong way."

"That's what makes me so charming."

A hint of a smile flickered across her lips. "That's not exactly how I would describe you."

Before she could say any more, lights from the private airport hangar popped up on the horizon surrounded by a ten-foot chain-link fence. A sudden splash of life in the otherwise dense brush that covered Bexar County south of the Alamo City. Ochoa cut the headlights and stopped by a locked access gate five hundred yards from the hangar. She pulled a pair of binoculars from under the seat and studied a plane parked near the fuel pump. "It looks like a Beechcraft King Air. Nice."

"You know planes?"

"I learned to fly in high school. My dad was a pilot. I always thought I'd follow in his footsteps."

"What happened?"

"I found something I liked better."

"My grandpa was a pilot. I still have his plane. A Cessna 172."

"I love those. It's a workhorse." She was looking through the binoculars. "There's Russell."

"Is Maya with him?"

"I can't see her, but there are three or four females inside the hangar. I count six men besides that. All armed. The plane's being prepped for takeoff. This wasn't a planned departure. You must have really rattled his cage."

"That's what I do best. How many passengers will that plane hold?"

"Ten people with a full tank of gas and gear. It's a smuggler's dream. If Russell gets off the ground, he's gone. He can be in Mexico City in two or three hours."

"That's not gonna happen."

Ochoa reached for her police radio and keyed the mic. "This is Detective Ochoa."

"What're you doin'?"

"Calling for backup."

I opened the car door. "They'll never make it in time."

"Damn you, Fischer. Wait."

I shut the door quietly and hustled toward the fence. Muffled voices came over her radio from inside the car. I guessed she'd called in San Antonio's finest, but I couldn't wait. I jogged down the dark fence line to the edge of the building. The front gate was open, and I knelt in the waist high Johnson grass and crawled forward on my hands and knees. One thug with an AR-15 stood guard at the gate. He was nervously puffing on a cigarette and blowing smoke into the cold night air. I started to back up and bumped into Ochoa crawling up behind me. I turned and held my index finger over my lips, then pointed at the guard.

She nodded, and I motioned for her to follow me to the far end of the building. The Beechcraft engines fired up, adding a cover noise for our movements. The gas tank was full. Time was running out. It was now or never.

"Over the fence," I whispered.

"No, wait for backup."

"You can wait." I grabbed the fence and hoisted myself up. Sharp pain shot through my arms. Ochoa saw me flinch and the grimace on my face.

"Do you ever follow orders? I thought you were in the military." She slung the shotgun over her shoulder and grabbed the fence wire.

I shrugged and kept climbing. I cleared the top strand of barbwire and dropped down on the inside.

Ochoa was hard on my heels. She was quick and agile and moved like a gymnast.

"You've done this before," I said.

"We do occasionally go after bad guys."

We jogged to the open back door of the hangar. A half dozen small four-seater planes filled the space with room for maybe half a dozen more. Russell Stevens stood in a small waiting area on the opposite end surrounded by four men. Two had AR-15s. The young females were seated. One wore a gold dress. Maya.

"She's here," I whispered. "The one in the gold dress."

I motioned for Ochoa to follow me, ducked back out the door, and jogged in the shadow along the outside of the building. I crouched down at the front corner. Ochoa did the same. She had the shotgun ready, and her face was all business. The revving Beechcraft engines told me I was right about the SAPD. They would be too late.

I inched forward to the edge of the building. The hangar opening was around the corner. The Beechcraft stood thirty yards away with the stairs extended to the tarmac. A harsh single floodlight on a pole lit the area. A guard holding an AR at the low ready shouted to someone inside the plane.

I was close enough to see the faces of the people in the waiting area. Russell wore a bomber jacket, his hair in a ponytail and a smug expression on his face. One of the other guards joined his partner on the tarmac. The two others guarded the girls.

Maya sat with her legs crossed, chewing on her index finger, the gold dress sparkling in the floodlight. Whatever circumstances led to this point didn't really matter. If I failed, she'd be wearing that gold dress or one just like it for a long time and entertaining Russell's perverted guests like the girls on the tapes.

I thought about the encounter in the warehouse. She had shouted a warning. Her attitude had changed. The defiance in her voice was gone and replaced by fear. She'd wanted to help me, wanted me to escape the Dragon and stay alive. If what I was about to do was going to work, she would need to trust me. I was going to ask her to choose between me and Russell Stevens. I hoped when the moment came, she'd make the right choice.

"Now would be a good time for your backup to arrive," I whispered to Ochoa.

She shrugged and inched closer to the edge so she could see the plane and the hangar opening. "You were right. What's plan B?"

"We need to separate the girls from the boys."

She studied the waiting area and the plane. "I've got an idea. Wait here." She took off running for the back door.

I aimed the AR's iron sights toward the man near the plane. The weapon was cold and deadly and gave me a measure of confidence. I'd fired thousands of rounds through rifles just like it and it felt like an old friend.

Suddenly, the hangar went dark. Ochoa had found the light switch or the electrical line. Dragon pulled a pistol from the shoulder holster inside his jacket. A loud boom echoed through the metal building. Ochoa had fired her shotgun. The light from the runway cast deep shadows inside the hangar.

The two men with rifles ran through the shadows toward the back door. I hoped Ochoa was ready for them. It was my turn. I put the iron sights on the thug by the Beechcraft and squeezed the trigger. He dropped like a sack of corn. The sharp pop from the rifle was drowned out by the plane engines.

Another shotgun blast boomed inside the hangar.

Russell shouted: "Check outside." He pointed in my direction.

One of the men took off running. I stood and pressed my back against the building, listening to the footsteps approaching. When he cleared the edge of the building, I jammed the rifle butt in his throat. The man went down, clutching his windpipe.

The odds were better now. I looked around the corner into the hanger. The two men who disappeared after Ochoa hadn't returned. Russell walked over to Maya, grabbed her by the neck, and jerked her to her feet.

"Is that you, Fischer!" he yelled. He pressed his pistol into Maya's ear.

There was nothing else to do now but confront him. I leaned the AR against the side of the building, pulled my Springfield, and stepped out into the open.

"Let her go, Russell," I shouted over the engine noise.

He turned toward me, using Maya as a shield. The other thug had his pistol out and took several steps to Russell's right. I quickly closed the distance between us, stopping ten feet in front of Russell and Maya.

"I told you it was over. The police are on their way. Drop the weapon and let her go."

"Fuck you, Fischer. She's mine. The plane is fueled and ready. You can't stop me." He took a step toward the Beechcraft, keeping Maya between us.

"I brought the money," I yelled.

He jammed his pistol harder into the side of her head. A trickle of blood ran down Maya's cheek. "Liar," he shouted.

I lowered my pistol to waist level. Maya was shaking like a leaf, her tight gold dress shimmering in the lights. "Two million is a lot of money," I said. The Beechcraft engine roared. "I told you I'd trade it for the girl."

He was thinking about it. He couldn't pretend two million dollars didn't matter. I caught and held Maya's eyes with my own. We stared at each other. *If I could get her to move…*

She mouthed, *Help me, please.*

It was all I needed from her. I nodded once and mouthed, *Drop.*

She buckled her knees and sank like a rock.

In one smooth practiced motion, I brought my .45 up and squeezed the trigger.

CHAPTER FORTY-EIGHT

I woke with a pulsing headache and a throat full of South Texas sand. The sterile white room smelled of antiseptic mixed with cleaning fluid and blood. A tube connected my right arm to a bag of saline solution. I was in a hospital room and not a jail cell. I hated both, but I knew I had a better chance of escaping from the former. I remembered being threatened with arrest. This could be the first step on my way to incarceration. An electronic beep and a low rumbling caught my attention. I eased my head sideways. The beep told me my heart still worked and the rumbling told me I still had one friend. Skeeter sprawled on an undersized chair beside the bed. He was sound asleep and snoring like an idling diesel engine. I hadn't passed on to the afterlife. For the second time in a couple of months, I'd awakened in a hospital. The staff probably already printed a permanent name tag for the door.

How I got here, I had no idea. I'd pushed the limits of my physical endurance in order to find a young girl named Maya. Had I saved her? Had I held out long enough to finish the mission? The last thing I remembered was a brute named Russell Stevens holding her by the neck and jamming a pistol against her head.

I tried to speak but what came out was a hoarse whisper. "Skeeter." It was barely loud enough for me to hear. I reached for the water glass on the table and sucked on the straw, trying to wash the sand away. "Skeeter." I tried again. This time I heard my own voice.

Skeeter stirred and opened his eyes. "Well, it's about damn time." He sat up and rubbed his face with his hands. "You had everyone worried. The doc said you were about two quarts low on fluid." He stood and stepped to the side of the bed. "Don't do that shit again, man. I don't like comin' to see you in the hospital."

He saw the plastic cup was empty and filled it with water from a jug on the table. I sipped greedily through the straw, not remembering when water had tasted so good. When the sand in my throat flushed away, I said: "What happened? Maya. Is she…?" I couldn't finish. If I hadn't done my job, I would never forgive myself.

"She's safe. Just down the hall. The doc said they were gonna keep her for a couple of days for observation."

"Is she okay?"

"She went through the wringer. But she's tough. Already asking when she can get out. You don't remember what happened?"

I leaned back and closed my eyes, resting my head against the hospital pillows. The image of Russell's head exploding emerged from my memory like an apparition. I remembered telling Maya to duck and drawing my .45. I hadn't wanted to kill Russell, but I wasn't sorry that I did. He'd murdered two innocent girls and probably messed up more lives than I could count. I wasn't gonna feel guilty over spilling his blood. The last thing I remembered was swinging my aim to the remaining thug and hearing the explosion from Ochoa's shotgun. The man crumpled to the concrete. After that, I must have passed out.

"Ochoa's been to see her," Skeeter said. "You were out of it. She wanted me to call when you woke up."

"How long have I been here?"

"Two days"—he looked at his wristwatch—"and four hours. Lucky and Sarge stopped by too. Lucky said not to stay here too long. There's a new heavyweight prospect he wants you to spar with." Skeeter chuckled. "I told him not to expect you too soon. We got a bet going for how long it will be before you jump back in the ring."

"What'd you take?"

"I said four weeks. Lucky said three."

"What about Sarge?"

"He said you'd be back in action in ten days."

I took another sip of water. The headache receded to a dull roar. I closed my eyes thinking about Detective Ochoa. She'd followed me over the fence and took out two of Russell's thugs when the SAPD backup didn't arrive in time. Now, I wondered if she wanted to arrest me.

"What'd Detective Ochoa want?"

"You thinkin' she gonna arrest you?" Skeeter said, reading my mind.

"She did mention that last time I saw her."

He let out a deep baritone chuckle. "You really don't know women."

"What're you talkin' 'bout?"

"She likes you, man. She stood right here and told me she'd never met anyone like you."

"Bullshit," I said.

"It's true. You want my advice, let Kelly go. She's never gonna come around to your way of doing business."

"And a San Antonio police detective would?"

"She was in that hanger with you, man. She talked the DA outta pressing charges. You gotta friend on the SAPD, and she's hot. That's a combination that don't come along very often." He told me Ochoa had gone through Russell's stash of blackmail tapes and wasted no time getting warrants for the men on camera, who included an assortment of local politicians, policemen, and one former congressman from El Paso. All the local and state agencies wanted a piece of the action. The FBI was in the process of tracking down the rest of the girls who were scattered across Texas, Louisiana, New Mexico, and Arizona. Many of them came from Mexico, but there were others like Maya who had wandered away from home and gotten swept up in a life that was more than they bargained for. The Dragon preyed on vulnerable young girls wherever he could find them.

"What'd she tell the DA?"

"That she found the money and the tapes at the scene. Russell was gonna flee the country. That makes all the evidence admissible."

His cell phone beeped. "Yeah, he's up," he said into the phone. "It's Ochoa. She wants to talk to you." He handed me the phone and winked. "Don't say anything stupid," he whispered.

"I'm I still wanted?"

"Maybe. We can have that conversation in person."

I detected a hint of innuendo, but I didn't want to press it in case I was misreading her.

"Skeeter tells me you're cleaning up Russell's outlaw network."

"Well, the local stuff. The money and drugs are linked to Mexico."

"Cartel?"

"More than likely. That's not my department."

"And I'm clear?"

"I had to do some fast-talking to the DA to get her to look at the tapes. You almost screwed up the entire case. She doesn't like you very much. Your ex-girlfriend works there now, and she argued for throwing the book at you."

"What's your opinion."

"I think you pushed the envelope. But you got the job done. Russell Stevens would have skipped town if it weren't for you."

I didn't know what to say. "Sometimes I even impress myself."

"Now, I know you're feeling better." She laughed. "There's one more fat cat on Russell's extortion tapes. We saved him for last. We're going out there now to take him into custody. Are you up for a drive?"

I sat up. "Going out where?"

"Fredericksburg."

"Who is it?"

"Are you comin' or not?"

I sat up and swung my feet off the bed. "Pick me up in front of the hospital. I'm on my way downstairs."

"What's up?" Skeeter asked, taking his phone back.

"I'm outta here." I pulled the IV needle out of my arm.

"I don't think the doc—"

I cut him off. "Ochoa found a Fredericksburg connection to Russell Stevens. She's goin' out there now to take him into custody. I don't wanna miss that." I stood up on the cold tile floor. My head swam, and I grabbed the metal bedframe for support.

"Who is it?"

"She wouldn't say, but I have a good idea."
"I'll get the nurse," he said.
"Don't bother. Just find my clothes."
"You're gonna cost me my bet."

CHAPTER FORTY-NINE

Outside, the sky was gray and overcast and the temperature hovered near fifty. Not cold by Wyoming standards, but everyone in Central Texas was wearing a jacket. Detective Ochoa picked me up and we drove the back roads through Boerne and Sisterdale. The oak and maple trees along the old highway added orange and yellow hues above the dry fall grass. The rolling limestone and granite hills took on a darker shade of green as the foliage prepared for winter hibernation. It was a welcome sight. I loved this time of year, and it was good to be out of the hospital and out of the city.

I studied Ochoa as she drove. Something was different about her. She was more relaxed than when we'd met outside the burning warehouse. That was understandable, but there was something more. She smelled of rose pedals and citrus and something spicy that I couldn't quite identify. She wore her shoulder-length hair loose and curled on the ends. Her faded Wrangler jeans showed off her curves and were neatly tucked into black cowboy boots. Her badge and pistol hung from a turquoise belt that matched her short leather jacket.

I couldn't help comparing her to Kelly. They were both smart and determined females who had not only survived, but thrived, in law enforcement. Not an easy thing to do in the Texas good ol' boy network. And they were both sexy. I had to admit it. The thought made me feel a little guilty and reminded me that I needed to call Kelly. I'd promised her I would let her know when it was all over. There hadn't been time. I woke up in the hospital, and now I was on my way to Fredericksburg with Ochoa. That phone call would have to wait. Besides, I needed time to decide what to say. I wasn't sure where our relationship stood or where it was going. Perhaps it was over already, and I was the last to know. It had happened before with Sylvia. When I thought I was saving her life from a ruthless politician, it turned out she was sleeping with him. I didn't think Kelly had another boyfriend, but I owed her a phone call at least before moving on.

"Are you studying me?" Ochoa asked, keeping her attention on the road.

I smiled. "Yeah, you cleaned up nice."

"You smell like bleach and antibacterial soap," she said with a straight face.

"Thanks, I try to stay clean."

Her sudden laugh tinkled like the entry bells on a country store.

"You gonna tell me who we're goin' after?"

"Be patient."

"Why not let the locals take care of the arrest? Or is it one of the local cops?"

"Why let them have all the fun? And no, it definitely isn't a cop. I said be patient. The locals will be there along with the DPS. I'm having the perp transported back to San Antonio. That's where the crime took place."

She was gonna make me wait, so I sat back and enjoyed the view. The farm fields in the Pedernales River valley were plowed under and ready for winter. Huge round bales of hay wrapped in blue plastic dotted the landscape. I unrolled my window a few inches and breathed in the mixture of fresh hay and wet cedar.

"You love this country, don't you?" she said.

"It's in my blood."

She slowed down for a closer look at an unusually large ten-point whitetail deer standing inside the barbwire fence.

"You won't see him in a couple of weeks."

"Why's that?" she asked.

"Hunting season starts soon."

"That's right. Sergeant Vera tells me your place is a great place to hunt."

"Sergeant Vera is a big gossip."

"That's true. Especially when it comes to you."

"What did he say?"

"He said you were a straight shooter. That you're honest to a fault, stubborn as hell, and never give up."

I wondered if he was setting me up. "Hugo Vera's been a family friend for a long time." Then it hit me. Vera was playing matchmaker. I wondered if he'd suggested Ochoa pick me up for the drive to Fredericksburg.

"Did Vera put you up to this?"

She glanced at me and smiled. "You mean did he suggest I pick you up?"

I nodded.

"He did suggest it, to prove to me he wasn't full of shit about you."

"And is he?"

"The jury's still out." She focused on the road. "The first time we met, you were wearing a bloody tuxedo shirt and handcuffs. It wasn't exactly a good first impression."

"You were with your corrupt partner who was responsible for my recently deceased client."

She nodded. "The second time was in the hospital after you'd killed my partner and his corrupt boss. Most of the department wanted your head mounted on the station wall."

"That included you."

"That's true. It was your word against some very powerful people."

"And I was right."

"Yes." She nodded again and glanced at me. "Now this."

I didn't know where her thoughts were going, so I shrugged and kept silent.

"Do you ever just have a normal weekend? Maybe kick back at home and grill steaks?"

I laughed. "Are you inviting me over for dinner?"

She stopped at a red light and remained silent. We faced the Willkommen to Fredericksburg sign that reminded everybody this was a German-themed tourist attraction. Her smile faded and she turned serious.

I found myself on the receiving end of her withering detective stare. "You know that money you took from Russell Stevens belonged to the Gulf Cartel?"

"I heard that."

"They don't forget that kind of money."

"What're you sayin'?"

"Watch your six."

"You know something specific?"

She pursed her lips. "No. I'm just saying, be careful. You've made a lot of enemies. I don't wanna see you get hurt."

I nodded, not sure what to say. I'd pissed off some powerful people in my short career as a private investigator, but then that was the nature of the job. I wasn't in it to make friends. The light turned green, and she turned east on Main Street.

"Is Kelly out of the picture?"

The question caught me off guard. She wasn't beating around the bush. Kelly had asked the same question about Sylvia when we'd met in Lubbock and were waiting for her lab to run the DNA test for Danny Allison. I remembered being just as uncomfortable. At the time, in my mind at least, the question wasn't settled, and I didn't want to play with two women's affections. It turned out the relationship with Sylvia was over. I just didn't know it yet. I wondered if the same thing were true now with Kelly.

She tapped her fingers on the steering wheel. The temperature inside the car seemed to increase. I started to speak, but she cut me off.

"It's okay. You don't have to answer that now."

Skeeter was right about one thing. I didn't know anything about women. We drove in silence until she pulled the Ford Taurus into the parking lot of Mike Bauer's winery. Three state trooper SUVs along with the sheriff's pickup and two local police cruisers were there waiting for us. Officer Zeller stood by one of the cruisers. He was juggling a blueberry kolache and a cup of coffee.

"I'll be damned. Mike Bauer?" I shouldn't have been surprised, but I was.

"We got him on tape enjoying himself with one of Russell's young girls."

"That explains a lot. What about his son, Owen?"

"We questioned him. He claimed he didn't know what Russell was going to do with Maya, and he's still seventeen. It will be up to the DA if she wants to file charges. But I think he'll walk."

"I have a recommendation for him."

"Join the Marines?" she asked.

"Why not? His football career is over. No university program will touch him. Everybody needs a second chance."

"He'll end up like you."

"Is that such a bad thing?"

The country store bells rang again. It was a pleasant sound that I could get used to.

"Hey, Les," I said when I got out of the Taurus.

"Hey, yourself." He licked powdered sugar from his fingers. "What're you doin' here?"

"I was gonna ask you the same thing."

"My town. My jurisdiction."

Ochoa stepped between us. "I'm Detective Ochoa," she said. "We spoke on the phone."

Zeller held out his sticky hand. Ochoa didn't take it.

"The sheriff's inside with Mike," he said, chinning toward the front entrance and wiping his hand on his pants.

I turned to follow Ochoa inside.

"Not you," Zeller said. "Just the detective."

Ochoa shrugged and hustled inside, leaving me with Les.

"No hard feelings," I said.

"You don't know, do you?"

"What?" I said.

"Your mom's in there with Mike."

I shook my head. I'd hoped she'd gone back to Colorado. "Why should that bother me?"

"Just thought you'd wanna know."

Zeller pinched the pastry bag from the front seat of his cruiser. He held it out to me. I wasn't really hungry but took one anyway. I recognized the white bag as coming from the German Bakery. They had the best kolaches in town. He offered it like a peace pipe at an Indian treaty meeting. The Comanches offered tobacco; the Fredericksburg police offered pastry.

"We're not real close," I said.

"I gathered that." He grinned, showing his blueberry-stained teeth.

We stood chewing in silence. Mike was finished in Fredericksburg. It wasn't Helen's style to give support when the ones around her needed it. She'd left my dad when he was elected sheriff—said she couldn't stand the long nights at home waiting for the phone call. It sounded like a good excuse, but it didn't explain why she left her son.

"You gonna keep doin' the private eye thing in San Antonio?" Zeller asked.

"Gotta make a livin' somehow," I said.

"What're ya gonna do with the home place?"

"I'll keep it as long as I can pay the taxes."

"That's good," he said. "It wouldn't be the same without a Fischer in town." He was trying to bury the hatchet. He would never admit that he was wrong about Maya and Bauer, but at least he wasn't going to arrest me.

"You got a place to go huntin' this year?" I asked.

Les grinned again, as if he'd been waiting for me to bring it up.

Before he could respond, the posse burst through the winery door. At the same time, a San Antonio news van pulled into the parking lot. A cameraman jumped out with his camera rolling, followed by a young female reporter in a long red coat and carefully coiffed TV hair. Les sprang into action with his hands up and instructed them to stay behind the barrier set up thirty feet from the front door.

Mike Bauer led the posse, his hands cuffed behind his back. A burly state trooper followed. Mike's face looked as white as the new limestone bricks supporting the winery porch. He saw the camera rolling and tried to duck his head. Too late. It was the second time he'd been caught on camera in a compromising position.

Ochoa and two other state troopers followed, along with the county sheriff and one of his deputies. She stood out among the well-fed law enforcement good ol' boys like a female reporter in an NFL locker room but wasn't intimidated in the least.

Helen appeared at the entrance beside Brenda, the teen server who'd tried to push the Bauer wine. Helen put a hand on her shoulder and gave Brenda a little shove out of the way just as the news camera swept across the building. She wasn't protecting her; Helen wanted a solo pose for the camera. She put her hand over her mouth in fake concern. Tears would be next. The perfect victim. She was too easy to read.

"Hey, Mike," I yelled over the commotion.

Mike looked up and saw me. His eyes had lost the bravado of our last visit.

"I'm gonna hang on to the ranch. Thanks for the offer."

"Fuck you, Fischer! You did this to me," Mike yelled.

The burly trooper guided Mike into the back seat of the SUV. Zeller answered questions on camera for the TV reporter, putting on a serious expression and clearly enjoying the attention.

Ochoa joined me in the parking lot. "Pervert denied everything. Said you set him up."

"Does he know about the video?"

"He does now."

"Nicky," Helen called from the porch in a singsong voice.

"*Nicky?*" Ochoa repeated. "You know her?" she asked, watching Helen clamber down the steps.

"No," I said.

"Nicky, can we talk?" Helen hurried toward us.

"Let's go," I said, opening the driver's side door and gesturing for Ochoa to get in.

"You just gonna ignore her?" she asked.

"Yes," I said.

Ochoa got in, and I closed her door. Helen caught me before I could get to the passenger side door.

"Did you have anything to do with what happened to Mike?" Helen asked breathlessly. She was blocking my path to the passenger door in full view of Ochoa.

"Not in the way you think. Mike's guilty. He's goin' to prison."

Her face fell like a kid who'd dropped her ice cream cone on the hot pavement.

"You'll need to find another sugar daddy," I said.

"Don't be cruel. I'm still your mother." She glanced through the windshield at Ochoa. "Who's this?"

"An SAPD detective. She handled the case."

"Nicky, I need to talk to you. Is there somewhere we can go?"

"No, Helen. There's nowhere we can go." I stepped around her and opened the car door.

"Please," she said. "Don't make me beg."

I'd heard that line before. I wasn't going to fall for it again. I sat down in the passenger seat. Helen stood at the open door holding her hands palms up. Tears streaked her makeup.

"She's your mother?" Ochoa whispered.

I felt Ochoa's stare on one side of my face and Helen's on the other. I was trapped and didn't want to face either of them. "Yes and no. It's complicated." I knew I sounded defensive. Both kept staring, making me feel guilty. I sighed and turned to Helen. I knew I was opening a can of worms, but the pressure was too great. "Come by the ranch next week. We'll talk."

"Thank you, Nicky. I wanted to—"

I nudged her out of the way and closed the door.

"Okay, I talked to her," I said, turning to Ochoa. "Let's go."

She started the engine. "Sergeant Vera was right about one thing."

"What's that?"

"You are as stubborn as a mule."

EPILOGUE

I rolled my F-150 to a stop at Helmut's front gate. The sun was out and reflected off the iron cowboy kneeling in front of the large cross, giving the gate ornament a golden glow. Maybe the metal cowboy's prayer had been answered. Maya sat in the passenger seat, looking a few pounds heavier and healthier than when I'd first seen her at the trap house in west San Antonio. The two-week stay in the hospital had been good for her. I wondered if she was thinking about the iron cowboy or what lay beyond in the house up the hill. She tapped her fingers nervously on the center console. It was her choice to come back to Fredericksburg. Luckily, the drugs the Dragon gave her hadn't done lasting physical damage, but it would take her some time to get over the mental aspects of the ordeal. The fact that she wanted to go back to her grandpa's ranch in rural Gillespie County said a lot about her. It wouldn't be easy. Ochoa had suggested a rehab facility. She knew of one in Bastrop County, east of Austin. They took girls under nineteen who had been rescued from thugs like Russell Stevens. They had a charter school and provided counseling to ease the recovery process. Maya said she wanted to give her grandfather's ranch a try first.

Without a word, Maya got out to open the gate. The cold air reddened her brown cheeks, and the north wind flicked the ends of her raven hair. She paused for a long moment to study Helmut's barren hay pasture and the limestone hills beyond covered with dark green live oak and cedar trees.

Woodsmoke rose from the single-story ranch house. Another norther had swept down from Canada and dropped the temperature into the thirties. Good news for the deer hunters whose season started in the morning.

"You have my number," I said when she'd climbed back in the cab and closed the door. "Detective Ochoa left you hers too." I waited for her to speak, but she was silent on the drive to the house. Helmut had wanted to visit her in the hospital, but I told him to wait and give Maya time to recover. She needed to make up her own mind. I wasn't going to force her to live with her grandfather. That wasn't my mission. I only wanted her to get away from Russell Stevens so she could make her own choice.

Before we reached the yard, Sam jumped off Helmut's front porch and sprinted toward my pickup. Helmut's dog pack followed, but they stayed a step behind him, sensing the connection between their newest pack member and the intruder. I stopped and opened the back door. Sam jumped in, and I let the other dogs follow us to the house. He stuck his wide Labrador head between the front seats and licked my face before turning his attention to Maya.

"Maya, this is General Sam Houston."

Sam wasted no time nudging his head against hers and lapping at her chin. She giggled and scratched him behind the ears.

"Is he always this friendly?"

"Apparently, he is. Lately he's been a little more leery of strangers, but he's made an exception with you."

"What's this scar?" She studied the patch of pink skin where a .22 bullet had almost ended his life.

"That's why he's been a little more leery of strangers. It's from a .22 bullet. Someday I'll tell you about it."

I parked facing the front porch. When I reached for my door handle, Maya touched my arm. "Wait." She studied the worn porch where generations of the Geisler family had stood. I wondered if she was having second thoughts.

Helmut held the front curtain back and peeked out. I'd known him all my life and had never seen him get particularly sentimental, but I thought I saw a tear in his eye as he gazed at his granddaughter. Maya had changed him. This young woman from California had stormed into Gillespie County and touched the lives of everyone she met.

"Do you wanna leave?" I asked.

Maya squeezed my arm. "No. I'll stay. Thank you for not giving up on me." She leaned over Sam's head and kissed me on the cheek. "I won't ever forget what you did." For the first time since I'd known her, her face was full of hope and determination.

Helmut stepped out the door with his silver Stetson hat pulled low over his eyes and his flannel-lined barn coat buttoned to his chin. He was the nineteenth century, and Maya was the twenty-first. The two had gone head-to-head like two billy goats in the barnyard. Now they would have to blend the past and the future to live together.

"Come in out of the cold," Helmut called. "The coffee's on."

Maya smiled. She jumped out, ran up the steps, and into her grandpa's arms.

THE END

If you enjoyed this Nick Fischer adventure, please stop by Amazon and write a quick review. Your support will be much appreciated.

Sign up for G.D.'s newsletter for a FREE copy of his latest short story and updates on new releases at GDObermiller.com.

Visit G.D. Online:
Facebook.com/GDObermiller
x.com/GDObermiller
Instagram.com/GDObermiller

Thank you for reading *The Girl from Cali.* Check out the other exciting books in the series.

RIVER WALK MURDER (book one)

Stonewalled by a dirty cop working for a corrupt politician, the family of a dead woman found in the San Antonio River turns to Nick Fischer for justice.

RODEO REQUIEM (book three) Available May 25, 2026

A rodeo cowboy turns up dead at the San Antonio rodeo clutching an empty snuff can inscribed with Nick Fischer's name and filled with painkillers. Was it a cry for help—the young cowboy was a wounded veteran—or was it murder? Nick finds himself on the wrong side of the law, again, as he races to clear his name and catch the killer before it's too late.

ACKNOWLEDGMENTS

I would like to thank my daughter Ruby and sister MaryAlice, who continue to chide and encouraged me through the writing process, and Jiaen for putting up with me. Also, I would like to thank my editor, Lisa Gilliam, for her continued patience and guidance. Prost!

The historical events mentioned in this book are derived from three main sources of historical research: *A Fate Worse Than Death:* Indian Captivities in the West, 1830-1885, by Gregory Michno and Susan Michno, *Myth, Memory, and Massacre:* The Pease River Capture of Cynthia Ann Parker, and *Empire of the Summer Moon* by S.C. Gwynne.

I would also like to acknowledge Pastor Joseph A. Travers and his organization, Saved In America, for being true heroes in the battle to rescue trafficked and exploited children. If you know someone in need of their services or would like to donate to the organization, contact SavedInAmerica.org.

G.D. Obermiller is a fifth-generation Texan who has worked as a cowboy, served as a Navy Corpsman, and taught college English. He's the author of four previous novels, several screenplays, and a one-act play produced in Austin, Texas. He currently lives in San Antonio with his daughter and faithful Labrador retriever.

www.ingramcontent.com/pod-product-compliance
Lightning Source LLC
Chambersburg PA
CBHW030826310726
48980CB00006B/653/J

* 9 7 9 8 9 9 3 8 5 8 8 0 7 *